# THE SORCERESS

{ *The Secrets of* THE IMMORTAL NICHOLAS FLAMEL }

www.kidsatrandomhouse.co.uk

# ALSO BY MICHAEL SCOTT

## *The Alchemyst*

## *The Magician*

# THE
# SORCERESS

{ *The Secrets of* THE IMMORTAL NICHOLAS FLAMEL }

*Michael Scott*

DOUBLEDAY

THE SORCERESS
A DOUBLEDAY BOOK
978 0 385 61312 5 (hardback)
978 0 385 61313 2 (trade paperback)

Published in the US by Delacorte Press,
an imprint of Random House Children's Books
a division of Random House, Inc.

Published in Great Britain by Doubleday,
an imprint of Random House Children's Books

Delacorte Press edition published in 2009
This edition published 2009

5 7 9 10 8 6 4

The Random House Group Limited supports the Forest Stewardship Council (FSC),
the leading international forest certification organization. All our titles that are printed
on Greenpeace-approved FSC-certified paper carry the FSC logo. Our paper
procurement policy can be found at www.rbooks.co.uk/environment.

Mixed Sources
Product group from well-managed
forests and other controlled sources
www.fsc.org  Cert no. TT-COC-2139
© 1996 Forest Stewardship Council

Set in Galliard

RANDOM HOUSE CHILDREN'S BOOKS
61–63 Uxbridge Road, London W5 5SA

www.kidsatrandomhouse.co.uk
www.rbooks.co.uk

Addresses for companies within The Random House Group Limited can be found at:
www.randomhouse.co.uk/offices.htm

THE RANDOM HOUSE GROUP Limited Reg. No. 954009

A CIP catalogue record for this book is available from the British Library.

Printed in the UK by CPI Mackays, Chatham, ME5 8TD

For Courtney,
*ex animo*

I am tired now, so tired.

And I am aging fast. There is a stiffness in my joints, my sight is no longer sharp and I find I have to strain to hear. Over the past five days I have been forced to use my powers more times than I have used them in the entire previous century, and that has speeded up the aging process significantly. I estimate that I have aged by at least a decade—perhaps more—since last Thursday. If I am to live, I have to retrieve the Book of Abraham, and I cannot—I *dare* not—risk using my powers again.

But Dee has the Codex, and I know that I will be forced yet again to use my waning aura.

I must, if we are to survive.

Every time I use it I grow closer to death . . . and once I die, and Perenelle, too, no one will stand against Dee and the Dark Elders. When we die, the world will end.

But we are not dead yet.

And we have the twins. The real twins this time, the true twins of legend with auras of pure gold and silver. While the twins survive, there is still hope.

We are about to enter London. I fear this city above all others, for it is at the very heart of Dee's power. The last time Perenelle and I were here, in September 1666, the Magician almost burned the city to the ground trying to capture us. We've never been back. London has attracted Elders from around the globe: there are more of them in this city than in any other on earth. Elders, Next Generation and immortal humans move freely and unnoticed through the streets, and I know of at least a dozen Shadowrealms scattered across the British Isles.

More ley lines meet and converge over these Celtic lands than over any other country, and I pray that with the twins'

Awakened powers, we can use those lines to return to San Francisco and my Perenelle.

And here too is Gilgamesh the King, the oldest immortal human in the world. His knowledge is incalculable and encyclopedic. It is said that he was once the Guardian of the Codex, that he even knew the mythical Abraham who created the book. Legend has it that Gilgamesh knows all the elemental magics—though, strangely, he has never possessed the power to use them. The king has no aura. I've often wondered what that must be like: to be aware of so many incredible things, to have access to the wisdom of the ancients, to know the words and spells that could return this world to the paradise it once was . . . and yet to be unable to use them.

I have told Sophie and Josh that I need Gilgamesh to train them in the Magic of Water and find us a ley line that will take us home. But they do not know that it is a desperate gamble; if the king refuses, then we will be trapped in Dee's domain, with no possibility of escape.

Nor have I told them that Gilgamesh is quite, quite insane . . . and that the last time we met, he thought I was trying to kill him.

*From the Day Booke of Nicholas Flamel, Alchemyst*
*Writ this day, Monday, 4th June,*
*in London, the city of my enemies*

MONDAY, *4th June*

## CHAPTER ONE

"*I* think I see them."

The young man in the green parka standing directly beneath the huge circular clock in St. Pancras station took the phone away from his ear and checked a blurred jpeg on the rectangular screen. The English Magician had sent the image a couple of hours ago: date-stamped June 04, 11.59.00, its colors washed and faded, the grainy picture looked like it had been taken by an overhead security camera. It showed an older man with short gray hair, accompanied by two fair teens, climbing onto a train.

Rising up on his toes, the young man scanned the station for the trio he'd briefly glimpsed. For a moment he thought he'd lost them in the milling crowd, but even if he had, they wouldn't get far; one of his sisters was downstairs, and another was on the street outside, watching the entrance.

Now, where had the old man and the teenagers gone?

Narrow pinched nostrils flared as he sorted through the countless scents in the station. He identified and dismissed the mixed stink of too many humani, the myriad perfumes and deodorants, the gels and pastes, the greasy odor of fried food from the station's restaurants, the richer aroma of coffee, and the metallic oily tang of the train engines and carriages. Nostrils opened unnaturally wide as he closed his eyes and tilted his head back. The odors he was seeking were older, wilder, unnatural. . . .

There!

Mint: just the merest suggestion.

Orange: no more than the vaguest hint.

Vanilla: little more than a trace.

Hidden behind small rectangular sunglasses, his blue-black pupils dilated. He sniffed the air, tracing the gossamer threads of scent through the vast train station. He had them now!

The older man from the image on his phone was striding down the station concourse directly toward him. He was wearing black jeans and a scuffed leather jacket and carried a small overnight case in his left hand. And just as in the picture taken earlier, he was followed by two blond teenagers alike enough to be brother and sister. The boy was taller than the girl, and they both wore backpacks.

The young man snapped a quick picture with his cell phone camera and sent it to Dr. John Dee. Although he had nothing but contempt for the English Magician, there was no point in making an enemy of him. Dee was the agent of one

4

of the more senior and certainly the most dangerous of all the Dark Elders.

Pulling the hood of his green parka over his head, the young man turned away as the trio drew near him, and dialed his sister, who was waiting downstairs. "It's definitely Flamel and the twins," he murmured into the phone, speaking the ancient language that had eventually become Gaelic. "They're heading in your direction. We'll take them when they get onto Euston Road."

Snapping his phone shut, the young man in the hooded parka set off after the Alchemyst and the American twins. He moved easily through the early-afternoon crowd, looking like just another teenager, anonymous and unnoticed in his sloppy jeans, scuffed sneakers and overlarge coat, his head and face concealed by a hood, eyes invisible behind the dark sunglasses.

Despite his appearance, however, the young man had never been remotely human. He and his sisters had first come to this land when it was still joined to the European mainland, and for generations they had been worshipped as gods. He bitterly resented being ordered around by Dee—who was, after all, nothing more than a humani. But the English Magician had promised the hooded boy a delectable prize: Nicholas Flamel, the legendary Alchemyst. Dee's instructions were clear; the boy and his sisters could have Flamel, but the twins must not be touched. The boy's lips twisted. His sisters would easily capture the twins, while he would have the honor of killing Flamel. A coal black tongue darted out of the

5

corner of his mouth to lick his lips at the thought. They would feast off the Alchemyst for weeks. And, of course, they would keep the tastiest morsels for Mother.

Nicholas Flamel slowed, allowing Sophie and Josh to catch up with him. Forcing a smile, he pointed to the thirty-foot-tall bronze statue of a couple embracing beneath the clock. "It's called *The Meeting Place*," he said loudly, and then added in a whisper, "We're being followed." Still smiling, he leaned into Josh and murmured, "Don't even think about turning around."

"Who?" Sophie asked.

"What?" Josh said tightly. He was feeling nauseous and dizzy; his newly Awakened senses were overwhelmed by the scents and sounds of the train station. A throbbing headache pulsed at the base of his skull, and the light was so bright he wished he had a pair of sunglasses.

"Yes—'What?' is the better question," Nicholas said grimly. He raised a finger to point to the clock, as if he were talking about it. "I'm not sure what's here," he admitted. "Something ancient. I felt it the moment we stepped off the train."

"Felt it?" Josh asked, disoriented, and getting more confused by the second. He hadn't felt this sick since he'd got heatstroke in the Mojave Desert.

"A tingle, like an itch. My aura reacted to the aura of whoever—whatever—is here. When you have a little more control of your own auras, you'll be able to feel the same."

Tilting her head back, as if she were admiring the metal-

and-glass latticework ceiling, Sophie slowly turned. Crowds swirled around them. Most seemed to be locals—commuters—though there were plenty of tourists, many stopping to have their pictures taken in front of *The Meeting Place* statue or with the huge clock in the background. No one seemed to be paying her and her companions any particular attention.

"What will we do?" Josh asked. He was starting to feel panicked. "I can boost Sophie's powers," he babbled, "just like I did in Paris—"

"No," Flamel snapped, gripping Josh's arm with iron fingers. "From now on, you can only use your powers as an absolute last resort. As soon as you activate your aura, you will alert every Elder, Next Generation and immortal within a ten-mile radius to your presence. And here, in England, just about every immortal you encounter is allied with the Dark Elders. Also, in this land, it could awaken others, creatures best left sleeping."

"But you said we're being followed," Sophie protested. "That means Dee already knows we're here."

Flamel urged the twins to the left, away from the statue, hurrying them toward the exit. "I would imagine there are watchers in every airport, seaport and railway station across Europe. Although Dee might have suspected that we'd head to London; the instant either of you activates your aura, he'll know for certain."

"And what will he do then?" Josh asked, turning to look at Flamel. In the harsh overhead lights, the new lines on the Alchemyst's forehead and around his eyes were sharp.

Flamel shrugged. "Who knows what he is capable of

doing. He is desperate, and desperate men do terrible things. Remember, he was on top of Notre Dame. He was prepared to destroy the ancient building just to stop you . . . prepared to kill you to prevent you leaving Paris."

Josh shook his head, confused. "But that's what I don't understand—I thought he wanted us alive."

Flamel sighed. "Dee is a necromancer. It is a foul and horrible art that involves artificially activating a dead body's aura and bringing that body back to life."

An icy coldness washed over Josh at the thought. "You're saying he would have killed us and brought us back to life?"

"Yes. As a last resort." Flamel reached out and squeezed the boy's shoulder gently. "Believe me, it is a terrible existence, the merest shadow of life. And remember, Dee saw what you did, so he now has some inkling of your powers. If there were any doubts in his mind that you are the twins of legend, they have vanished. He *has* to have you. He needs you." The Alchemyst poked Josh in the chest. Paper rustled. Beneath his T-shirt, in a cloth bag hanging around his neck, Josh carried the two pages he'd torn from the Codex. "And above all else, he needs those pages."

The group followed the signs for the Euston Road exit, and were swept along by a crowd of commuters heading in the same direction. "I thought you said there would be someone to meet us," Sophie said, looking around.

"Saint-Germain told me he'd try and contact an old friend," Flamel muttered. "Maybe he couldn't get in touch."

They stepped out of the ornate redbrick train station onto

Euston Road and stopped in surprise. When they'd left Paris just over two and a half hours ago, the skies had been cloudless, the temperature already creeping into the seventies, but in London it felt at least ten degrees cooler and it was raining hard. The wind whipping down the road was cold enough to make the twins shiver. They turned and ducked back into the shelter of the station.

And that was when Sophie saw him.

"A boy in a green parka, with the hood pulled up," she said suddenly, turning to Nicholas and concentrating fiercely on his pale eyes. She knew that if she looked away, she would involuntarily glance at the young man who had been hurrying after them. She could still see him from the corner of her eye. He was loitering close to a pillar, staring at the cell phone in his hand, fiddling with it. There was something wrong about the way he was standing. Something unnatural. And she thought she caught the faintest scent of spoiled meat on the air. Her nose wrinkled. Closing her eyes, she concentrated on the odor. "It smells like something rotten, like roadkill."

The smile on the Alchemyst's face grew strained. "Wearing a hood? So, that's who's been following us." The twins heard the slightest tremor in his voice.

"Except he's not a boy, is he?" Sophie asked.

Nicholas shook his head. "Not even close."

Josh took a deep breath. "Well then, do you want me to tell you that there are now two more people wearing green hooded parkas, and they're both heading this way?"

9

"Three?" Flamel whispered in horror. "We've got to go." Grabbing the twins' arms, he pulled them out into the sleeting rain, turned to the right and dragged them down the street.

The rain was so cold it took Josh's breath away. Pellets of hard water stung his face. Finally, Flamel pulled both twins into an alley, out of the downpour. Josh stood catching his breath. He brushed his hair back out of his eyes and looked at the Alchemyst. "Who are they?" he demanded.

"The Hooded Ones," the Alchemyst said bitterly. "Dee must be desperate, and more powerful than I thought if he can command them. They are the Genii Cucullati."

"Great," Josh said. "That tells me everything I need to know." He looked at his sister. "Have you ever heard . . . ," he began, and then stopped, seeing the expression on her face. "You have!"

Sophie shivered as the Witch of Endor's memories flickered at the edges of her consciousness. She felt something sour at the back of her throat, and her stomach twisted in disgust. The Witch of Endor had known the Genii Cucullati— and she had loathed them. Sophie turned to her brother and explained. "Flesh eaters."

# CHAPTER TWO

The streets were empty, the squall having driven most people into the station or the nearby shops. Traffic on Euston Road had ground to a halt, and windshield wipers beat furiously. Horns blared, and a nearby car alarm began to howl.

"Stay with me," Nicholas ordered, then turned and darted across the road, weaving through the stopped traffic. Sophie followed close behind. Josh paused before he stepped off the curb, and looked back at the station. The three figures had gathered together in the entrance, their heads and faces hidden by the hoods of their coats. As the water stained the parkas dark green, Josh could have sworn they briefly took on the appearance of cloaks. He shivered, and this time the chill came from more than just the icy downpour. Then he turned and darted across the road.

Head ducked against the driving rain, Nicholas led the twins between vehicles. "Hurry. If we can put enough distance between us, the smells of the traffic and the rain might wash away our scents."

Sophie glanced over her shoulder. The hooded trio had left the shelter of the station and were closing in fast. "They're coming after us," she panted, voice rising in alarm.

"What do we do now?" Josh asked.

"I've no idea," Flamel said grimly. He stared down the long straight road. "But if we stay here, we're dead. Or at least I am." His teeth flashed in a humorless smile. "Dee will still try to get you both alive, I'm sure." Flamel glanced around, then spotted an alleyway to the left and motioned for the twins to follow him. "This way. We'll try and lose them."

"I wish Scatty were here," Josh muttered, truly realizing the magnitude of their loss. "She'd be able to deal with them."

It was dry in the narrow high-walled alleyway. Blue, green and brown plastic trash cans lined one wall, while the remains of wooden pallets and overflowing black plastic trash bags were piled against the other. The smell was foul, and a wild-haired cat sat on top of one bag, methodically shredding it with her claws. The cat didn't even look up as Flamel and the twins ran by. A heartbeat later, however, when the three hooded figures entered the alleyway, the cat arched its back, fur bristling, and disappeared into the shadows.

"Do you have any idea where this leads?" Josh asked as they raced past a series of doors to their left, obviously the rear entrances to businesses on the main road.

"None at all," Flamel admitted. "But as long as it takes us away from the Hooded Ones, it doesn't matter."

Sophie looked back. "I don't see them," she announced.

12

"Maybe we've lost them." She trailed Nicholas around a corner only to run straight into him when he stopped suddenly.

Josh then rounded the corner, narrowly missing the two. "Keep going," he gasped, dodging the pair to take the lead. And then he realized why they'd stopped: the alley ended in a tall red brick wall topped with curling razor wire.

The Alchemyst spun and put his finger to his lips. "Not a sound. They might have run past the alley altogether. . . ." A flurry of cold rain spattered onto the ground and carried with it a peculiar rancid smell: the foul scent of spoiled meat. "Or maybe not," he added as the three Genii Cucullati loped silently around the corner. Nicholas pushed the twins behind him, but they immediately took up positions on either side of him. Instinctively, Sophie moved to his right and Josh to his left. "Stand back," Flamel said.

"No," Josh said.

"We're not going to let you face these three alone," Sophie added.

The Hooded Ones slowed, then spread out to block the alleyway and stopped. They stood unnaturally still, faces concealed by the overlarge hoods.

"What are they waiting for?" Josh murmured, his voice barely above a whisper. There was something about the way the figures stood, the way they held themselves: something that suggested an animal. He'd seen a National Geographic documentary in which an alligator had been waiting in a river for deer to cross. It too had stayed completely still—until it had exploded into action.

Abruptly, a sound like snapping wood cracked shockingly

loudly across the quiet alleyway, followed by what seemed to be the sound of cloth tearing.

"They're changing," Sophie breathed.

Beneath the green coats, muscles rippled and spasmed, arching the creatures' spines, pushing their heads forward. Arms visibly lengthened, and the hands that poked out of the overlong sleeves were now thickly furred and tipped with ragged curling black claws.

"Wolves?" Josh asked shakily.

"More bear than wolf," Nicholas answered quietly, looking around the alleyway, eyes narrowed. "And more wolverine than bear," he added as the vaguest hint of vanilla touched the air.

"And no threat to us," Sophie announced, suddenly standing straighter. Raising her right hand, she pressed the thumb of her left hand against the gold circle burned into the flesh of her wrist.

"No," Nicholas snapped, reaching out to push the girl's hand down. "I've told you; you cannot use your powers in this city. Your auras are too distinctive."

Sophie shook her head indignantly. "I know what these things are," she said firmly. Then a tremor crept into her voice. "I know what they do. You can't expect us just to stand here while these things eat you. Let me take care of them—I can cook them to a crisp." Her anger quickly turned to excitement at the prospect, and she smiled. For an instant her bright blue eyes winked silver and her face became hard and sharp, making her look far older than her fifteen years.

The Alchemyst's smile was grim. "You could do that. And

I doubt we'd get a mile down the road before something much more lethal than these creatures caught up with us. You have no idea what walks these streets, Sophie. I'll take care of it," he insisted. "I'm not entirely defenseless."

"They're going to attack," Josh said urgently, interpreting the creatures' body language, watching how they moved into an assault pattern. Somewhere at the back of his mind, he found himself wondering how he knew this. "If you're going to do something, you need to do it now."

The Genii Cucullati had spread out, each taking up a position before Flamel and the twins. The creatures were hunched over, their backs arched, parkas stretched across broad chests, bulging shoulders and muscular arms. In the shadow of their hoods, blue-black eyes glowed over jagged teeth. They spoke to each other in what sounded like yips and growls.

Nicholas pushed up the sleeves of his leather jacket, revealing the silver link bracelet and the two frayed multi-colored friendship bracelets he wore around his right wrist. Twisting off one of the simple string bracelets, he rolled it between the palms of his hands, brought it to his lips and blew on it.

Sophie and Josh watched as he tossed the little ball onto the ground in front of the Hooded Ones. They saw the colored strands fall into a muddy puddle directly in front of the largest of the creatures and braced themselves for an explosion. Even the terrifying creatures scrambled back from the tiny pool, claws slipping on the pavement.

And nothing happened.

15

The sound that came from the largest creature might have been a laugh.

"I say we fight," Josh said defiantly, though he was shaken by the Alchemyst's failure. He'd seen Flamel throw spears of pure energy, he'd watched him create a forest out of a wooden floor—he'd been expecting something spectacular. Josh glanced over at his sister and knew that she was thinking exactly the same thing he was. In Flamel's aging and weakened state, his powers were fading. Josh nodded slightly and saw Sophie tip her head in return, then flex her fingers. "Nicholas, you saw what we did to the gargoyles," Josh continued, sure of his sister's and his own powers. "Together, Sophie and I can stand against anyone . . . and anything."

"The line between confidence and arrogance is very fine, Josh," Flamel said quietly. "And the line between arrogance and stupidity even finer. Sophie," he added, without looking at her, "if you use your power, you condemn us to death."

Josh shook his head. He was disgusted at Flamel's obvious weakness. Stepping away from the older man he shrugged off his backpack and tugged it open. Sticking up out of one side of the backpack was a thick cardboard tube, usually used to carry posters and rolled maps. Ripping off the white plastic cap, he reached in, grabbed the bubble-wrapped object inside and pulled it out.

"Nicholas . . . ?" Sophie began.

"Patience," Flamel whispered, "patience . . ."

The largest of the Hooded Ones dropped to all fours and took a step forward, filthy long-nailed claws clicking on the pavement. "You have been given to me," the beast said in a voice that was surprisingly high-pitched—almost childlike.

"Dee is very generous," Flamel said evenly. "Though I am surprised that the Genii Cucullati would deign to work for a humani."

The creature took another clicking step closer. "Dee is no ordinary humani. The immortal Magician is dangerous, but he's protected by a master infinitely more so."

"Perhaps you should fear me," Flamel suggested with a thin smile. "I am older than Dee, and I have no master to protect me—nor have I ever needed one!"

The creature laughed and then, without warning, leapt for Flamel's throat.

A stone sword hissed through the air, slicing cleanly through the parka hood, cutting away a huge chunk of green cloth. The creature yelped and twisted its entire body in midair, curling away from the returning blade, which slashed across the front of the coat, chopping through buttons and destroying the zipper.

Josh Newman stepped directly in front of Nicholas Flamel. He was holding the stone sword he'd pulled from the cardboard tube in both hands. "I don't know who you are, or what you are," he said tightly, voice trembling with adrenaline and the effort of holding the weapon steady. "But I'm guessing that you know what this is?"

The beast backed away, blue-black eyes fixed on the gray blade. Its concealing hood was gone, cut to ribbons, the remnants hanging around its shoulders, revealing its head. There was nothing even vaguely human about the planes and angles of its face, Josh noted, but it was extraordinarily beautiful. He'd been expecting a monster, but the head was surprisingly small, with huge dark eyes sunk deep behind a narrow brow ridge, cheekbones high and sharp. The nose was straight, nostrils flaring. The mouth was a horizontal slash that now hung slightly open to reveal misshapen yellowed and blackened teeth.

Josh's eyes flickered left and right at the other creatures. They too were focused on the stone sword. "This is Clarent," he said quietly. "I fought the Nidhogg in Paris with this weapon," he continued. "And I've seen what it does to your kind." He moved the sword slightly and felt it tingle, the hilt growing warm in his hands.

"Dee did not tell us that," the creature said in its childlike voice. It looked over Josh's shoulder to the Alchemyst. "It is true?"

"Yes," Flamel said.

"Nidhogg." The creature almost spat the word. "And what happened to the legendary Devourer of Corpses?"

"Nidhogg is dead," Flamel said shortly. "Destroyed by Clarent." He stepped forward and put his left hand on Josh's shoulder. "Josh killed it."

"Killed by a humani?" it said incredulously.

"Dee has used you, betrayed you. He didn't tell you we had the sword. What else has he not told you about: did he mention the fate of the Disir in Paris? Did he tell you about the Sleeping God?"

The three creatures slipped back into their own language, yipping and growling among themselves; then the largest turned to regard Josh again. A black tongue danced in the air. "These things are of little consequence. I see before me a frightened humani boy. I can hear his muscles straining as he struggles to hold the sword steady. I can taste his fear on the air."

"And yet, despite the fear you can smell, he still attacked you," Flamel said quietly. "What does that suggest?"

The creature's shoulders moved in an awkward shrug. "That he's either a fool or a hero."

"And you and your kind have always been vulnerable to both," Flamel said.

"True, but there are no more heroes left in the world. None to attack us. Humani no longer believe in our kind. That makes us invisible . . . and invulnerable."

Josh grunted as he brought the tip of the sword up. "Not to Clarent."

The creature tilted its head and then nodded. "Not to the Coward's Blade, that is true. But there are three of us and we are fast, so fast," it added with a grin that exposed its jagged teeth. "I think we can take you, boy; cut the sword from your hands before you even know it's—"

Instincts Josh didn't know he possessed warned him that the creature was going to attack the moment it stopped speaking. Then it would all be over. Without thinking, he jabbed straight out in a thrust Joan of Arc had taught him. The blade hummed as the point stabbed at the monster's exposed throat. Josh knew that all he needed to do was to scratch the horror with the sword: a single cut had all but destroyed Nidhogg.

Laughing, the creature danced back out of range. "Too slow, humani, too slow. I saw your knuckles strain and whiten the moment before you thrust."

And at that instant Josh knew they had lost. The Genii Cucullati were just too fast.

But over his left shoulder, he heard Flamel chuckle.

Josh stared directly at the creature. He knew that the last thing he could do was turn around, but he wondered what had amused the Alchemyst. He looked closely at the Hooded One. But nothing had changed . . . except that when the monster had darted out of range, it had landed in the puddle of dirty water.

"Has fear driven you mad, Alchemyst?" the creature demanded.

"You must know the Elder Iris, the daughter of Electra?" Flamel asked conversationally, and stepped around Josh. The Alchemyst's narrow face had turned hard and expressionless, lips a thin line, pale eyes closed to little more than slits.

The creature's blue-black eyes widened in horror. It looked down.

The dirty water curling around the creature's feet had suddenly bloomed with a rainbow of colors bleeding out of the ragged strands of Flamel's woven bracelet. The Genii Cucullati attempted to leap back, but its two front paws were stuck fast in the puddle. "Release me, humani," it screeched, its childlike voice filled with terror. The creature frantically tried to push itself free. Digging in with its claws, it tried to get traction, but the tip of one of its rear legs touched the edge of the pool and it howled once more. It yanked its paw back and a curling claw ripped off, stuck at the edge of the water. The creature barked and its two companions darted forward to grab hold of it, attempting to pull it away from the swirling colored liquid.

"Decades ago," Flamel continued, "Perenelle and I rescued Iris from her sisters and in return, she gave me these bracelets. I watched her weave them out of her own rainbow-hued aura. She told me that one day they would bring a little color into my life."

Twisting swirls of color began to creep up the Genii Cucullati's leg. Black nails turned green, then red, then filthy purple fur changed to shimmering violet.

"You will die for this," the creature snarled, its voice even higher, bright blue eyes wide with terror.

"I'll die someday," Flamel agreed, "but not today, and not by your hand."

"Just you wait till I tell Mother!"

"You do that."

There was a pop, like a bubble bursting, and abruptly the rainbow colors raced up the monster's body, bathing it in light. Where the two others held it, the color spread to the claws and washed up over their skins, turning the green parkas into spectacular multicolored coats. Like oil on water, the colors shifted in mesmerizing patterns, forming new bizarre shades and incandescent hues. The creatures managed

21

a single terrified howl of terror, but their cry was cut short and they slumped onto the sidewalk in a heap. As they lay unmoving on the ground, the riot of colors quickly flowed out of their flesh, returning their coats to their former drab green, and then their bodies started to change, bones cracking, muscles and sinews re-forming. By the time the color had seeped back into the pool, the creatures had resumed their semblance of humanity.

Rain spattered along the length of the alleyway, and the surface of the multicolored puddle danced and shattered with the drops. For a single instant a perfect miniature rainbow appeared over it before fading away, leaving the puddle its previous muddy brown.

Flamel stooped to pluck the remains of the friendship bracelet from the street. The entwined threads were now off-white, leached of all color. He straightened and looked back over his shoulder at the twins. Flamel smiled. "I'm not quite as helpless as I look. Never underestimate your enemy," he advised. "But this victory is yours, Josh. You saved us. Again. It's becoming quite a habit: Ojai, Paris and now here."

"I didn't think—" Josh began.

"You never think," Sophie interrupted, squeezing his arm.

"You acted," Flamel said. "That was enough. Come; let's get out of here before they're discovered."

"Aren't they dead?" Sophie asked, stepping around the creatures.

Josh quickly wrapped Clarent in the bubble wrap and shoved it back into the cardboard tube. Then he pushed the tube into his backpack and heaved the bag onto his shoulders.

"What happened?" he asked. "That colored water. What was that?"

"A gift from an Elder," Flamel explained, hurrying down the alleyway. "Iris is called the goddess of the rainbow because of her multicolored aura. She also has access to the Shadowrealm waters of the river Styx," he finished triumphantly.

"And that means?" Josh asked.

Flamel's grin was savage. "The living cannot touch the waters of the Styx. The shock overloads their systems and knocks them unconscious."

"For how long?" Sophie asked, glancing back at what looked like a bundle of cloth in the middle of the alleyway.

"According to the legends—a year and a day."

# CHAPTER THREE

*T*he enormous dining room shimmered in the late-afternoon sunshine. Slanting sunbeams ran golden on polished wood panels and bounced off the waxed floor, sparking highlights from a full suit of armor standing in the corner and picking out spots of color from display cases of coins that traced more than two millennia of human history. One wall was entirely covered with masks and helmets from every age and continent, their empty eye sockets looking down over the room. The masks surrounded an oil painting by Santi di Tito that had been stolen from the Palazzo Vecchio in Florence centuries earlier. The painting that now hung in Florence was a perfect forgery. The center of the room was dominated by a huge scarred table that had once belonged to the Borgia family. Eighteen high-backed antique chairs were arranged around the time-stained table. Only two were occupied, and the table was bare except for a large black phone, which looked out of place in the antique-filled room.

Dr. John Dee sat on one side of the table. Dee was a small neat Englishman, pale-skinned and gray-eyed. He was wearing his customary charcoal three-piece suit, the only touch of color in the pattern of tiny gold crowns on his gray bow tie. He usually wore his iron gray hair pulled back into a tight ponytail, but it now hung loose around his shoulders, curling down to touch his triangular goatee. His dark-gloved hands rested lightly on the wooden table.

Niccolò Machiavelli sat facing John Dee. The physical difference between the two men was startling. While Dee was short and pale, Machiavelli was tall, his complexion deeply tanned, emphasizing the one trait both men shared: cold gray eyes. Machiavelli kept his snow-white hair short and had always been clean-shaven, and his tastes tended toward a more elegant style. His black suit and white silk shirt were clearly custom-made, and his deep crimson tie was woven through with threads of pure gold. It was his portrait on the wall behind him and he looked little older now than he had when it had been painted, more than five hundred years before. Niccolò Machiavelli had been born in 1469; technically he was fifty-eight years older than the Englishman. He had actually died the year Dee was born, in 1527. Both men were immortal, and they were two of the most powerful figures on the planet. Over the centuries of their long lives, the immortals had learned to detest one another, though now circumstances required them to be uneasy allies.

The two men had been sitting in the dining room of Machiavelli's grand town house off the Place du Canada in Paris for the past thirty minutes. In that time neither had spoken a word. They had each received the same summons on their cell phones: the image of a worm swallowing its own tail—the Ouroborus—one of the oldest symbols of the Dark Elders. In the center of the circle was the number thirty. A few years ago they would have received such summonses by fax or mail, decades ago by telegram and messenger, and earlier still on scraps of paper and parchment, and they would have been given hours or days to prepare for a meeting. Now the summons came by phone and the response was measured in minutes.

Although they were expecting the call, each jumped when the speakerphone in the center of the table buzzed. Machiavelli reached out to spin the phone around and check the caller ID before answering. An unusually long number beginning with 31415—he recognized it as a portion of pi—scrolled off the screen. When he hit the Answer button, static howled and crackled before dying away to a soft breezelike whisper.

*"We are disappointed."* The voice on the phone spoke an archaic form of Latin that had last been used centuries before the time of Julius Caesar. *"Very disappointed."* It was impossible to tell whether the voice was male or female, and at times it even sounded as if two people could be talking together.

Machiavelli was surprised; he had been expecting to hear his own Dark Elder master's scratchy voice—he'd never heard this speaker before. But Dee had. Although Dee's face remained

26

impassive, the Italian watched as the muscles tightened in the English Magician's jaw and he straightened almost imperceptibly. So, here was Dee's mysterious Dark Elder master.

*"We were assured that all was in readiness . . . we were assured that Flamel would be captured and slain . . . we were assured that Perenelle would be disposed of and that the twins would be apprehended and delivered into our hands. . . ."*

The voice trailed away into static.

*"And yet Flamel remains free. . . . Perenelle is no longer imprisoned in a cell, though she is trapped on the island. The twins have escaped. And we still do not have the complete Codex. We are disappointed,"* the disembodied voice repeated.

Dee and Machiavelli looked at one another. People who disappointed the Dark Elders tended to disappear. An Elder master had the power to grant human subjects immortality, but it was a gift that could be withdrawn with a single touch. Depending on how long the human had been immortal, sudden and often catastrophic old age raced through the body, centuries of time aging and destroying flesh and organs. In a matter of heartbeats, a healthy-looking human could be reduced to a pile of leathery skin and powdered bones.

*"You have failed us,"* the voices whispered.

Neither man broke the silence that followed, fully aware that their very long lives were now hanging by a thread. They were both powerful and important, but neither was irreplaceable. The Dark Elders had other human agents they could send after Flamel and the twins. Many others.

Static crackled and popped on the line, and then a new voice spoke. *"And yet, let me suggest that all is not lost."*

27

Centuries of practice kept Machiavelli's face expressionless. Here was the voice he'd been expecting, the voice of his Elder master, a figure who had briefly ruled Egypt more than three thousand years ago.

*"Let me suggest that we are closer now than we have ever been. We have cause for hope. We have confirmed that the humani children are indeed the twins of legend; we have even seen some demonstration of their powers. The cursed Alchemyst and his Sorceress wife are trapped and dying. All we have to do is to wait, and time, our greatest friend, will take care of them for us. Scathach is lost and Hekate destroyed. And we have the Codex."*

*"But not all of it,"* the male-female voice whispered. *"We still lack the final two pages."*

*"Agreed. But it is more than we have ever had. Certainly enough to begin the process of calling back the Elders from the most distant Shadowrealms."*

Machiavelli frowned, concentrating hard. Dee's Elder master was reputedly the most powerful of all the Elders, and yet here was his own master arguing and debating with him or her. The line crackled, and the male-female voice sounded almost petulant.

*"But we lack the Final Summoning. Without it, our brothers and sisters will not be able to take that last step from their Shadowrealms into this world."*

Machiavelli's master responded evenly. *"We should still be gathering our armies. Some of our brethren have ventured far from this earth; they have even gone beyond the Shadowrealms into the Otherworlds. It will take them many days to return. We need to call them back now, draw them into the Shadowrealms that border this earth, so that when the time is right, a single step will take them into this world and we can move as one to reclaim the planet.*"

Machiavelli looked at Dee. The English Magician's head had titled slightly to one side, eyes half closed as he listened to the Elders. Almost as if he felt Machiavelli's gaze on him, Dee opened his eyes and raised his brows in a silent question. The Italian shook his head slightly; he had no idea what was happening.

"*This is the time foreseen by Abraham when he first created the Codex,*" Machiavelli's master continued. "*He had the Sight, he could see the curling strands of time. He foretold that this age would come—he called it the Time of the Turning, when order would be returned to the world. We have discovered the twins, we know the whereabouts of Flamel and the last two pages from the Codex. Once we have the pages we can use the twins' powers to fuel the Final Summoning.*"

The line crackled with static, and in the background Machiavelli clearly heard a murmur of assent. He realized that there were others listening in on the line, and he wondered how many of the Dark Elders had gathered. He bit down hard on the inside of his cheek to prevent himself from smiling at the image of the Elders, in their assorted guises and aspects—human and inhuman, beast and monster—listening intently on cell phones. Machiavelli chose his moment when there was a break in the murmuring voices and spoke carefully, stripping all emotion from his voice, keeping it neutral and professional.

"Then can I suggest that you allow us to complete our

tasks. Let us find Flamel and the twins." He knew he was playing a dangerous game now, but it was clear that there was dissension in the ranks of the Elders, and Machiavelli had always been expert at manipulating such situations. He had clearly heard the need in his master's voice. The Elders desperately wanted the twins and the Codex: without them, the rest of the Dark Elders would not be able to return to the earth. And at that instant he recognized that both he and Dee were still valuable assets. "The doctor and I have formulated a plan," he said, and then fell silent, waiting to see if they would take the bait.

"*Speak, humani,*" the male-female voice rumbled.

Machiavelli folded his hands and said nothing. Dee's eyebrows shot up and he pointed at the phone. *Speak,* he mouthed.

"*Speak!*" the voice snarled, static howling and popping.

"You are not my master," Machiavelli said very quietly. "You cannot command me."

There was a long hissing sound, like steam escaping. Machiavelli turned his head slightly, trying to identify the noise. Then he nodded: it was laughter. The other Elders were amused by his response. He had been correct; there was dissension in the ranks of the Elders, and though Dee's master might be all-powerful, that did not mean he was liked. Here was a weakness Machiavelli could exploit to his advantage.

Dee was staring at him, gray eyes wide with horror and maybe even admiration.

The line clicked, the ambient background noise changed and then Machiavelli's master spoke, amusement clearly audible in his gravelly voice. *"What do you propose? And be careful, humani,"* he added. *"You too have failed us. We were assured that Flamel and the twins would not leave Paris."*

The Italian leaned toward the phone, his smile triumphant. "Master. I was instructed to do nothing until the English Magician arrived. Valuable time was lost. Flamel was able to contact allies, find shelter and rest." Machiavelli was watching Dee carefully as he spoke. He knew the Englishman had contacted his Elder master, and that master in turn had ordered Machiavelli's master to tell the Italian to do nothing until Dee arrived. "However," he pressed, having made his point, "this delay worked to our advantage. The boy was Awakened by an Elder loyal to us. We have some idea of the twins' powers and we know where they've gone." He could barely keep the smugness out of his voice. He looked at Dee sitting across the table and nodded quickly. The English Magician took the hint.

"They are in London," John Dee continued. "And Britain, more than any other land on this earth, is *our* country," he stressed. "Unlike in Paris, we have allies there: Elders, Next Generation, immortals and humani servants who will aid us. And in England there are others, loyal to none but themselves, whose services can be bought. All of these resources can be directed to finding Flamel and the twins." He finished and leaned forward, staring intently at the phone, waiting for an answer.

The line clicked and went dead. Then an irritating busy signal filled the room.

Dee stared at the phone with a mixture of shock and

anger. "Have we lost the connection or have they just hung up on us?"

Machiavelli hit the Speaker button, silencing the noise. "Now you know how I feel when you hang up on me," he said quietly.

"What do we do now?" Dee demanded.

"We wait. I would imagine they are discussing our futures."

Dee folded his arms over his narrow chest. "They need us," he said, trying—and failing—to sound confident.

Machiavelli's smile was bitter. "They use us. But they do not need us. I know of at least a dozen immortals in Paris alone who could do what I do."

"Well, yes, *you* are replaceable," Dee said with a self-satisfied shrug. "But *I* have spent a lifetime chasing Nicholas and Perenelle."

"You mean you've spent a lifetime failing to catch them," Machiavelli said, his voice neutral, and then added with a sly smile, "So close, and yet always so far."

But any reply Dee was about to make was cut off when the phone rang.

*"This is our decision."* It was Dee's Elder master speaking, the male-female voices blending together into one slightly discordant voice. *"The Magician will follow the Alchemyst and the twins to England. Your instructions are explicit: destroy Flamel, capture the twins and retrieve the two missing pages. Use whatever means necessary to achieve this objective; we have associates in England who are indebted to us. We will call in*

*those debts. And Doctor . . . if you fail us this time, then we will temporarily remove the gift of immortality and allow your humani body to age to its very limit . . . and then, at the moment before your death, we will make you immortal again."* There was a rasp that might have been a chuckle or an indrawn breath. *"Think about how that will feel: your brilliant mind trapped in an ancient and feeble body, unable to see or hear clearly, unable to walk or move, in constant pain from a score of ailments. You will be forever ancient and yet undying. Fail us and this will be your destiny. We will trap you in this aged fleshy shell for an eternity."*

Dee nodded, swallowed hard and then said with as much confidence as he could muster, "I will not fail you."

*"And you, Niccolò . . ."* Machiavelli's Elder master spoke. *"You will travel to the Americas. The Sorceress is loose on Alcatraz. Do whatever you must to secure the island."*

"But I have no contacts in San Francisco," Machiavelli protested quickly, "no allies. Europe has always been my domain."

*"We have agents all across the Americas. Even now they are moving westward to await your arrival. We will instruct one to guide and assist you. On Alcatraz, you will find an army of sorts sleeping in the cells, creatures the humani will recognize from their darkest nightmares and foulest myths. It was not our intention to use this army so soon, but events are moving quickly now, much faster than we anticipated. Soon it will be the Time of Litha, the summer solstice. At midsummer, the twins' auras will be at their strongest and the barriers between this world and*

33

*the myriad Shadowrealms at their weakest. It is our intention to reclaim the world of the humani on that day."*

Even Machiavelli was unable to keep his face expressionless. He looked at Dee and found that the Magician too was wide-eyed with shock. Both men had worked for the Dark Elders for centuries and had always known that they intended to return to the world they had once ruled. Still, it was startling to discover that after years of waiting and planning, it was about to happen in just over three weeks' time.

Dr. John Dee leaned closer to the phone. "Masters—and I know I speak for Machiavelli when I say this—we are delighted that the Time of the Turning is almost upon us and that you will soon return." He swallowed hard and took a quick breath. "But if you will allow me to caution you: the world you are returning to is not the world you left. The humani have technology, communications, weapons . . . they will resist," he added hesitantly.

*"Indeed they will, Doctor,"* Machiavelli's master said. *"So we will give the humani something to focus on, something to use up their resources and consume their attention. Niccolò,"* the voice continued, *"when you have retaken Alcatraz, rouse the monsters in the cells and then loose them on the city of San Francisco. The destruction and terror will be indescribable. And when the city is a smoking ruin, allow the creatures to wander as they will. They will ravage across America. Mankind has always been fearful of the dark: we will remind him why. There are similar caches of creatures already hidden on every continent; they will be released at the same time. The world will quickly dissolve into madness and chaos. Entire armies will be wiped out, so that*

34

*there will be none to stand against us when we return. And what will be our first action? Why, we will destroy the monsters and be hailed by the humani as their saviors.*"

"And these beasts are in Alcatraz's cells?" Machiavelli asked, appalled. "How do I rouse them?"

"*You will be given instructions when you reach the Americas. But first, you have to defeat Perenelle Flamel.*"

"How do we know she is still there? If she has escaped her cell, surely she will have fled the island?" The Italian was aware that his heart was suddenly pounding; three hundred years ago he had sworn vengeance on the Sorceress. Was he now about to be given an opportunity for revenge?

"*She is still on the island. She has released Areop-Enap, the Old Spider. It is a dangerous foe, but not invincible. We have taken steps to neutralize it and ensure that Perenelle will remain there until you arrive. And Niccolò*"—the Elder's voice turned hard and ugly—"*do not repeat Dee's mistake.*"

The Magician straightened.

"*Do not attempt to capture or imprison Perenelle. Do not talk to her, bargain with her or try to reason with her. Kill her on sight. The Sorceress is infinitely more dangerous than the Alchemyst.*"

35

# CHAPTER FOUR

The early-morning sky over Alcatraz was the color of dirty metal. Flecks of ice-cold rain hissed across the island, and the churning sea pounding against the rocks sent bitter salty foam high into the air.

Perenelle Flamel ducked back into the shelter of the ruin of the Warden's House. She rubbed her hands up and down her bare arms, brushing away droplets of salty moisture. She was wearing a light sleeveless summer dress, now soiled with mud and rust, but the tall elegant woman wasn't cold. Although she'd been reluctant to use her waning powers, she had adjusted her aura, bringing her body temperature up to a comfortable level. She knew if she got too cold, she wouldn't be able to think clearly, and she had a feeling she was going to need all her resources in the hours to come.

Four days ago, Perenelle Flamel had been kidnapped by John Dee and imprisoned on Alcatraz. Her guard, a sphinx, had been chosen for its special ability to feed off others' auras—the energy fields that surround every living thing. The English Magician had hoped the sphinx would drain Perenelle's aura and prevent her from escaping, but as Dee had done so often in the past, he had underestimated Perenelle's abilities and powers. With the help of the island's guardian ghost, the Sorceress had been able to escape the sphinx. It was only then that she discovered the island's terrible secret: Dee had been collecting monsters. The prison cells were filled with horrific creatures from all over the earth, creatures most humans believed existed only in the darkest corners of myth and legend. But the most surprising discovery had lain in the hidden tunnels deep beneath the island. There, trapped behind magical symbols older than even the Elders, she had found the creature known as Areop-Enap, the Old Spider. The two had formed an uneasy alliance and defeated the Morrigan, the Crow Goddess, and her army of birds. But they knew that worse was to come.

"This weather is not natural," Perenelle said softly, the merest trace of her French accent audible in her voice. She breathed deeply and grimaced. To her heightened sense of smell, the wind coming in off San Francisco Bay was tainted with the odor of something foul and long dead, a sure sign that it was abnormal.

Areop-Enap was perched high on a wall of the empty building. The enormous bloated spider was busy sheathing the shell of the house with a sticky white web. Millions of spiders, some as big as plates, others little more than specks of dirt, scuttled across the massive web in an undulating dark shadow, adding their own layers of silk to the dripping web. Without turning its head, the Elder swiveled two of its eight eyes to focus on the woman. It raised one of its thick legs straight up in the air, gray-tipped purple hair waving in the breeze. "Aye, something's coming . . . but not Elder, and not humani, either," it lisped.

"Something's already here," Perenelle said grimly.

Areop-Enap turned to look down at Perenelle. Eight tiny eyes were perched on the top of its eerily humanlike head. It had no nose or ears, and its mouth was a horizontal slash filled with long poisonous fangs. The savage teeth gave it a curious lisping speech. "What happened?" it asked suddenly, dropping to the ground on a gossamer thread.

Perenelle picked her way across the stone floor, trying to avoid the knotted strands of spiderweb that stuck to everything they touched. They had the consistency of chewing gum. "I was down at the water's edge," she said quietly. "I wanted to see how far we were from land."

"Why?" Areop-Enap asked, stepping closer to the woman, towering over her.

"I learned a spell many years ago from an Inuit shaman. It changes the consistency of running water, turning it to something like thick sticky mud. Effectively, it allows you to walk on water. Inuits use it when they're hunting polar bears out on ice floes. I wanted to see if it worked on warm salt water."

"And?" Areop-Enap asked.

"I didn't get a chance to try it." Perenelle shook her head. Gathering her long mane of black hair in her hands, she pulled it over her shoulder. Usually, she wore it in a tight thick braid, but it hung loose now, and it was shot through with more silver and gray than even the day before. "Look."

Areop-Enap stepped closer. Each of its legs was thicker than the woman's torso, and tipped with a hooked spike, but it moved without making a sound.

Perenelle held out a hank of hair. A four-inch-long chunk had been neatly cut from it. "I was leaning over the water, gathering my aura to try the spell, when something came up out of the water with barely a ripple. Its jaws sliced right through my hair."

Old Spider hissed softly. "Did you see it?"

"A glimpse, nothing more. I was too busy scrambling back up the beach."

"A serpent?"

Perenelle reverted to the French of her youth. "No. A woman. Green-skinned, with teeth . . . lots of tiny teeth. I caught the flash of a fish's tail as it dipped back into the water." Perenelle shook her head and dropped her hair, settling it back over her shoulder, then looked up at the Elder. "Was it a mermaid? I've never seen one of the seafolk."

"Unlikely," Areop-Enap muttered. "Though it might have been one of the wilder Nereids."

"The sea nymphs . . . but they are far from home."

"Yes. They do prefer the warmer waters of the Mediterranean, but the oceans of the world are their home. I've encountered them everywhere, even amongst the icebergs of the Antarctic. There are fifty Nereids, and they always travel together . . . which suggests to me that this island is most likely completely surrounded. We'll not escape by sea. But that is not the greatest of our concerns," Areop-Enap lisped. "If the Nereids are here, then that probably means that their father, Nereus, is close as well."

Despite her warmth, a shiver ran up Perenelle's spine. "The Old Man of the Sea? But he lives in some distant watery Shadowrealm and only rarely ventures to this realm. He hasn't come to our world since 1912. What would possibly bring him back?"

Areop-Enap bared its teeth in a savage grin. "Why, you, Madame Perenelle. You are the prize. They want your knowledge and your memories. You and your husband are amongst the rarest of humans: you are immortals without Elder masters controlling you. And now that you are trapped on Alcatraz, the Dark Elders will do their utmost to ensure that you not leave here alive."

Blue and white static crackled down the length of Perenelle's hair, which slowly rose and extended out behind her in a shimmering black halo. Her eyes blazed cold and green and an ice white aura bloomed around her, filling the interior of the ruined house with stark light. A dark wave of spiders scuttled into the shadows. "Do you know how many Dark Elders and their kith and kin have attempted to kill me?" Perenelle demanded.

Areop-Enap shrugged, an ugly movement of all its legs. "Many?" it suggested.

"And do you know how many are still alive?"

"Few?" Areop-Enap suggested.

Perenelle smiled. "Very few."

# CHAPTER FIVE

"Wait up. My phone is ringing."

Sophie ducked into a doorway, fished in her pocket and pulled out her cell phone. The battery had died in Hekate's Shadowrealm, but the Comte de Saint-Germain had found her a charger that worked. Tilting the screen, she peered at the unusually long number. "I don't know who it is," she said, looking from her brother to Nicholas.

Josh looked over his sister's shoulder. "I don't recognize the number," he added

"What does it begin with?" Nicholas asked, squinting, trying to focus on the screen.

"Zero, zero, three, three . . ."

"That's the country code for France," Flamel said. "Answer it; it can only be Francis."

"Or Dee or Machiavelli," Josh said quickly. "Maybe we should—"

But before he could finish, Sophie had pressed the Answer button. "Hello?" she said cautiously.

"It's me!" Saint-Germain's voice was light and accentless, and Sophie could tell he was outside by all the noise in the background. "Let me speak to the old man. And don't tell him I said that!"

Sophie bit back a grin and handed the phone to the Alchemyst. "You were right; it's Francis. He wants to talk to you."

Nicholas pressed the phone to one ear and covered the other with his hand, trying to block out the noise of the traffic. *"Allô?"*

"Where are you?" Saint-Germain asked in Latin.

Nicholas looked around, trying to orient himself. "On Marylebone Road, just coming up to Regent's Park tube station."

"Hang on; I've got someone on the other line." Nicholas heard Saint-Germain move away from the phone and relay the information in rapid-fire archaic French. "OK," he said a moment later. "Continue straight down the road and then wait outside St. Marylebone Church. You will be picked up."

"How will I know the driver is working for you?" Nicholas asked.

"A good point. Do you have reason to believe this conversation may be monitored?"

"Both the Italian and the Englishman certainly have the resources," the Alchemyst said carefully.

"That is true."

"And there was an unwelcoming committee waiting for us. I would imagine they reported in before they came after us."

"Ah." Saint-Germain paused and then said carefully, "I am assuming you took care of the problem discreetly."

"Very discreetly. But . . ."

"But?" Saint-Germain asked.

"Although I used none of my aura, a certain amount of power was released. That's sure to have attracted attention, especially in this city."

There was another pause; then Saint-Germain said, "OK, I've just sent the driver a text. Let me remind you of a party I held in Versailles in February 1758. It was my birthday, and you gave me a vellum-bound book from your personal library as a present."

Nicholas's lips curled in a smile. "I remember."

"I still have the book. The driver will tell you the title," he continued, raising his voice over the rattle of hammering in the background.

"What's all the noise?" Flamel asked, slipping back into English.

"Workmen. We're trying to shore up the house. Apparently, there is the very real danger that it will collapse into the catacombs below, and probably take half the street with it."

Nicholas lowered his voice. "Old friend. I cannot tell you how sorry I am for the trouble I brought to your home. I will of course pay for the damage."

Saint-Germain chuckled. "Please do not trouble yourself. It's not costing me anything. I've sold the exclusive rights to the story to a magazine. The fee more than takes care of the repairs, and the press coverage is invaluable; my new album is shooting up the download charts . . . if that is not a contradiction," he added with a laugh.

"Which story?" Nicholas asked, glancing quickly at the twins.

"Why, the gas explosion that damaged my house, of course," Saint-Germain said lightly. "I must go. I will keep in touch. And old friend"—he paused—"be careful. If there is anything you need—anything—then you know how to get in touch with us."

Nicholas hit the Off button and handed the phone back to Sophie without a word. "He said—"

"We heard." The twins' Awakened senses had allowed them to clearly hear both sides of the conversation. "A gas explosion?" Sophie asked.

"Well, he could hardly say the damage was caused by some sort of primeval dinosaur, could he?" Josh teased. "Who'd believe him?" Shoving his hands in his pockets, he hurried after Flamel, who was already striding down the street. "Come on, sis."

Sophie nodded. Her brother had a point. But she was also beginning to see how the Elders had managed to keep their existence a secret for so long. Mankind simply didn't want to believe that there was magic in the world. Not in this age of science and technology. Monsters and magic belonged to the primitive uncivilized past, and yet in the last few days she'd seen that every day there was evidence for magic. People reported impossibilities all the time; they saw the strangest

44

things, the most bizarre creatures . . . and no one believed them. They couldn't all be wrong, lying, confused or misguided, could they? If the Dark Elders and their servants were in positions of power, then all they would have to do was dismiss the reports, ignore them or—as had just happened in Paris—ridicule them in the media. Soon even the people who had made the reports, the very people who had seen something out of the ordinary, would begin to doubt the evidence of their own senses. Just yesterday the Nidhogg, a creature that supposedly existed only in legend, had rampaged through Paris's narrow streets, leaving a trail of devastation. It had crashed across the Champs-Elysées and ripped apart a section of the famous quayside before plunging into the river. Dozens of people must have seen it; but where were their stories, their statements? The press had reported the event as a gas explosion in the ancient catacombs.

And then all the gargoyles and grotesques on Notre Dame had come alive and crawled down the building. Using Josh's aura to enhance her own, Sophie had used Fire and Air magic to reduce the creatures to little more than shattered stone . . . and yet how had it been reported in the press?

The effects of acid rain.

As they'd sped through the French countryside on the Eurostar, they'd read the online coverage on Josh's laptop. Every news organization in the world had some story about the events, but they'd all told versions of the same lie. It was only on the wilder conspiracy Web sites and blogs that sightings of Nidhogg had been reported, along with shaky mobile-phone footage of the monster. Dozens of postings

45

dismissed the videos and stills as fake, comparing them to images of Sasquatch and the Loch Ness monster that had been proven false. Only now, of course, Sophie was beginning to suspect that both of those creatures were probably real too.

She hurried to catch up with Flamel and her brother.

"Stay close, Sophie," Nicholas said. "You have no idea of the danger we're in."

"So you keep telling us," she muttered, though right now she couldn't figure out how things could get any worse.

"Where are we going?" Josh asked. He was still dizzy after the adrenaline rush, and now he was starting to feel shaky as well.

"Just down here," Nicholas said, nodding toward a white stone church on their left.

Sophie caught up with her brother and noticed that he was pale and there was a light sheen of sweat on his forehead. She gripped his arm and squeezed lightly. "How are you doing?" She knew what he was going through: the noise, the smells, the sounds of the city were starting to overwhelm his recently Awakened senses. She'd experienced the same shocking sensory overload when Hekate had Awakened her. But while the Witch of Endor and Joan had helped her control the wash of emotions and sensations, there was no one to help her brother.

"I'm fine," Josh said quickly. "OK, not so well," he admitted a moment later, seeing the look of disbelief on his sister's face. She'd been through the same transformation; she knew what he was feeling. "It's just that everything . . ." He struggled to find the words.

"It's just too much," Sophie finished for him.

Josh nodded. "Too much," he agreed. "I can even taste the car exhaust."

"Everything adjusts," she promised, "and it gets easier. Or maybe you just get used to it."

"I don't think I could ever get used to this," he said, dipping his head and squinting against the brilliant sunshine breaking through the blue-black clouds. Sunlight sparkling on the wet streets sent painful daggers into his eyes. "I need sunglasses."

"That's a good idea." Sophie trotted ahead a few steps. "Nicholas, wait up," she called.

But though the Alchemyst glanced over his shoulder, he didn't stop. "We cannot delay," he snapped, and continued at a brisk pace.

Sophie stopped in the middle of the street and pulled her brother to a halt with her. Nicholas had walked half a dozen paces before he realized that the twins were no longer behind him. He stopped and turned, waving them forward. They ignored him, and when he strode back to them there was something dark and ugly about the set of his face. "I've no time for this nonsense."

"We need sunglasses for Josh, and for me too," Sophie said, "and water."

"We'll get them later."

"We need them now," she said firmly.

Nicholas opened his mouth to spit out a reply, but Josh took a step forward, bringing him close to the Alchemyst. "We need them now." There was something like arrogance in his voice. Standing on the parvis in front of the cathedral in Paris, feeling the raw power flow through his body, watching the animated stone gargoyles shatter to dust, he had realized just how powerful he and his sister were. At this moment they might need the Alchemyst, but he needed them also.

Nicholas looked into the boy's bright blue eyes, and whatever he saw in them made him nod and turn back to a row of shops. "Water and sunglasses," he said. "Any particular color sunglasses?" he asked sarcastically.

"Black," the twins answered in unison.

Sophie stood with Josh outside the shop. She was exhausted, but she knew Josh was feeling even worse. Now that the rain had blown over, the street was beginning to fill up. People of a dozen different nationalities walked past, chatting in a variety of languages.

Sophie suddenly tilted her head to one side, brow creasing in a frown.

"What's wrong?" Josh asked immediately.

"Nothing's wrong," she said slowly, "it's just that . . ."

"What?"

"I thought I recognized some of the words those people were speaking."

Her brother turned to follow her gaze. Two women in the long flowing abaya of the Middle Eastern countries, their heads covered and their faces hidden behind burkas, chatted together animatedly.

"They're sisters. . . . They're going to see a doctor just

around the corner in Harley Street . . . ," Sophie said in wonder.

Josh turned to hear better and pushed his hair back off his ear. Concentrating hard, he managed to isolate the voices of the two women. "Sophie, I can't make out a word they're saying; I think they're speaking Arabic."

Two smartly dressed businessmen walked past, heading toward Regent's Park tube station. They were both on mobile phones.

"The one on the left is talking to his wife in Stockholm," Sophie continued, her voice now little more than a whisper. "He's sorry he missed his son's birthday party. The one on the right is talking to his head office, also in Sweden. He wants some spreadsheets e-mailed."

Josh turned his head again, ignoring the traffic and the myriad other noises of the city. Suddenly, he found that by focusing on the two businessmen, he could pick up individual words. His hearing was so acute that he could even hear the tinny voices on the other end of the cell phone. Neither man was speaking English. "How can you understand?" he asked.

"It's the Witch of Endor's knowledge," Nicholas said. He had stepped out of the shop in time to hear Josh's question. He pulled two pairs of identical cheap sunglasses from a paper bag and handed them over. "Not designer, I'm afraid."

Sophie slipped the dark glasses onto her face. The relief was immediate, and she could see by her brother's expression that he felt the same. "Tell me," she said. "I thought it was just a lot of ancient stuff she passed on to me. I didn't realize any of it would be useful."

Nicholas handed over two bottles of water, and the twins fell into step beside him as he hurried down the street toward St. Marylebone Church. "The Witch passed on all her knowledge to you when she wrapped you in the shroud of air. It was, I'll admit, too much for you to handle. But I'd no idea she was going to do it," he added quickly, seeing the scowl appear on Josh's face. "It was totally unexpected and completely out of character. Generations ago, priestesses would study with the Witch all their lives to be rewarded with only the tiniest fragment of her knowledge."

"Why did she give it all to me?" Sophie asked, confused.

"It's a mystery," he admitted. Spotting a gap in the traffic, the Alchemyst hurried the twins across Marylebone High Street. They were close enough now to see the elegant façade of the church ahead of them. "I know Joan helped sift through the Witch's knowledge for you."

Sophie nodded. In Paris, while she'd slept, Joan of Arc had taught her techniques for controlling the jumble of arcane and obscure information that washed through her brain.

"I believe that what is happening now is that the Witch of Endor's memories and knowledge are gradually being absorbed into your own memories. Rather than simply just knowing what the Witch knows, you will also know *how* she knows it. In effect, her memories are becoming yours."

Sophie shook her head. "I don't understand."

They had finally reached the church. Nicholas climbed two steps and looked up and down the road, quickly scanning the passersby, twisting to look out toward Regent's Park before turning back to the twins. "It's like the difference between watching a game and playing the game. When you met Saint-Germain," he added, "you instantly knew what the Witch knows about him, right?"

Sophie nodded. It had come to her in a flash that the Witch of Endor neither liked nor trusted the Comte de Saint-Germain.

"Think about Saint-Germain now," the Alchemyst suggested.

She looked at her brother, who shrugged, eyes invisible behind his own dark glasses. Sophie turned over her right wrist. On the underside of her arm was a gold circle with a red dot in the center. Saint-Germain had painlessly burned the tattoo into the flesh of her wrist when he'd taught her about the Magic of Fire. Thinking of Saint-Germain brought a sudden flood of memories: brilliantly intense physical memories. Sophie closed her eyes and in an instant she was in another time, another place.

*London, 1740.*

She was standing in an enormous ballroom, wearing a gown that was so heavy it felt as if it was pressing her into the ground. It was amazingly uncomfortable, biting and pinching, squeezing, constricting and contracting everywhere. The air in the ballroom stank of candle wax and too many perfumes, of overflowing toilets, cooked food and unwashed bodies. A crowd of people swirled around her, but as she moved forward, they unconsciously moved out of her way, clearing a path to the somberly dressed young man with the startling blue eyes. It was Francis, the Comte de Saint-Germain. He was speaking in Russian with a nobleman from the court of the infant emperor, Ivan VI. She found she understood what he was saying. The nobleman was hinting that Peter the Great's youngest daughter, Elizabeth, might soon seize power and that there would be business opportunities for a man of Saint-Germain's skills in St. Petersburg. The count slowly turned to look at her. Taking her hand in his, he bowed over it and said in Italian, "It is an honor to finally meet you, madam."

Sophie's eyes blinked open and she swayed. Josh's arm shot out to catch hold of her. "What happened?" he demanded.

"I was there . . . ," Sophie whispered. She shook her head quickly. "Here, in London. More than two hundred fifty years ago. I saw everything." She reached out to squeeze his arm. "I could feel the clothes I was wearing, smell the stink of the room, and when Saint-Germain spoke in Russian I understood him, and then, when he talked to me in Italian, I understood that, too. I was there," she repeated still awed by her new memories.

"The Witch of Endor's memories are becoming *your* memories," Nicholas said. "Her knowledge is becoming yours. Eventually, all that she knows, you will know."

Sophie Newman shivered. Then she suddenly thought of something disturbing. "But what happens to me?" she asked. "The Witch has thousands of years of memories and experiences; I've only got fifteen and a half years, and I don't remember all of them. Could her memories crowd mine out?"

Nicholas blinked hard. Then he slowly nodded. "I hadn't thought of that, but yes, you're right, they could," he said very quietly. "We'll have to ensure that that does not happen."

"Why?" the twins asked together.

Nicholas came down the steps to stand beside them. "Because we are nothing more than the sum of our memories and experiences. If the Witch's memories crowd out yours, then you will in effect *become* the Witch of Endor."

Josh was horrified. "And what happens to Sophie?"

"If that happens, there will be no more Sophie. There will only be the Witch."

"Then she did it deliberately," Josh said, anger raising his voice enough to attract the attention of a group of tourists photographing the church's clock face. His twin nudged him and he lowered his voice to a hoarse whisper. "That's why she gave Sophie all her knowledge!" Nicholas started to shake his head, but Josh pressed on. "Once her memories take over completely, then she has a newer, younger body, rather than her old blind body. You can't deny it."

Nicholas closed his mouth and turned away. "I have to . . . I have to think about this," he said. "I've never heard of anything like this happening before."

"But you never heard of the Witch giving all her knowledge to one person before, did you?" Josh demanded.

Sophie caught the Alchemyst's arm and stepped in front of him. "Nicholas, what do we do?" she asked.

"I've no idea," he admitted with an exhausted sigh. And in that moment, he looked ancient, with lines etched deeply onto his forehead and around his eyes, creases alongside his nose, deep grooves between his eyebrows.

"Then who *would* know?" she snapped, a note of fear in her voice.

"Perenelle," he said, and then nodded fiercely. "My Perenelle will know what to do. We've got to get you back to her. She'll be able to help. In the meantime, you've got to concentrate on being Sophie. You've got to focus on your own identity."

"How?"

"Think about your past, your parents, your schools, people you've met, friends, enemies, places you've visited." He turned to Josh. "You've got to help. Ask your sister questions about the past, about everything you've done together, the places you've been. And Sophie," he added, turning to look at the girl, "every time you begin to experience one of the Witch of Endor's memories, deliberately focus on something else, a memory of your own. You have to fight to keep the Witch's memories from overwhelming yours until we find a way to control this."

Suddenly, a black London cab pulled up to the curb and the passenger window slid down. "Get in," a voice commanded from the shadows.

No one moved.

"We don't have all day. Get in." There was a hint of North Africa in the rich timbre of the voice.

"We didn't call a cab," Flamel said, desperately glancing up and down the road. St Germain had said he was sending someone to them, but the Alchemyst had never imagined it was going to be anything as ordinary as a London taxi. Was this a trap? Had Dee caught up with them? He looked over his shoulder at the church. The door was open. They could dart up the steps into the sanctuary of the church, but once inside, they would be trapped.

"This car was specially ordered for you, Mr. Flamel." There was a pause and the voice added, "The author of one of the most boring books I have ever read, *The Philosophic Summary*."

"Boring?" Nicholas yanked the door open and pushed the twins into the gloom. "It's been acknowledged for centuries as a work of genius!" Climbing in, he slammed the door. "Francis probably told you to say that."

"You'd better buckle up," the driver commanded. "We've got all sorts of company heading this way, none of it friendly and all of it unpleasant."

# CHAPTER SIX

The man's enormous bulk filled the front seat. He swiveled around to look at them through the glass separating the driver from the passengers, and the twins realized that it wasn't fat that made him so large, it was muscle. A sleeveless black-and-white striped shirt stretched tightly across his massive chest, and he was so tall that his smooth-shaven head brushed the top of the car's cabin. His skin was a deep rich brown, matching the color of his eyes, and his teeth looked almost too white to be natural. There were three short horizontal scars on each cheek just below his eyes. "You're barely in the country and you've managed to stir up quite a hornets' nest," he said, his voice a deep rumble. "On the way down here, I spotted some things that haven't walked this earth for generations." He grinned. "I'm Palamedes, by the way." Then he shook his head. "And don't ever call me Pally."

"Palamedes?" Flamel asked in astonishment, leaning forward to get a better look at the driver. "Palamedes? The Saracen Knight?"

"The same," the driver said, turning away, locking the steering wheel and screeching back into traffic without signaling. Car horns blared and tires squealed behind him. He held up his cell phone. "Francis gave me just the barest details. Usually, I don't get involved in the disputes between the various Elder factions—it's safer that way—but once he told me it was to do with the legendary twins"—his eyes watched them in the rearview mirror—"then I knew I had no choice."

Josh reached down and squeezed his sister's hand hard. He wanted to distract her; he didn't want her thinking about Palamedes. Even though Josh had never heard of him, he had no doubt that the Witch's knowledge would tell Sophie about their driver. The man was huge, built like a linebacker or a professional wrestler, and he spoke English with a strange accent. Josh thought it might even be Egyptian. Four years ago, the entire Newman family had traveled to Egypt. They'd spent a month touring the ancient sites, and the man's lilting accent was similar to the ones he'd heard then. Josh leaned forward for a closer look at the man. Massive short-fingered hands gripped the steering wheel—and then he noticed that the man's wrists were thickened and his knuckles swollen and hard with calluses. Josh had seen similar hands on some of the sensei he'd trained with; they were usually signs of someone who had studied karate, kung fu or boxing for years.

"Hang on." Palamedes made an illegal U-turn and headed

back the way they'd come. "Just sit back and stay in the shadows," he warned. "There are so many cabs on the street that they're practically invisible; no one even looks at them. And besides, they won't be expecting you to return this way."

Josh nodded. It was a clever strategy. "Who are 'they'?" he asked.

Before Palamedes could answer, Nicholas suddenly stiffened, staring out the window.

"You see them?" Palamedes asked in a deep rumble.

"I see them," the Alchemyst whispered.

"What?" Sophie and Josh said simultaneously, sitting forward, following the Alchemyst's gaze.

"The three men on the opposite side of the street," he said shortly.

A trio of shaven-headed, pierced and heavily tattooed young men swaggered down the center of the road. In their stained blue jeans, dirty T-shirts and construction boots, they looked threatening, but not particularly otherworldly.

"If you squint," Flamel explained, "you should be able to see their auras."

The twins closed their eyes to little more than slits, and they immediately saw the ugly gray tendrils of smoky light that flowed off the trio. The gray was shot through with purple.

"Cucubuths," Palamedes explained.

The Alchemyst nodded. "Very rare. They are the offspring of a vampire and a Torc Madra," Flamel told the twins. "They often have tails. They're mercenaries, hunters. Blood drinkers."

"And as dumb as dirt." Palamedes pulled up beside a bus, shielding the car from the cucubuths. "They'll trace your scent as far as the church; then it will vanish. That will confuse them. With luck, they'll end up arguing with one another and start fighting."

The car slowed, then stopped as the lights changed.

"There, at the traffic lights," Nicholas whispered.

"Yes, I passed them on the way down here," Palamedes said.

The twins scanned the intersection but saw nothing out of the ordinary. "Who?" Sophie asked.

"The schoolgirls," Palamedes rumbled.

Two red-haired and pale-skinned young women were chatting, waiting for the lights to change. They were alike enough to be sisters and seemed to be wearing school uniforms. Both were carrying expensive-looking handbags.

"Don't even look at them," Palamedes warned. "They're like beasts; they can sense when they're being watched."

Sophie and Josh stared hard at the floor, concentrating fiercely on not thinking about the two girls. Nicholas picked up a newspaper he'd found on the backseat and held it open in front of his face, focusing on the most boring item he could find, the international exchange rates.

"They're crossing right in front of the car," Palamedes murmured, turning to look back into the cabin, hiding his face. "I'm sure they wouldn't recognize me, but I don't want to take the risk."

The lights changed and Palamedes pulled away with the rest of the traffic.

"Dearg Due," Flamel said, before the twins could ask the question. He swiveled to look through the rear window. The girls' red hair was still visible as they disappeared into the crowd. "Vampires who settled what became the Celtic lands after the Fall of Danu Talis."

"Like Scatty?" Sophie asked.

Nicholas shook his head. "Nothing like Scatty. These are most definitely not vegetarian."

"They were heading toward the church too," Palamedes said, chuckling. "If they encounter the cucubuths, that should make for an interesting meeting. They hate one another."

"Who would win?" Sophie asked.

"Dearg Due, every time," Palamedes said with a cheery smile. "I fought them in Ireland. They're vicious fighters, impossible to kill."

They continued down Marylebone Road before turning left onto Hampstead Road. Traffic slowed to a crawl, then finally ground to a halt. Somewhere ahead of them horns blared, and an ambulance wail started up. "We might be here for a while." Palamedes pulled the emergency brake and twisted in his seat once again to look at the twins and Flamel. "So you're the legendary Nicholas Flamel, the Alchemyst. I've heard a lot about you over the years," he said. "None of it good. Do you know, there are Shadowrealms where your very name is used as a curse?"

The twins were startled by the vehemence in the man's voice. They were unsure whether he was joking.

Palamedes focused on the Alchemyst. "Death and destruction follow in your wake—"

"The Dark Elders have been ruthless in their attempts to stop me," Flamel said slowly, with a definite chill in his voice.

"—as do fires, famines, floods and earthquakes," Palamedes rumbled on, ignoring the interruption.

"What are you suggesting?" Nicholas asked pointedly, and for an instant there was a whiff of mint in the back of the taxi. He leaned forward, resting his elbows on his knees, hands clasped in a tight knot.

"I am suggesting that perhaps you should have chosen less populated places to live out your long life. Alaska, maybe, or Mongolia, Siberia, the Outback or some far reaches of the Amazon. Places without people. Without victims."

An icy silence descended on the back of the car. The twins looked at one another, and Josh raised his eyebrows in silent question, but Sophie shook her head imperceptibly. She pressed her index finger to her earlobe; Josh got the message: listen, say nothing.

"Are you suggesting I've caused the deaths of innocent people?" Flamel asked very softly.

"Oh yes."

Color flushed Flamel's pale face. "I have never—" he began.

"You could have disappeared from this world," Palamedes pressed on, deep voice vibrating through the cab. "You faked your own death once, you could have done it again, and made a home someplace remote and inaccessible.

You could even have slipped into one of the Shadowrealms. But you didn't; you choose to remain in this world. Why is that?" Palamedes asked.

"I have a duty to protect the Codex," the Alchemyst snapped, genuine anger in his voice, the scent of mint stronger now, filling the air.

Car horns started to blare again, and Palamedes swiveled in the seat, released the brake and drove on.

"A duty to protect the Codex," he repeated, staring straight ahead. "No one forced you to become the Guardian of the book. You took that role gladly and without question . . . just like all the other Guardians before you. But you were different from your predecessors. They went into hiding with it. But not you. You stayed in this world. And because of that, many humani have died: a million in Ireland alone, more than one hundred and forty thousand in Tokyo."

"Killed by Dee and the Dark Elders!"

"Dee followed you."

"And if I had surrendered the Book of Abraham," Flamel said evenly, "then the Dark Elders would have returned to this world and the earth would have learned the true meaning of the word *Armageddon*. Ripping open the Shadowrealms would have sent shock waves across the earth, bringing with it hurricanes, earthquakes and tsunami. Millions would die. Pythagoras once calculated that perhaps half the earth's entire population would be destroyed just by the initial event. And then the Dark Elders would have come pouring back into this world. You've met some of them, Palamedes; you know what they are like, you know what they are capable of. If they ever return to this planet, it will be a catastrophe of global proportions."

"They say it will herald a new Golden Age," the driver replied mildly.

Josh watched Flamel's face for his reaction; Dee had made the same claims.

"That is what they say, but it is untrue. You've seen what they've done as they've tried to take the Book from me. People have died. Dee and the Dark Elders have no regard for human life," Flamel argued.

"But have you, Nicholas Flamel?"

"I don't like your tone."

In the rearview mirror, Palamedes' smile was ferocious. "I don't care whether you like it or not. Because I really do not like you, nor those others like you, who think they know what is best for this world. Who appointed you the guardian of the humani?"

"I am not the first; there were others before me."

"There have always been people like you, Nicholas Flamel. People who think they know what's best, who decide what people should see and read and listen to, who ultimately try to shape how the rest of the world thinks and acts. I've spent my entire life fighting against the likes of you."

Josh leaned forward. "Are you with the Dark Elders?"

But it was Flamel who answered. His voice was scornful. "Palamedes the Saracen Knight has not taken sides in centuries. He is similar to Hekate in that respect."

"Another of your victims," Palamedes added. "You brought ruin to her world."

63

"If you dislike me so much," Flamel said icily, "then what are you doing here?"

"Francis asked me to help, and despite his many faults, or perhaps because of them, I consider him a friend." The taxi driver fell silent, and then his brown eyes flickered in the rearview mirror to look over Sophie and Josh. "And, of course, because of this latest set of twins," he added.

Sophie broke in and asked the question that was forming on her brother's lips. "What do you mean, the *latest* set?"

"You think you're the first?" Palamedes barked a laugh. "The Alchemyst and his wife have been looking for the twins of legend for centuries. They've spent the past five hundred years collecting young men and women just like you."

Sophie and Josh looked at one another, shocked. Josh lurched forward. "What happened to the others?" he demanded.

Palamedes ignored the question, so the boy rounded on Nicholas. "What happened to the others?" he repeated, his voice cracking as it rose almost to a shout. For a single heartbeat his eyes blinked gold.

The Alchemyst looked down, then slowly and deliberately peeled Josh's fingers off his arm where he had grabbed him.

"Tell me!" Josh could see the lie forming behind the immortal's eyes and shook his head. "We deserve the truth," he snapped. "Tell us."

Flamel took a deep breath. "Yes," he said finally. "There have been others, it is true, but they were not the twins of legend." Then he sat back in the seat and folded his arms across his chest. He looked from Josh to Sophie, his face an expressionless mask. "You are."

"What happened to the other twins?" Josh demanded, voice trembling with a combination of anger and fear.

The Alchemyst turned his face away and stared out the window.

"I heard they died," Palamedes said from the front seat. "Died or went mad."

# CHAPTER SEVEN

$\mathcal{T}$he flaking sign had originally said CAR PARTS, but the second *R* had fallen off and had never been replaced. Behind a tall concrete wall tipped with shards of broken glass and curls of razor wire, hundreds of broken rusted cars rested one atop the other in precariously balanced towers. The wall surrounding the car yard was thick with peeling posters advertising long-past concerts, year-old "just released" albums and countless indy groups. Ads had been pasted over each other to create a thick multicolored layer, then covered again in graffiti. It was almost impossible to see the DANGER—KEEP OUT and NO TRESPASSING signs.

Palamedes pulled the car up to the curb about a block away from the heavily chained entrance and turned off the engine. Wrapping both arms over the top of the steering wheel, he leaned forward and carefully took in his surroundings.

Flamel had fallen asleep, and Sophie was lost in thoughts that occasionally turned her pupils silver. Josh pushed himself out of his seat and crouched on the floor behind the glass partition. "Is that where you're taking us?" Josh asked, nodding toward the car yard.

"For the moment." Palamedes' teeth flashed in the gloomy interior of the car. "It might not look like much, but this is probably the safest place in London."

Josh looked around. The redbrick houses on either side of the narrow road were dilapidated beyond repair, and the whole area was shabby and run-down. Most of the doors and windows had been boarded over, and some had even been bricked up. Every pane of glass was broken. The rusted hulk of a burnt-out car squatted on concrete blocks by the side of the road, and nothing moved on the streets. "I'm surprised this area hasn't been redeveloped or anything."

"It will be, eventually," Palamedes said ruefully. "But the present owner is prepared to sit on the land and let it appreciate in value."

"What will happen when he sells it?" Josh asked.

Palamedes grinned. "I'll never sell it." His thick right index finger moved, pointing straight ahead. "There used to be a car factory here, and there was full employment in these streets. When the factory closed in the 1970s, the houses began to empty as people died off or moved away looking for work. I started buying up the properties then."

"How many do you own?" Josh asked, impressed.

"All of them for about a mile in every direction. A couple hundred houses."

"A couple hundred! But that must have cost you a fortune."

"I've lived on this earth since before the time of Arthur. I've made and lost several fortunes. My wealth is incalculable . . . the hardest part is hiding it from the taxman!"

Josh blinked in surprise; he never imagined an immortal having problems with the government. Then he realized that in these times of computers and other surveillance technology, it must be increasingly difficult to remain in hiding from the authorities. "Do people live here?" he asked. "I don't see anyone. . . ."

"You won't. The *people*"—he used the word carefully—"who live in my houses only come out at night."

"Vampires," Josh murmured.

"Not vampires," Palamedes said quickly. "I have no time for the blood drinkers."

"What then?"

"Larvae and lemurs . . . the undead and the not-dead."

"And what are they?" Josh asked. He was guessing that larvae did not mean insect young and that lemurs were not the long-tailed primates he'd seen in zoos.

"They are . . ." Palamedes hesitated, then smiled. "Nocturnal spirits."

"Are they friendly?"

"They are loyal."

"So why are we waiting?" Josh asked. It was clear that Palamedes wasn't going to tell him anything else. "What are you looking for?"

"Something out of the ordinary."

"So what do we do?"

"We wait. We watch. Have a little patience." He glanced back at Josh. "By now much of the immortal world knows that the Alchemyst has discovered the legendary twins."

Josh was surprised by how direct the knight was being with him. "You didn't seem too sure about that earlier. Do you think we are?" he asked quickly. He needed to find out what Palamedes knew about the twins and, more importantly, about the Alchemyst.

But Palamedes ignored the question. "It doesn't matter if you are the legendary twins or not. What matters is that Flamel believes it. More importantly, Dee believes it also. Because of that, an extraordinary series of events has been put in motion: Bastet is abroad again, the Morrigan is back on this earth, the Disir brought the Nidhogg to Paris. Three Shadowrealms have been destroyed. That hasn't happened in millennia."

"Three? I thought it was just Hekate's realm that was destroyed." Scathach had spoken of other Shadowrealms, but Josh had no idea just how many existed.

Palamedes sighed, clearly tired of explanations. "Most of the Shadowrealms are linked or intersect with one another through a single gate. If anything happens to the Shadowrealm, the gate collapses. But the Yggdrasill, the World Tree, stretched up from Hekate's realm into Asgard and down deep into Niflheim, the World of Darkness. All three winked out of existence when Dee destroyed the tree, and I know that the gates to another half dozen have collapsed, effectively sealing off that world and its inhabitants. Dee added a few enemies to the long list of people—both human and inhuman—who hate and fear him already."

"What will happen to him?" Josh asked. Despite all he'd been told about the Magician, he found he still had a niggling admiration for him . . . which was more than he had for the French Alchemyst at the moment.

"Nothing. Dee is protected by powerful masters. He is completely focused on bringing the Elders back to this earth by any means possible."

Josh still didn't get that. "But why?" he asked.

"Because he is that most dangerous of foes: he is absolutely confident that what he is doing is right."

There was a flash of movement out of the corner of Josh's eye and he turned to see a huge dun-colored dog loping down the center of the street, running on the white line. It looked like a cross between an Irish wolfhound and a Borzoi, a Russian wolfhound. It raced past the taxi, right up to the gates of the car yard, then padded back and forth, sniffing the ground.

"Flamel's arrival has stirred up many ancient things," Palamedes continued, watching the dog intently. "I saw creatures today I thought had left this earth entirely, monsters that gave birth to humani's darkest legends. You should also know that Dee has posted a huge bounty on your heads. My spies tell me he wants you and your sister taken alive. Interestingly, he no longer wants Flamel alive; he will accept proof of his death. That is a major change. Elders, Next Generation, immortals and their humani servants are all converging on London. Just keeping the rabble from each other's throats is going to be a huge job; I've no idea how Dee is going to do it." Palamedes suddenly turned the engine back on, inching the car forward. "We're clear," he announced.

"How do you know?"

Palamedes pointed to where the dog sat before the gates, facing them. He hit a button on the dashboard and the gates started to slide open.

"The dog," Josh answered his own question. "Except it's not really a dog, is it?"

Palamedes grinned. "That's no dog."

# CHAPTER EIGHT

*A*ll the hair on Areop-Enap's enormous body suddenly stood on end, individual strands quivering. "Madame Perenelle," it said. "I am going to suggest something that may seem shocking."

Perenelle turned toward the Elder. Behind it, incalculable numbers of spiders scattered across the enormous wall of web the ancient creature had created. "It's hard to shock me."

"Do you trust me?" Areop-Enap asked.

"I do," Perenelle said without hesitation. Once, she would have considered the Old Spider an outright enemy, but now she knew where its allegiances lay—with the humans. And it had proven itself in the battle with the Morrigan and her flocks. "What do you want to do?"

"Be still and do not panic," Areop-Enap said with a toothy smile. "This is for your own good." Abruptly, a thick blanket of web fell across the Sorceress, enveloping her from head to foot. A wave of spiders flowed up off the ground over the woman, quickly sheathing her in silk, cinching the cloak tight to her body with sticky threads. "Trust me," Areop-Enap said again.

Perenelle remained perfectly still, although her every instinct was to fight against the web, to tear it apart, to allow her aura to bloom and crisp it to blackened dust. She kept her mouth clamped tightly shut. She had fought monsters and seen creatures from the darkest edges of mankind's legends, but she still found the thought of a spider crawling into her mouth absolutely repulsive.

The Old Spider's head swiveled, and a long leg rose, hair gently blowing as it tested the air. "Prepare yourself," Areop-Enap said. "They're coming. So long as the web remains unbroken, you are protected."

Perenelle was now completely sheathed in a thick cocoon of white silken spiderweb. She had worn the finest silk before, but this was different. It was like being tightly wrapped in a soft blanket, incredibly comfortable but slightly constricting. The web was thinner around her mouth and eyes, so that she could breathe and see, but it was like looking through a gauze curtain. She felt a jolt, and suddenly she was hoisted up into the air and tucked into a corner. A wave of black spiders immediately swept over her, securing the cocoon tightly to the walls and the metal girders that buttressed the house. From her new vantage point, she could look down over the room to where Areop-Enap squatted in the middle of the floor. Perenelle realized that the dark carpet beneath the Elder was a mass of thousands—maybe even millions—of spiders. The floor rippled and pulsed under Areop-Enap, which was facing north, toward Angel Island, now lost in early-morning mist. Shifting in the cocoon, Perenelle strained to look in the same direction. From her perch she could see out over the water. There were storm clouds massing on the horizon, thick and blue-black; she expected to see them spike and flash with lightning. But through the silk covering her face, she saw that this cloud was twisting, turning in on itself . . . and it was racing closer. In less than a dozen heartbeats, it had flowed over the north end of Alcatraz.

And then it started to rain.

There was no roof on the ruined Warden's House. Thick black drops fell out of the cloud and spattered against Perenelle's web cocoon . . . and stuck.

And the Sorceress abruptly realized that these were not raindrops—they were flies.

Huge bluebottles and houseflies, squat fruit flies, narrow horseflies, soldier flies and robber flies rained down over the island, hitting and sticking to her web cocoon.

Before Perenelle even had a chance to call out in disgust, individual spiders were darting across the web and had commenced wrapping the struggling flies in silk.

Perenelle looked up. The huge cloud was almost upon them. But now she could see that it was not a cloud at all. The initial shower of insects was only a taste of what was to come. The roiling mass was flies, millions of them, crane flies and black flies, mosquitoes and tiny midges, squat botflies and red-eyed pomace flies.

The insects exploded against Alcatraz in a dark buzzing

sheet. The first wave were caught by the white silken cobwebs, which quickly turned dark and heavy with the weight of the struggling insects. Perenelle watched the webs around her quickly rip and tear as more and more flies crashed against them. Hordes of spiders rolled over the trapped flies and were quickly locked in an ancient battle. The silk-sheathed walls heaved with wriggling spiders and desperately struggling flies, until it looked as if the sides of the building were alive, pulsing and throbbing.

The flies whirled around Areop-Enap, and the few that found Perenelle were trapped by the protective web around her. Faintly, she could hear their buzzing as they attempted to escape.

More and more waves of flies washed in over the island, and the spiders—Perenelle hadn't realized there were so many—swarmed over them. An incalculable number of flies had attached themselves to Areop-Enap, completely coating the Old Spider, until it resembled a huge buzzing ball. The Elder's massive leg lashed out of the heaving mass, scattering a wave of dead husks, but countless more took their places. The Elder leapt up and then crashed to the ground, crushing thousands more beneath its huge body.

And still more came in an endless dark surge.

Then, suddenly, Perenelle noticed that the walls and floor had stopped moving and rippling. Focusing hard through the gauzy curtain in front of her eyes, she saw something that shocked her: the spiders were dying. She watched a black-and-white zebra spider sink two iridescent blue fangs into an enormous crane fly that was stuck to its sticky web. The fly thrashed about, desperate to escape, but then, abruptly, the spider shuddered and stiffened. Both creatures died at the same time. And it was happening again and again: the moment the spiders bit into the flies, they died. It took a lot to frighten the Sorceress, but suddenly, she began to feel the first twinges of disquiet.

Whoever or *whatever* had sent the flies had poisoned them.

And if a single fly could kill a spider, then what could the huge mass do to Areop-Enap?

Perenelle had to do something. All around her, millions of spiders were dying, poisoned by the flies. Areop-Enap had disappeared beneath the dark mass. It was still heaving with the Old Spider's struggling and thrashing about, but as the Sorceress watched, she realized that the struggles were becoming weaker. Areop-Enap was ancient and primal but not completely invulnerable. Nothing—Elder, Next Generation, immortal or human—was completely indestructible. Not even Areop-Enap. Perenelle herself had once brought an ancient temple down on the spider's head and it had shrugged off the attack—yet could it survive billions of poisonous flies?

But Perenelle was caught. Areop-Enap had tucked her high on the wall, out of harm's way. If she were to cut through the web cocoon, she would fall at least twenty feet to the floor below. The impact probably wouldn't kill her, but it might snap an ankle or break a leg.

And how was she going to defeat a plague of flies?

Looking out over the island, she saw yet another curling

thread of insects coming in on the breeze. Once they reached Alcatraz, it would all be over. The wind carried the faintest hum, like the sound of a distant chain saw.

Wind.

Wind had carried the insects onto the island . . . could Perenelle also use it to drive them away?

But even as the thought crossed her mind, Perenelle realized that she didn't know enough of wind lore to control the element with precision. Perhaps if she'd had time to prepare and her aura were fully charged, she would have attempted to raise some type of wind—a typhoon, maybe, or a small tornado—in the heart of the island and sweep it clean of flies, and probably spiders, too. But she couldn't risk it now. She needed to do something simple . . . and she needed to do it quickly. All the spiders had stopped moving. Millions of flies had died, but millions more remained, and they were swarming over Areop-Enap.

So if she couldn't drive the flies off the island, could she lure them away? Someone was controlling the insects—a Dark Elder or immortal, who must have first poisoned them, then set the tiny mindless insects on the island. Something had drawn them here. Perenelle's eyes snapped wide in realization. So something would have to draw them away. What would attract millions of flies?

What did flies like?

Behind the gauze web, Perenelle smiled. For her five hundredth birthday on the thirteenth of October in 1820, Scathach had presented her with a spectacular pendant, a single piece of jade carved into the shape of a scarab beetle.

More than three thousand years previously, the Shadow had brought it back from Japan for the boy king Tutankhamen, but he'd died a day after she'd presented it to him. Scathach had despised Tutankhamen's wife, Ankhesenamen, and hadn't wanted her to have it, so she'd broken in to the royal palace late one night just before the boy king was embalmed and taken it back. When Scathach had given her the jade, Perenelle had joked, "You're giving me a dung beetle."

Scathach had nodded seriously. "Dung is more valuable than any precious metal. You cannot grow food in gold."

And flies were attracted to dung.

But there was no dung pile on the island, and to catch the flies' attention, she would have to create an exceptionally strong odor. Perenelle immediately thought of the beautiful plants of the arum family. Some of them stank abominably of dung. There was the cactuslike desert herb the carrion flower: beautiful to look at, but it reeked of something long dead. And there was skunk cabbage, and the world's largest flower, the giant rafflesia, the stinking corpse lily, with its putrid odor of rotting meat. If she could replicate that scent, she might be able to lure the flies away.

Perenelle knew that at the heart of all magic and sorcery was imagination. It was this gift for intense concentration that characterized the most powerful magicians; before attempting any great piece of magic, they had to clearly *see* the end result. So before she concentrated on creating the smell, she needed to think about a location that she could see in every detail. Places flickered at the edges of Perenelle's consciousness. Places she had lived, places she knew. In her long life she'd had the opportunity to visit so much of the world. But what she needed now was someplace reasonably close, a location she knew well, and one where there was not a huge human population.

The San Francisco Dump.

She'd only been to the dump on one previous occasion. Months ago, she'd helped one of the bookshop's employees move to a new apartment. Afterward, they'd driven south toward Monster Park and the dump on Recycle Road. Always sensitive to smells, Perenelle had caught the distinctively acrid—though not entirely unpleasant—smell of the dump when they'd turned onto Tunnel Avenue. As they'd got closer, the stink had become eye-watering and the air had filled with the sound of countless seabirds calling.

Perenelle drew upon that memory now. Fixing the dump clearly in her imagination, she visualized a huge clump of stinking, corpse-smelling flowers in the very heart of the refuse and then she imagined a wind carrying the foul stink northward toward Alcatraz.

The stench of something long rotten wafted over the island and a rippling wave coursed through the massed flies.

Perenelle focused her will. She visualized the sprawling dump scattered with blooms: calla and carrion flowers poking through the rubbish, giant red and white spotted rafflesia thriving amid the junk, and the air filling with the noxious scents, mingling with the dump's own fetid odor. Then she imagined a wind pushing the scent north.

The smell that washed over the island was eye-wateringly foul. A wave pulsed through the thick carpet of flies. Some rose buzzing into the air, circled aimlessly but then dropped back onto Areop-Enap.

Perenelle was tiring, and she knew that the effort was aging her. Drawing in a deep breath, she made one final effort. She had to move the flies before the second swarm joined them. She concentrated so hard on the foul stench that her normally odorless ice white aura shimmered and took on the hint of putrefaction.

The sickening stink that flowed over the island was a nauseating mixture of fresh dung mixed with long-spoiled meat and the rancid odor of sour milk.

The flies rose from Alcatraz in a solid black blanket. They hummed and buzzed like a power station and then, as one, set off heading south toward the source of the stench. The departing insects encountered the second huge swarm as it was just about to descend on the island and both groups mingled in an enormous solid black ball; then the entire mass turned and flowed south, following the rich soupy scent.

Within moments, there was not a living fly left on the island.

Areop-Enap shook itself free of tiny carcasses and then slowly and stiffly climbed the wall, sliced the web holding Perenelle in place and lowered her gently to the ground on a narrow spiral of thread. Perenelle allowed her aura to flare for a millisecond and the cocoon of spiderweb, now dotted and speckled with trapped flies, crisped to dust. She threw back her head, pushed her damp hair back off her forehead and neck and breathed deeply. It had been suffocatingly warm in the web.

"Are you all right?" she asked, reaching out to stroke one of the Elder's huge legs.

Areop-Enap swayed to and fro. Only one of its eyes was open, and when it spoke, its normally lisping speech was slurred almost beyond comprehension. "Poison?" it asked.

Perenelle nodded. She looked around. The ruins were thick with the husks of flies and spiders. She suddenly realized she was standing ankle-deep in the tiny corpses. When all this was over, she'd have to burn her shoes, she decided. "The flies were deadly. Your spiders died when they bit into them. They were sent here to kill your army."

"And they succeeded," Areop-Enap said sadly. "So many dead, so many . . ."

"The flies that attacked you also carried poison," Perenelle continued. "Individually, their bites were unnoticeable, but Old Spider, you have been bitten millions—perhaps even billions—of times."

Areop-Enap's single open eye blinked slowly closed. "Madame Perenelle, I must heal. Which means I must sleep."

Perenelle stepped closer to the huge spider and brushed the husks of dead flies from its purple hair. They crackled to dust at her touch. "Sleep, Old Spider," she said gently. "I will watch over you."

Areop-Enap staggered awkwardly into the corner of the room. Two huge legs swept a section of the floor clean of dead spiders and flies, and then it attempted to spin a web. But the silk was thin, threadlike and slightly discolored. "What did you do with the flies?" Areop-Enap asked, struggling to create more web.

"Sent them south on a wild-scent chase." Perenelle smiled. Her right hand flashed out, her aura flared and Areop-Enap's thin spiderweb suddenly grew and thickened. The Old Spider settled itself into the corner of the room in its nest and began again to spin a web around itself.

"Where?" Areop-Enap asked suddenly. Its single open eye was almost closed, and Perenelle could see where incalculable numbers of weeping sores had appeared on the creature's body from the poisonous bites.

"The San Francisco Dump."

"Few will make it there . . . ," Areop-Enap mumbled, "and those who do will find plenty to distract them. You saved my life, Madame Perenelle."

"And you saved mine, Old Spider." The huge ball of web was almost complete. The silk had already started to turn rocklike, and only a small hole at the top remained. "Sleep now," Perenelle commanded, "sleep and grow strong. We are going to need your strength and wisdom in the days to come."

With a tremendous effort, Areop-Enap opened all its eyes. "I am sorry to leave you alone and defenseless."

Perenelle sealed the spider Elder into the huge cocoon of web, then turned and strode across the room. The tiniest breeze swept the floor clean before her. "I am Perenelle Flamel, the Sorceress," she said aloud, unsure whether Areop-Enap could hear her. "And I am never defenseless."

But even as she was saying the words, she clearly heard the note of doubt creep into her own voice.

# CHAPTER NINE

*O*n the western shore of Treasure Island in San Francisco Bay, a young-looking man sat on the hood of a bright red 1960 Thunderbird convertible. Short and slight, he was wearing blue jeans with the ends ragged and frayed and both knees worn to threads. The wolf's-head graphic on his T-shirt was faded to little more than a ghostly pattern, and his cowboy boots were scuffed and needed new soles and heels. His unkempt appearance, long hair and stubbly beard were in stark contrast to the gleaming car he was sitting on, which looked as if it had just been driven out of the showroom. The young man had twenty-nine dollars and change in his wallet; the car was worth at least one thousand times that.

Next to him on the hood of the car was an ancient antique Anasazi pottery bowl, decorated in elegant black-and-white angular geometric patterns. A thick liquid filled the bowl, a mixture of honey, flaxseed oil and water, and reflected in the liquid was the figure of Perenelle Flamel striding across Alcatraz, the black blanket of spider and fly corpses opening up before her in a wave.

So this was the legendary Perenelle Flamel. The young man moved his finger clockwise over the liquid and his bright blue eyes sparkled, turning briefly crimson, the hint of cayenne filling the air. The image of Perenelle zoomed in. He watched her stop and frown, the lines in her forehead deepening, and she looked around quickly, almost as if she knew that someone was watching her. He waved his hand and the liquid trembled, the image dissolving. Folding his arms across his thin chest, the man turned his face to the west, where Alcatraz was hidden in the gloom. It seemed as if everything he had heard about the woman was true: Perenelle was that most lethal of combinations, both beautiful and deadly.

He was momentarily at a loss. Should he attack again, or should he wait? Lifting his hand to his face, he breathed deeply and his aura glowed a deep purple-red, a shade darker than the Thunderbird, and the salt sea air was tainted with the odor of red pepper. He still had enough power left to do . . . what?

Calling the flies had been relatively easy; an Indian shaman had taught him that trick, and it had saved his life on more than one occasion. Poisoning the flies had been his Elder master's suggestion, and his master had even supplied the pool of poisoned water in Solano County, north of the city. The plan was to destroy Areop-Enap's army of spiders and murder the Elder. And it had almost succeeded. The mass of spiders were dead, and the Old Spider was very close

84

to death. But at the last minute something had drawn the flies away from Alcatraz in a great pulsing cloud. In the oily liquid in the scrying bowl, the young man had seen the silver-white flicker of Perenelle's aura, and knew she'd been responsible. His thin face twisted in a grimace and he bit nervously into his bottom lip. He'd been assured that she was weakened, incapable of any display of her powers. Obviously, that information had been incorrect.

The thick liquid began to bubble and cloud, then to hiss and steam away; the scrying spell had a limited life span. Slipping off the hood of the car, the young man tossed the sticky remnants onto the ground, then carefully washed out the bowl with a bottle of water and dried it with a chamois cloth before putting it in the trunk of the car, nestling it in a small foam-filled metal suitcase. The bowl was one of the most precious objects he owned, and even when he'd been desperately poor, he'd never thought about selling it.

Sitting in the red leather interior of the car, he opened a manila envelope and read through the file he'd been sent by encrypted e-mail. A severe-looking white-haired man glared out of a black-and-white photograph. He'd been caught mid-stride as he crossed a street. The Eiffel Tower loomed over the rooftops in the background, and the date stamp on the bottom of the photograph revealed that it had been taken on Christmas Eve, six months ago. Idly, the young man wondered why the Dark Elders were watching one of their most trusted agents. This was the man they were sending to work with him: the European immortal Niccolò Machiavelli. The Elders' instructions had been unambiguous—he was to offer

Machiavelli every assistance. He wondered if the Italian was anything like John Dee. He'd met Dee briefly and didn't like him; he was one of those arrogant European immortals who thought they were better than anyone else, just because they were older than the United States. But reading through Machiavelli's file, he found himself liking the man more and more. Ruthless, cunning and scheming, he was described as the most dangerous man in Europe.

He'd help Machiavelli, of course. He didn't really have any choice; going against the Dark Elders was tantamount to a death wish. Personally, he didn't believe he needed the Italian. Tossing the file on the floor, he turned the key in the ignition, pushed hard on the accelerator and spun the wheel, and the car fishtailed into a semicircle, billowing dust and grit in its wake.

Billy the Kid had never needed anyone.

# CHAPTER TEN

The scrap yard was a maze.

Towering alleyways of rusting metal, with barely enough space for the car to drive through, stretched from the entrance in every direction. A solid barrier of tires, hundreds deep, leaned precariously out over the narrow spaces. There was one wall composed entirely of car doors, another of hoods and trunks. Engine blocks stained with dripping oil and grease were piled in a tower next to a bank of exhaust pipes that had been driven into the ground, making them look like an abstract sculpture.

Palamedes eased the black London cab deeper into the mountainous warren of crushed cars. Sophie was completely awake now. She sat forward on the seat, looking through the window, eyes wide. In its own way, the scrap yard was as extraordinary as Hekate's Shadowrealm. Although it looked chaotic, she instinctively knew that there was probably a pattern to it. Something fluttered to her right and she turned quickly, catching a glimpse of movement in the shadows. She was turning back when she saw a shadow shift and blink away. They were being followed, yet despite her enhanced senses, she couldn't catch sight of the creatures, though she got the impression that they moved upright like humans. "Is this a Shadowrealm?" she asked aloud.

Beside her, Flamel stirred awake. "There are no Shadowrealms in the center of London," he mumbled. "Shadowrealms exist on the edges of cities."

Sophie nodded—she'd known that, of course.

Palamedes swung the car in a tight left-hand turn that led to an even narrower alleyway. The ragged metal walls were so close they almost scraped the car doors. "We're not in the center of the city anymore, Alchemyst," he said in his deep bass voice. "We're in the slightly disreputable suburbs. And you're wrong, too; I know two Elders who have small Shadowrealms situated in the heart of the city of London, and there are entrances to at least another three that I know of, including the best-known one, in the pool behind Traitor's Gate."

Josh craned his neck to look up at the towering walls of metal. "It's like a . . ." He stopped. Somewhere at the back of his mind, the twisting layout fell into place and he abruptly realized what he was seeing. "It's a castle," he whispered. "A castle made of crushed metal and flattened cars."

Palamedes' laugh was a loud bark that startled both twins. "Hah. I'm impressed. There's not many alive today who would recognize it. This layout is based upon a design created by the great Sébastien Le Prestre de Vauban himself."

"That sounds like a wine," Josh murmured, still mesmerized by what he discovered.

"I met him once," Flamel said absently. "He was a famous French military engineer." He twisted in the seat to look out the rear window. "Just looks like junked cars to me," he said, almost to himself.

Sophie looked curiously at her brother—how had he known that the jumble was actually a castle? But then, looking up at the walls of cars, the pattern she'd glimpsed earlier fell into place and she could see the shape of the castle, the battlements and towers, the narrow spaces where defenders could fire down onto any attackers. A shape moved behind one of the spaces and vanished.

"Over the years we've built up the cars like the walls of a castle," Palamedes continued. "The medieval castle builders knew a lot about defense, and de Vauban brought all that knowledge together to create the strongest defenses in the world. Then we took the best of all styles. There are mottes and baileys, outer wards and an inner ward, a barbican, towers and keeps. The only entrance is through this single narrow alleyway, and it is designed to be easily defensible." His huge hand moved toward the wrecked cars. "And behind and between and within the walls there are all sorts of nasty traps waiting."

The car vibrated as it ran onto metal. The twins both slid over to the windows and looked out to discover that they'd driven onto what looked like a bridge of narrow metal pipes suspended over a thick bubbling black liquid.

"The moat," Josh said.

"Our modern version of a moat," the Saracen Knight agreed. "Filled with oil instead of water. It's deeper than it looks and is lined with spikes. If anything falls in . . . well, let's just say that they're not climbing out. And of course we can set it ablaze with the flick of a switch."

"We?" Josh asked quickly, glancing at his sister.

"We," the knight confirmed.

"So there are others like you here?" Josh asked.

"I am not alone," Palamedes agreed with a quick grin, teeth white against his dark face.

He drove on, past the bridge, and another alleyway curved and ended at a solid metal wall of crushed and flattened cars. It was thick with blood-colored rust. Palamedes slowed but didn't stop. He pressed a button on the dashboard and the entire wall shuddered and silently slid to one side, leaving just enough space for the car to slip through. Once they were inside, the thick rusted gate slid silently back into position.

Beyond the gate was a broad area of churned and muddy ground, dotted with water-filled potholes. In the center of the sea of mud was a long rectangular metal hut set up on concrete blocks. The hut was dilapidated and filthy, its windows covered with wire mesh, and the rust that dappled the metal walls made it look diseased. Curls of barbed wire ran around the edges of the roof. Two sorry-looking flags—a British Union Jack and a red dragon on a green and white background—flapped on slightly bent poles. Both flags were ragged and in need of washing.

Sophie bit the inside of her cheek to keep a straight face. "I was expecting something . . ."

". . . nicer?" Josh finished. His twin raised her hand and he high-fived her.

"Nicer," she agreed. "It looks kind of depressing."

Josh noticed a pack of rangy wild dogs lurking in the shadows under the hut. They were the same color and breed as the huge dun-colored dog he'd spotted earlier, but these were smaller and their coats were dull, the fur matted. There was a spark of crimson light and he squinted hard: were the dogs' eyes red?

Nicholas straightened. He yawned and stretched as he looked around, then murmured, "Why all the security, Palamedes? What are you afraid of?"

"You have no idea," Palamedes said simply.

"Tell me." Nicholas rubbed his face and sat forward, elbows on his knees. "We are on the same side, after all."

"No, we're not," Palamedes said quickly. "We may have the same enemies, but we are not on the same side. Our aims are quite different."

"How are they different?" Flamel asked. "You fight the Dark Elders."

"Only when we have to. You seek to prevent the Dark Elders from returning to this world, whereas I, and my brother knights, go into the Shadowrealms and bring back those humans who have become trapped there."

Josh looked from Flamel to Palamedes, confused. "What brother knights?" he asked. "Who?"

Flamel took a deep breath. "I think Palamedes is referring to the Green Knights," he said.

Palamedes nodded. "Just so."

"I heard rumors . . . ," the Alchemyst muttered.

"Those rumors are true," Palamedes said shortly. He pulled the car in beside the long metal-roofed hut and shut off the engine. "Don't step into any of the potholes," he advised as he pushed open the door. "You don't want to know what lives in them."

Sophie climbed out first, blinking hard behind her sunglasses in the late-afternoon sunshine. Her eyes felt gritty and sore, and there was a ticklish dry patch at the back of her throat. She wondered if she was coming down with a cold. Even though she'd been desperately trying *not* to think about Palamedes, some of the Witch's memories had percolated into hers, and she realized she knew a little about him. He was an immortal human gifted with the special ability to move freely through the Shadowrealms and yet remain unaffected by them. Few humans who went into the artificial worlds the Elders created ever returned. Human history— both ancient and modern—was full of people who had simply disappeared. Those very few who had somehow returned, or been brought back, often found that hundreds of years had passed on earth even though only a few nights had slipped by in the Shadowrealms. Many who came back were mad or had come to believe that the Shadowrealm was the real world while this earth was nothing more than a dream. They spent their entire lives trying to return to what they thought was the real world.

"You're thinking again." Josh jerked her elbow, distracting her.

Sophie smiled. "I'm always thinking."

"I meant you were thinking about stuff you shouldn't. The Witch's stuff."

"How can you tell?"

Josh's smile turned grave. "For an instant, just an instant, the pupils of your eyes turn silver. It's scary."

Sophie wrapped her arms around her body and shivered. She looked around at the walls of cars surrounding the rust-dappled hut. "It's a bit grim, isn't it? I thought all these Elders and immortals lived in palaces."

Josh turned in a complete circle, but when he looked back at her there was a grin on his face. "Actually, I think it's kind of cool. It's like a metal castle. And it seems to be incredibly secure, too. There's no way to even get close to this place without tipping off the guards."

"I caught glimpses of something moving as we drove through the maze," Sophie said.

Josh nodded. "Earlier, Palamedes told me that the houses in all the streets surrounding this place are empty. He owns them all. He said there are something called larvae and lemurs in them."

"Guardians."

"I saw a huge dog. . . ." He nodded toward the pack of dogs lying completely still under the hut. "It was like those, only bigger, cleaner. It seemed to be patrolling the streets. And you've seen the defenses," he added excitedly. "There's a single heavily guarded entrance that funnels everything into a narrow alleyway. So no matter how big whatever army you have is, only two or three soldiers can attack at any one time. And they're also vulnerable from above because of the battlements."

Sophie reached out and squeezed her brother's arm tightly. "Josh," she said sharply, blue eyes wide with concern. She'd never heard her brother talk like this before. "Stop it. How come you know so much about castle defenses . . . ?" Her voice trailed off, the ghost of an unsettling idea flickering at the corner of her mind.

"I don't know," Josh admitted. "I just . . . sort of . . . know it. It's like when we were in Paris—I knew that Dee and Machiavelli had to be on high ground controlling the gargoyles. And then, earlier today, when those three creatures were going to attack . . ."

"The Genuii Cucullati," Sophie murmured absently, turning to watch Nicholas climb stiffly out of the cab. When she saw him reach in to pull out Josh's backpack, she noticed that his knuckles looked slightly swollen. Aunt Agnes, back in Pacific Heights in San Francisco, had arthritis, and her knuckles were also swollen. The Alchemyst was aging fast.

"Yes, them. I knew that they were moving into an attack pattern by their body language. I knew that the center one would charge first and come at us straight on, while the other two would try to flank us. I knew if I could stop him, it might distract the others and give us a chance to escape." Josh stopped suddenly, realizing what he was saying. "How did I know that?" he wondered aloud.

"Mars," Sophie whispered. She nodded. "It has to have

come from the God of War." The girl shuddered; she and her brother were changing. Then she shook her head slightly: they had already changed.

"Mars. I . . . I remember," Josh whispered. "When he was Awakening me he said something at the end, something about giving me a gift that I might find useful in the days to come. And then he rested his hand on the top of my head and I felt this incredible heat flow through me." He looked at his twin. "What did he give me? I don't have any strange memories, like the ones the Witch gave you."

"I think you should probably be grateful you don't have his memories," Sophie said quickly. "The Witch knew Mars and despised him. I would imagine most of his memories are foul. Josh, I think he's given you his military knowledge."

"He's made me a warrior?" Even though the thought was creepy, Josh was unable to keep the note of delight from his voice.

"Maybe even something better," Sophie said, her voice soft and distant, eyes flashing silver. "I think he's made you a strategist."

"And that's good?" He sounded disappointed

Sophie nodded quickly. "Battles are won by men. Wars are won by strategists."

"Who said that?" Josh asked, surprised.

"Mars did," Sophie said, shaking her head to clear the sudden influx of memories. "Don't you see? Mars was the ultimate strategist; he never lost a battle. It's an amazing gift."

"But why did he give it to me?" Josh asked the question Sophie was thinking.

Before she could answer, the door to the long metal hut suddenly creaked open and a figure in soiled mechanic's overalls bustled down the steps. Small and slight, with stooped shoulders and a long oval face, the man blinked nearsightedly at the cab. He had a wispy mustache, and although the top of his head was bald, the hair over his ears and at the back of his head flowed down onto his shoulders.

"Palamedes?" he snapped, clearly irritated. "What is the meaning of this?" His English was crisp and precise, each word enunciated clearly. He saw the twins and stopped short. Pulling a pair of oversized black-framed glasses from a top pocket, he pushed them onto his face. "Who are these people?" And then he turned and spotted Nicholas Flamel at about the same time the Alchemyst saw him.

Both men reacted simultaneously.

"Flamel!" The small man shrieked. He turned and darted back toward the hut, scrambling and falling on the metal steps.

Nicholas grunted something in archaic French, tore open Josh's backpack and wrenched Clarent from the cardboard map tube. Holding it in a tight two-handed grip, he swung it around his head, the edge of the blade keening and humming through the air. "Run," he shouted to the twins, "run for your lives! It's a trap!"

# CHAPTER ELEVEN

*B*efore Sophie or Josh could react, Palamedes reared up behind the Alchemyst and his two huge hands locked onto Flamel's shoulders. The two immortals' auras blazed and crackled, the Alchemyst's bright green mingling with the knight's darker olive green. The acrid metal-and-rubber-tainted air of the car yard was suffused with the clean odor of mint and the spicy warmth of cloves. Flamel struggled to swing Clarent around, but the knight tightened his grip and pushed, driving the Alchemyst to his knees, fingers biting into the flesh, pinching nerves. The sword dropped from Flamel's hand.

Sophie spread the fingers of her right hand wide and prepared to call up the element of fire, but Josh caught her arm and pulled it down. "No," he said urgently, just as the pack of dogs boiled out from beneath the hut and swarmed around them. The animals moved in complete silence, lips bared to reveal savage yellow teeth and lolling tongues that were forked like snakes'. "Don't move," he whispered, squeezing his twin's hand. The dogs were close enough for him to see that their eyes were completely red, without a trace of white or pupil. Teeth clicked, and he felt wet lips brush against his fingers. The animals exuded a stale musty odor like rotting leaves. Although the dogs weren't large, they were incredibly muscled—one bumped against Josh's legs, knocking him forward into Sophie. The twins' auras sparked and the dog pressing against Josh's legs tumbled away, hair bristling.

"Enough!" Palamedes' voice boomed and echoed across the car lot. "This is no trap." The knight leaned over Nicholas, his huge hands still locked onto each shoulder, pushing him into the ground. "I may not be your ally, Alchemyst," Palamedes rumbled, "but I am not your enemy. All I have left now is my honor, and I promised my friend Saint-Germain that I would take care of you. I'll not betray that trust."

Flamel tried to shake himself free, but Palamedes' grip was unbreakable. The Alchemyst's aura sparkled and flared, then suddenly fizzled out, and he slumped in exhaustion.

"Do you believe me?" Palamedes demanded.

Nicholas nodded. "I believe you—but, why is *he* here?" With a look of absolute disgust on his face, the Alchemyst raised his head to look at the small man cowering just inside the hut, peering around the corner of the door.

"He lives here," Palamedes said simply.

"Here! But he's—"

"My friend," the knight said shortly. "Much has changed." Loosening his grip, Palamedes caught Nicholas by both shoulders and heaved him to his feet. Spinning him around, the knight straightened his rumpled leather jacket; then he snapped a word in an incomprehensible language and the animals surging around the twins flowed back to the shelter of the hut.

Josh glanced down at the sword on the ground and wondered if he was fast enough to reach it. He looked up and found Palamedes' deep brown eyes watching him. The knight smiled with a flash of white teeth and dipped down to pluck Clarent from the mud. "I've not seen this for a long time," the knight said softly, his accent thickening, hinting again at his Middle Eastern origins. The moment he touched it, his aura bloomed into life around him, and for an instant he was sheathed in a long hauberk of black chain mail, complete with a close-fitting hood that covered his arms to his fingertips and finished low on his thighs. Each link of the chain mail winked with tiny reflections. As his aura faded, Clarent's stone blade shimmered red-black, like oil on water, and a sound, like the wind through long grass, sighed across the blade.

"No!" The dark stone blade winked bloodred again, and Palamedes drew in a deep shuddering breath and suddenly dropped the sword, a sheen of sweat on his dark skin. The weapon stuck point-first in the muddy ground, swaying to and fro. The mud immediately hardened in a circle around the tip of the sword, dried and then split and cracked. Palamedes rubbed his hands briskly together, then brushed them against his trousers. "I thought it was Excal—" He rounded on Flamel. "What are you doing with this . . . thing? You must know what it is?"

The Alchemyst nodded. "I've kept it safe for centuries."

"You kept it!" The knight clenched his hands into huge fists. Veins popped out along his forearms and appeared on his neck. "If you knew what it was, why didn't you destroy it?"

"It is older than humanity," Flamel said quietly, "even older than the Elders or Danu Talis. How could I destroy it?"

"It's loathsome," Palamedes snapped. "You know what it did?"

"It was a tool; nothing more. It was used by evil people."

Palamedes started to shake his head.

"We needed it to escape," the Alchemyst said firmly. "And remember, without it, the Nidhogg would still be alive and rampaging through Paris."

Josh stepped forward, pulled the sword from the ground and wiped the muddy tip of the blade on the edge of his shoe. There was the briefest hint of oranges in the air, but the smell was bitter and faintly sour. The moment the boy touched the hilt, a wash of emotions and images hit him:

*Palamedes, the Saracen Knight, at the head of a dozen knights in armor and chain mail. They were battered, their armor scarred and broken, weapons chipped, shields dented. They were fighting their way through an army of primitive-looking beastlike men, trying to get to a small hill where a single*

100

*warrior in golden armor desperately battled against creatures that were a terrible cross between men and animals.*

*Palamedes shouting a warning as a huge creature rose up behind the lone warrior, a creature that was shaped like a man but had the curling horns of a stag on its head. The horned man raised a short stone sword and the warrior in gold fell.*

*Palamedes standing over the fallen warrior, gently removing the sword Excalibur from his hand.*

*Palamedes racing through a marshy swampland, pursuing the staglike creature. Beasts came at him—boarmen and bearmen, wolfmen and goatmen—but he cut through them with Excalibur, the sword blazing, leaving arcs of cold blue light in the air.*

*Palamedes standing at the bottom of an impossibly sheer cliff, watching the horned man climb effortlessly to the top.*

*And at the top, the creature turning and holding aloft the sword he'd used to kill the king. It dripped and steamed with crimson-black smoke. And it was almost a mirror of the sword in the Saracen Knight's hand.*

Josh drew in a deep shuddering breath as the images faded. The horned man had been holding Clarent, Excalibur's twin. Opening his eyes, he looked at the weapon, and in that instant, he knew why Palamedes had snatched up the blade. The two swords were almost identical; there were only minor differences in the hilts. The Saracen Knight had assumed the stone sword was Excalibur. Concentrating fiercely on the gray blade, Josh tried to focus on what he'd just seen—the warrior in the golden armor. Had that been . . . ?

A stale unwashed smell assaulted Josh's nose and he

turned to find the bald man they'd glimpsed earlier standing close to him, squinting shortsightedly behind his thick black-rimmed glasses. His eyes were a pale washed-out blue. And he stank. Josh coughed and took a step back, eyes watering. "Man, you could use a bath!"

"Josh!" Sophie said, shocked.

"I do not believe in bathing," the man said in his clipped accent, the voice completely at odds with his appearance. "It damages the natural oils in the body. Dirt is healthy."

The small man moved from Josh to Sophie and looked her up and down. Josh noticed that his sister blinked hard and wrinkled her nose. Then she clamped her mouth tightly shut and stepped back.

"See what I mean?" Josh said. "He needs a bath." He brushed dirt off the sword blade and took a step closer to his sister. The man looked harmless, but Josh could tell that something about him angered—or was it frightened?—the Alchemyst.

"Yeah." Sophie tried not to breathe in through her nose. The stench from the man was indescribable: a mixture of stale body odor, unwashed clothes and rank hair.

"I will wager you are twins," the man asked, looking from one to the other. He nodded, answering his own question. "Twins." He reached out with filthy fingers to touch Sophie's hair, but she slapped his hand away. Her aura sparked and the stench around the man briefly intensified.

"Don't touch me!"

Flamel stepped between the man in the mechanic's overalls

and the twins. "What are you doing here?" he demanded. "I thought you were dead."

The man smiled, revealing shockingly bad teeth. "I'm as dead as you are, Alchemyst. Though I am better known."

"You two have obviously met before," Josh said.

"I've known this"—Nicholas hesitated, lines and wrinkles creasing his face—"this person since he was a boy. In fact, I once had high hopes for him."

"Would someone like to tell us who this is?" Josh demanded, looking from the Alchemyst to Palamedes and back again, waiting for an answer.

"He was my apprentice, until he betrayed me," Flamel snapped, almost spitting the words. "He became John Dee's right hand."

The twins immediately backed away from the man, and Josh's grip tightened on the sword.

The bald man tilted his head to one side, and the expression on his face became lost and indescribably sad. "That was a long time ago, Alchemyst. I've not associated with the Magician for centuries."

Flamel stepped forward. "What changed your mind? Was he not paying you enough to betray your wife, your family, your friends?"

Pain flickered in the man's pale blue eyes. "I made mistakes, Alchemyst, that is true. I've spent lifetimes attempting to atone for them. People change. . . . Well, most people," he said. "Except you. You were always so sure of yourself and your role in the world. The great Nicholas Flamel was never wrong . . . or if he was, he never admitted it," he added very softly.

The Alchemyst swung away from the man to look squarely at the twins. "This," he said, arm waving toward the small man in the soiled overalls, "is Dee's former apprentice, the immortal human William Shakespeare."

# CHAPTER TWELVE

Standing framed in the doorway of his impressive town house, Niccolò Machiavelli watched Dr. John Dee climb into the sleek black limousine. The smartly dressed driver closed the door, nodded to Machiavelli, then climbed into the driver's seat. A moment later the car pulled away from the curb, and, as the Italian had guessed, Dee neither looked back nor waved. Machiavelli's stone gray eyes followed the car as it merged into the evening traffic. It was just about to pull out from the Place du Canada when an anonymous-looking Renault took up a position three cars behind it. Machiavelli knew the Renault would follow Dee's car for three blocks and then be replaced by a second and then a third car. Cameras mounted on the dashboard would relay live pictures to Machiavelli's computer. He would have Dee followed every moment he remained in Paris. His instincts, honed by centuries of survival, were warning him that Dee was up to something. The English Magician had been far too eager to leave, refusing Machiavelli's offer of a bed for the night, claiming he had to get to England immediately and resume the search for Flamel.

It took an effort to push closed the heavy hall door with its thick bulletproof glass, and Machiavelli suddenly realized that it was little things like this that made him miss Dagon.

Dagon had been with him for almost four hundred years, ever since Machiavelli had found him, injured and close to death, in the Grotta Azzurra on the Isle of Capri. He'd nursed Dagon back to health, and in return the creature had become his manservant and secretary, his bodyguard and, ultimately, his friend. They had traveled the world and had even ventured into some of the safer Shadowrealms together. Dagon had shown him wonders, and he in turn had introduced the creature to art and music. Despite his brutish appearance, Dagon had had a voice of extraordinary beauty and purity. It was only in the latter half of the twentieth century, when Machiavelli had first heard the haunting notes of whale songs, that he had recognized the sounds the creature was capable of making.

Machiavelli had allowed no one to get close to him for almost half a millennium. He'd been in his early thirties when he'd married Marietta Corsini in 1502, and over the next twenty-five years they'd had six children together. But when he had become immortal, he'd been forced to "die" to conceal the truth that he would never age. The Dark Elder who had made him immortal hadn't told him at the time that such a ruse would be necessary. Leaving Marietta and the children

106

had been one of the hardest things he'd ever done, but he'd looked out for them for the remainder of their lives. He'd also watched them age, sicken and perish: this was the dark side of the gift of immortality. When Marietta finally died, he'd attended her funeral in disguise and then visited her grave in the dead of night to pay his last respects and swear an oath that he would always honor his marriage vows and never remarry. He'd kept that promise.

Machiavelli strode down a wood-paneled corridor and pressed his palm against a bronze bust of Cesare Borgia on a small circular table. *"Dell'arte della guerra,"* he said aloud, voice echoing in the empty hallway. There was a click and a section of the wall slid back to reveal Niccolò's private office. When he stepped into the room, the door hissed shut and recessed lights came to glowing life. He'd had a room like this—a private, secret place—in every home he'd ever lived in. This was his domain. During their life together, Marietta hadn't been allowed access to his private chambers in any of their homes, and over the centuries even Dagon had never stepped into one. In years past the room would have been accessed via secret passages and protected with spiked and bladed traps, and later with many locks and intricate hand-carved keys. Now, in the twenty-first century, it was safe within a bombproof casing and secured with palm- and voice-print technology.

The room was a perfect soundproof cube. There were no windows, and two walls were covered with books he had collected down through the centuries. Leather bindings stood beside dusty buckram and yellowed vellum were shelved side by side. Rolled parchment and stitched hide rested alongside brightly colored modern paperbacks. And all the books, in one way or another, had to do with the Elders. Absently, he straightened a four-thousand-year-old Akkadian tablet, pushing it back on top of a printout from a mythology Web site. Whereas Flamel was obsessed with preventing the Dark Elders from returning to this world and Dee was equally determined that the world return to its masters, Machiavelli focused on discovering the truth behind the enigmatic rulers of the ancient earth. One of the lessons he had learned in the court of the Medici was that power came from knowledge, so he had become determined to discover the Elders' secrets.

The wall facing the doorway was completely taken up with a series of computer screens. Machiavelli hit a button and they all lit up, each one showing a different image. There were assorted views of Paris and images from a dozen of the world's capitals, and a quartet of screens carried live national and international news from around the world. One screen, larger than the rest, showed a moving grainy gray image. Machiavelli sat down in a high-backed leather chair and stared at the screen, trying to make sense of what he was seeing.

It was a live video feed from the car trailing Dee.

Machiavelli ignored the black limousine in the center of the picture and concentrated on the streets. Where was Dee going?

The Magician had told him that he was heading to the airport, where his private jet was being refueled. He was going to fly to England and resume the hunt for the Alchemyst. The corners of Machiavelli's mouth curled in a smile. Dee was clearly not heading toward the airport; he was heading back into the city. The Italian's instincts had been correct: the Magician was up to something.

Keeping one eye on the screen, Machiavelli opened his laptop, powered it on and ran his index finger through the integrated fingerprint reader. The machine completed the boot sequence. If he had used any other finger to log on, a destructive virus would have overwritten the entire hard drive.

He quickly read through the encrypted e-mails coming in from his London-based agents and spies. Another ironic smile twisted his thin lips; the news was not good. In spite of everything Dee had done, Flamel and the twins had disappeared, and the trio of Genii Cucullati the Magician had sent after them had been discovered in a side street close to the train station. They were all in a deep coma, and the Italian suspected that it would be 366 days before they awoke. It seemed the English doctor had underestimated the Alchemyst yet again.

Machiavelli sat back in the chair and put his hands together, almost in an attitude of prayer. The tips of his index fingers pressed against his lips. He had always known that the image Flamel projected—that of a bumbling, slightly absent-minded, vaguely eccentric old fool—was a smokescreen. Nicholas and Perenelle had survived everything the Dark Elders and Dee had thrown at them over the centuries by a combination of cunning, skill, arcane knowledge and a healthy dose of luck. Machiavelli believed that Flamel was intelligent, dangerous and completely ruthless.

However, whereas Nicholas was wily, even he admitted that Perenelle was far cleverer than he was. Machiavelli's smile faltered: this was the woman he had been sent to kill, the woman his own Dark Elder master had described as being infinitely more dangerous than the Alchemyst. He sighed. Killing someone as powerful as the Sorceress was not going to be easy. But he had absolutely no doubt that he could do it. He had failed once before, but that was because he'd made the same grave error Dee had just made: he had under-estimated his enemy.

This time Machiavelli would be ready for the Sorceress. This time he *would* kill her.

But first he had to get to America. Machiavelli's fingers flew across the keys as he logged on to a travel Web site. Un-like Dee, who preferred to use his private jet, Machiavelli had decided to take a commercial flight to America. He could use one of the French government jets, but that would attract at-tention, and Machiavelli had always preferred to work behind the scenes.

He needed a direct flight to San Francisco. His options were limited, but there was a nonstop out of Paris at 10:15 a.m. the following morning. The flight was just over eleven hours long, but the nine-hour time difference meant that he would arrive on the West Coast at around 12:30 p.m. local time.

The Air France flight had no First Class seats so he booked l'Espace Affaires—Business Class. It was certainly ap-propriate. This trip was, after all, business. Machiavelli clicked forward through his purchase and chose seat 4A. It was at the back of the Business Class cabin, but when the plane landed and the door opened, he would be first off. When the e-mail confirmation popped into his in-box, he forwarded a copy of his flight details to the Dark Elders' principal agent on the West Coast of America: the immortal human Henry Mc-Carty.

Machiavelli had researched the man thoroughly. During his brief life McCarty had been better known as William H. Bonney or Billy the Kid. Born in 1859, immortal at twenty-two years old—or dead, according to the history books. Machiavelli shook his head in wonder. It was very unusual for a human to become immortal at such an early age; most of the immortals he'd encountered through the centuries were older. Despite years of research, Machiavelli still had no idea why certain people were chosen by the Elders to receive the gift. There had to be a pattern or a reason, but he had come across kings, princes, vagabonds and thieves who had nothing in common except that they had been granted immortality—and therefore were in the employ of the Elders. Less than a handful had become immortal before they were in their forties. So, to have been granted immortality at twenty-two, Billy the Kid must be very special indeed.

A flash of movement caught his attention and Machiavelli looked up at the screen tracking Dee.

The cars had stopped, and even as Machiavelli watched, Dee climbed out of the back of the limousine without giving the driver time to scuttle around to open the door. The Magician walked away from the limousine, then paused and turned to look back at the car behind him. In the instant when Dee gazed directly into the camera, Machiavelli realized he'd known he was being followed. The Magician smiled, then disappeared out of frame, and the Italian hit a speed dial that connected him with the driver of the second car. "Status?" he snapped. There was no need to identify himself.

"We've stopped, sir. The subject has just exited the vehicle."

"Where?"

"We're on the Pont au Double. The subject is heading for Notre Dame."

"Notre Dame!" Machiavelli said softly. Only yesterday, he had stood on the roof of the great cathedral with Dee, and together, they had brought the gargoyles and grotesques to terrifying life and watched them crawl down the wall to where Flamel, the twins, Saint-Germain and a mysterious woman had crouched on the parvis in front of the cathedral. The animated stone creatures should have crushed the humans, but the attack had not gone according to plan.

Flamel and his companions had fought back. Absently, the Italian rubbed his leg where he'd been struck by a silver arrow of pure auric energy. A star-shaped black bruise covered his thigh from knee to hip, and he knew he would be walking with a limp for weeks. It had been the twins who had saved them, the twins who had destroyed the gargoyles and grotesques of Notre Dame.

Machiavelli had stood in silence, seeing for himself the evidence that Sophie and Josh were indeed the twins of legend. It had been an amazing demonstration of power. Although the girl had learned only the very basics in two of the elemental magics—Wind and Fire—it was obvious that her natural skill was extraordinary. And when the twins had combined their auras to heighten and intensify the girl's powers, he had realized that Sophie and Josh Newman were truly exceptional.

Machiavelli's public relations department had released the story that the destruction of the cathedral's stonework was caused by acid rain and global warming. And even now teams of archaeologists and students from the universities of Paris were working to clear the parvis. The square was sealed off behind strips of tape and metal barricades.

The Italian stared hard at the screen, but it revealed nothing. Why had Dee gone back to that place?

"Should we follow?" The driver's voice crackled with static.

"Yes," Machiavelli said quickly. "Follow, but do not approach and do not apprehend. Keep this line open."

"Yes, sir."

Machiavelli waited impatiently, eyes fixed on the static image of the car on the screen. The driver spoke urgently to the men in the other two cars, ordering them to take up positions by the side entrances to the great cathedral. The main doors, which opened out onto the square, were closed. The immortal watched as the driver passed in front of the dashboard camera and disappeared off to the left, phone pressed to his ear. "He's heading for the cathedral," the driver said breathlessly. "He's gone inside. There's no way out," he added quickly.

The ambient sound changed as the man ran indoors. Footsteps echoed, doors slammed; then Machiavelli heard the tinny sounds of excited voices. He listened to the driver grow louder, more demanding, more insistent, but he could not make out the words. Moments later, the driver came back on the phone. "Sir: there are some architects and planners here to examine the damage. The subject would have had to come right past them, but they say no one has entered the cathedral in the last hour." A note of fear crept into the man's voice; Machiavelli's reputation for ruthlessness was legendary, and no one wanted to report a failure. "I know it's impossible, but I think . . . we—we've lost him." The man's voice faltered. "I . . . I have no idea how, but it looks like . . . he's not in the cathedral. We'll seal off the building and get some more men for a search. . . ."

"Negative. Let him go. Return to base," Machiavelli said very softly, and hung up. He knew where Dee was. The Magician wasn't in the cathedral. He was *under* it. He'd returned to the catacombs beneath the city. But the only thing in the ancient City of the Dead was the Elder Mars Ultor.

And yesterday, Dee had entombed the Elder in bone.

# CHAPTER THIRTEEN

The stink of frying food wafted across the junkyard, completely dispelling the odors of metal and oil and the wet musky scent of the dogs.

Flamel was standing on the bottom step to the hut. Even with the extra height, he had to look up into the knight's face. The man the Alchemyst had introduced as William Shakespeare had gone inside and slammed the door with enough force to shake the entire building. Moments later black smoke had started to leak from the chimney. "He cooks when he's upset," Palamedes had explained.

Josh swallowed hard, then pinched his nose shut, forcing himself to breathe through his mouth as the smoke from the building drifted around them. Already sickened by his Awakened senses, he knew that he had to get away from the smell of smoke and grease or he was going to throw up. He saw his sister looking at him, eyes wide with concern, and he jerked his head to one side. She nodded, then coughed, eyes watering as more smoke eddied around them. Stepping carefully, avoiding the booby-trapped potholes in the muddy ground, the twins quickly moved away from the dilapidated metal building. Josh rubbed the heel of his hand across his lips. He could actually taste the cooking oil and grease on his tongue. "Whatever it is," he muttered, "I'm not eating it." He glanced sideways at his sister. "I guess there are a few disadvantages to having Awakened senses."

"Just a few." She smiled. "I thought I was getting used to it," she added.

"Well, I'm not," Josh sighed. "Not yet, anyway." The Elder Mars had Awakened him only the previous day—though it felt like a lifetime ago—and he was still completely overwhelmed by the assault on his senses. Everything was brighter, louder and a lot smellier than it had ever been before. His clothing felt harsh and heavy against his skin, and even the air left a bitter taste on his lips.

"Joan told me that after a while, we'll be able to blank out most of the sensations and only concentrate on what we need to know," Sophie said. "Remember how sick I was when Hekate first Awakened me?"

He nodded. Sophie had been so weak that he'd had to carry her.

"It doesn't seem to have hit you so hard," she said. "You look pale, though."

"I feel sick," Josh said. He nodded toward the hut, where a plume of gray-black smoke was curling from the crooked

116

chimney, leaking the stink of bubbling fat and rancid oil into the air. "And that's not helping. I wonder, would it smell as bad if our senses weren't Awakened?"

"Probably not." She attempted a joke. "Maybe this was why human senses dulled over time. It was all just too much to handle."

Flamel suddenly looked over at the twins and raised an arm. "Stay close; don't wander off," he called. Then, followed by Palamedes, he climbed the remainder of the steps and jerked open the door. The two immortals disappeared into the gloomy interior and slammed the door behind them.

Sophie glanced at her twin. "Looks like we're not invited." Although she kept her voice carefully neutral, Josh could tell she was angry; she always sucked in her lower lip when she was irritated or upset.

"Guess not." Josh pulled the neck of his T-shirt up over his nose and mouth. "What do you think's going on in there? You think if we got closer we'd be able to hear what they're talking about?"

Sophie looked quickly at him. "I'm sure we would, but do you really want to get any closer to that stink?"

Josh's eyes narrowed as a thought struck him. "I wonder . . ."

"What?"

"Maybe that's why the smell is so bad," he said slowly. "They must know we won't be able to take it and it'll keep us away."

"You really think they'd go to all that trouble? What—so

they can talk about us?" Sophie looked at her brother again and her eyes winked briefly silver. "That's not your idea, Josh."

"What do you mean it's not my idea?" he demanded. "I thought of it." He paused and then added, "Didn't I?"

"For one, it's too smart," Sophie argued. "And it sounds like something Mars would think. From what I can tell from my memories—or the Witch's—there was a time when he thought everyone was after him."

"And were they?" Josh asked. Although the Elder was terrifying, he couldn't help feeling incredibly sorry for him. When Mars Ultor had touched him, Josh had felt the smallest bit of the warrior's unending pain. It was unbearable.

"Yes," Sophie said, eyes blinking silver, her voice now little more than a whisper. "Yes, they were. By the time he became Mars Ultor—the Avenger—he was one of the most hated and feared men on the planet."

"Those are the Witch's memories," Josh said. "Try not to think about them."

"I know." She shook her head. "But I can't help it. It all sort of creeps in around the edges of my mind." She shuddered and wrapped her arms around her body. "It's scaring me. What happens . . . what happens if her thoughts take over mine? What happens to *me*?"

Josh shook his head. He had no idea. Even the thought of losing his twin was terrifying. "Think about something else," Josh insisted. "Something the Witch couldn't know."

"I'm trying, but she knows so much," Sophie said miserably. She spun around, trying to focus on their surroundings

118

and ignore the strange and foreign thoughts at the back of her mind. She knew she should be strong, she needed to be strong for her brother, but she couldn't get past the Witch's memories. "Everyone I look at, everything I see, reminds me how things have changed. How am I supposed to think of something ordinary when all this is happening? Look at us, Josh: look at where we are, look at what's happened to us. Everything has changed . . . changed completely."

Josh nodded. He shifted the map tube on his shoulder, the heavy sword rattling inside. From that very first moment back in the bookshop when he'd popped his head up over the edge of the cellar and seen Flamel and Dee fighting with spears of green and yellow energy, he'd known the world would never be the same again. That had been—what?—four days ago, but in those four days, the world had turned upside down. Everything he'd thought he knew was a lie. They had met myths, fought legends; they had traveled halfway around the world in the blink of an eye to fight a primeval monster and watch stone carvings come to lumbering life.

"You know," Sophie said suddenly, "we really should have taken last Thursday off."

Josh couldn't resist a grin. "Yeah, we should have." He'd spent weeks trying to talk Sophie into taking a day off so they could visit the Exploratorium, the science museum close to the Golden Gate Bridge. Ever since he'd heard about it, he'd desperately wanted to see Bob Miller's famous *Sun Painting,* a creation of sunlight, mirrors and prisms. Then his smile faded. "If we'd done that, then none of this would have happened."

"Exactly," Sophie said. She looked at the towering metal walls of rusting cars, the pockmarked muddy landscape and the red-eyed dogs. "Josh, I want things the way they were. Ordinary." She turned back to her twin, her eyes catching and holding his. "But you don't," she said flatly.

Josh didn't even bother trying to deny it. His sister would know he was lying; she always did. And she was right: even though he was exhausted and barely able to cope with his Awakened senses, he didn't want things to go back to the way they'd been; he didn't want to go back to being ordinary. He'd been ordinary all his life—and when people did notice him, they only saw him as half of a set of twins. It was always Josh *and* Sophie. They went to summer camp together, went to concerts and movies together and had never spent a holiday apart. Birthday cards were always addressed to the two of them; party invitations came with both of their names on them. Usually, it didn't really bother him, but over the past few months, it had all started to grate on him. What would it be like to be seen as an individual? What if there were no Sophie? What if he was just Josh Newman, not half of the Newman twins?

He loved his sister, but this was his chance to be different, to be an individual.

He'd been jealous of Sophie when her senses had been Awakened and his hadn't. He'd been scared of her when he'd seen her do battle, in control of impossible powers. He'd been terrified for her when he'd seen the pain and confusion the Awakening had caused. But now that his own senses were Awakened and the world had turned sharp and brilliant, he'd had a momentary glimpse of his potential and he was beginning to understand what he might become. He'd experienced the Nidhogg's thoughts and Clarent's impressions, he'd caught fleeting glimpses of worlds beyond his imagination. He knew—beyond any shadow of a doubt—that he wanted to go to the next stage and be trained in the elemental magics. He just wasn't sure he wanted to do it with the Alchemyst. There was something *wrong* with Nicholas Flamel. The revelation that there had been other twins before them had been shocking and disturbing, and Josh had questions—hundreds of questions—but he knew he wasn't going to get a straight answer from the Alchemyst. Right now he didn't know who to trust—except Sophie—and the realization that she would prefer not to have her powers was a little frightening. Even though his Awakened senses had given him a pounding headache and a sick sour stomach, had made his throat raw and his eyes gritty, he wouldn't give them up. Unlike his twin, he realized, he was glad he hadn't taken Thursday off.

Josh pressed his hand to his chest. Paper rustled under his T-shirt, where he still wore the two pages he'd snatched from the Codex. A thought occurred to him. "You know," he said softly, "if we had gone to the Exploratorium, then Dee would have kidnapped Nicholas and Perenelle and he'd have the entire Codex. He probably would've already brought the Dark Elders back from their Shadowrealms. The world might have already ended. There's no *ordinary* to go back to, Soph," he finished in an awed whisper.

The twins stood in silence, trying to comprehend it all.

The very idea was terrifying: it was almost incomprehensible that the world they knew could end. Back on Wednesday they would have laughed at the idea. But now? Now they both knew that it could have happened. And worse—they knew it might still happen.

"Or at least, that's what Nicholas says," Josh added, unable to keep the bitterness out of his voice.

"And you believe him?" Sophie asked, curious. "I thought you didn't trust him."

"I don't," Josh said firmly. "You heard what Palamedes said about him. Because of Flamel, because of what he did and didn't do, hundreds of thousands of people have died."

"Nicholas didn't kill them," Sophie reminded him. "Your *friend*," she said sarcastically, "John Dee, did that."

Josh turned away and looked at the metal hut. He had no answer to that because it was the truth. Dee himself had admitted to setting fire and plague loose on the world in an attempt to stop the Flamels. "All we know is that Flamel has lied to us right from the very beginning. What about the other twins?" he asked. "Palamedes said Flamel and Perenelle had been *collecting* twins for centuries." Even saying the word *collecting* made him feel queasy and uncomfortable. "Whatever happened to them?"

A gust of icy wind whipped across the junkyard, and Sophie shivered, though not because of the cold air. Staring hard at the metal hut, not looking at her brother, she spoke very slowly, picking her words with care. She could feel herself growing angry. "Since the Flamels are *still* looking for twins, that means all the others . . . what?" She spun around to look at her brother and found he was already nodding in agreement.

"We need to know what happened to the other twins," he said firmly, voicing exactly what she was thinking. "I hate to ask, but does the Witch know?" he said carefully. "I mean, do you know if the Witch knew?" He still found it hard to grasp that the Witch of Endor had somehow passed all her knowledge on to his sister.

Sophie paused for a second, then shook her head again. "The Witch doesn't seem to know a lot about the modern world. She knows about the Elders, the Next Generation and some of the oldest human immortals. She'd heard about the Flamels, for instance, but she'd never met them before Scatty brought him there with us. All I know is that she's been living in and around Ojai for years, without a phone, a TV or radio."

"OK, then forget about it, don't even think about her again." Josh picked up a pebble and tossed it against the wall of crushed cars. It rattled and bounced and a shape flickered behind the metal. The red-eyed dogs raised their heads and watched him carefully. "You know, I just had a thought . . . ," he said slowly.

Sophie watched him, silent.

"How did I end up working for the Flamels, a couple who collect twins, and you end up in the coffee shop across the road? It can't be a coincidence, can it?"

"I guess not." Sophie nodded, the tiniest movement of

her head. She'd started thinking the same thing the second Palamedes had mentioned the other twins. It couldn't be a coincidence. The Witch didn't believe in coincidence, nor did Nicholas Flamel, and even Scatty said she believed in destiny. And then of course there was the prophecy. . . . "Do you think you got the job because he *knew* you had a twin?" she asked.

"After the battle in Hekate's Shadowrealms, Flamel told me that he'd only started to suspect that we were the twins mentioned in the prophecy the day before."

Sophie shook her head. "I hardly remember anything about that day."

"You were asleep," Josh said quickly, "exhausted after the battle." The memory of the fight chilled him; it was the first time he had seen how alien his sister had become. "Scatty said that Flamel was a man of his word and told me that I should believe him."

"I don't think Scatty would lie to us," Sophie said but even as she was speaking, she wondered if these were her thoughts or the Witch's.

"Maybe she didn't." Pressing both hands to his face, Josh rubbed his fingers over his forehead, pushing back his over-long blond hair. He was trying to remember exactly what had happened last Thursday. "She wasn't agreeing with him when he said he hadn't known *who* we were. He said that everything he'd done had been for our own protection: I'm thinking she was agreeing with *that*," he finished. "And the last thing Hekate said to me before the World Tree burned was 'Nicholas Flamel never tells anyone everything.' "

Sophie closed her eyes, trying to blank out the sights and sounds of the junkyard, concentrating hard now, thinking back to early April, when they'd both started the part-time jobs. "Why did you go for that particular job?" she asked.

Josh blinked in surprise, then frowned, remembering. "Well, Dad saw an ad in the university newspaper. *Assistant Wanted, Bookshop. We don't want readers, we want workers.* I didn't want to do it, but Dad said he'd worked in a bookshop when he was our age and that I'd enjoy it. I sent in a résumé and was called for an interview two days later."

Sophie nodded, remembering. While Josh was in the bookshop, she'd gone across the road to wait for him in a small coffee shop. Bernice, the owner of The Coffee Cup, had been there talking to a striking-looking woman who Sophie now knew was Perenelle Flamel. "Perenelle," Sophie said so suddenly that Josh looked around, half expecting to see the woman behind him. He would not have been surprised.

"What about her?"

"On the day we got our jobs. You were being interviewed in the bookshop and I was having a drink. Bernice was talking to Perenelle Flamel. While Bernice was making my chai latte, Perenelle started a conversation with me. I remember her saying that she hadn't seen me in the neighborhood before, and I told her I'd come along because you'd been called for an interview in the bookshop." Sophie closed her eyes, thinking back. "She didn't say then that she was one of the owners of the shop, but I remember her asking me something like, 'Oh, I saw you with a young man outside. Was that your boyfriend?' I told her no, it was my brother. Then she said, 'You look very alike.' When I told her we were twins, she smiled, then she quickly finished her drink and left. She crossed the street and went into the bookstore."

"I remember when she came in," Josh agreed. "I didn't think the interview was going particularly well. I got the impression that Nicholas—or Nick . . . whatever his name is—was looking for someone older for the job. Then Perenelle came in, smiled at me, and called him to the back of the shop. I saw them both looking at me. Then she left the store as quickly as she'd arrived."

"She came back into The Coffee Cup," Sophie murmured. Then she stopped as memories and events slotted into place. When she spoke again, her voice was barely above a whisper. "Josh, I just remembered something. She asked Bernice if she was still looking for staff. She suggested that if my brother was working across the street, it would be perfect if I was working at The Coffee Cup. Bernice agreed and offered me the job on the spot. But you know what, when I turned up for work the next day it was the strangest thing. I could swear that Bernice looked a little surprised to find me there. I even had to remind her that she'd offered me the job the                                                    day before."

Josh nodded. He remembered his sister telling him that. "Do you think Perenelle somehow made her give you the job? Could she do that?"

"Oh yes." Sophie's eyes turned briefly silver. Even the

Witch of Endor acknowledged Perenelle as an extraordinarily powerful Sorceress. "So do you think we got the jobs because we're twins?" she asked again.

"I have no doubt about it," Josh said angrily. "We were just another set of twins to be added to the Flamels' collection. We've been tricked."

"What are we going to do, Josh?" Sophie asked, her voice as hard as her brother's. The thought that the Flamels had somehow used them made her feel sick to her stomach. If Dee hadn't showed up in the shop, then what would have happened to them? What would the Flamels have done to them?

Catching Sophie's hand, Josh pulled his sister behind him toward the stinking metal hut, stepping carefully around the potholes. The dogs sat up, heads swiveling to follow them, red eyes glowing. "There's no going back. We have no choice, Soph: we have to see this through to the end."

"But what is the end, Josh? Where does it end . . . *how* does it end?"

"I have no idea," he said. He stopped and turned to look directly into his sister's blue eyes. He took a deep breath, swallowing his anger. "But you know what I do know? This is all about us."

Sophie nodded. "You're right. The prophecy is about us, we're gold and silver, we're special."

"Flamel wants us," Josh continued, "Dee wants us. It's time to get some answers."

"Attack," Sophie said, hopping over a muddy puddle.

"When I knew him—I mean, when the Witch knew him—Mars always said that attack was the best form of defense."

"My football coach says the same thing."

"And your team didn't win a single game last season," Sophie reminded him.

They had almost reached the hut when a wild-eyed William Shakespeare appeared, a blazing frying pan clutched in both hands.

# CHAPTER FOURTEEN

Without a second thought Josh shrugged the map tube off his shoulder and shook out the sword. It settled easily into his hand, his fingers wrapping around the stained leather hilt. He took a step forward, putting himself between Shakespeare and his sister.

The immortal didn't even look at them. He turned the blazing pan upside down and shook out the contents. What looked like half a dozen blackened sausages dropped onto the muddy ground. They hissed and sizzled but continued to burn, spiraling sparks into the air. One of the red-eyed dogs came out from beneath the hut, and a long forked tongue snatched up a chunk of still-burning meat and swallowed it whole. The flames turned its eyes to rubies, and when it licked its lips, curls of gray smoke leaked from the corner of its mouth.

Shakespeare bent down and roughly patted the dog's

head. He was about to turn and climb the steps when he spotted the twins. The dull evening light reflected off his overlarge glasses, turning them to silver mirrors. "There was a little mishap with our evening meal," he said, a quick smile revealing his bad teeth.

"That's OK. We weren't that hungry," Sophie said quickly. "And I'm trying to give up meat."

"Vegetarians?" Shakespeare asked.

"Sort of," Sophie said, and Josh nodded in agreement.

"There might be some salad inside," the immortal said vaguely. "Neither Palamedes nor I are vegetarians. There's fruit," he added. "Lots of fruit."

Josh nodded. "Fruit would be perfect." Even the thought of meat set his stomach churning.

Shakespeare seemed to notice the sword in Josh's hand for the first time. "Keep up your bright swords," he murmured. Stepping forward, he produced a surprisingly pristine white handkerchief, pulled off his glasses and started to polish them. Without the thick lenses, Sophie noticed, he looked more like the image of the famous playwright she'd seen in her textbooks. He put his glasses back on and looked at Josh. "It is Clarent?"

Josh nodded. He could feel it tremble slightly in his hands and was aware of a slow warmth soaking into his flesh.

Shakespeare leaned forward, his long narrow nose inches from the tip of the blade, but he made no attempt to touch it. "I saw its twin many times," he said absently. "The blades are identical, but the hilts are slightly different."

"Was this when you were with Dee?" Sophie asked shrewdly.

Shakespeare nodded. "When I was with the doctor," he agreed. He reached out and tentatively touched the tip of the blade with his index finger. The dark stone sparkled and rippled with a tracery of pale yellow, as if a liquid had been poured down the blade, and there was a hint of lemon in the air. "Dee inherited Excalibur from his predecessor, Roger Bacon, but this was really the weapon he wanted to find. The twin blades are older than the Elders and were ancient long before Danu Talis was raised from the seas. Individually, the swords are powerful, but legend has it that together they have the power to destroy the very fabric of the earth itself."

"I'm surprised Dee didn't find it," Josh said a little breathlessly. He could feel the sword buzzing in his hands, and strange images floated at the edge of his consciousness. Somehow he knew that these were Shakespeare's memories.

*A circular building in flames . . .*

*A pitifully small grave, and a young girl standing over the opening, tossing in a handful of dirt . . .*

*And Dee. A little younger than Josh remembered him; his face unlined, his hair dark and full, his goatee without a hint of gray.*

"The Magician always believed the sword had been lost in a lake deep in the Welsh mountains," Shakespeare continued. "He spent decades hunting for it there."

"Flamel found it in a cave in Andorra," Sophie said. "He believed Charlemagne hid it there in the ninth century."

131

Shakespeare smiled. "So the Magician was wrong. It is gratifying to know that the doctor is not always correct."

Sophie stepped out from behind Josh and pushed down his arm. The wind coming across the sword blade moaned. "Are you really . . . really William Shakespeare? The Bard?" she asked. Even after all she had seen and experienced over the past few days, she still found the idea awe-inspiring.

The man stepped back and executed a surprisingly elegant sweeping bow, leg outstretched, head bent almost to waist level. "Your servant, my lady." The whole effect was slightly ruined by the stench of stale body odor that rolled off him. "Please call me Will."

Sophie wasn't sure how to react. "I've never met anyone famous before . . . ," she started, and then stopped when she realized what she was saying.

Shakespeare straightened. Josh coughed and backed away, eyes watering. "You have met Nicholas and Perenelle Flamel," Shakespeare said in his precise English, "Dr. John Dee, the Comte de Saint-Germain and, of course, Niccolò Machiavelli," he continued. "And no doubt you encountered the charming Jeanne d'Arc."

"Yes," Sophie said with a shy smile, "we met all of them. But none of them are as famous as you are."

William Shakespeare took a moment to consider, and then he nodded. "I am sure Machiavelli and certainly Dee would disagree. But yes, you are correct, of course. None of them would have my"—he paused—"my profile. My work has thrived and survived, whereas theirs is not quite so popular."

"And did you really serve Dee?" Josh asked suddenly, realizing that here was an opportunity to get some answers.

Shakespeare's smile faded. "I spent twenty years in Dee's service."

"Why?" Josh asked.

"Have you ever met him?" Shakespeare replied.

Josh nodded.

"Then you will know that Dee is that most dangerous of enemies: he truly believes that what he is doing is right."

"That's what Palamedes said," Josh murmured.

"And it's true. Dee is a liar, but I came to understand that he *believes* the lies he tells. Because he wants to believe, he *needs* to believe."

A quick spattering of rain rattled across the junkyard, pinging off the crushed metal cars.

"But is he right?" Josh asked quickly, ducking as big drops of rain hit the side of the metal hut. He reached out and grabbed the man's arm, and instantly his aura flared bright brilliant orange, while a pale yellow aura outlined the man's body. Orange and lemon mingled, and while the results should have been pleasant, the two odors were sour and tainted by Shakespeare's unwashed smell.

*Dee, younger, his face unlined, hair and beard dark, staring into an enormous crystal, a young wide-eyed William Shakespeare by his side.*

*Images in the crystal . . .*

*Lush green fields . . .*

*Orchards laden down with fruit . . .*

*Seas churning with fish . . .*

"Wait—you think Dee should bring the Elders back to this world?"

William Shakespeare started for the stairs. "Yes," he said, without turning around. "My own research has led me to believe it may be the right decision."

"Why?" the twins demanded.

The Bard rounded on them. "Most of the Elders have abandoned this world. The Next Generation toy with humani and use the earth as both a playground and a battleground, but the most dangerous of all are we humani. We are destroying this world. I believe we need the Dark Elders to return so that they can save the earth from our destruction."

Stunned, the twins looked at one another, completely confused now. Josh spoke first. "But Nicholas said the Dark Elders want humans as food."

"Some do. But not all Elders eat flesh; some feed off memories and emotions. It seems a small price to pay for a paradise without famine, without disease."

"Why do we need the Dark Elders?" Sophie asked. "Between the Alchemyst and Dee and the others like them, surely they must possess enough power and knowledge to save the world?"

"I do not believe so."

"But Dee is powerful . . . ," Josh began.

"You cannot ask me anything about Dee; I have no answers."

"You spent twenty years with him; you must know him better than anyone on this earth," Sophie protested.

"No one truly knows the Magician. I loved him like a father, like an older brother. He was all that I admired, all that I wanted to be." A single tear suddenly appeared under the immortal's thick glasses and rolled down his cheek. "And then he betrayed me and killed my son."

# CHAPTER FIFTEEN

In the catacombs deep beneath the city of Paris, Dr. John Dee fastidiously brushed dust off the arm of his suit, tugged at his cuffs and straightened his bow tie. He snapped his fingers and a sulfurous yellow ball blossomed before him, bobbing at head height. It exuded the smell of rotten eggs, but its stench was so familiar that Dee no longer even registered the foul odor. Dirty yellow light splashed across two arching columns of polished bones that had been shaped to resemble a doorframe. Beyond the opening there was utter blackness.

Dee stepped into the underground chamber to face a frozen god.

In his long lifetime the Magician had experienced wonders. He had come to accept the extraordinary as ordinary, the strange and wonderful as commonplace. Dee had seen the legends of the Arabian Nights come to life, had fought with monsters from Greek and Babylonian myth, had traveled through realms that people believed were lies created by the travelers Marco Polo and Ibn Battutah. He knew that the myths of the Celts and the Romans, the Gauls and the Mongols, the Rus, the Viking and even the Maya, were more than stories—they were based on fact. The gods of Greece and Egypt, the spirits of the American plains, the jungle totems and the Japanese Myo-o had once lived. Now they were remembered as little more than fragments of myths and snatches of legend, but John Dee knew that they had once walked this earth. They were part of an Elder race who had ruled the world for millennia.

One of the greatest of the Elders was Mars . . . and less than twenty-four hours earlier, Dee had encased him in a tomb of solid bone.

The Magician stepped into a vast but low-ceilinged circular chamber, the floating light painting everything sallow, the color of pale butter, and looked around the chamber. Although he'd known about its location for decades, he'd never had a reason to venture down to face the Sleeping God before, and everything had happened so quickly yesterday that he hadn't had a chance to examine the sepulchre. He ran his hand down a section of the smooth wall beside the door, the scientist within him recognizing the materials: collagen fiber and calcium phosphate. The walls here were not stone—they were bone. Dee spotted two indentations against the far wall. Between them were two dimpled depressions, and suddenly he knew what he was seeing and realized where he was. He was looking at a set of eyes and a nose. The chamber had not been hollowed from a single piece of bone, as he'd thought—

he was *inside* an enormous skull. Terrifyingly, the skull looked almost human. Dee felt a shiver run down his spine; he'd never encountered them, but he'd heard stories of Shadow-realms inhabited by cannibal giants. Yesterday, the walls had been smooth and polished; today they looked like a candle that had been left too close to a fire. Long-frozen stalactites of bone dripped like sticky toffee from the ceiling; huge bubbles had been caught and frozen as they popped; dribbles and streams of thick liquid curled in ornate patterns.

In the center of the room was a long rectangular raised stone plinth splashed and spattered with globules of what looked like yellow wax. The ancient slab was cracked in two.

And on the floor before the plinth was a gray statue partially encased in yellow. It depicted an enormous man on hands and knees, caught as he attempted to climb to his feet. The figure was dressed as a warrior, wearing the metal and leather armor of the ancient past, his left arm outstretched, fingers splayed wide, while his right arm was buried in the floor up to his wrist. His body from the waist down also disappeared into the ground. On the figure's back, two hideous child-sized creatures had been frozen as they'd attempted to leap forward on goatlike hooves. Stick-thin, ribs and bones visible, their mouths gaped to reveal maws filled with jagged teeth, and their outstretched hands were tipped with dagger-sharp claws.

Gathering up his coat so that it would not brush the floor, and hitching up his trousers, Dee hunkered down for a closer look at the statues. The piece looked like something from a museum, a classical sculpture by Michelangelo or Bernini,

138

perhaps—Phobos and Deimos on the back of Mars Ultor. Dee moved his hand and the ball of light floated over the satyrs' heads. The detail was incredible; every strand of hair had been preserved, the drool caught on their chins, and one of them—Phobos, he thought—even had a cracked nail. But these were no statues; yesterday, they had been savage living creatures, and Mars had loosed them on him. It would have been a terrible death. The satyrs fed off panic and fear . . . and over the centuries Dee had learned that there was much to fear. The knowledge of what the Elders could do to him always sent queasy swells of panic through his stomach. Phobos and Deimos would have feasted for months.

The Magician leaned forward to look at the helmet that completely covered Mars's head. Beneath the yellow coating of hardened bone, the gray stone was still visible. It sparkled like granite, but this was no natural rock. For a single instant, Dee felt something like pity for the Dark Elder. The Witch of Endor had caused his aura to become visible and to harden, stonelike, around his body, trapping him within an impossibly heavy crust. If the god peeled it off, his aura bubbled up like lava and hardened again immediately. Mars, who had once roamed the world and been worshipped as a god by a dozen nations under scores of names, had been practically immobile for millennia. Dee found himself wondering what crime the God of War had committed that had so offended the Witch that she had condemned him to this lingering undeath. It must have been terrible indeed. Then the Magician's lips twitched in a smile as a thought struck him. Reaching out, he rapped his knuckles on the helmeted head. The sound was dull and flat in the bone-wrapped chamber. "I know you can hear me," Dee said conversationally. "I was just thinking that this seems to be your destiny," he continued. "First the Witch trapped you in your own aura, and then I wrapped you in solid bone."

Wisps of black smoke suddenly curled from the Dark Elder's helmet.

"Ah, good," Dee murmured. "For a moment there I thought I'd lost you."

Eyes blazed crimson in the blackness behind the helmet. "I am not so easy to kill." Mars's voice was a gravelly rasp, touched with an indefinable accent.

Dee straightened and dusted off his spotless knees. "You know, every Elder I've killed has said that. But there is blood in your veins. And what lives can be slain." He showed his small teeth in a tiny smile. "Admittedly, you are difficult—in fact, well-nigh impossible—to kill, but it can be done. I know. I've done it. Why, less than a week ago, I slew Hekate."

The interior of the helmet glowed bright red for an instant and the glow faded. Locked in place by granite and bone, Mars could not move, and yet Dee could clearly feel the Elder's eyes on him. Black smoke curled up out of the slit in his helmet, and where his eyes should have been were now two crimson balls flecked with blue. "Have you come back to gloat, Magician?"

"Not intentionally." Dee walked behind the trio of statues, examining them from every angle. "But now that I'm here, I might as well gloat anyway." He ran his hands across the Elder's shoulder, and Dee felt his own aura flicker as the

140

merest buzz of energy crackled through him. Even buried beneath a sheath of stone and bone, the Elder's aura was powerful.

"When I escape," Mars rumbled, "as I surely will, you will be my first priority. Even before I discover the whereabouts of the Witch of Endor, I will find you, and my vengeance will be terrible."

"I'm scared," Dee said, sarcasm heavy in his voice. "The Witch has kept you locked in stone for millennia. You've not managed to shake off that curse yet. And you know that if anything happens to the Witch, then the spell dies with her, leaving you trapped like this forever." The Magician moved around in front of the Elder again. "Perhaps I should have the Witch killed. Then you will never escape."

There was a peculiar snuffling sound within the helmet, and it took the Magician a few moments to realize that the Elder was laughing. "You! Kill the Witch? I was called the God of War; my powers were terrible. And yet I could not kill her. If you move against her, Magician, she will do something horrible to you—and ensure that your agony lasts a millennium. She once reduced an entire Roman legion to figures about the size of her fingernail, and then strung them together on a silver wire so that she could wear them as a necklace. She kept them alive for centuries." The Elder chuckled, a sound like grinding stone. "She used to collect amber paperweights; within each one was a person who had displeased her. So yes, go and attack the Witch! I am sure she will be particularly creative with your punishment."

Dee crouched down before the Elder's head. He laced

141

the fingers of his hands together and stared into the smoking dark interior of the stone helmet. Two crimson dots glowed back at him. The Magician moved his fingers and the globe of yellow light came down and settled behind his head. He hoped the harsh light would blind Mars, but the two red orbs stared at him, unblinking. With a flick of his wrist, Dee dismissed the light, sending it bobbing close to the ceiling, where it softened and faded, painting the room in sepia. "I have come here to make you an offer," Dee said after a long moment of silence.

"There is nothing you can offer me."

"There is one thing," Dee said confidently.

"Did you come of your own accord, or were you sent by your masters?" Mars asked.

"No one knows I am here."

"Not even the Italian?"

Dee shrugged. "He may suspect, but there is nothing he can do." He stopped and then waited. Dee was a great believer in silence. In his experience, people often spoke to fill the quiet.

"What do you want?" Mars asked eventually.

The Magician dipped his head to hide a smile. With that single question, Dee knew that the Elder would give him exactly what he wanted. The Englishman had always prided himself on his imagination—it was part of what made him one of the most powerful magicians and necromancers in the world—but even he could not comprehend what it must be like to be trapped for centuries in a hard stone shell. He had heard the desperation in the God of War's voice the previous day when he had pleaded with Sophie to lift the curse, and it had given him an idea.

"You know that I am a man of my word," Dee began.

Mars said nothing.

"True, I have lied, cheated, stolen and killed, but all with one single intention: to bring the Elders back to this world."

"The end justifies the means," Mars grumbled.

"Just so. And you know that if I give you my word, my oath, then I will carry through with my promise. Yesterday, you said you could read my intent clearly."

"I know that in spite of your faults—or possibly even because of them—you are an honorable man, though it is a peculiar definition of honor," Mars said. "So yes, if you give me your word, I will believe you."

Dee stood up quickly and walked around behind the statue, so that Mars could not see the triumphant grin on his face. "The Witch of Endor will never lift your curse, will she?"

Mars Ultor remained quiet for a long time, but Dee made no move to break the silence. He wanted to give the Elder time to think through what he'd just said; he needed him to admit that he was doomed for all eternity to wear the stone shell.

"No," the god finally admitted in a ghastly whisper. "She will not."

"Maybe someday I will learn what you did to earn such punishment."

"Maybe. But not from me."

"So you are trapped . . . or maybe not."

"Explain yourself, Magician."

Dee started walking counterclockwise around the frozen Elder. He kept his voice low and unemotional as he outlined his plan. "Yesterday, you Awakened Josh, the sun twin. You touched him; you are connected to him."

"Yes, there is a connection," Mars agreed.

"The Witch touched the moon twin, gifted her with the Magic of Air, and also poured her complete compendium of knowledge into her," Dee continued. "Yesterday, you said that the girl must know the spell that would free you."

"And she said she did," Mars whispered.

Dee slapped his hand off the statue's shoulder as he spun to crouch in front of it. Electrical energy snapped around the room. "And she refused you! But would she refuse you if her brother's life—wait, better still, her parents' lives—were in danger? Would she? Could she?"

The smoke curling from behind the Elder's full-face visor turned white, then gray-black. "Even knowing me, knowing what I am, what I did, what I am capable of, she still faced me down to rescue her brother," Mars said very slowly. "I believe she would do anything to save her brother and her family."

"Then here is my oath to you," Dee continued. "Find the boy for me, and I swear I will bring the girl, her brother and their parents here to stand before you. When she is faced with their deaths, I guarantee she will free you of this terrible curse."

# CHAPTER SIXTEEN

*F*rom the outside, the long metal structure sitting in the middle of the muddy clearing had looked dilapidated and run-down, but like everything else in the junkyard, it was just a façade. Inside, it was neat and spotlessly clean. One end of the room was used for cooking and eating; a sink, a fridge and a stove sat next to a table. The middle section of the hut contained a tiered desk holding a desktop computer hooked up to two matching screens, while at the far end of the hut, a large flat-screen TV faced two leather couches. A trio of low metal towers held dozens of DVDs.

When the twins followed Shakespeare inside, they realized immediately that they had walked in on an argument. Flamel and Palamedes were standing at either end of the small wooden kitchen table, the knight with his arms folded across his massive chest, Flamel with his hands clenched into fists. The air was sour with their mixed auras.

"I think you should wait outside," Nicholas said quietly, looking from Josh to Sophie, then turning back to the knight. "We'll be done in a few moments."

Sophie moved to leave, but Josh pushed her forward into the hut. "No. I think we should wait here," he said firmly. He looked from Palamedes to the Alchemyst. "If you have anything to say, you should say it in front of us. After all, this is about us, isn't it?" He glanced sidelong at his sister. "We're the . . . what's the word?" he asked.

"The catalyst," she supplied.

Josh nodded. "The catalyst," he said, though that wasn't the word he had been hunting for. He looked around the room, eyes lingering on the computer, and then turned to his twin. "I just hate it when adults send you out of the room when they're talking about you, don't you?"

Sophie agreed. "Hate it."

"We weren't talking about you," Flamel said quickly. "This has nothing to do with you, actually. This has to do with a little unfinished business between Mr. Shakespeare and me."

"Right now," Josh said, stepping into the room, concentrating hard on keeping his voice even and preventing it from trembling, "just about everything that happens concerns us." He looked directly at the Alchemyst. "You've nearly killed us. You've changed our lives ir . . . irev . . . irevo . . ."

"Irrevocably," Sophie said.

"Irrevocably," Josh said. "And if you two have a problem, then it's our problem and we need to know about it."

Sophie put her hand on Josh's shoulder and squeezed encouragingly.

Palamedes grinned, a quick flash of white teeth. "The boy has spirit. I like that."

Nicholas's face was an impassive mask, but his pale eyes were clouded. A vein throbbed on his forehead. Folding his arms across his chest, he nodded toward Palamedes. "If you must know, then, I have no argument with the Saracen Knight." He moved his head slightly, indicating the smaller man in the stained overalls, who was now standing before an open fridge, pulling out bags of fruit. "I have a problem with this man. A major problem."

Shakespeare ignored him. "What will you have to eat?" he asked, looking at the twins. "I know you do not want any meat, but we have plenty of fruit, fresh this morning. And Palamedes picked up some nice fish in Billingsgate Fish Market earlier." He dumped several bags of fruit into the sink, then turned the taps on full. Water thundered into the metal sink.

"Just the fruit," Sophie said.

Palamedes looked at the twins. "This dispute has nothing to do with you," he said. "It goes back centuries. But yes, I agree that you are affected by it. We all are." He turned back to the Alchemyst. "If we are to survive, then we—all of us—must put aside old arguments, old habits. However," he rumbled, "let me suggest that we discuss this after we eat."

"We want some answers now," Josh said. "We're tired of being treated like children."

The knight bowed and looked at the Alchemyst. "They have a right to answers."

Nicholas Flamel rubbed his hands against his face. There were bruise-colored bags under his eyes, and the wrinkles on his forehead had deepened. Sophie noticed that tiny spots had started to appear on the backs of his hands. The Alchemyst had said that he would age at the rate of at least a year for every day that passed, but she thought he looked at least ten years older than he had a week ago. "Before we go any further," Nicholas said, his French accent more evident now that he was tired, "I must admit I am uncomfortable discussing anything in front of . . ." He raised his head and looked at Shakespeare. "That man."

"But why?" Sophie asked, frustrated. She pulled out a wooden chair and collapsed into it. Josh took the chair beside her. The knight remained standing a moment longer, then he too sat. Only the Alchemyst and the Bard still stood.

"He betrayed Perenelle and me," Flamel snarled. "He sold us out to Dee."

The twins turned to look at the Bard, who was arranging grapes, apples, pears and cherries on plates. "This much is true," he said.

"Because of him, Perenelle was wounded and nearly died," the Alchemyst snapped.

The twins looked at the Bard again. He nodded. "It was in 1576," Shakespeare said quietly, looking up from the table, his pale blue eyes magnified behind his glasses, huge with unshed tears.

Josh sat back in astonishment. "You're arguing about

148

something that happened more than four hundred years ago?" he asked incredulously.

Shakespeare turned to speak directly to Sophie and Josh. "I was but twelve years old, younger than you are now." His lips moved, revealing his yellowed teeth. "I made a mistake— a terrible mistake—and I've spent centuries paying for it." He glanced back to Flamel. "I was apprenticed to the Alchemyst. He was running a small bookshop in Stratford, where I grew up."

Josh turned to look at Nicholas.

"He did not treat me well."

Flamel's head rose quickly and he opened his mouth to respond, but Shakespeare pressed on.

"I was not uneducated; I had attended the King's New School, and I could read and write English, Latin and Greek. Even then, at that early age, I knew I wanted to be a writer, and I prevailed upon my father to find me a position in Mr. Fleming's bookshop." Shakespeare's eyes were fixed on the Alchemyst now, and his language and even his accent were changing, becoming formal, almost archaic. "I wanted to read and learn and write; Mr. Fleming had me sweeping floors, running errands, carrying parcels of books across town."

The Alchemyst opened his mouth again but then closed it, saying nothing.

"And then Dr. Dee appeared in Stratford. You should know that he was famous then. He had served two queens, Mary and Elizabeth, and survived with his head still on his shoulders, which was no mean feat in those days. He was close to Elizabeth—it was said that he had even chosen the date for her coronation. He was reputed to have the largest library in England," Shakespeare continued, "so it was entirely natural that he called upon the Flemings' bookshop. Surprisingly, the Flemings, who rarely left the premises and never the town, were not at home that day. The shop was in the charge of one of their assistants, a horse-faced man whose name I have never been able to remember."

"Sebastian," Flamel said softly.

Shakespeare's damp eyes fixed on the Alchemyst's face and he nodded. "Ah yes, Sebastian. But Dee was not interested in him. He spoke to me, in English first, then Latin, then Greek. He asked me to recommend a book—I suggested Ovid's *Medea,* which he purchased—and then he asked me if I was happy in my present position." Shakespeare's pale blue eyes locked onto Flamel's. "I told him I was not. So he offered me an apprenticeship. Given the choice between a lowly position as a bookseller's assistant and an apprenticeship with one of the most powerful men in England, how could I refuse?"

Josh nodded. He would have made the same choice himself.

"So I became Dee's apprentice. More than that, perhaps: I came to believe that he even regarded me as a son. What is undeniable is that he created me."

Sophie leaned forward over the table, confused. "What do you mean, he created you?"

Shakespeare's eyes clouded with sadness. "Dee saw something in me—a hunger for sensation, a yearning for adventure—and offered to train and educate me in ways the

Flemings—the *Flamels*—either would not or could not. True to his word, the Magician showed me wonders. He took me to worlds beyond comprehension, he fed my imagination, allowed me access to his incredible library, which gave me the language to shape and describe the worlds I had experienced. Because of Dr. John Dee I *became* William Shakespeare the writer."

"You've missed the bit where he asked you to creep into our home at dead of night and steal the Codex," Nicholas Flamel said icily. "And when you failed, he accused us of being Spanish spies. Fifty of the Queen's Men surrounded the bookshop and attacked without warning. Sebastian was injured and Perenelle was struck with a musket ball in the shoulder, which almost killed her."

Shakespeare listened to the words and nodded very slowly. "Dee and I were not in Stratford when that happened, and I only learned about it much, much later," he said in a raw whisper. "And by then it was too late, of course. I was deep under Dee's spell: he had convinced me that I could become the writer I wanted to be. Even though it sounded impossible, I believed him. My father was a glove maker and wool merchant; there were no writers, no poets or playwrights or even actors in my family." He shook his head slightly. "Perhaps I should have followed my father into the family business."

"The world would have been a poorer place," Palamedes said quietly. The Saracen Knight was watching Shakespeare and the Alchemyst closely.

"I married. I had children," Shakespeare continued,

151

speaking more quickly now, focused only on Flamel. "A girl first, my beautiful Susanna, then two years later, the twins, Hamnet and Judith."

Sophie and Josh straightened, glancing quickly at one another; they hadn't ever heard about Shakespeare's twins.

There was a long pause and finally the immortal Bard sucked in a deep shuddering breath. He spread his long-fingered hands on the wooden table and stared hard at them. "I discovered then why Dee was interested in me. He had somehow known that I would have twins, and he believed that they were the legendary twins prophesied in the Codex. In 1596, I was in London and no longer living at home in Stratford. Dee visited my wife and offered to educate the twins. She foolishly agreed, even though by that time, ugly rumors were beginning to circulate about the doctor. A few days later, he attempted to have Hamnet Awakened. The Awakening killed him," he finished simply. "My son was eleven years old."

No one spoke into the long silence that followed, the only sound the pattering of rain on the metal roof.

Finally, Shakespeare looked up and stared at Flamel. His eyes were brimming and there were tears on his cheeks. He came around the table until he was standing directly in front of the Alchemyst. "A foolish boy betrayed you out of ignorance and stupidity. Ultimately, I paid for that action with the life of my son. Nicholas, I am not your enemy. I hate Dee in ways you cannot even begin to understand." Shakespeare gripped the Alchemyst's arm, fingers tightening. "I have waited a long time to meet you. Between us, we know more

152

about the Magician than anyone else on this planet. I am tired of running and hiding. It is time to pool our knowledge, to work together. It is time to take the fight to Dee and his Dark Elders. What say you?" he demanded.

"It's a good strategy," Josh said, before Flamel could answer. He was aware, even as he spoke, that he had no idea what he was talking about. It was Mars speaking. "You've spent a lifetime running; Dee won't expect you to change tactics."

Palamedes rested his huge forearms on the table. "The boy is right," he sighed. "The Magician has effectively trapped you here in London. If you run, he will capture you."

"And if we stay here, he'll capture us," Josh said quickly.

Nicholas Flamel looked around the table, obviously troubled by what he'd heard. "I'm not sure . . . ," he said finally. "If only I could speak to Perenelle; she would know what to do."

Shakespeare grinned delightedly for the first time since they'd arrived. "I think we can arrange that."

# CHAPTER SEVENTEEN

*P*erenelle Flamel stood framed in the doorway and stared down into the gloom. The heavy metal door that had once sealed this opening lay on the ground behind her, battered and twisted, ripped off its hinges by the weight of the spiders that had surged out of the prison cells below. With Areop-Enap's retreat to its cocoon, the surviving arachnids had vanished, and all that remained on the surface of Alcatraz were the dried-up husks of dead flies and the shells of spiders. She wondered who—or what—had sent the flies. Someone powerful, certainly; someone who was probably even now plotting their next move.

Perenelle tilted her head to one side and pushed her long black hair back over her ear, closed her eyes and listened. Her hearing was acute, but she could pick up nothing moving. And yet the Sorceress knew the cells were not empty. The island's prison was full of blood drinkers and flesh eaters, ve-tala, minotaur, Windigo and oni, trolls and cluricauns—and, of course, the deadly sphinx. The sunlight had recharged Perenelle's aura, and she knew she could handle the lesser creatures—though the minotaur and the Windigo would give her some problems—but she was fully aware that she could not deal with the sphinx. The eagle-winged lion fed off mag-ical energy; just being close to it would drain her aura, leav-ing her helpless.

Perenelle pressed her hand to her growling stomach. She was hungry. The Sorceress rarely needed to eat anymore, but she recognized that she was burning a lot of energy and needed calories to fuel it. If Nicholas were there it would not be a problem; many times on their travels, he had used his al-chemical skills to transmute stones into bread, and water into soup. She knew a couple of horn-of-plenty spells she'd learned in Greece that would give her enough to eat, but casting them would mean using her aura, whose distinctive signature would draw the sphinx upon her.

She'd encountered no humans on the island—she doubted any could have survived a single night on Alcatraz with their sanity or body intact. She remembered reading a newspaper report recently—about six months ago—that had said Alcatraz had been acquired by a private corporation and was closing to the public. The state park was going to be turned into a multimedia living history museum. Now that she knew Dee owned the island, she guessed that that wasn't the truth. Worse, though, with no humans having been on the island for at least six months, it was looking less and less likely she'd discover anything edible left behind. It wouldn't be the first time she'd gone hungry in her long life.

The Magician had gathered an army in the cells, creatures from every nation and the myths of every race. Without exception, they were the monsters who had been the source of human nightmares for millennia. And if there was an army, that meant a war was coming. Perenelle's full lips curled in a wry smile. So it looked as if she was the only human on Alcatraz . . . along with assorted mythical beasts, nightmare monsters, vampires and werebeasts. There were Nereids in the sea, a vengeful Crow Goddess locked up in a cell deep below the island and an incredibly powerful Elder or Next Generation attacking her from somewhere on the mainland.

Perenelle's smile faded; she was sure she'd been in worse situations at some time in her past, but right now she couldn't remember when. And she'd always had Nicholas with her. Together, they were unbeatable.

The tiniest breeze blew up from below, ruffling her hair, and then dust motes whirled and a shape flickered in the gloom. Perenelle darted back out into the sunlight, where she was strongest. She doubted it was the sphinx; she would have smelled its unmistakable odor: the musky scent of lion, bird and serpent.

A shape materialized in the doorway, taking on depth and substance as the light hit it, a figure composed of red rust particles and the shining scraps of spiderweb: it was the ghost, Juan Manuel de Ayala, the discoverer and Guardian of Alcatraz. The specter bowed deeply. *"It is good to see you hale and well, madame,"* he said in archaic, formal Spanish.

Perenelle smiled. "Why, did you think I would be joining you as a spirit?"

A semitransparent de Ayala floated in the air and considered the question carefully; then he shook his head. *"I knew that if you had fallen on the island, you would not have remained here. Your spirit would have gone wandering."*

Perenelle nodded in agreement, eyes clouding in sorrow. "I would have gone to find Nicholas."

The perfect teeth that the ghost sailor had never possessed in life flashed in a grin. *"Come, madame, come: I think there is something you should see."* He turned and floated back down the stairs. Perenelle hesitated; she trusted de Ayala, but ghosts were not the brightest creatures and were easily fooled. And then, thinly and faintly, Perenelle caught the scent of mint—little more than a suggestion—on the damp salty air. Without a second's hesitation, the Sorceress followed the ghost into the shadows.

# CHAPTER EIGHTEEN

*N*icholas Flamel sat in front of the two matching LCD computer screens. William Shakespeare sat on his left while Josh hovered over their shoulders, trying to keep as far away from the English immortal as possible and breathe only through his mouth. When Shakespeare moved, he trailed an odor in his wake, but when he sat still, the stink gathered around him in a thick cloud. Palamedes and Sophie had gone outside to feed the dogs.

"Trust me; it is quite simple," Shakespeare explained patiently, eyes huge behind his glasses, "the merest variation of the scrying spell Dee taught me over four hundred years ago."

"Should I mention at this point that the computer is turned off?" Josh interjected, suddenly realizing what apparently no one else had. "Only the screens are on."

"But we only need the screens," Shakespeare said enigmatically. He looked at the Alchemyst. "Dee always used a reflective surface for scrying. . . ."

"Scrying?" Josh frowned. He'd heard Flamel use the same word. "What do you mean?"

"From the ancient French word *descrier*," Shakespeare murmured, "meaning 'to proclaim' or 'to show.' In Dee's case, it meant 'to reveal.' When I was with him, he carried a mirror everywhere."

Flamel nodded. "His famous 'shew-stone,' or magical lens. I've read about it."

"He demonstrated it to Queen Elizabeth herself at his home at Mortlake," Shakespeare said. "She was so terrified by what she saw that she ran from the house and never returned. The doctor could look into the lens and focus in on people and places across the world."

Flamel nodded. "I've often wondered what it was."

"That sounds like TV," Josh said quickly. And then he realized he was talking about something in the seventeenth century.

"Yes, very like television, but without a camera at the other end to transmit the picture. It was a scrap of Elder technology," Shakespeare added, "a gift from his master. I believe it was an organic lens activated by the power of his aura."

"Whatever happened to it?" Flamel wondered aloud.

Shakespeare smiled, tight-lipped. "I stole it from him the night I ran away. I had a mind to keep it for myself and mayhap even use it against him. But then I realized that if it linked Dee to his master, it probably linked his master to me. I dropped it in the Thames at Southwark, close to where we later built the Globe Theatre."

"I wonder if it's still there," Flamel muttered.

"No doubt it is lost beneath centuries of silt and mud. But never mind that; Dee could—and did—use any highly polished surface to scry—mirrors, windows, glass, polished crystals—but then he discovered that liquids worked better. By applying his aura to a liquid, he could alter its properties, turn it reflective and use it to look at people and places from across the globe or from other times and places. With enough time and preparation, he could even look into the closest Shadowrealms. He could also use it to see through the eyes of animals or birds. They became his spies."

"He is astonishing," Flamel agreed, shaking his head in wonder. "If only he'd chosen to work with us, against the Dark Elders."

"The doctor usually used pure springwater, though I have known him to use snow, ice, wine or even beer. Any liquid will do." Leaning forward, Shakespeare tapped the black plastic frame around the computer screen. "And what do we have here . . . but liquid crystal?"

The Alchemyst's pale eyes widened and he nodded slowly. From under the neck of his T-shirt, he pulled the tiny pair of pince-nez he wore around his neck on a string and popped them onto his nose. "Of course," he whispered. "And the properties of liquid crystal can be altered by applying an electrical or a magnetic charge. That changes the orientation of

160

the crystals." He snapped his fingers and a tiny green spark no bigger than a pinprick appeared on his index finger. The foul-smelling hut was touched by the sharp fragrance of mint, and a curling smokelike pattern immediately rolled down both screens. Flamel moved his finger and both screens flashed white, then green, then abruptly turned into dull mirrors that reflected his face, framed by Shakespeare and Josh. "I would never have thought of that. That's genius!"

"Thank you," Shakespeare muttered, sounding a little embarrassed by the praise, blotches of color on his pale cheeks.

"What will you use as a mirror on the other end?" Flamel asked.

"Spiderweb," the Bard said, surprisingly. "I've found that whether it be in a palace or a hovel, there are always spiderwebs. The threads are always sticky with liquid, and they make excellent magical mirrors."

Flamel nodded again, obviously impressed.

"Now all we need is something that links you to Madame Perenelle."

Nicholas peeled off the heavy silver bracelet that wrapped around his right wrist. "Perenelle made this for me herself," he explained, laying it on the table. "A little more than a century ago, a masked bounty hunter chased us across America. His guns were loaded with silver bullets. I think he thought us werewolves."

"Werewolves and silver bullets!" Shakespeare coughed a quick laugh and shook his head. "Lord, what fools these mortals be!"

"I thought silver bullets worked against werewolves," Josh said, "but I'm guessing not?"

"No," Flamel said. "I've always preferred vinegar."

"Or lemon," Shakespeare said, "and pepper is a very reasonable alternative." He saw Josh's puzzled look and added, "Spray it on them or throw it into their eyes and nose. They will stop and sneeze and that will give you time to escape."

"Vinegar, lemon and pepper," Josh muttered. "I'll remember to add them to my werewolf-hunting kit. And if I don't find any werewolves, I can always make a salad," Josh said sarcastically.

Shakespeare shook his head. "No, no, you would need a good olive oil for a salad," he said seriously, "and olive oil is ineffective against any of the Wereclans."

"Though very useful against bruxa and strega," Flamel murmured absently as he created swirling fractal-like patterns on the two LCD screens.

"I was not aware of that," Shakespeare said. "And how would one use—"

"What happened to the bounty hunter?" Josh interrupted, frustrated, trying to bring the conversation back on track.

"Oh, Perenelle ended up rescuing him from a tribe of Oh-mah."

"Oh-mah?" Josh and Shakespeare asked together.

"Sasquatch . . . Saskehavis," Flamel said, and for an instant, an image of a tall, primitive-looking, powerfully built human appeared on the screen. It was covered in long reddish hair and carried a huge club made from a gnarled tree root. "Big Foot," he added.

"Big Foot. Of course." Josh shook his head. "So you're saying there are Big Foot—Big *Feet*—in America?"

"Of course," Flamel said dismissively. "When Perenelle rescued the bounty hunter from the Oh-mah," he continued, stroking the bracelet, "he presented her with his silver bullets as a gift." A green spark crawled across the metal. "I watched her melt down the silver bullets with her aura and shape each link. . . ." The scent of mint filled the hut again. Picking up the bracelet, the Alchemyst closed his fist around the metal band. "She always said that a little of her was in this bracelet."

And abruptly both LCD screens blinked and the trio found they were looking at Perenelle Flamel.

# CHAPTER NINETEEN

*E*ven without de Ayala to guide her, the smell of mint would have drawn Perenelle deeper into the cells. Crisp and clean, it blanketed the stench of the decaying building and the ever-present tang of salt. There was another scent in Alcatraz now: the zoolike stench of too many animals crowded together.

De Ayala stopped before the entrance to a cell and drifted to one side, revealing a huge intricate spiderweb filling the opening. The circular web glistened with trembling liquid droplets. The odor of mint was strongest here.

"Nicholas?" Perenelle whispered, puzzled. It was the distinctive deliciously familiar scent of her husband's aura . . . but what was it doing here? She tried to peer beyond the web, into the cell. "Nicholas?" she whispered again.

Abruptly, each individual droplet in the web shimmered

and coalesced. The spiderweb turned briefly reflective, so that it was as if she were looking into a huge mirror, and then it faded and darkened, revealing the intricate pattern beneath. A crackling green thread curled across each delicate strand and she distinctly heard Nicholas's voice—*"She always said that a little of her was in this bracelet"*—the instant before the web came to glowing life again and three astonished-looking faces appeared out of the gloom, staring at her.

"Nicholas!" Perenelle's voice was a ragged whisper. She fought hard to keep her aura from blazing. This was impossible—but then, that was the world she lived in. Instinctively, she knew this was a form of scrying, using the liquid on the spiderweb as a viewing source . . . and she also knew that her husband should not have been able to do this; he'd never mastered this particular art. But Nicholas was always surprising her, even after more than six hundred years of marriage. "Nicholas," she whispered. "It is you!"

"Perenelle! Oh, Perenelle!"

The joy in Nicholas's voice took her breath away. The Sorceress blinked back tears, then focused hard on her husband, examining him critically. The lines on his forehead had deepened, and there were new wrinkles around his eyes and nose, the bags under his eyes were bruise black and his hair was silvered, but it didn't matter: he was alive. She felt something shudder and relax inside her. The sphinx had taunted her that Nicholas was doomed; the Morrigan had said the Nidhogg was loose in Paris. Perenelle had been almost afraid to even think about Nicholas and what might have happened to him. But here he was: looking older, certainly; tired, definitely; but very much alive!

The boy, Josh, was there also, just behind Nicholas. He too looked tired. His forehead was smudged and his hair wild, but otherwise he seemed well. She could see no sign of Sophie. And where was Scathach? Perenelle kept her face expressionless as she shifted her gaze to the man sitting beside her husband. He was vaguely familiar.

"I've missed you," Nicholas said. He lifted his right hand, fingers spread wide. Half a world away, Perenelle unconsciously mimicked the gesture, her fingers matching his. She was careful not to touch the spiderweb, conscious that she might break the connection.

"You are unharmed?" Nicholas's voice was little more than the tiniest whisper, and his image flickered as the web undulated in the breeze that blew in from the open door at the other end of the corridor.

"I am unharmed and well," she said.

"Quickly, Perry, there is not much time. Where are you?"

"I'm not far from home; I am on Alcatraz. And you?"

"Farther afield than you, I'm afraid. I am in London."

"London! The Morrigan told me you were in Paris."

Nicholas smiled. "Ah, but that was yesterday; today we are in London, but not for long, if I can help it. Can you leave the island?"

"Unfortunately not." She smiled sadly. "This is Dee's island. There is a sphinx loose in the prison corridors, the cells are full of monsters and the seas are guarded by Nereids."

"Stay safe: I will come for you," Nicholas said firmly.

166

Perenelle nodded. She had absolutely no doubt that the Alchemyst would try to get to her; whether he would arrive in time was another matter. "I know you will." They had lived together for so long and, for most of the last century, in such relative comfort and obscurity, and with so little contact with Elders or Next Generation, that she sometimes forgot that his knowledge was incalculable. "Have you a plan?"

"In Paris, I retrieved our old map of the world's ley lines," he said quickly, eyes twinkling with mischief. "There is a line somewhere on Salisbury Plain that will take us directly to Mount Tamalpais. We'll head there when . . ." He hesitated.

Perenelle caught the hesitation and felt a surge of alarm. "*When?* What are you up to, Nicholas?"

"There's something I have to do in London first," he said. "Someone I want the children to meet."

She immediately thought of a dozen names, none of them good. "Who?"

"Gilgamesh." Perenelle opened her mouth to protest, but the stony look on her husband's face stopped her. His eyes flashed and his head moved almost imperceptibly toward Josh. "I'm going to ask him to teach the children the Magic of Water."

"Gilgamesh," she repeated, "the King." Forcing a smile to her lips, she added, "Give him my regards."

"I'll do that." Flamel nodded. "I'm sure he'll remember you. And I'm hoping he will direct us to the ley line that will take us home," he added.

"Tell me quickly, Nicholas: is all well? Are the children safe?"

"Yes. The twins are here with me," Nicholas said. "Both have been Awakened, and Sophie has received both the Magic of Air and the Magic of Fire. Unfortunately, Josh has not yet received any training."

Perenelle was watching Josh as her husband spoke. Even without the wavering image, she sensed, rather than saw, his disappointment.

"There is much to tell you," Flamel continued.

"Obviously. But Nicholas, you are forgetting your manners," Perenelle chided him. "You have not introduced me to . . ." Recognition dawned even as she was about to ask the question. "Is that Master Shakespeare?"

The man next to Nicholas bowed as deeply as he could from his sitting position. "Your humble servant, madam."

Perenelle remained silent. She felt the twinge in her shoulder where she'd been shot in the attack following Shakespeare's betrayal, but unlike Nicholas, she had never held any grudge against the boy. She knew how dangerously persuasive Dee could be. Finally, she inclined her head. "Master Will. You are looking well."

"Thank you, madam. Almost four hundred years ago, I wrote a line in your honor—'*Age cannot wither her, nor custom stale her infinite variety*'—it seems that line still holds true. You are as beautiful as ever." He drew in a quick shuddering breath. "I owe you an apology, madam. Because of what I did, you were nearly slain. I made a mistake."

"You chose the wrong side, Will."

"I know that, madam." The sadness in the immortal's voice was almost palpable.

"But you did not make a mistake: surely the mistake would have been *remaining* on that side?" she asked lightly.

The Bard smiled and bowed his head, silently thanking her.

"Perry, I have wronged Mr. Shakespeare. He is no friend to the Magician." Nicholas waved his hand. "And he has made this communication possible."

Perenelle bowed. "Thank you, Will. I cannot tell you how grateful I am to see Nicholas safe and well."

Color touched Shakespeare's cheeks and flowed up over his balding head. "It is my pleasure, madam."

"And you, Josh. How are you?"

The boy nodded. "Good, I guess. Really good."

"And Sophie?"

"Great. She learned Fire and Air. You should have seen what we did to the gargoyles at Notre Dame."

Perenelle turned her green eyes on her husband, and her eyebrows rose in a silent question.

"As I said, much to tell you." The Alchemyst leaned forward. He started off speaking in English but slipped into the French of his youth. "We were trapped, surrounded, facing the Guardians of the City. The boy fed the girl's aura with his own—silver and gold together. Their power was incredible: they defeated the combined magic of Dee and Machiavelli. Perenelle, we have them: finally, we have the twins of legend!"

The spiderweb rippled as a sudden foul gust blew down the corridor. Nicholas's image dissolved into a million tiny faces, each one reflected in the droplets on the web. Then the drops flowed back together again and the reflective surface reappeared.

*"Madame . . . ,"* de Ayala whispered urgently, *"something approaches."*

"Nicholas," Perenelle said quickly. "I've got to go."

"I'll get to you as fast as I can," the Alchemyst responded.

"I know you will. Just be careful, Nicholas. I can see age upon your face."

"Perry, a last word of advice, please," Nicholas added. "Mr. Shakespeare thinks that we need to stand and fight. But we are in the heart of Dee's London and desperately outnumbered. What do you think we should do?"

"Oh, Nicholas," Perenelle said softly in the forgotten Breton dialect of her long-lost youth. Something subtle happened to the bones and angles of her face, turning them hard. Her green eyes took on a glasslike appearance, and she reverted to English. "There is a time to run and a time to stand and face the enemy. Nicholas, often have I urged you to stop and fight. You have half a millennium of alchemical knowledge to use against Dee and his Dark Elders. But you've always told me you couldn't—you were waiting to find the twins. Well, now you have them. And you've told me they are powerful. Use them. Strike a blow at the heart of Dee's empire, let him see that we are not entirely defenseless. It's time, Nicholas, time to stand and fight."

The Alchemyst nodded. "And you. Can you stay safe until I get to you?"

Perenelle had just started to nod when the horror leapt through the spiderweb, teeth and claws extended toward her face.

# CHAPTER TWENTY

The Alchemyst, Josh and Shakespeare saw Perenelle start to nod . . . and then the image shattered into pixels, but not before they had all seen the flash of curled claws. Instinctively, all three jerked back from the screens.

"What . . . what happened?" Josh asked, confused. The left screen was completely black, but the right was speckled with clumps of sparkling red and green spots.

Flamel's left hand locked into a white-knuckled fist around the silver bracelet. Mint green fire danced across the metal as the fingertips of his right hand pressed against the monitor. The LCD cycled through a rainbow of colors, and then ten narrow and irregular colored streaks appeared on the blackness, long wavering vertical strands that gave tantalizing glimpses of an empty corridor on the other side of the world. But there was no sign of Perenelle.

"What was that?" Josh asked.

Shakespeare shook his head. "I have no idea." Then he curled his right hand into a claw and reached toward the screen. Five of the narrow colored bands matched up with his fingers. "Something leapt at Madame Perenelle and slashed at her. It must have come at her through the web." He tapped the glass with a fingernail. "It looks like we're still connected through the torn shreds of web. I can try again."

"Is she . . . is she OK?" Josh asked, worried. He noticed that the silver bracelet was now in two halves; its center had melted into flat silver droplets. "Nicholas?"

Flamel said nothing. He was trembling, his face bloodless and gaunt, lips outlined in blue. The word *Perenelle* formed on his lips, but he didn't say it aloud.

The screen image wavered . . . and then they saw Perenelle.

She was backing away from them, hands spread protectively before her. A long scratch ran across her bare shoulder and down one arm, the flesh red and angry-looking.

"Perenelle," Flamel whispered, the sound escaping in a ragged gasp.

And then they saw it. A creature was moving slowly down the stone corridor, advancing on the Sorceress. Josh had never seen anything like it before: it was both beautiful and horrific in equal measure. The creature was about his height, and while the plump red-cheeked face was that of a young man, the body was skeletal, bones and ribs clearly visible through gray-white skin. Talons that were a cross between human feet and birds' claws click-clacked across the floor, and although it had human hands, its nails were long and black, sharply curled, like a cat's. Huge leathery bat's wings grew out of its bony spine and dragged along the floor behind it.

And then a second figure appeared. It was a female. Gossamer black hair framed her delicately beautiful face. But if anything, her body was even more emaciated than the boy's. Her wings were ragged and torn, and she dragged her left leg behind her.

"Vetala," Flamel whispered in horror. "Blood drinkers, flesh eaters."

Another figure appeared before Perenelle. Vague and insubstantial, this one looked human and male. His hands rose into threatening fists and he moaned.

Flamel's aura bloomed bright green around his body, and the smell of mint was overpowering. "I've got to help her," he said desperately.

Suddenly, Palamedes burst through the door into the hut. "Your aura—douse it now!" he commanded.

Wide-eyed, Sophie was at the knight's heels, while behind her the red-eyed dogs crowded in the doorway and began to bark and growl.

"Perenelle's in trouble," Josh said, looking at Sophie. He knew his sister really liked the woman.

"Flamel: stop!" the knight shouted.

But the Alchemyst ignored him. Rolling the halves of the ruined silver bracelet into the palm of his left hand, he closed his fingers over them and brilliant emerald green light engulfed his fist. Then he pressed his right hand to the LCD screen. "Perenelle!" he called.

Flamel's mint odor was blanketed by the warmer spice of

cloves as the knight clamped his hands onto the Alchemyst's shoulders. "You've got to stop, Nicholas. You'll bring destruction down on top of us!"

Abruptly, the Alchemyst's aura flared even brighter, flaming first to brilliant emerald, then luminescent jade and finally a deep olive green. The knight was flung backward away from Nicholas, a suit of chain mail forming over his body even as he crashed against the wall with enough force to dent the metal. Green fire crawled across the links of his armor. "Will—stop him!" Palamedes shouted, his accent thick with fear. "Break the link!"

"Master, please . . ." Shakespeare grabbed the Alchemyst's sleeve and tugged. Tiny bitter-green flames immediately coursed up his arm, sending him staggering back, beating at the cold fire.

Josh crouched beside the Alchemyst, staring at the screen. "What are you trying to do?" he demanded.

"Strengthen Perenelle's aura with my own," Nicholas said desperately. "The vetala will tear her apart. But I fear I'm not strong enough." The terror in his voice was clear.

Josh looked up at his sister, saw her head move in the tiniest of nods and then turned to Nicholas. "Let me help," he said.

"Let *us* help," Sophie added.

The twins took up positions on either side of the Alchemyst, Sophie on his right, Josh on his left, and each placed a hand on his shoulder. Josh looked at his sister and asked, "Now what do we do?"

And then the mixture of scents in the room became

overpowering, almost nauseating: orange and vanilla, clove and mint, mingling with the odors of fried food, stale body odor and the ripe smell of damp dogs.

The Saracen Knight shouted, but his words were lost as the twins' auras crackled around them, gold and silver, sizzling and spitting as they touched the Alchemyst's now dull green aura, which immediately flared and brightened, sparkling with gold motes and silver threads.

"Alchemyst," Palamedes shouted desperately, "you have doomed us all!"

"Perenelle!" Nicholas cried, splaying his fingers against the working monitor. Coiling threads of green, yellow and silver spiraled down his arm, wrapped around each finger and disappeared into the screen.

The screen to the right cracked down the middle, thick black smoke curling upward, and then Perenelle's voice, thin and high, was clearly audible.

"Nicholas! Stop! Stop now!" She sounded terrified.

In the left-hand monitor they saw her ice white aura shimmer into existence around her and then quickly wink out.

"Nicholas!" Perenelle screamed. "You have killed me!"

And then the screen melted into a stinking puddle of bubbling plastic and molten glass.

# CHAPTER TWENTY-ONE

*D*r. John Dee strolled into the arrivals concourse in London City Airport. He was unsurprised to see a man in a two-piece black suit, white shirt and dark glasses, holding a card with the name DEE neatly printed on it. The Magician had phoned ahead and let the London offices of Enoch Enterprises know he was arriving.

"I am Dr. John Dee," he said, handing the man his small overnight bag but holding on to his laptop bag.

"Yes, sir, I recognized you. Follow me, please."

Dee thought he could hear a trace of the Middle East in the man's accent; he was almost positive it was Egyptian. He followed the man to an anonymous black limousine parked directly outside arrivals in the no-parking zone. The driver pulled open the rear door and stepped back, and in that instant, Dee's nostrils caught a familiar scent and he abruptly realized that this car and driver had not come from his company. For a heartbeat he thought about turning and running . . . but then he realized he had nowhere to go. "Thank you," he said politely, sliding into the darkened interior. The door shut with a soft pneumatic click. The odor in the enclosed compartment was enough to take his breath away. He sat quietly and heard the thump when his suitcase was put into the trunk; moments later, the car pulled smoothly and silently away from the curb.

The Magician put his laptop bag beside him, then turned to look at the hooded figure he knew would be sitting at the other end of the leather seat. Forcing a smile to his face, he bowed slightly. "Madam, I must say I am surprised—and delighted, of course—to see you here."

The shape in the gloom moved and cloth rustled. Then the interior light clicked on, and Dee, though he had been alerted by the smell to what he was going to see, started at the terrifying sight of the huge lioness's head inches from his own. The light gleamed off vicious-looking incisors and glistened off thick whiskers. The Dark Elder Bastet raised her head and glared at him with her huge yellow slit-pupiled eyes. "I am really beginning to dislike you, Dr. John Dee," she growled.

The doctor forced himself to smile, then lowered his gaze from the sharp teeth and brushed an invisible speck of dust off his sleeve. "You are in the majority, then; a lot of people dislike me. But fair is fair," he added lightly, "I dislike a lot of people. In fact, most people. But, believe me, madam, I have nothing but your best interests at heart."

The light clicked off and Bastet became invisible in the gloom.

A thought struck Dee and he asked, "I thought your aversion to iron prevented you from using modern conveniences like cars."

"Iron is not toxic to me, unlike some of the other Elders. I can tolerate it for short periods of time. And much of this vehicle is carbon fiber."

Dee nodded gravely, filing away the information that iron was not toxic to all Elders. He'd always assumed that it was the coming of iron that had driven the Elders out of this world. After more than four hundred years in their service, there was still so much he did not know about them.

The car slowed, then stopped. Through the dark tinted window Dee could just about make out the glowing red traffic light. He waited until the light changed to green before trusting himself to speak again. "Can I ask what I have done to anger you?" he murmured, pleased that he'd managed to keep his voice from trembling. Bastet was a First Generation Elder and one of the original rulers of Danu Talis. After the sinking of the island, she had been worshipped for generations in Egypt, and countries and peoples from the Incas to the Chinese honored cats in memory of the time she had walked the ancient humani world.

Dee heard paper rustle and pages turn and he realized that the Elder was reading in complete darkness.

"You are trouble incarnate, Dr. Dee. I can smell it coming

off you like that ridiculous sulfur aura you prefer." There was the sound of paper being slowly and methodically shredded. "I have perused your file. It does not make for inspiring reading. You may be our premier agent in this world, but I would argue you have been particularly useless. You have failed again and again in your mission to capture the Flamels, and have left a trail of death and destruction in your wake. You are tasked with protecting the Elders' existence, and yet three days ago you destroyed not just one but three interlinked Shadowrealms. This latest adventure in Paris has come close—dangerously close—to revealing our presence to the humani. You even permitted the Nidhogg to rampage through the streets."

"Well, that really was Machiavelli's idea . . . ," the Magician began.

"Many Elders have called for your destruction," Bastet continued in a deep growl.

The sentence shocked Dee into silence. "But I serve the Dark Elders loyally. I have done so for centuries," he argued plaintively.

"Your methods are crude, antiquated," the cat-headed Elder went on. "Consider Machiavelli: he is a scalpel, neat and precise; you are a broadsword, crude and blundering. You once almost burned this very city to the ground. Your creatures killed a million humani in Ireland. One hundred and thirty thousand died in Tokyo. And despite this loss of humani life, you still failed to secure the Flamels."

"I was told to capture the Flamels and the Codex by any

means possible. That was the priority," Dee snapped, anger making him reckless. "I did what I had to do to achieve that goal. And three days ago, let me remind you, I delivered the Book of Abraham the Mage."

"But even there you failed," Bastet whispered coldly. "The Codex was incomplete, lacking the final two pages." The Elder's breathing changed and Dee was suddenly aware in the darkness that her meat-tainted breath was dangerously close to his face. "Magician, you enjoy the protection of a powerful Elder—perhaps the most powerful of us all—and that has kept you alive thus far," Bastet pressed on. Huge glowing yellow eyes appeared out of the gloom, the pupils as narrow as knife blades. "When others called for your punishment or death, your master has protected you. But I wonder— and I am not alone in this—why does an Elder use such a flawed tool?"

The words chilled him. "What did you call me?" he finally managed to whisper. His mouth was dry and his tongue felt huge in his mouth.

Bastet's eyes blazed. "A flawed tool."

Dee felt breathless. He tried to calm his thundering heart. It had been more than four hundred years since he'd last heard those three words, but they'd remained vividly etched in his memory. He'd never forgotten them. In many ways they had shaped his life.

Turning his face away from the stink of Bastet's breath, Dee rested his forehead against the cool glass and looked out into the night flashing past in streaks of light. He was driving through the heart of twenty-first-century London, and yet when he closed his eyes and remembered the last time he had felt this way, the last time he had heard those words, he felt as if he were back in the city of Henry VIII.

Memories, long buried but never forgotten, came flooding back, and he knew the Elder's use of those three bitter words could not have been accidental. She was letting him know just how much she knew about him.

It was April 23, 1542, a cold showery day in London, and John Dee was standing before his father, Roland, in their house on Thames Street. Dee was fifteen years old—and looked older than his years—but at that moment he felt like a ten-year-old. He had locked his hands into fists behind his back and was unable to move, afraid to speak, breathless, heart thundering so hard it was actually shaking his entire body. He knew if he moved he would fall over, or turn and run like a child from the room, and if he spoke he would break down and weep. But he would not show any weakness in front of Roland Dee. Over his father's right shoulder, through the tiny diamond-paned window, John could see the top of the nearby Tower of London. Standing still and silent, he allowed his father to continue reading.

John Dee had always known he was different.

He was an only child, and it had been obvious from an early age that he was gifted with an extraordinary ability for mathematics and languages; he could read and write not only English, but also Latin and Greek, and had taught himself French and a little German. John was entirely devoted to his mother, Jane, and she always sided with him against his domineering father. Encouraged by his mother, John had set his sights on attending St. John's College, Cambridge. He had thought—had hoped—that his father would be delighted, but Roland Dee was a textile merchant who held a minor position in Henry's court and was almost fearful of too much education. Roland had seen what happened to educated men at court: it was too easy to upset the king, and men who did that too often ended up in prison or dead, stripped of their lands and fortune. John knew his father wanted him to take over the family business, and for that he needed no further education than the abilities to read and write and add up a column of figures.

But John Dee wanted more.

On that April day in 1542, he had finally plucked up the courage to tell his father he was attending college, with or without his permission. His grandfather, William Wild, had agreed to pay the fees, and Dee had enrolled without his father's knowledge.

"And if you go to this school, what then?" Roland demanded, bushy beard bristling with rage. "They will fill your head with useless nonsense. You will learn your Latin and Greek, your mathematics and philosophy, your history and geography, but what use is that to me, or to you? You will not be content with that. You will seek more knowledge, and that will send you down some dark paths, my boy. You will never be satisfied, because you will never know enough."

"Say what you will," the fifteen-year-old boy had managed to answer. "I am going."

"Then you will become like a knife that is sharpened so often it becomes blunt: you will become a flawed tool . . . and what use have I for a flawed tool?"

Dr. John Dee opened his eyes and focused once more on the streets of modern London.

He had rarely spoken to his father after that day, even when the old man was locked up in the Tower of London. Dee had gone to Chelmsford, and then to the newly founded Trinity College, and quickly established a reputation for himself as one of the most brilliant men of his age. And there were times when he remembered his father's words and realized that Roland Dee had been right: his quest for knowledge was insatiable, and it had taken him down some very dark and dangerous paths. It had ultimately led him to the Dark Elders.

And somewhere at the back of his mind, in that dark and secret place where only the most hurtful memories are buried, lurked those three bitter words.

*A flawed tool.*

No matter what he achieved—his extraordinary successes, his amazing discoveries and uncannily accurate predictions, even his immortality and his association with figures who had been worshipped by generations as gods and myths—those three words mocked him, because he was secretly afraid that his father had been correct about that too. Perhaps he *was* a flawed tool.

Clearing his throat, he lifted his forehead from the

window, fixed a quizzical smile on his face and turned back to the dark interior of the car. "I was not aware that you had a file on me."

Leather squeaked as Bastet changed position. "We have files on every immortal and mortal humani who is in our service. Yours happens to be bigger than all the rest combined."

"I'm flattered."

"Don't be. It is, as I have said, a litany of failures."

"I am disappointed that you should view it that way," Dee said softly. "Luckily, I do not answer to you. I answer to a higher authority," he added, with the smile still fixed on his face.

Bastet hissed like a cat with its tail caught.

"But enough of these pleasantries," the Magician continued, rubbing his hands quickly together. "What brings you to London? I thought you had returned to your Bel Air mansion after our adventure in Mill Valley."

"Earlier today I was contacted by someone from my past." The Dark Elder's voice was a low angry rumbling. "Someone I thought long dead, someone I never wanted to talk to again."

"I'm not sure what this has to do with me . . . ," the Magician began.

"Mars Ultor made contact with me."

Dee straightened. Now that his eyes had adjusted to the gloom, he could just about make out Bastet's cat head silhouetted in black against the lighter rectangle of the window. "Mars spoke to you?"

"For the first time in centuries. And he asked me to help you."

Dee nodded. When he had left the catacombs earlier, the Elder had still not responded to his offer to bring the twins back to Paris and force Sophie to lift the curse.

Cloth rustled and the cat smell of the Goddess grew stronger. "Is it true?" she asked, close enough to make Dee recoil from her foul breath.

The Magician turned away, blinking tears from his eyes. "Is . . ." He coughed. "Is what true?"

"Can you release him? The Witch cursed him; that is a curse she will not lift."

One of the reasons the English Magician had survived in the lethal court of Queen Elizabeth and for centuries afterward was that he never made a promise he could not keep, or a threat he didn't intend to carry out. He took a moment to consider his response, careful to keep his face neutral. Although it was dark in the back of the car, he knew that it made no difference to the cat-headed Elder. She could easily see in the dark. "The Witch transferred all her knowledge and lore into the girl, Sophie, who we now know to be one of the twins of legend. The girl even admitted that she knew how to reverse the spell, but when Mars asked her—begged her—to do so, she refused. All I have to do is give her a good reason not to refuse the next time we ask." Dee's cruel lips twisted in a smile. "I can be very persuasive."

The Dark Elder grunted.

"You don't sound very happy about that. I would have

thought you would be thrilled to have someone like Mars back in your ranks."

The Elder laughed, an ugly sound. "You know nothing about Mars Ultor, the Avenger, do you?"

The Magician took a moment before replying. "I know some of the myths," he admitted.

"Once he was a hero; then he became a monster," Bastet said slowly. "A force of nature, untamable, unpredictable and deadly beyond belief."

"You don't seem to like him very much."

"Like him?" Bastet echoed. "I love him. And it is precisely because I love him that I do not want him abroad in the world again."

Confused, Dee shook his head. "I would have thought we needed Mars in the coming battle."

"His rage is liable to devastate this world and every adjoining Shadowrealm . . . and then either some humani hero or warrior Elder will be forced to destroy him utterly. At least in the catacombs, I know where he is and I know he is safe."

Dee tried to make sense of what he was hearing. "How can you claim that you love him and yet want him condemned to that living death?"

Dee felt, rather than heard, the swish of nails as they arced through the air before his face. The leather seat popped and hissed as it was punctured. When she spoke, the Elder's voice was trembling with emotion. "The humani nations called Mars by many names through the ages. I called him Horus . . . and he is my baby brother."

187

Stunned, Dee sat back in the seat. "But why then did the Witch curse him?" he asked. "You're suggesting that this curse actually protects him."

"Because she loved him even more than I did. The Witch of Endor is his wife."

# CHAPTER TWENTY-TWO

*Vetala.*

The Sorceress backed away from the creature that had come through the web. It had obviously been sleeping in the cell beyond. She had caught the hint of movement in the last instant before it had appeared, but she hadn't been quick enough to escape its flailing claws. A ragged nail had sliced her flesh, and her shoulder and arm stung as if they had been burned. She knew she needed to get back into the sunshine as quickly as possible and wash out the wound. Perenelle shuddered to think what foulness might be hiding under the vetala's fingernails.

Behind the vampire, the spiderweb hung in ragged tatters. Tiny green sparks danced across the web, and she wondered if these were what had awakened the creature. Each strip still showed a sliver of Nicholas, Josh and Shakespeare.

And then the second creature stepped through the dangling threads of web.

Perenelle noted that the two creatures were alike enough to be twins. Their faces were beautiful, with fine delicate Indian features, flawless skin and enormous liquid brown eyes. She knew that they would usually keep their black bat wings wrapped around them, concealing their emaciated gray-skinned bodies and clawed hands and feet until the moment before they struck.

Backing down the corridor, Perenelle stepped slowly away from the vetala, desperately trying to remember what she knew about them. They were primitive and beastlike, creatures of the night and darkness, and like many of the vampire clan who were nocturnal, they were photosensitive and could not stand sunlight.

She needed to reach the stairs behind her . . . but she dared not turn her back to run.

De Ayala appeared behind the two vetala. The ghost raised both hands and flowed through the creatures. It moaned, a long terrifying howl of utter despair and absolute loneliness that echoed and reechoed off the damp stones. The vetala ignored the ghost. Their huge eyes were focused on the Sorceress, mouths slightly parted to reveal perfectly white teeth, chins damp with saliva. De Ayala winked out of existence and then doors slammed and rattled above their heads with enough force to send dust drifting down on top of them. The vetala didn't even react. They simply continued to inch ever forward.

*"Madame, I cannot help you,"* de Ayala said desperately, appearing alongside the Sorceress. *"It is as if they know I am a ghost and powerless to harm them."*

"They look hungry," Perenelle murmured, "and they know they cannot eat you." She stopped, suddenly noticing that the shreds of spiderweb behind the vampires had started to glow a dull lambent green. She caught fragmentary glimpses of her husband outlined in his aura.

*"Perenelle."*

Nicholas's voice was the merest gossamer whisper. There was a flicker of movement alongside him, and then his aura flared, bright enough to shed a dull green glow through the rags of web over the corridor on Alcatraz.

The Sorceress knew a dozen spells that would defeat the vampire, but to use them meant activating her aura . . . and that would bring the sphinx. She continued backing away; once she reached the stairs, she was going to turn and run and hope to make it to the door before the creatures brought her down. She thought she could make it. These were forest creatures; their claws were designed for soft earth and tree bark, and she had seen how their long nails slipped on the stone floor. Their folded wings were also awkward and cumbersome. Perenelle took another step back, moving toward the lighted rectangle of the door behind her. Now that she could feel the heat of the sun on her back, she knew she was close to the steps.

And then, in the shreds of dangling web, she saw Sophie and Josh standing on either side of her husband. They were all staring intently at her, frowning hard. Nicholas's aura glowed bright emerald. On his right-hand side, Sophie blossomed silver, and Josh, on his left, bloomed gold. The spiderweb glowed like a lantern and the entire corridor lit up.

*"Perenelle."*

The two vetala turned, hissing like cats at the sound and sudden light, and Perenelle saw her husband reach out to her, fingers wide. Light particles danced at the end of his fingertips . . . and at that moment, she knew what he was going to do.

"Nicholas! Stop! Stop now!" she screamed.

Coiling spirals and twisting circles of crackling silver, green and gold energy spun from the tattered web. Hissing and spitting, they bounced off the walls and ceiling and then gathered around Perenelle's feet, creating a puddle of light that gradually sank into the stones. The Sorceress gasped as a warm wave of energy flowed up her legs and through her chest and exploded into her head. Images danced at the corner of her mind; thoughts and memories that were not hers.

*The Eiffel Tower ablaze with lights . . .*

*The Nidhogg rampaging through the streets . . .*

*Valkyries in white armor . . .*

*The same women trapped in ice . . .*

*Gargoyles slithering down off Notre Dame . . .*

*The hideous Genii Cucullati advancing . . .*

Unbidden, her aura shimmered into existence around her, ice white and glacial, and her hair spread in a dark sheath behind her.

"Nicholas," Perenelle shouted as the web blackened to dust and her aura faded to nothing. "You have killed me!"

And then, howling through the very stones of Alcatraz, came the triumphant cry of the sphinx.

Even the vetala turned and fled.

# CHAPTER TWENTY-THREE

$\mathcal{I}$n a stinking flurry of flapping wings, the sphinx appeared at the end of the corridor, huge lion paws scraping along on the floor. Crouching low, belly to the ground, the creature spread her eagle's wings and screamed triumphantly in a language that predated the first Egyptian pharaoh. "You are mine, Sorceress. I will feast off your memories and then eat your bones." The sphinx's head was that of a beautiful woman, but her eyes were slit-pupiled and the tongue that waved in the air was long, black and forked. Closing her eyes, she threw back her head and drew in a deep shuddering breath. "But what's this . . . what's this?" Her tongue darted, tasting the air. She took a couple of steps down the corridor, claws clicking on stone. "How can this be? You are powerful . . . powerful indeed . . . too powerful." And then she stopped, her flawless face creasing into an ugly frown. "And strong." Her voice faltered. "Stronger than you should be."

Perenelle had half turned to make a dash for the stairs, but then she suddenly stopped and turned back to face the sphinx. The corners of her eyes crinkled and the tiniest of smiles curled her lips, turning her face cruel. Bringing her hand up to her face for a closer look, she gazed at it in wonder as a glasslike glove grew over each finger and down into her palm. The glass turned from transparent to translucent and then opaque. "Why, of course I am," she whispered. And then she laughed aloud, the shocking sound echoing off the walls. "Thank you, Nicholas; thank you, Sophie and Josh!" she shouted.

The woman's smile frightened the sphinx, but her laughter terrified her. The creature took a tentative step forward, then backpedaled. Despite her fearsome appearance and appalling reputation, the sphinx was a coward. She had grown up in a time of monsters, and it was fear and cowardice that had kept her alive through the millennia.

The Sorceress faced the creature and brought her palms together, thumb against thumb, fingers touching. Suddenly, her aura blazed white light, bleaching the entire corridor of color, and then crackled around her in a protective oval of harshly reflective mirrorlike crystals. Every crumbling brick, each rusting pipe, the mold-spattered ceiling, the tattered cobwebs and the crumbling metal cell-door bars were picked out in exquisite detail. Long angular shadows stretched down the corridor toward the sphinx, though Perenelle herself cast no shadow.

The woman flung out her right hand. A globe of white light that almost looked like a snowball burst from her palm and bounced once, twice on the floor, bounced again and then rolled to a stop between the filthy paws of the sphinx.

"And what am I supposed to do about this?" the creature snarled. "Catch it in my mouth and bring it back to you?"

Perenelle's smile was terrifying as her hair rose in a dark cloud behind her.

The sphere started to grow. Spinning, twisting, turning, sparkling ice crystals grew in layers on it. The air temperature abruptly plummeted and the sphinx's breath plumed white on the air.

The sphinx was a creature of the desert. All her long life, she had known arid heat and searing sunshine. Certainly, in the weeks since she had been tasked with guarding Alcatraz, she had grown used to the chill of the prison island, the damp bite of the bay's rolling fog banks, the sting of rain, the bitter winds. But she had never experienced cold like this. This was a chill so extreme that it burned. Countless tiny crystals erupted out of the glowing sphere and alighted on her flesh like fiery embers. A snowflake no bigger than a dust mote landed on her tongue: it was like sucking a hot coal. And still the ball grew bigger.

Perenelle took a step closer. "I should thank you."

The sphinx stepped back.

"If I had turned and run, you would have chased me down. But when you reminded me that I was more powerful than before, I realized the gift my husband and the twins had given me."

The sphinx screeched like a feral cat as the icy air bit

and stung her human face. "Your powers will not last. I will drink them."

"You will try," Perenelle said quietly, almost gently. "But to do that you need to concentrate and focus on me. And personally, I have always found it hard to concentrate when it is cold." She smiled again.

"Your aura will fade." The sphinx's needle-sharp teeth began to chatter. Thin curls of ice were forming on the wall.

"True. I have a minute, perhaps less, before my aura fades back to normal. But I have enough time."

"Enough time?" The creature shuddered. Frost now coated the sphinx's chest and legs; her pale cheeks turned red, her lips blue.

"Enough time to do this!"

The snowball was now the size of a large pumpkin. The sphinx lashed out at it, an enormous lion's paw cutting through the frozen crystals. When she jerked her paw back, the skin and nails were burned black by the intense chill.

"A shaman on the Aleutian Islands taught me this pretty spell," Perenelle said, moving closer to the sphinx. The creature immediately tried to back away, but the floor was slick with crackling ice and her feet shot out from beneath her, sending her crashing to the ground. "The Aleut are the masters of snow and ice magic. There are many different types of snow," the Sorceress said. "Soft . . ."

Feather-soft snowflakes curled out of the spinning ball and flurried around the sphinx, hissing onto her skin, burning and melting the moment they touched.

"Hard . . ."

Stone-sharp chips of ice danced away from the ball, stinging the sphinx's human face.

"And then there are blizzards."

The ball erupted. Thick snow blasted against the creature, coating her chest and face. She coughed as the freezing crystals swirled into her mouth. Feet scrabbling, she attempted to back away, but the entire hallway was now a sheet of ice. The sphinx raised her wings, but they were weighted down beneath a thick coating of frost and could barely move.

"And of course, hail . . ."

Pea-sized chips and chunks of ice battered the ancient creature. Snow pellets and hailstones ricocheted out of the spinning ball, puncturing tiny holes in her wings.

Howling, the sphinx turned and fled.

An ice storm pursued her, hail bouncing and pinging off the floor, shattering against the ceiling, rattling off the metal cell doors. Inch-thick ice bloomed along the length of the corridor, metal bars shattered with the intense chill, bricks crumbled to dust and whole chunks of ceiling collapsed under the weight of the heavy ice.

The sphinx had almost reached the end of the corridor when it collapsed around her, burying her under tons of rock and metal. And then the cracking and snapping ice flowed over it all, sealing the rubble beneath eighteen inches of iron-hard permafrost.

Perenelle staggered as her aura winked out of existence.

*"Bravo, madame,"* the ghost Juan Manuel de Ayala murmured, appearing out of the gloom.

The Sorceress leaned against a wall, breathing in great heaving gasps. She was trembling with exertion, and the effort had left her with aching joints and stiff muscles.

*"Have you killed her?"*

"Hardly," Perenelle said tiredly. "Slowed her down, irritated her, frightened her. I'm afraid it will take more than that to kill a sphinx." She turned and slowly climbed the stairs, leaning heavily on the wall.

*"The snow and ice was impressive,"* de Ayala said, floating backward up the stairs so that he could admire the solid plug of glacier at the end of the corridor.

"I was going to try something else, but for some reason, I had an image of two warrior women trapped in ice; they looked like Valkyries. . . ."

*"A memory?"* de Ayala suggested.

"Not one of mine," Perenelle whispered, then sighed with relief as she stepped out into the glorious morning sunshine. With the last remnant of her aura, she trailed her fingers across her wounds, cleansing them. Then, closing her eyes, she tilted her face to the light. "I think they were Sophie's memories," she said in wonder. Then she stopped, a sudden thought chilling her. "Valkyries and the Nidhogg abroad in the world again," she said in wonder. Instinctively, the Sorceress turned to the east and opened her eyes. What was happening to Nicholas and the children? How much trouble were they in?

# CHAPTER TWENTY-FOUR

"Alchemyst," Palamedes shouted desperately, "you have doomed us all!"

Flamel lay slumped before the destroyed screens. His skin was the color of yellowed parchment, there were new wrinkles around his eyes and the lines etched into his forehead had deepened. When he turned to look at the Saracen, his eyes were glassy and unfocused, the whites tinged with green.

"I told you not to use your aura," the knight snarled. "I warned you." Palamedes rounded on Shakespeare. "Prepare for battle. Alert the guards." The Bard nodded and hurried outside, the red-eyed dogs silent now, fanning out around him in a protective shield. The knight's chain-mail armor appeared ghostlike around his huge frame, then solidified. "What did I say, Alchemyst? Death and destruction follow you. How many will die tonight because of you?" he shouted before he raced out the door.

Josh blinked black spots from in front of his eyes. He saw his sister swaying and caught her arm. "I'm exhausted," he said.

Sophie nodded in agreement. "Me too."

"I could actually feel the energy flowing up through my body and down my arm," he said in wonder. He looked at his fingertips. The skin was red and there were water blisters forming over his fingerprints. He helped his twin to a chair and sat her down, then knelt in front of her. "How do you feel?"

"Drained," Sophie mumbled, and Josh noticed that her eyes were still flat, mirrored silver discs. He was disturbed to see a distorted image of himself reflected in them. It was such a tiny change to her body, and yet it lent her face a sinister and almost alien appearance. As he watched, the silver gradually faded and the normal blue returned. "Perenelle?" she said, but her mouth was dry and the words came out thickly. "What happened to her?" she whispered hoarsely, then added, "I need some water."

Josh was getting to his feet when Shakespeare appeared by his side with two glasses of muddy-colored liquid. "Drink these."

Josh accepted both glasses but took a tentative sip of his first before handing it to his sister. He made a face. "Tastes sweet. What's in it?"

"Just water. I took the liberty of adding a spoonful of natural honey to each," the immortal said. "You have just used a lot of calories and burned through much of your bodies' natural sugars and salts. You will need to replace them as quickly as possible." He smiled crookedly, showing his bad teeth. "Consider it the price of magic." He placed a third glass, larger than the others, swirling with brown honey, on the table by the Alchemyst. "And you too, Nicholas," he said gently. "Drink quickly. There is much to do." Then he turned and hurried out into the night.

Sophie and Josh watched Nicholas raise the glass to his lips and sip the sticky liquid. His right hand was trembling and he caught it with his left and held it steady. He saw them looking at him and tried to smile, but it came out more like a grimace of pain. "Thank you," he whispered, his voice raw. "You saved her."

"Perenelle," Sophie repeated. "What happened?"

Nicholas shook his head. "I don't know," he admitted.

"Those creatures . . . ," Josh began.

"Vetala," Nicholas said.

"And what looked like a ghost," Sophie added.

Nicholas finished the water and put the glass down with a shudder. "Actually, that gives me cause for hope," he said, and this time his smile was genuine. "Perenelle is the seventh daughter of a seventh daughter. She can communicate with the shades of the dead; they hold no fear for her. Alcatraz is an isle of ghosts, and ghosts are mostly harmless."

"Mostly?" Josh said.

"Mostly," Nicholas agreed. "But none can harm my Perenelle," he added confidently.

"Do you think anything has happened to her?" Sophie said, just as Josh opened his mouth to ask the same question.

There was a pause, and then Flamel answered. "I don't think so. We saw her aura flare. Augmented by our auras—yours especially—she would be briefly powerful."

"But what did she mean when she said you had killed her?" Sophie asked, her voice stronger now.

"I do not know," he said quietly. "But this I am sure of: if anything had happened to her, I would know. I would feel it." He came slowly and stiffly to his feet, pressing his hands into the small of his back. He looked around the empty hut and nodded toward the twins' backpacks. "Get your stuff; we need to get out of here."

"And go where?" Josh demanded.

"Anywhere away from here," Nicholas said. "Our combined auras will have acted like a beacon. I'll wager every Elder, Next Generation and immortal in London is heading this way right now. That's what has Palamedes so upset."

Sophie stood. Josh reached out to steady his sister, but she shook her head. "I thought you were going to stay and fight," she said to Nicholas. "That's what Perenelle wanted you to do, and isn't that what Shakespeare and Palamedes both said we should do also?"

Flamel climbed down the steps and waited until the twins had joined him outside in the cool night air before he replied. He looked at Josh. "And what do *you* think? Stay and fight or flee?"

Josh looked at him in astonishment. "You're asking me? Why?"

"You are our tactician, inspired by Mars himself. If anyone

knows what to do in a battle, it is you. And, as Perenelle reminded me, you two are the twins of legend: you are powerful indeed. So tell me, Josh, what should we do?"

Josh was about to protest that he had no idea . . . but even
as he was shaking his head, he suddenly *knew* the answer.
"With no idea what's coming at us, it's impossible to say." He
looked around. "On the one hand, we are secure behind a
cleverly designed and booby-trapped fortress. We know there
is a protective zone around the castle and that the houses are
occupied by creatures loyal to the knight. I'm sure that
Shakespeare and Palamedes have other defenses. But if we do
stay and fight, we'll be stuck here, and since this is Dee's
country, there will be time for him to bring in reinforce-
ments, completely trapping us." He looked at his sister. "I say
we run. When we fight, we need to do it on our terms."

"Well said." The Alchemyst nodded. "I agree. We run
now and live to fight another day."

Palamedes appeared out of the darkness, trailing the scent
of cloves. His transformation into the Saracen Knight who
had fought with King Arthur was now complete. He was
dressed from head to foot in smooth black metal plate armor
over a suit of black chain mail. A chain-link coif completely
protected his head and neck and spread over his shoulders.
Over that was a smooth metal bascinet helmet with a long
nose guard. A curved shamshir sword dangled by his side and
an enormous claymore sword was strapped to his back. The
armor made the already-huge man look monstrous. Before
he could speak, Shakespeare hurried up, five of the red-eyed

dogs silently following him. "How bad is it?" Palamedes rumbled.

"Bad," Shakespeare murmured. "A little while ago, a few individuals—immortals, mainly, and some humani bounty hunters—entered the streets patrolled by the larvae and the lemurs. They did not get far." Shakespeare's aura crackled dull yellow and the air was touched with lemon. A suit of modern police body armor grew over the immortal's soiled mechanic's overalls. He carried a mace and chain loosely in his left hand, the studded head of the mace trailing in the mud. One of the dogs licked it with its forked tongue. "The larvae and lemurs are our first line of defense," he continued, looking from the Alchemyst to the twins. "They are loyal, but none too bright. And once they feed, they'll sleep. The attackers will be at the walls before midnight."

"The castle will hold," Palamedes said confidently.

"No castle is completely impregnable," Josh said simply, and then stopped as a huge red-eyed shape loomed out of the night. Everyone turned to follow his gaze. It was the largest of the dogs. Its fur was matted with filth and there was a long cut on its back dangerously close to its spine.

"Gabriel!" Shakespeare cried.

In the space of a single heartbeat, between one step and the next, the dog transformed. Muscle flowed, bones popped and cracked and the dog reared up on its two hind legs, neck shortening, the planes and angles of its face and the line of its jaw shifting. The dog became an almost-human-looking young man with long dun-colored hair. Curling purple-blue tattoos spiraled on his cheeks, ran down his neck and spread across his bare chest. He was barefoot, wearing only rough-spun woolen trousers with a red and black check pattern. Bloodred eyes peered from beneath badly cut bangs.

"Gabriel, you're hurt," the Bard said.

"A scratch," the dogman answered. "Nothing more. And the creature who did it to me will do nothing more." He spoke in a singsong accent that Sophie recognized as Welsh.

One by one the dogs standing around Shakespeare blinked into a human shape.

"Are you Torc Allta?" Josh asked, remembering the creatures that had guarded Hekate's Shadowrealm.

"They are kin to us," Gabriel said. "We are Torc Madra."

"Gabriel Hounds," Sophie said, eyes sparkling silver. "Ratchets."

Gabriel turned to look at the girl, his forked tongue tasting the air like a snake's. "It has been a long time since we were called by that name." The tongue appeared again. "But you are not entirely human, are you, Sophie Newman? You are the Moon Twin, and young, young, young to be carrying the knowledge of ages within you. You stink of the foul witch, Endor," he said dismissively, turning away, nose wrinkling in disgust.

"Hey, you can't talk to my—" Josh began, but Sophie jerked his arm, pulling him back.

Ignoring the outburst, Gabriel turned to Palamedes. "The larvae and lemur have fallen."

"So soon!" cried the Saracen Knight. Both he and Shakespeare were visibly shaken. "Surely not all?"

"All. They are no more."

"There were nearly five thousand . . . ," Shakespeare began.

"Dee is here," Gabriel said, his voice little more than a growl. "And so too is Bastet." He rolled his shoulders and grimaced as the wound on his back opened.

"There is something else, though, isn't there?" Flamel said tiredly. "The Dark Elders' followers and Dee's agents in the city are a ragtag alliance of opposed factions who would just as soon fight one another as go into battle together. To kill the larvae and lemurs would take an army, trained and organized, loyal to one leader."

Gabriel inclined his head slightly. "The Hunt is abroad."

"Oh no." Palamedes drew in a great ragged breath and shrugged the longsword from his back.

"And their master," Gabriel added grimly.

Josh looked at his sister, wondering if she knew what the Torc Madra was talking about. Her eyes were flat silver discs and there was an expression not of fear but almost of awe on her face.

"Cernunnos has come again," Gabriel said, a note of absolute terror in his voice. And then, one by one, all the ratchets threw back their heads and howled piteously.

"The Horned God," Sophie whispered and she started to shiver. "Master of the Wild Hunt."

"An Elder?" Josh asked.

"An Archon."

# CHAPTER TWENTY-FIVE

"*I* was told this Perenelle woman was trapped, weak, defenseless," Billy the Kid said firmly into the narrow Bluetooth microphone that ran along the line of his unshaven jaw. "That's just not true." Through the Thunderbird's bug-spattered windshield, he could clearly see Alcatraz across the bay. "And I think we have a problem. A big problem."

Half a world away, Niccolò Machiavelli listened carefully to the voice on the speakerphone as he packed his overnight bag. He couldn't remember the last time he had packed for himself; Dagon had always taken care of that. "And why are you calling me?" Machiavelli asked. He packed a third pair of handmade shoes, then decided two pairs were enough and took them out of the case again.

"I'll be straight with you," Billy admitted reluctantly. "I

didn't think I needed you. I was sure I'd be able to take care of the woman myself."

"A mistake that has cost many their lives," Machiavelli mumbled in Italian; then he reverted to English. "And what changed your mind?"

"A few minutes ago, something happened on Alcatraz. Something odd . . . something powerful."

"How do you know? You're not on the island."

The Italian clearly heard the awe in the American immortal's voice. "I felt it—from three miles away!"

Machiavelli straightened. "When? When exactly?" he demanded, checking his watch. Crossing the room, he opened his laptop and ran his index finger across the fingerprint reader to bring it back to life. He'd received a dozen encrypted e-mails from his spies in London, reporting that something extraordinary had happened. The e-mails had come in at 8:45 p.m., just over a quarter of an hour ago.

"Fifteen minutes ago," Billy said.

"Tell me exactly what happened," Machiavelli said. He pressed a button on the side of his phone that started to record the conversation.

Billy the Kid climbed out of the car and raised a pair of battered military green binoculars to his deep blue eyes. He had parked close to the Golden Gate Bridge; ahead and to his right the distant island looked calm and peaceful, basking under a cloudless noon sky, but he knew that the image was deceptive. He frowned, trying to remember precisely what had happened. "It was . . . it was like an aura igniting," he explained. "But powerful, more powerful than any I've ever encountered in my life."

Machiavelli's voice was surprisingly clear on the transatlantic line. "A powerful aura . . ."

"Very powerful."

"Was there an odor?"

Billy hesitated, instinctively breathing in, but he smelled only the ever-present salt of the sea and the bitter tang of pollution. He shook his head, then, realizing that Machiavelli could not see him, spoke. "If there was, I don't remember. No, I'm sure there wasn't."

"How did you experience it?"

"It was cold, so cold. And it sparked my own aura. For a few minutes I had no control." Billy's voice shook a little. "I thought I was going to burn up."

"Anything else?" Machiavelli asked, keeping his voice calm, willing the American to focus. Every immortal human knew that an uncontrolled aura could completely consume the human body it wrapped around; the process was known as spontaneous human combustion. "Tell me."

"Lucky I was parked when it happened; if I'd been driving I would have wrecked the car. I went completely blind and totally deaf. Couldn't even hear my own heartbeat. And when I could hear again, it sounded as if every dog in the city was howling. All the birds were screaming too."

"Perhaps it was the sphinx slaying the Sorceress," the Italian murmured, and Billy frowned, his sensitive ears picking up what might have been a note of regret in the man's voice. "I understand she has been given permission to kill the woman."

"That's what I thought too," Billy said. "I've got a scrying bowl. Anasazi pottery, very rare, very powerful."

"The best, I'm told," Machiavelli agreed.

"When I got my aura back under control, I immediately tried to scry the island. I got a glimpse, just a quick image of the Sorceress standing against a wall in the exercise yard. She was sunning herself, as calm as you please. And then—and I know this is impossible—she opened her eyes and lifted her face to look up . . . and I swear she saw me."

"It may well be possible," Machiavelli murmured. "No one knows the extent of the Sorceress's powers. And then . . . ?"

"The liquid in my scrying bowl froze into a solid chunk of ice." The Kid looked down onto the passenger seat, where the fragments of the ancient bowl lay wrapped in the morning's newspaper. "It shattered," he said, a note of despair in his voice. "I've had that bowl a long time." And then his voice hardened. "The Sorceress is still alive, but I can't sense the sphinx. I think Perenelle has killed her," he said, in awe.

"That too may be possible," Machiavelli said slowly. "But it is unlikely. Let us not jump ahead. All we know for certain is that the Sorceress is still alive."

The Kid drew in a deep breath. "I thought I could take Perenelle Flamel on my own; now I know I can't. If you have any special European magic or spells, then it's time to bring them." Billy the Kid laughed, but there was nothing humorous in the sound. "We're only going to get one chance to kill this Sorceress; if we fail, then we won't be leaving the Rock alive."

Niccolò Machiavelli found himself nodding in agreement. He wondered if the American knew that the Morrigan had also gone missing. But what the Kid could not know was that at the precise moment the aura had been pulsing out from the island, a similar energy had blinked to life in North London. Machiavelli quickly skimmed the e-mails he'd received; they were all reporting on what had to be an incredibly powerful aura bursting to life.

. . . *more powerful than any I have ever encountered before . . .*

. . . *comparable to an Elder's aura . . .*

. . . *reports of auras spontaneously flaring on Hampstead Heath and Camden Road and in Highgate Cemetery . . .*

Interestingly, two e-mails reported the distinctive odor of mint.

Flamel's signature.

Machiavelli shook his head in admiration. The Alchemyst must have connected with Perenelle. Scrying was relatively simple, and while it usually worked best over short distances, the Flamels had married in 1350, and they had lived together for more than 650 years. The connection between them was very strong, and it stood to reason that they should be able to make that connection over thousands of miles. But scrying should not have activated Flamel's and Perenelle's auras in such a dramatic way. Unless . . . unless Perenelle had been in danger and the Alchemyst had fed her aura with his own. Machiavelli frowned. But Nicholas was weakening; that process should have—would have—killed him.

The twins!

Niccolò Machiavelli shook his head in disgust. He must be getting slow in his old age, he thought. It had to be connected to the twins. He had seen them work together at Notre Dame to defeat the gargoyles. They must have given Flamel some of their strength, and he, in turn, had somehow managed to connect to Alcatraz and Perenelle. That was why the aura's signature was so strong.

"Why did you contact me?" Machiavelli wondered aloud.

"You weren't my first call," the Kid admitted. "But I can't get in touch with my master. I thought I should warn you . . . and I hoped that maybe you had some way of defeating this Perenelle Flamel. Have you ever met her?"

"Yes." Machiavelli smiled bitterly, remembering. "Just the once. A long time ago: in the year 1669. Dee had lost track of the Flamels after the Great Fire in London, and they had fled to continental Europe. I was holidaying in Sicily when I spotted them entirely by chance. Nicholas was ill, laid low with food poisoning, and I ensured that the local physician added some sleeping potion to his medicine. In my arrogance I thought I could defeat Perenelle first and then go after the Alchemyst." The Italian held his left hand up to the light. A fine tracery of scars was still visible across his flesh, and there were others on his shoulders and back. "We fought for an entire day—her sorcery against my magic and alchemy. . . ." His voice trailed away into silence.

"What happened?" Billy asked eventually.

"The energies we released caused Mount Etna to erupt. I almost died on the island that day."

Billy the Kid lowered the binoculars, then turned his back to the bay and sat down on a low stone wall. He stared at his battered cowboy boots; the leather was scuffed and torn, almost worn through in places. It was time to get a new pair, but that meant driving down to a shoemaker he knew in New Mexico, who still crafted boots and shoes to the traditional pattern. Billy had some friends in Albuquerque and Las Cruces, others in Silver City, where he'd grown up, and Fort Sumner, where Pat Garrett had shot him down.

"I could raise a gang," he said slowly. He expected the Italian to object and was surprised when he heard nothing. "It would be just like in the old days. I know some immortals—a couple of cowboys, a Spanish conquistador and two great Apache warriors—who are loyal to us. Maybe if we all attacked the island together . . ."

"It is a good idea, but you would probably be condemning your friends to death," Machiavelli said. "There is another way." The line crackled. "There is an army on the island—an army of monsters. I think that rather than attacking Perenelle, we should simply awaken the slumbering beasts. Many have slept under enchantment for a month or more; they will be hungry . . . and will go in search of the nearest warm-blooded meal: Madame Perenelle."

Billy the Kid nodded, and then a thought struck him. "Hey, but won't we be on the island too?"

"Trust me," Machiavelli said. "Once we awaken the sleeping army, we will not be hanging around. I will see you tomorrow at twelve-thirty p.m. local time, when my plane lands. If everything goes according to plan, Perenelle will not live to see out the day."

# CHAPTER TWENTY-SIX

*D*r. John Dee was terrified.

Standing beside him, Bastet drew a sharp breath and shivered, and Dee realized that she too was scared. And that frightened him even more.

Dee had known fear before and had always welcomed it. Fear had kept him alive, had sent him running when others had stood and fought and died. But this was no ordinary terror: this was a bone-deep, stomach-churning, flesh-crawling repulsion that left him bathed in icy sweat. The cold analytical part of his mind recognized that this was not a rational fear; this was something stronger, something primal and ancient, a terror lodged deep in the limbic system, the oldest part of the human brain. This was a primeval fear.

In his long life Dee had encountered some of the foulest of the Elders, ghastly creatures that were not even vaguely human. His research and travels had led him into some of the darkest Shadowrealms, places where appalling nightmare creatures floated in emerald skies or tentacled horrors writhed in bloodred seas. But he had never been this frightened. Black spots danced at the corners of his vision and he realized he was breathing so hard he was hyperventilating. Desperately attempting to calm his breathing, he concentrated on the source of his fear—the creature striding down the middle of the empty North London street.

Most of the streetlights were dead, and the few that were not shed a ghastly sodium glow over the figure, painting it in shades of yellow and black. It stood close to eight feet tall, with massive arms and legs that ended in goatlike hooves. An enormous rack of six-pointed antlers curled out of each side of its skull, adding at least another five feet to its height. It was wrapped in mismatched hides of animals long extinct, so that Dee found it hard to tell where the skins ended and the creature's hairy flesh began. Resting on its left shoulder was a six-foot club shaped from the jawbone of a dinosaur, one side ragged with a line of spiky teeth.

This was Cernunnos, the Horned God.

Fifteen thousand years ago, a frightened Paleolithic artist had daubed an image of this creature on a cave wall in southwest France, an image that was neither man nor beast, but something caught in between. Dee realized that he was probably experiencing the same emotions that ancient man had felt. Just looking at it made him feel small, inconsequential, puny.

He had always believed that the Horned God was just another Elder—maybe even one of the Great Elders—but earlier that day Mars Ultor had revealed something shocking, something quite terrifying. The Horned God was no Elder. It was something older, far older, something that existed at the very edges of myth.

Cernunnos was one of the legendary Archons, the race that had ruled the planet in the incredibly distant past. Yggdrasill had been a seed when the Horned God had first walked the world, Nidhogg and its kin only newly hatched, and it would be hundreds of millennia before the first humani appeared.

The Horned God stepped forward and light washed across its face.

Dee felt as if he had been punched in the stomach. He'd been expecting a mask of horror, but the creature was beautiful. Shockingly, unnaturally beautiful. The skin of its face was deeply tanned, but smooth and unlined, as if it had been carved out of stone, and oval amber eyes glowed within deep-sunk sockets. When it spoke, its full-lipped mouth barely opened and its long throat remained still.

"An Elder and a humani, a cat and its master, and which is the more dangerous, I wonder?" Its voice was surprisingly soft, almost gentle, though completely emotionless, and although he heard it speak in English, Dee was sure he could hear the buzzing of a hundred other languages saying the same words in his head. Cernunnos came closer and then bent on one knee, first to stare at Bastet and then to look down on Dee. The Magician looked into the Horned God's eyes: the pupils were black slits, but, unlike a serpent's, they were horizontal, like flat black lines. "So you are Dee." The buzzing voices swirled in Dee's head.

The Magician bowed deeply, unwilling to look into the amber eyes, desperately trying to control his fear. A peculiar musky odor enveloped the Archon, the smell of wild forests and rotting vegetation. Dee was struck with the scent and realized it probably had something to do with the emotions he felt. He had seen worse creatures, certainly more shocking creatures, so what was it about the Horned God that terrified him so much? He focused on the savage-looking club the ancient creature was leaning on. It looked like the jaw of a sarcosuchus, the supercroc from the Cretaceous Period, and he found himself wondering just how old the Archon was.

"We are delighted by your presence," Bastet hissed loudly. Dee thought he could hear the tremor of fear in her voice.

"I do not think so," Cernunnos said, straightening.

"We—" Bastet began, but suddenly the huge club swung around and came to a stop, its teeth inches from her feline skull.

"Creature: do not speak to me again. I am not here by choice. You." Cernunnos turned its amber eyes on Dee. "Your Elder masters have invoked an ancient debt that has existed between us going back to the dawn of time. If I assist you, then my debt to them is wiped clean. That is the only reason I am here. What do you need?"

Dee took a deep breath. He bowed again, and then bit down hard on the inside of his cheek to prevent himself from smiling. An Archon was putting itself at his command. When he spoke, he was pleased that his voice was steady and controlled. "How much have you been told?" he began.

"I am Cernunnos. Your thoughts and memories are mine to read, Magician. I know what you know; I know what you have been, I know what you are now. The Alchemyst, Flamel, and the children are with the Saracen Knight and the Bard behind their makeshift metal fortress. You want me and the Wild Hunt to force an entrance for you." Although the Archon's face remained an unwrinkled mask, Dee imagined he heard what might be a sarcastic note in the Horned God's voice.

The Magician bowed again, attempting to control his thoughts. "Just so."

The Archon turned its huge head to look at the metal walls of the used-car lot. "Promises have been made to me," it rumbled. "Slaves. Fresh meat."

Dee hurried on. "Of course. You can have Flamel, and anyone else you want. I need the children and the two pages from the Codex that remain in Flamel's possession." Dee bowed again. With the power of the Horned God and the Wild Hunt it commanded, he could not fail.

"I am instructed to tell you this," Cernunnos said softly, moving its head slightly, looking down on the Magician, amber eyes glowing in its dark face: "that if you fail, your Elder masters have given you to me. A gift, a little recompense for arousing me from my slumbers." The huge horned head tilted to one side, and horizontal pupils expanded to turn its eyes black and bottomless. "I have not had a pet in millennia. They do not tend to last long before they turn."

"Turn?" Dee swallowed hard.

A wave of stinking fur, claws, teeth and eyes made yellow by the lights flowed down the streets, boiling out of the houses, leaping through windows, flattening fences, pushing up through sewers. Filthy foul-smelling creatures gathered in a huge silent semicircle behind the Archon. They had the bodies of enormous gray wolves . . . but they all had human faces.

"Turn," Cernunnos said. Without moving its body, its head swiveled at an impossible angle to regard the silent army behind it, and then it looked back at Dee. "You are strong. You will last at least a year before you become part of the Wild Hunt."

# CHAPTER TWENTY-SEVEN

*P*alamedes rounded on the Alchemyst. "See what you have done!" Anger had thickened his accent, making his words almost unintelligible.

Flamel ignored him. He turned to Shakespeare. "There is an escape route?" he asked calmly.

The Bard nodded. "Of course. There's a tunnel directly under the hut. It comes up about a mile away in a disused theater." He smiled crookedly. "I chose the location myself."

Flamel turned to Sophie and Josh. "Get your stuff. Let's go; we can be well away before the Horned God arrives." Before either of them could object, the Alchemyst had caught the twins each by an arm and pushed them back toward the hut. Josh angrily shook off the immortal, and Sophie jerked herself free. The Alchemyst was about to object when he realized that neither Palamedes nor Shakespeare had moved. He turned to look at the smaller man. "Quickly; you know what the Horned God is capable of, and once the Wild Hunt have tasted blood, even it will have little control over them."

"You go," Shakespeare said. "I will stay here. I can hold them and give you the time you need to escape."

Nicholas shook his head. "That is madness," he said desperately. "You will not escape. Cernunnos will destroy you."

"Destroy my body, possibly." Shakespeare smiled. "But my name is and will always be immortal. My words will never be forgotten as long as there is a human race."

"And if the Dark Elders return, then that might be sooner than you think," Flamel snapped. "Come with us," he said, and then added gently, "Please."

But the Bard shook his head. His aura crackled warm and pale around his body, filling the air with lemon. Modern armor flickered into plate armor and chain mail before finally settling into the ornate and grotesque armor of the Middle Ages. He was fully wrapped in shining yellow metal, smooth and curved, designed to deflect any blow, spikes jutting from his knees and elbows. He pushed back the visor on the helm that encased his head, pale eyes glowing, magnified behind the glasses he still wore. "I will stay and fight alongside the Gabriel Hounds. They have been loyal to me for centuries; now I will be loyal to them." He smiled, his teeth a ruined mess in his mouth.

"William . . . ," Flamel whispered, shaking his head.

"Alchemyst, I am not entirely defenseless. I have not lived this long without learning some magic. Remember, at the heart of all magic is imagination . . . and there was never a greater imagination than mine."

"Nor a greater ego," Palamedes interjected. "Will, this is a battle we cannot win. We should go, regroup and fight another day. Come with us." There was almost a note of pleading in the Saracen Knight's voice.

The immortal Bard shook his head firmly. "I'm staying. I know I cannot win. But I can hold them here for hours . . . maybe even until the dawn. The Wild Hunt cannot run abroad during the hours of sunlight." He looked at the Alchemyst. "This is something I have to do. I betrayed you once; let me now make amends."

Nicholas stepped forward and gripped the Bard's armor-clad arm with enough force to bring both their auras fizzing alight. "Shakespeare: knowing what I know now, I would be honored to stand and fight with you. But let us do as Palamedes says: let us choose our battles. You do not have to do this for me."

"Oh, but I'm not doing this just for you," Shakespeare said. He turned his head slightly, glancing sidelong at the silent twins. "I am doing this for them." Armor squeaking and creaking, he stepped closer to Sophie and Josh and looked into each of their faces. Now he smelled strongly of lemon, sharp and clean, and they could see their own reflections in the shining armor. "I have witnessed their powers. These are the twins of legend, of that I have no doubt. Those of us loyal to the Elders have a duty to train these twins, to nurture them and bring them to their full potential. There is a time coming when they will need their powers . . . indeed, when the very world will need them." Stepping back, he shook his head, his eyes huge and damp behind his glasses.

"And I am also doing this for Hamnet, my dear dead son. My twin boy. His sister was never the same after his death, though she lived for many years thereafter. I was not there to help him, but I can help you."

"You can help us by leaving with us," Sophie said softly. "I know what's coming." She shuddered as dark disturbing images appeared at the edges of her consciousness.

"Cernunnos and the Wild Hunt." Shakespeare nodded, and then he looked around at the Gabriel Hounds, some still in their dog shapes, though most had now assumed their human guises. "Wolfmen against dogmen. It will be an interesting battle."

"We need you," Josh said urgently.

"Need me?" Shakespeare looked surprised. "Why?"

"You know so much. You could teach us," he said quickly.

The Bard shook his head, armor winking. He lowered his voice and spoke directly to Josh and Sophie. "The Alchemyst knows more—much more—than I. And Sophie has access to the knowledge of the ages; she knows more than she thinks. You do not need me. I cannot teach you the elemental magics. That is your priority: if you are to have any chance of surviving the days to come, you need to master the five pure magics."

"Five!" Josh looked startled. "I thought there were only four elements." He looked at Sophie. "Air and Fire, and then Water and Earth."

"Four elements?" Shakespeare smiled. "You're missing Aether, the fifth magic. The most mysterious, the most powerful of all. But to master it, you have to first control the other four." He lifted his head, turned to the Alchemyst and raised his voice. "Go now. Take them to Gilgamesh the King. And Nicholas," he added gravely, "be careful. You know what he is like."

"What is he like?" Josh asked quickly, suddenly nervous.

The Bard turned pale blue eyes on Flamel. "You have not told them?" He looked at the twins and then dropped his visor, completely masking his face. When he spoke again, his voice echoed hollowly. "The king's noble mind is over-thrown. He is mad. Quite, quite mad."

Josh rounded on the Alchemyst. "You never said—"

And then a sound filled the night. It was the bellow of a stag: ancient and primal, the bestial coughing echoed off the metal walls and trembled up through the ground, setting the puddles vibrating and shivering.

In response, Sophie's aura appeared unbidden around her body, automatically molding itself into protective armor; Josh's aura blinked into existence as a weak gold shadow around his head and hands.

The damp oily odor of rusting cars and the wet fur of the Gabriel Hounds was suddenly swamped by a repellent stink. The twins immediately recognized the smell from a working vacation they had spent with their parents in Peru: it was the putrid odor of the jungle, heavy with the cloying scent of rot and damp, of decaying trees and noxious deadly flowers.

And then Cernunnos and the Wild Hunt attacked.

# CHAPTER TWENTY-EIGHT

*J*osh suddenly realized he had Clarent in his hands, though he had no memory of pulling the sword from the map tube. The leather-wrapped hilt was warm and dry in his sweat-dampened palms, and he felt a tickle like an insect on his skin. The ancient weapon crackled, wisps of gray-white smoke coiling off the blade as the tiny crystals set into the stone winked with red and black light.

A flood of feelings and ideas almost overwhelmed him. They weren't his thoughts, and because he'd handled the sword before and experienced its emotions, he didn't think they belonged to the sword. These feelings were new and strange. He felt . . . different: confident, strong, powerful. And angry. Above all else he felt a terrible anger. It burned in the pit of his stomach, making him double over in pain. He could actually feel the heat flowing up from his stomach into his chest and down through his arms. His hands grew almost uncomfortably hot, and then the smoke leaking off Clarent changed color, turning an ugly red-black. The sword twitched in his hands.

The pain disappeared, and as he straightened, Josh found that he was not afraid. All the fears of the past five days were gone.

He looked around, taking in the defenses and the number of defenders. He had no idea of the scale of the army they faced, and although the metal fortress was well made, he instinctively knew it would not hold till the dawn. It was designed to stand against human attackers. He automatically looked up, trying to gauge the time from the position of the stars, but they were hidden behind a layer of amber-tinted clouds . . . and then he remembered that he was wearing a watch. Eight-twenty-five. At least nine hours till dawn, when the Wild Hunt would retreat to their twilight Shadowrealm.

Tapping the stone blade against the palm of his left hand, he looked around, eyes narrowing. How would he attack a place like this? Scathach would know; the Warrior Maid would be able to tell him what they were up against and where the first attack would occur. He was guessing that the attackers had not brought siege engines, so storming the walls would be both time-consuming and costly. The Horned God would need to create an opening. . . .

And then Josh suddenly realized that he didn't need the Warrior Maid to instruct him. He already knew. Sophie had been right: when Mars had Awakened him, he'd passed on his martial knowledge.

Josh turned to watch Palamedes and Shakespeare. The Gabriel Hounds had clambered up along the metal walls and joined those others already on the metal parapets. In total there were perhaps a hundred warriors, and Josh knew that there were not enough. They were all armed with bows and arrows, crossbows and spears. Why no modern weapons? he wondered. The archers had a handful of arrows in their quivers, the spearmen two or three spears apiece. Once they had fired their arrows and thrown their spears, they were useless. They would have to stand and wait for their attackers.

Josh found himself turning toward the gate, and almost of its own accord his hand came up, pointing the tip of the sword at the entrance. He knew that the weakest part of any fortress was its gate. Josh's lips twisted in an ugly smile. "He will concentrate his attack here," he said to no one in particular, staring hard at the gate, and a coil of gray-black smoke curled off the blade, almost in agreement. This was where the Horned God would attempt to create its opening.

At that moment a blow struck the gates with enough force to set the walls ringing. Cars shifted and moved in their tall stacks. Another blow, as if from a battering ram, vibrated through the night. Somewhere off to the right, a car toppled and crashed to the ground. Glass shattered.

The stag cried out again, a sound of raw power.

Clarent seemed to react to the sound. It twitched and actually turned in Josh's palm. Heat coiled around his wrist, and suddenly his aura crackled orange.

"Josh . . . ," Sophie whispered.

Josh turned to look at his twin and saw that she was staring at his hands. He looked down. A pair of gauntlets had appeared on his hands where they gripped the hilt of the stone sword. They looked like soft leather gloves, and they were stained and worn, the leather scraped, dappled with what looked like dirt and mud.

Another tremendous blow struck the gate.

"We don't have enough troops to hold the walls," Josh said, thinking aloud. He pointed with Clarent. "Palamedes and Shakespeare should open the gates. The Gabriel Hounds can pick off the attackers as they bunch up in the narrow entrance."

Flamel stepped forward and reached out for Josh. "We need to get out of here."

The moment his fingers touched the boy's shoulder, Josh's aura intensified around him, yellow threads of power crawling across his chest and arms. The Alchemyst jerked his fingers back as if they had been burned. The stone sword glowed briefly gold, then faded to an ugly red-speckled black as a wash of emotions took Josh by surprise.

*Fear. A terrible all-consuming fear of beastlike creatures and shadowy humans.*

*Loss. Countless faces, men, women and children, family, friends and neighbors. All dead.*

*Anger. The overriding emotion was one of anger—a simmering, all-consuming rage.*

The boy slowly turned to look at the immortal. Their eyes locked. Josh immediately knew that these new emotions had nothing to do with the sword. He had held Clarent before and had come to recognize the peculiarly repulsive nature of its memories and impressions. He knew that what he'd just experienced were the Alchemyst's thoughts. When the man had touched him, he'd felt Flamel's fear, loss and anger, and something else also: for a single instant there had been the vaguest ghostly impression of children . . . lots of children, in the clothes and costumes of a dozen countries from across the centuries. And as the immortal human had jerked his hand away, Josh had been left with the impression that all the children had been twins.

Josh took a step toward the Alchemyst and stretched out his hand, fingers spread wide. Perhaps if he just touched Nicholas and held on tightly, he'd finally have some answers. He would know the truth about the immortal Nicholas Flamel.

The Alchemyst took a step back from Josh. Although his lips still curled into a smile, Josh saw the older man's hands close into fists and caught the suggestion of light as his fingernails turned green. A suggestion of mint touched the air, but it was sour and bitter.

Another crash shook the car yard and the gate vibrated in its frame. Metal screeched and sang as the Wild Hunt launched themselves, scratching and clawing at the walls. Josh hesitated, torn between forcing a confrontation with the Alchemyst and dealing with the assault. Something his father had once said to him popped into his head. They'd been walking on the banks of the Tennessee River and talking about the Civil War Battle of Shiloh. "It's always best to fight just one battle at a time, son," he'd said. "You win more that way."

Josh turned away. He needed to talk to Sophie, tell her what he'd experienced, and then, together, they would confront Flamel. He darted toward Palamedes. "Wait," he called, "don't fire!"

But before he could stop Palamedes, Josh heard the Saracen Knight's deep voice, loud and clear across the junkyard.

"Fire!"

The archers on the parapets released their arrows, which keened and whispered as they cut through the air and disappeared into the night.

Josh bit his lip. They should be conserving their ammunition, but he had to acknowledge that the Saracen Knight knew his tactics. Arrows first, then spears, with the powerful but short-range crossbows held in reserve for close-quarters combat.

"Spears," the Saracen Knight called. "Fire!"

The Gabriel Hounds flung their tall leaf-bladed spears down from the walls.

Josh tilted his head, listening, focusing with his enhanced senses, but he heard no sound from the attacking forces. It seemed incredible, but the Wild Hunt were moving and fighting in absolute silence.

"We need to go," Nicholas said urgently.

Josh ignored him. Then he heard ragged talons and teeth tear at the metal, ripping away fencing, slashing at the piled cars.

"Arrows," Shakespeare called from another section of the wall. "Loose!"

Another tremendous blow shook the gate.

"The gate," Josh shouted, his voice strong and commanding. "They're going to come in through the gate!"

Both Palamedes and William Shakespeare turned to look at the boy.

Clarent blazed red-black in the boy's hand as he pointed. "Concentrate on the gate. That's where they will try and break through."

Palamedes shook his head, but the Bard immediately started moving the Gabriel Hounds under his command toward the gate.

Clarent glowed bright red, twitching in his hand, and Josh unwittingly took a step forward, almost as if the sword was pulling him closer to the enemy.

"One more blow," he murmured.

# CHAPTER TWENTY-NINE

"*O*ne more blow," Dee muttered.

Dee and Bastet had stood in silence and watched the Wild Hunt fling themselves at the metal walls. Unlike normal wolves, these creatures moved without barking or even growling; the only sound was the clicking of their claws on the pavement. Most loped on four legs, but some ran on two, stooped and hunched over, and Dee wondered if here was the source of the werewolf legend. The dogs, the Gabriel Hounds, had always protected the humani; the wolves of the Wild Hunt had always hunted them.

About a hundred of the more agile wolves had clawed their way over the fence and up along the stacked cars. And then the defenders had appeared at the parapets. Arrows whistled into the first row of the Wild Hunt, and the moment the arrows touched the human-faced wolves, the creatures *changed*. Dee glimpsed apemen, Roman centurions, Mongol warriors, Neanderthal cavemen, Prussian officers and English Roundheads . . . and then they crumbled to dust on the air.

"Cernunnos is wasting his troops," Bastet said shortly. She had stepped back into the shadows and was almost completely invisible, bundled up in a long black leather coat.

"It's a distraction," the Magician said aloud, not looking at the Elder. It was the first time she had spoken since she had been shamed by the Archon, and Dee could almost feel the rage coming off her in slow waves. The Magician doubted that anyone—or anything—had ever spoken to the Elder like that and survived. He was also conscious that he had witnessed her humiliation; Bastet would never forget that. From the corner of his eye, he could see the great cat head turning to look down on him.

"Those attacking the walls are just a distraction," he added quickly, explaining himself. "The main assault will take place at the gate." He paused, then asked: "I am presuming nothing can harm the Archon?"

Bastet's eyes narrowed to slits. "It lives," she hissed. "And so it can die."

"I thought the Archons were only stories," he said quickly. Dee wondered just how much the cat-headed goddess knew about the creature.

The Elder was quiet for a moment before she answered. "In my youth I was taught that at the heart of every story is a grain of truth," she said.

Dee found it hard to imagine the cat-headed goddess as a youngster; he had a sudden absurd image of a fluffy white kitten. Had Bastet ever been young—or had she been born, or hatched, fully grown? There was so much he wanted to know. His eyes narrowed as he looked across the street toward Cernunnos. And now here was a new mystery: the Archon. Dee had spent several lifetimes investigating the legends of the Elders. Occasionally, he had come across fragments of stories about the mysterious race who had ruled the earth in the very distant past, long before the Great Elders raised Danu Talis from the seabed. It was said that the Elders had built their empires upon fragments of Archon technology and had even taken possession and settled some of the cites abandoned by the ancient race. But how had one become indebted to an Elder? Surely the Archons were more powerful than those who had come after them? The Elders, even the Next Generation, were infinitely more powerful than the humani who had followed them into the world.

The Magician watched the Archon lift its huge club and bring it around in a tremendous blow against the solid-looking metal door. The sound exploded into the night and a screech of white-hot sparks spewed into the air. The door shuddered and creaked, and when Cernunnos jerked the club free, it ripped away long strips of metal, leaving them dangling. The huge horned creature dropped the club, gripped both sides of the torn door and wrenched it apart, peeling back the metal as if it were as thin as paper.

Standing back, Cernunnos allowed the Wild Hunt to pour through the ragged opening. The creature turned to look at Dee and Bastet and its beautiful face lit up with a radiant smile. "Dinnertime," it said.

# CHAPTER THIRTY

*J*osh darted forward, taking up a position where he could watch the gate. He saw the thick metal bulge inward, then rip open, and caught a glimpse—a fleeting impression—of the huge horned creature that had torn the defenses apart with its bare hands. Clarent jerked in his grip again, attempting to pull him forward, closer to the action; Josh had to make an effort to stand still.

And then the Wild Hunt appeared.

They were smaller than he had imagined, but still bigger and broader than any wolves he had ever seen before. And behind the fur and filth, their faces were unquestionably human. The savage creatures surged through the opening, boiling over one another, teeth and claws slashing as they raced forward, but the narrow metal walls kept them bunched close together. There were no barks or growls; the

237

only sounds were the clicking of their claws and the snapping of teeth.

"Arrows," Josh whispered.

"Loose!" Palamedes called from the left-hand parapet, almost as if he'd heard.

A second wave of arrows rained down on the Wild Hunt. For an instant the creatures winked back into the forms they had worn as humans: Spartan warriors, blue-painted Celts, massive Vikings and tall Masai hunters. Then fur, flesh and bones dissolved into age-old dust. Those who came behind blinked grit from their yellow eyes, sneezing as it coated their muzzles.

"Fire!" Shakespeare shouted from the right-hand side.

A third wave of arrows scythed into the wolves. Samurai in full armor, ferocious Gurkas in jungle camouflage and primitive hominids turned from wolves to humans to dust in a heartbeat. Crusader knights in metal and German World War II officers in gray, French legionnaires in blue and savage Vandals in furs briefly assumed their human forms before they disappeared. Josh noticed that they all had smiles on their faces, as if they were relieved to finally be free.

"Three volleys: the Gabriel Hounds are out of arrows," Josh murmured.

"We've got to go now," Flamel snapped, coming around to stand in front of Josh.

"No," Josh answered quietly. "We're not leaving."

"You agreed it was better if we left," Flamel began. "We will fight them, but not today."

"I changed my mind," Josh said shortly. On one level—

thinking coldly, practically, logically—he knew that it made sense to run, hide and regroup. He looked for Shakespeare, finding him on a parapet, surrounded by the Gabriel Hounds. The Bard had been prepared to sacrifice himself, to buy time to allow the others to escape. That had nothing to do with logic; that had been an emotional decision. And sometimes emotion won more battles than logic. Clarent shivered in his grip and for the first time Josh caught momentary impressions of the lineage of warriors who had held the ancient blade, who had faced down terrible odds, fought monsters and demons, battled entire armies. Some—*many*—had died. But none had run. The stone blade whispered agreement in Josh's mind. A warrior didn't run.

"Josh . . ." Anger had crept into the Alchemyst's voice.

"We're staying!" Josh barked. He turned to look at Flamel, and something in the boy's face and eyes made the Alchemyst step back.

"Then you are putting yourself and your twin in terrible danger," Flamel said icily.

"I think we've been in terrible danger from the moment we met you," Josh said. Unconsciously, he lifted the smoking blade, moving it in the air between them, tracing two waving lines in the air. "We've spent the last couple of days running with you from danger to danger." His lips pulled back from his teeth in a frightening grin. "I think we should have been running *from* you."

The Alchemyst folded his arms, but not before Josh once again smelled bitter peppermint. "I am going to pretend you did not say that."

"But I did. And I meant it."

"You are overtired," Nicholas said quietly. "You have only recently been Awakened and have not had a chance to deal with that. Maybe a little of Mars's knowledge leaked into you, confusing you, and," he added, nodding to the sword, "you are carrying the Coward's Blade. I know what it can do, the dreams it brings, the promises it makes. It can even make a boy think he's a man." He stopped and took a quick breath and changed his tone, forcing the bitterness from his voice. "Josh, you're not thinking clearly."

"I disagree," Josh retorted. "For the first time I'm thinking very clearly. This—all this—is because of us." He looked over the Alchemyst's shoulder, concentrating on the Wild Hunt.

Flamel followed Josh's gaze and glanced behind him. "Yes," he agreed. "But not because of *you*, not because of Sophie and Josh Newman. This is because of what you are, and what you can become. This is just another battle in a war that has raged for millennia."

"Winning battles wins wars," Josh said. "My father once told me it's always best to fight one battle at a time. We're fighting this one."

"Maybe you should ask your sister," Flamel countered.

"He doesn't need to," Sophie said quietly. Drawn by the argument, she had come to stand behind her brother.

"So you're in agreement about this?" Flamel demanded.

"The two that are one," Sophie said, watching the Alchemyst's face. "Isn't that what we are?"

Josh turned to focus on the attack. The Gabriel Hounds

had thrown their spears and fired the last of their crossbow bolts. The metal corridor was now thick with swirling, cloying dust. Vague shapes moved in the cloud, but none of the enemy had broken through yet. Palamedes and Shakespeare had come down from the walls and were marshaling the hounds around the entrance to the alleyway. Josh suddenly looked up, realizing that the walls were vulnerable, and was unsurprised to see the first of the wolf heads appear over the parapets.

"If anything happens to either of you now," Flamel said desperately, turning away from Josh, concentrating on Sophie, "then everything we have done, everything we have achieved will have been for naught. Sophie, you have the Witch's memories. You know what the Dark Elders did to humanity in the past. And if they capture you and your brother and retrieve the last two pages of the Codex, then they will do that, and worse—much worse—to this world."

The immortal's words stirred horrible memories within Sophie, and she blinked away nightmare images of a devastated flooded earth. She took a deep breath and nodded. "But before they can do anything, the Dark Elders have to capture us." She held out her left hand and it turned into a solid silver glove. "And we're no longer ordinary, no longer entirely human, either," she added bitterly.

"Pull everyone back!" Josh yelled, and when he turned to look at his sister, she was shocked to see that his pupils had turned gold and were speckled with black and red that matched the hues on the stone sword he held. Mars's eyes had been red, she remembered. Josh reached out and, before she could say anything, caught her arm. "We'll pull them back behind the moat," he said. "Then we'll set the moat on fire."

Sophie blinked. She saw Josh, standing tall and straight, Clarent blazing in his left hand, and then her eyes silvered as the Witch's memories flooded her and she saw the ghostly image of Mars in red and gold armor superimposed over her brother. He too carried his sword in his left hand.

Josh spotted the Bard and drew in a deep breath. "Shakespeare!" Strong and commanding, his voice echoed in the silence, and both the Bard and Palamedes looked over. Josh waved and pointed to the walls, which were now gray with wolves pouring over the battlements. "Retreat! Get back behind the moat!"

The Bard started to shake his head, but the big knight simply caught the smaller man around the waist and slung him across his shoulders. Ignoring the kicking and protesting, the Saracen Knight turned and raced back toward Flamel and the twins, with the Gabriel Hounds, in both human and dog form, close at his heels.

"Well done," Palamedes said as he came level with Josh. "We were about to be overrun. You saved us." The Saracen Knight dumped Shakespeare off his shoulder, setting him upright on the ground. He pushed back his helmet and grinned at the immortal. "Oh, if only you were still writing, Will; think what a tale this would make." He looked over at Josh. "That's it. The last of the Gabriel Hounds are with us. Let's fire the moat."

"Not yet. Let them get closer before we set it alight,"

Josh said confidently. "That'll hold them." He stopped then and looked at Palamedes as doubts bubbled to the surface of his consciousness. "I mean . . . will it? Have you fought the Wild Hunt before?"

The huge knight nodded. "I've fought them. I've yet to see a living creature that will willingly cross fire. And despite his appearance, Cernunnos is part beast."

"They'll not cross it." A red-faced Shakespeare turned to look at them. His glasses were crooked on his face. "I added a tincture or two to the oils. Some minerals, herbs and exotic spices that the Elders and Next Generation find repulsive for some reason. The moat is lined with mercury, and I've also mixed iron ore and various oxides throughout the liquid. Not even Cernunnos will be able to pass through the flames."

"The Archon is coming," Sophie whispered, but no one heard her. She wrapped her arms tightly around her body to stop herself from shaking. The Witch of Endor had known Cernunnos; known him, feared him and hated him. The Witch had spent centuries searching for the remnants of Archon technology and had systematically destroyed them all, burning the metal books, melting down the artifacts, killing the storytellers who repeated the tales. She was trying to erase her memories of those who had ruled before the Elders. Now those memories threatened to overwhelm Sophie.

A monstrous shape moved in the dusty swirling remnants of the Wild Hunt, and Cernunnos stepped out of the metal alleyway. The creature moved slowly, unhurriedly, its huge club resting lightly on its left shoulder. Tendrils of white fire crawled across its antlers, sparking from one to the other, bathing its beautiful statuelike face in soft light. Tilting its head to one side, it curled its lips in a smile and spread its arms wide. Its mouth worked, but the words that formed in its listeners' heads were not in sync with its lips, and the sound was of a dozen voices talking together. The twins heard it speak in English with a precise Boston accent; in Flamel's head it was the French of his youth; Palamedes heard the voice in the lilting desert tongue of Babylon; while to Shakespeare's ears it spoke Elizabethan English. "I came to feast. I came for the twins. I even came here for a little amusement. I never realized I was coming to collect an old friend." Cernunnos stretched out its right hand, and the stone blade in Josh's grasp blazed red-black fire, dark cinders spiraling up into the night air. "You have something of mine, boy. Give me my sword."

Josh tightened his grip on the weapon. "It's mine now."

The Horned God's laugher was light, almost a giggle. "Yours! You have no idea what you're holding." Cernunnos strode forward, its huge goatlike hooves stamping into the mud. It stopped at the edge of the moat and its nostrils wrinkled, the first sign of an expression on its perfect face.

"I know what this is," Josh said. He took a step toward the Horned God. They were now separated by the six-foot-wide moat of thick black liquid. Josh was holding the sword in both hands, trying to keep it level and steady. The weapon was trembling, shivering in his grip. And then he realized that the vibration running up his arms into his shoulders was a regular pulse . . . like a heartbeat. As the delicious warmth flowed through his body and gathered in his chest and stomach, he felt strong and confident, afraid of nothing and no one. If Cernunnos attacked, Josh knew he'd be able to defeat him. "This is Clarent, the Sword of Fire," he said, his voice echoing and ringing. "I saw what it did to the Nidhogg. I know what it can do to you."

"Threatened by a humani boy," the Horned God said in wonder.

Josh stepped right up to the edge of the moat and stared at the creature across the swirling liquid. Fragments of thoughts danced through his mind, images of the time Cernunnos had carried the sword.

"There is a battle coming," Josh said loudly. "And I think I'm going to need this sword."

Cernunnos smiled. "Remember, it is also called the Coward's Blade," it said, planting its massive club on the ground and then leaning on it, its huge horned head pushed forward, amber eyes staring hard at Josh. "It is a cursed weapon. All who carry it are cursed."

"You carried it."

"Exactly," Cernunnos said. "And look at me. Once this world was mine to command; now I do another's bidding. The blade will poison you, ultimately even destroy you."

"You could be lying to me," Josh said simply, but somewhere at the back of his mind he knew the Archon was not lying.

"Why would I lie to you?" Cernunnos sounded genuinely confused. "I am neither Elder nor Next Generation. I have no need to lie to humani."

Sophie stepped forward to stand just behind her twin.

Behind his back, her thumb gently rested against the tattoo burned into her wrist. All she had to do would be to touch the red spot in the gold circle and it would bring her Fire magic to blazing life. The Horned God looked at her, eyes glowing as his pupils contracted to flat black lines. "We have met before," he said, a note of wonder in his voice, looking from face to face.

Shocked, the twins shook their heads.

"We have," the Horned God insisted.

"I think we'd remember," Sophie said.

"You're not exactly forgettable," Josh added.

"I know you," Cernunnos said firmly. "But that's a mystery we will solve later," he added as Nicholas, followed by Palamedes and Shakespeare, hurried over to join the twins. The Horned God looked at each of them in turn, starting and finishing with the Alchemyst. Straightening, he heaved up his dinosaur club and pointed it at Flamel. "Dinner," he said, and then the club moved to point to Palamedes. "Lunch." The club moved back across the Alchemyst's chest to point to Shakespeare. "A snack."

"I feel I should take insult," the Bard muttered.

The Horned God looked at him. "And your Gabriel Hounds will join with the Wild Hunt; the two ancient clans will be reunited." He raised his club. There was movement in the gloom behind the Archon and suddenly the massed wolves surged forward, jaws gaping.

Sophie closed her eyes, focused, pressed her thumb against the circular tattoo and created a tiny flaming ball in the palm of her hand. Digging her fingers into Josh's shoulders, she pulled him away from the edge of the moat as she dropped the burning golden globe into the thick black liquid.

It plopped onto the surface of the oil and floated for a second, then disappeared with a hiss of white steam.

"Oh," she whispered. She felt as if all the air had rushed out of her lungs, leaving her breathless and gasping. Although she had learned the Magic of Fire only the previous day, it had already become a *part* of her. She had fought the Disir and the gargoyles with it, but she realized she knew little about its properties. There was so much more she needed to know.

The silent Wild Hunt raced toward the moat. Josh suddenly went to one knee and plunged Clarent into the thick liquid. It instantly exploded, roaring alight with a dull boom that sent sticky black flames shooting skyward. The force of the explosion sent both Josh and Sophie spinning backward into the mud—and on the other side of the moat, the Wild Hunt tumbled over one another as they tried to get away from the flames. Some continued to slide forward on the wet ground, while others were pushed into the fire by the press of bodies from behind. They instantly disappeared into gritty black cinders.

"You will pay for that!" Cernunnos stabbed at Josh with his club. "And you, boy . . . I will have my sword!"

"Let me try this again." Sophie flicked her fingers and sent a thick stream of yellow fire across the Horned God's huge club, which began to blaze with the appalling stench of burning bone. "Didn't your mother ever tell you it's rude to point?"

# CHAPTER THIRTY-ONE

*P*erenelle Flamel stepped off the last rung of the rusting ladder and tilted back her head to look at the tiny circle of pale blue sky high above her. Then she frowned. What looked like a cloud was falling toward her, coming straight down the long shaft that connected the surface of Alcatraz to the old smugglers' tunnel deep beneath the island. The cloud twisted and coiled in on itself, then solidified into Juan Manuel de Ayala.

"*Madame Perenelle?*" the sailor asked in formal Spanish. "*What are you doing down here?*"

"I'm not entirely sure," Perenelle admitted. "I thought I might visit the Crow Goddess." Yesterday—was it only yesterday?—Perenelle and Areop-Enap had defeated the Morrigan, the Crow Goddess, and her army of birds. The Old Spider had wanted to feed the Morrigan to some of its bird-eating spiders, but Perenelle had refused and instead had asked the Elder to carry the thread-bound creature to the lightless cell deep under the island.

When Perenelle had originally freed Areop-Enap from the prison, she had dismantled an intricate pattern of spears set into the muddy floor outside the door. Each spearhead had been painted with an ancient Word of Power, which created a barrier unbreakable by any of the Elder race. When Areop-Enap had brought the tightly wrapped Morrigan into the cell, Perenelle had drawn upon her extraordinary memory to re-create the pattern of spears around the cave mouth. Then, using mud and shells, she had redrawn the complex patterns on the flat spearheads, locking the Morrigan behind Words of Power and symbols that predated the Elders. Only a human could free her; an Elder or Next Generation could not even approach the invisible and deadly spell spun by the primeval hex.

*"Madame,"* de Ayala said urgently. *"We need to get you off the island."*

"I know," Perenelle said, lips curling in disgust as her foot sank up to the ankle in stinking fishy mud. "I'm working on it. Did you see any Nereids?"

*"There were a dozen sunning themselves on the seaward rocks, and I saw another two around by the landing dock. I saw no sign of their father, Nereus, though I know he must be close by."* Wisps of the ghost streamed away as he wrapped his arms tightly around his body. *"They cannot come ashore . . . but he can. And will."*

Perenelle took a dozen squelching steps down the corridor. She glanced back at the ghost, surprised. "I did not know that."

*"The Nereids have women's bodies but the tails of fish. Nereus has legs of a sort. He sometimes comes ashore in lonely fishing villages to . . . to eat, or he'll creep aboard a boat at night and snatch an unwary sailor."*

Perenelle stopped and peered down the corridor. The far end of the tunnel sloped down into the sea, and she had a sudden image of the Old Man of the Sea crawling up the tunnel toward her. Shaking her head, dismissing the image, she snapped her fingers and created an inch-long candlelike white flame that floated just above the center of her forehead. Like the light on a miner's helmet, it cast a yellow-white beam ahead of her. Perenelle turned back to de Ayala. "Will you stand watch for me, warn me if anyone, or anything, is coming?"

*"Of course."* The ghost folded in the middle, attempting to bow without legs. *"But why are you here, madame? There is nothing down here but the Crow Goddess."*

Perenelle's smile lit up the gloom. "That's who I've come to see."

"Have you come to gloat?" The Morrigan's voice was a hoarse, almost masculine rasp.

"No," Perenelle said truthfully. Standing in the middle of the doorway, she crossed her arms over her chest and peered into the cell. "I've come down here to talk to you."

Areop-Enap had spun a beautiful circular orb web in the

center of the underground cell. The threads were about the thickness of Perenelle's little finger, and they shimmered liquid silver in the light from the tongue of fire bobbing above her head. Directly in the center of the web, arms outstretched, black-feathered cloak spread out around her, lay the Crow Goddess. It looked as if she were simply perching in midair and could swoop down at any moment.

"You do not look well," Perenelle said a moment later. In the soft light, Perenelle could see that the creature's alabaster skin had taken on a greenish hue. Her black leather suit had dried and cracked in long splits that exposed the goddess's pale skin. The silver studs set into her jerkin were stained and blackened, and the heavy leather belt around her waist was dripping with moisture, the round shields set into it tarnished the same green color as her face.

The Morrigan smiled and licked her black lips with the tip of her tongue. "And you have aged in the hours since we last spoke. We will die together, you and I."

Perenelle moved her hand and the tongue of flame floated closer to the Morrigan. The Crow Goddess tried to twist her head to one side, but it was held fast by the sticky silver web. Reflections appeared in her jet-black eyes, giving them the appearance of having pupils. There was the hint of bone beneath the flesh of her face.

"You look ill," Perenelle said. "You might go before me."

"The Symbols of Binding are poisoning me," the Morrigan snapped, "but no doubt you knew that."

Perenelle twisted to look at the curling square glyph she had painted onto the head of the nearest spear. "I did not. I know they kept Areop-Enap trapped in here, but she seemed otherwise unharmed."

"Areop-Enap is an Elder. I am Next Generation. How did you discover the Symbols?" the Morrigan asked, and gave a deep hacking cough. "Many of the Elders and most of the Next Generation believe that the Symbols of Binding and the Words of Power are nothing more than legend."

"I did not discover them. It was your friend Dee who used them to trap Areop-Enap in this same cell," the Sorceress said.

The Morrigan's dark lips twisted in disgust. "Dee? Dee knew those ancient Words?" She fell silent and then slowly shook her head.

"You do not believe me?" Perenelle asked.

"Oh no, on the contrary. I do believe you. I think I know the English Magician better than anyone else alive, yet the more I discover, the less I realize I know. He never gave me any indication that he had this ancient knowledge," she finished.

"And now you're wondering who taught him," Perenelle said shrewdly. "Areop-Enap said that there was someone with Dee—an Elder, she thought, but so powerful that even the Old Spider could not see them. They must have been protected by an intricate spell of concealment. No doubt it was Dee's masters."

"No one knows Dee's Elder master."

Perenelle blinked in surprise. "Not even you?"

The Morrigan's long white teeth pressed against her black lips. "Not me. No one knows, and those who are curious—Elder, Next Generation or humani—disappear. It is one of the great secrets . . . though the bigger secret is why his masters continue to protect him and keep him alive, despite his many disasters. For centuries he has failed to capture you and your husband." She coughed a quick gurgling laugh. "The Elders are neither kind nor generous, and certainly not forgiving. I've known humani to be reduced to dust for failing to bow deeply enough to them."

"Do you know what Dee intends to do with all the creatures on this island?"

The Morrigan regarded her silently.

Perenelle smiled. "Does it matter if I know . . . especially if we are both to die soon?"

The Crow Goddess tried to nod, but her head was stuck fast. "Dee was instructed to collect the creatures, but I am sure he does not know what the Elders intend to do with them."

"But you do," Perenelle guessed.

"I have seen something like this happen before, a long time ago even as you humani measure time. It is an army of sorts," the Crow Goddess said tiredly. "When the time is right, it will be loosed upon the city."

Perenelle gasped. She had a sudden image of the skies above San Francisco filled with ravenous vampires, the sewers crawling with boggarts and trolls, peists in the bay, Windigo and cluricauns in the streets. "There would be carnage."

"That is the idea," the Morrigan whispered. "How do you think the humani would react if they saw monsters of myth and legend in the streets and skies?"

"With terror, disbelief." Perenelle took a deep shuddering breath. "Civilization would fall."

"It has fallen before," the Morrigan said dismissively.

"And risen," Perenelle said quickly.

"It will not rise again. I have heard rumors that there are similar collections—armies, zoos, menageries, call them what you will—on every continent. I would imagine they will be loosed on the world on the same day. The humani armies will waste themselves and their weapons against the creatures . . . and then, when they are exhausted and weakened, those you call the Dark Elders will return to the earth." The Crow Goddess laughed, then broke into a quick racking cough. "Well, that is the plan. Of course, this cannot happen if Dee does not get the last two pages of the Codex. Without the Final Summoning, the Shadowrealms cannot be drawn into alignment." She coughed again. "I wonder what Dee's master has in store for him if he fails? Something cruel, no doubt," she added almost gleefully.

"But I thought he was your friend?" Perenelle said, surprised again. "You've worked with him down through the centuries."

"Never by choice," the Morrigan snapped. "I am commanded to do Dee's bidding by those Elders he serves." She attempted to turn in the sticky web, but the strands tightened, holding her closer. "And see where it has led me." A glistening black tear gathered at the corner of her eye and then rolled down her cheek. "I will die here today, poisoned by the Symbols of Binding, and I will never see the sky again."

Perenelle watched the black tear drip off the Morrigan's

chin. The moment it left her flesh, it turned into a snow-white feather, which floated gently to the ground. "Perhaps Dee will send someone to rescue you."

"I doubt that." The Crow Goddess coughed. "If I die it would be nothing more than an inconvenience. Dee would get a new servant from his Elder master and I would be forgotten."

"It seems we have both been betrayed by the Magician," Perenelle whispered. She watched another black tear fall from the Crow Goddess's face and curl into a white feather the moment it dripped off her chin. "Morrigan . . . I wish . . . I wish I could help you," Perenelle admitted, "but I'm not sure I can trust you."

"Of course you cannot trust me," the Morrigan retorted. "Free me now and I will destroy you. That is my nature." Her pale flesh had darkened to a deep blue-green, and tiny spots had popped up on her forehead and across her cheeks. She started to thrash about on the web, black feathers ripping from her cloak to join the small pile of white feathers on the ground below her feet. "It is time to die. . . ." Her eyes opened wide, black and empty, and then slowly, slowly, slowly, curls of red and yellow spiraled across the blackness, turning it a pale orange. Taking a great heaving breath, she closed her eyes and lay still.

"Morrigan?" Perenelle whispered.

The creature did not move.

"Morrigan?" Perenelle asked again. Even though this creature had been her enemy for generations, she felt stricken, appalled that she had stood there and allowed a legend to die.

Abruptly, the Morrigan's eyes snapped open. No longer black, they were now bright red, the color of fresh blood.

"Morrigan . . . ?" Perenelle took a step back.

The voice that came out of the Crow Goddess's lips was subtly different from her usual voice. Traces of an Irish or Scottish accent were clearly audible. "The Morrigan is sleeping now. . . . I am the Badb."

The creature's eyes slowly closed, then blinked open. Now they were a brilliant yellow.

"And I am Macha." The Celtic accent was even stronger, and the voice was deeper, harsher.

The creature's eyes closed again, and when they opened once more, one eye was a deep lustrous red, the other a bright yellow. Two voices rolled from the same mouth, slightly out of sync.

"And we are the Morrigan's sisters." The red and yellow eyes turned to look down at the Sorceress. "Let us talk."

# CHAPTER THIRTY-TWO

"I thought you were both dead," Perenelle Flamel said. She knew she should be frightened, but all she felt was relief. And curiosity.

The dancing tongue of flame floating above her head shed a warm yellow light over the dark figure of the Crow Goddess stuck to the enormous web. In the blistered green-skinned face, one red and one yellow eye looked down over the Sorceress and when the black lips moved, the two voices spoke as one. "Sleeping, perhaps. But not dead."

Perenelle nodded; it wasn't an unusual idea. She'd grown up in a world of ghosts, she saw the dead every day and spoke to them often, and yet she knew that the voices coming from the Morrigan's mouth were not those of spirits. This was something different. She tried to remember what she knew about the Crow Goddess. The creature was Next Generation, born after the sinking of Danu Talis. She had settled in the lands that would one day be called Ireland and Britain and had quickly come to be worshipped by the Celts as a goddess of war, death and slaughter. Like many of the Elders and Next Generation, she was a triune goddess: she had three aspects. Some Elders visibly altered with the passage of time—Hekate was cursed to physically change from a young girl to an old woman during the course of each day. Others changed with the phases of the moon or the seasons, while still other triune goddesses were simply different aspects of the same person. But from what she remembered, the Macha, the Badb and the Morrigan were three different creatures with different personalities . . . all of them savage and deadly.

"When Nicholas and I were in Ireland back in the nineteenth century, an old wise woman told me that the Morrigan had somehow killed you both."

"Not quite." For an instant both eyes turned red and the creature spoke with a single voice. "We were never three; we were always one."

Perenelle kept her face impassive, careful to remain neutral. "One body, three personalities?" she asked. Then she nodded. "So that was why the three sisters were never seen together."

"At different times of the month, depending on the phase of the moon, each of us would assume control of this body."

The eyes blinked yellow, the voice changed and the angle of bones beneath the flesh altered, making the face subtly different. "And there were certain times of year when one or the other of us held sway. Midwinter was always my time."

The left eye turned red, the right eye bright yellow and both voices returned. "But this body was usually under the control of our younger sister, the Morrigan." The creature started to cough with enough force to shake the web, and thick black liquid gathered on its lips. The red and yellow eyes flickered toward the pattern of spears behind Perenelle's back. "Sorceress, break the Symbols of Binding . . . they are poisoning us, killing us."

Perenelle looked over her shoulder. Outside the cave mouth the twelve wooden spears stretching across the corridor formed an interlocking series of triangles and squares. From the corner of her eye she could see a gossamer hint of the black light that buzzed between the metal spearheads upon which she had inscribed in wet mud the ancient Words of Power.

"Sorceress . . . please. Break the spell," the Crow Goddess whispered. "Our sister, the Morrigan, knows you . . . and respects you. She knows that you are strong and powerful . . . but never cruel."

Perenelle stepped back into the corridor and wrenched one of the spears from the mud, breaking the pattern. Instantly, the thrumming she'd been only vaguely aware of vanished and the bitter metallic-tasting air was filled with the normal smells of the underground tunnel: salt and foul mud, rotting fish and seaweed. Holding the spear tightly in both hands, the Sorceress returned to the cell. "This had better not be a trick," she warned. As she brought the spear closer to the Crow Goddess, the head began to glow. Then it popped alight, cold black-white light streaming from it. Perenelle touched the tip of the glowing spear to the small pile of feathers beneath the web and they sizzled, smoked, then curled and crisped. The stink of burning feathers made Perenelle's eyes water and drove her back out of the cell.

The goddess's eyes blinked in the curling smoke. "No trick . . ."

And then a shudder ran through the body caught in the web and the red and yellow colors flowed from the eyes, leaving them black and empty. "They lie!" the Morrigan screeched. "Do not listen to them!"

Perenelle raised the spear high, bringing the lustrous metal head almost level with the Crow Goddess's face. The black-white light washed over her green-tinged skin and the goddess squeezed her eyes shut and tried and failed to twist her head away. When she opened her eyes again, the red and yellow of the Badb and the Macha had returned. The eyes started flickering from color to color as the two sisters spoke.

"The Morrigan tricked us," the Badb said.

"Imprisoned us, enchanted us, cursed us . . . ," the Macha added.

"She used a foul necromancy spell she learned from Dee's predecessor to bind our spirits, enslave us, then render us powerless. . . ."

"We have been trapped under enchantment for centuries," red-eyed Macha said. "Able to see and hear all that our sister saw and heard, but unable to do anything, unable to move, to act. . . ."

"But the corrosive effect of the Symbols of Binding loosened the spell and allowed us to regain control of this flesh."

"What do you want?" Perenelle asked, curious, but strangely saddened by the story.

"We want to be free." The voices merged, the left eye still glowing red, the right burning yellow. "Our sister may be prepared to sacrifice herself. But we are not. Our sister may be in thrall to Dee and the Elders. We are not. We did not side with the humani after the fall of Danu Talis, but we did not fight against them either. In time, the humani even came to worship us, and their worship made us stronger. Every war they fought, every battle won or lost, they fed us with their pain and memories. They even mourned us when we disappeared from the World of Men. And that is more than any of our own clan, kith or kin did. None of them cared or raised an objection when the Morrigan bound us, trapped us, enchanted us. Sorceress, we owe loyalty to neither Elder nor Next Generation."

Perenelle pressed the butt of the spear on the muddy floor, holding the wood just below the metal head, and leaned on it. The muddy sigil pulsed softly, like a slowly beating heart, warm against the side of her face, and she could feel the faintest thrumming through the length of wood.

"Free us," the Crow Goddess continued urgently, "and we will be in your debt."

"It's a very tempting offer," Perenelle said. "But how do I know I can trust you? How do I know you will not set upon me the moment I free you?"

The web-trapped creature smiled, black lips drawing back

261

from long white teeth. "Because we will give you our word—the word of a warrior, the unbreakable word of the Crow Goddess," the yellow-eyed goddess snapped.

"And because you have the spear inscribed with the Archon glyph," the red-eyed goddess added.

"Archon?" Perenelle asked. She had heard the word perhaps twice before in her long lifetime.

"Before the Elders, the Twelve Archons ruled this planet."

"Before the Elders?"

"The world is older and wilder than you think." The Crow Goddess smiled. "Far older. Much wilder."

Perenelle nodded. "I have always believed that." The idea of the Archons was fascinating—Nicholas would love it—but she focused on more practical matters. "Can you carry me from the island?" she wondered aloud. Her grip tightened on the spear. Much depended on the creature's answer.

There was a moment's hesitation, and then the goddess said, "We cannot do that. As light as you are, you would be too heavy for us. Those of us, Elder and Next Generation, who have the ability to fly have almost hollow bones. We're not strong."

The Sorceress nodded and relaxed. She had already known the answer; nearly two centuries earlier, she had fought a nest of Next Generation harpies on the Palatine Hill above Rome in Italy. She'd discovered then that despite their ferocious appearance and deadly claws, they lacked physical strength. In the time it had taken Nicholas to find a sword and spear in their baggage, Perenelle had swatted them out of the air with her leather cloak and then used her whip, which was woven from a handful of snakes she had pulled from the Medusa's hair, to turn the creatures to stone. If the Crow Goddess had told her that they could carry her off the island, she would have known they were lying.

"At the moment when you thought our sister had died," the Crow Goddess continued, "we sensed your sorrow, your regret at her passing. Free us, Sorceress, and while we control this body, we will not move against you or yours. That is our oath to you."

Unlike her husband, Nicholas, who was a man of science, Perenelle Flamel was a creature of intuition. She always followed her instinct; it rarely failed her, and if she was wrong now and the Crow Goddess attacked her, then she was hoping that a combination of her power and the deadly spear would be effective against the creature.

"Give me your word, then," Perenelle demanded.

"You have it," the two voices buzzed. "We will not harm you. We owe you a debt of honor."

"Close your eyes," Perenelle commanded. She stepped forward, leveling the spear at the web. Gray-white smoke drifted in tall vertical lines and cobwebs hissed and sizzled as she pressed the spearhead to the sticky threads. She tried to cut the strands that would ease the bound Crow Goddess down gently, but then she remembered that this was a creature that was almost impervious to pain. The spear moved in a huge slashing X and the creature tumbled to the ground without a sound. Although free of the web, she was still tightly wrapped in thread.

The red and yellow eyes opened. "Careful, Sorceress," the Crow Goddess muttered as Perenelle approached, holding the spear in both hands. The eyes fixed on the smoking blade. "A cut could be lethal."

"I'll remember that," the Sorceress promised as she carefully, delicately sliced away the almost-invisible cocoon, then peeled it back and freed the Crow Goddess.

The creature surged to her feet and brushed strands of sticky web off her leather cuirass. Then she stretched, leather cracking as she spread her arms wide and arched her back. Both voices buzzed together. "Oh, but it is good to be alive again."

"Is there any danger that the Morrigan could reappear?" Perenelle asked, straightening up, holding tightly onto the spear. A single movement would bring it down on the Crow Goddess.

Eyes flowed from red to yellow, then back to red again. "We will keep our baby sister under control." Then the head snapped around to look at something over Perenelle's shoulder.

Even as she was turning, the woman found herself wondering if she was falling for the oldest trick in the book.

Juan Manuel de Ayala floated framed in the entrance to the cell. The ghost's eyes and mouth were empty holes, and long curling strands of his essence streamed off into the tunnel behind it like a wavering flag.

"What is it?" Perenelle demanded, immediately knowing

something was wrong. She waved the spear and the ghost briefly solidified as it looked away from the Crow Goddess and focused on the glowing metal head. "Trouble?"

"*Nereus has come.*" The ghost's voice was high with terror. "*The Old Man of the Sea is here.*"

"Where?" Perenelle demanded.

"*Here!*" the ghost shouted, and turned, his left arm rising to point into the gloom. "*He's just climbed up out of the sea at the other end of the tunnel. He's coming for you!*"

And then the stench of long-dead rotting fish and rancid blubber rolled down the length of the tunnel.

# CHAPTER THIRTY-THREE

Sparking, snapping and crackling, bright red flames roared
upward, dirty black oily smoke coiling and twisting into the
night air over the car yard. John Dee threw back his head and
breathed deeply; all he could smell was the stink of burning
rubber and oil, he could detect no magic on the air. "I'm
going inside," he said, looking at Bastet.

"I would not advise that," the cat-headed goddess
warned.

"Why not?"

The Dark Elder showed her teeth in what might have
passed for a terrifying smile. She pulled her long black coat
tighter around her narrow shoulders. "It would be a shame if
one of the Wild Hunt mistook you for an enemy or the Archon decided to make you one of his pack. He lost wolves
this night; he will need to replace them."

"I am not completely defenseless, madam," Dee said. From beneath his coat he pulled the short stone sword Excalibur and strode across the empty street toward the car yard. He stopped at the thick gates. The heavy metal was studded with punctures from the teeth on the Archon's club, and where the metal had split, it had been pulled apart and curled like aluminum foil. Dee brought the sword close to where the Archon would have touched the metal, but nothing happened. If Cernunnos had used any magical power, Excalibur would have reacted, but the blade remained cold and dark. Dee nodded; the creature had used brute strength to tear open the gates. He was beginning to wonder just how much auric or magical power Cernunnos possessed. Legend spoke of the Archons—and even the earliest Elders, the Great Elders, who had come after them—as being either giants or hideous monsters, and sometimes both. But they were never described as magicians or sorcerers. It was the Great Elders who had first developed those abilities.

Dee bit back a smile; now that he suspected that Cernunnos possessed little or no magical power, he was starting to feel more confident. The creature had suggested that it could read his mind, but it could have been lying. He tried to recall exactly what the Archon had said when it had first appeared.

"Your thoughts and memories are mine to read, Magician. I know what you know; I know what you have been, I know what you are now."

Well, that meant nothing. Cernunnos claimed he knew

Dee's thoughts but had not proved it in any way. Dee knew that his Elder had briefed the Archon.

"The Alchemyst, Flamel, and the children are with the Saracen Knight and the Bard behind their makeshift metal fortress. You want me and the Wild Hunt to force an entrance for you."

Cernunnos had not revealed anything new, either. It was merely repeating a fact—a fact Dee already knew—and then stating the orders it had received from the Elder. It had only made it sound as if it were reading Dee's thoughts.

Dr. John Dee laughed softly. The creature was certainly ancient, powerful and undoubtedly deadly. But suddenly, it didn't seem quite so frightening.

Gripping the sword tightly, he slipped through the entrance into the narrow metal alleyway. He could hear the fire; it was closer now, crackling and moaning, painting the walls in dancing darting shadows. Dee realized that with every step, he sent up billowing clouds of gritty dust. Squeezing his lips tightly shut, he pulled a white handkerchief from his pocket and pressed it to his mouth: he didn't want to breathe in the gritty remains of the Wild Hunt. He'd been a magician, a sorcerer, a necromancer and an alchemist for too long, and could easily imagine what foul properties the dust contained. He certainly didn't want them in his lungs.

He walked over stone-tipped wooden arrows and leaf-bladed spears and discovered that the ground was littered with short crossbow bolts. The sight took him back to his youth. He'd attended sieges, had studied warfare at the court of Elizabeth and could tell from the broken remains what had taken place: the defenders had trapped most of the Wild Hunt in the narrow alleyway and reduced them to dust. But why had they not held this position and continued to fire down and into the attackers? he wondered. Because they had run out of ammunition, he thought, answering his own question, and had been forced to withdraw to a more defensible position. Beneath the white handkerchief, Dee's lips broke into a broad smile. History had taught him that once the defenders started to retreat, the siege was coming to an end. Flamel and the others were trapped.

Emerging from the metal alleyway, he spotted the flaming moat. It completely encircled a mean-looking metal hut in the center of the camp. Dee hurried forward; he knew a dozen spells that would put out the fire, or he could transmute the oil into sand and use a separate Persian spell that would turn the sand into glass.

The Alchemyst and the twins stood on the opposite side of the fire, the boy and girl close together. Firelight turned their blond hair red and gold. Two other humani stood alongside them, one tall and bulky in black armor, the other short and slight in mismatched armor. Red-haired Gabriel Hounds, in both human and dog shapes, gathered protectively around the shorter man.

The Archon stood outlined before the dancing flames, firelight playing on its rack of antlers, while behind it what remained of the Wild Hunt waited patiently. The wolves' human faces tracked Dee's movements as he picked his way across the potholed expanse of mud. Without moving its body, Cernunnos twisted its head around to regard the Magician. The Horned God's eyes fixed on the stone blade in his hands, which had now started to leak a cold blue smoke.

"Excalibur and Clarent together in the same place," Cernunnos's buzzing voice murmured in Dee's skull. "These are indeed momentous times. Do you know when last these two swords were united?"

Dee was about to tell him that both swords had been in Paris the previous day but decided not to say anything to irritate the creature. A terrifyingly nasty plan was beginning to form at the back of his mind, something so incomprehensible that he was almost afraid to focus on the idea—just in case Cernunnos really could read his thoughts. Taking up a position to the left of the creature, he held Excalibur in his right hand and folded his arms across his chest. The glowing blue blade painted the left-hand side of his face in chill color. "I believe it was here, in England," Dee said. "When Arthur fought his nephew Mordred on Salisbury Plain. Mordred used Clarent to kill Arthur," he added.

"I killed Arthur," Cernunnos said softly. "Mordred too. And he was Arthur's son, not his nephew." The Horned God's head turned back to the fire. "You are a magician; I presume you can douse these flames?"

"Of course." A new smell permeated the already foul air: the rotten-egg stink of brimstone. "Can you not cross through the fire?" he asked, deliberately testing the limits of the Horned God's powers.

"The flames are laced with metal," Cernunnos said shortly.

270

Dee nodded. He knew from experience that some metals—especially iron—were poisonous to Elders. And to Archons, too, he'd just discovered. He wondered if the two races were related in any way; he had always assumed that while they were similar, they were separate, like Elders and humani.

"I can kill the fire," Dee answered confidently.

The Archon leaned forward, its ripe forest odor suddenly strong as it stared hard into the fire and beyond. Dee followed the direction of its gaze and found it was staring at the boy, Josh. "You can have the twins, Magician, and your pages. I claim the three immortal humani and the Gabriel Hounds for my own."

"Agreed," Dee said immediately.

"And Clarent. I claim the Sword of Fire."

"Of course you can have it," Dee said without hesitation. He deliberately allowed his aura to blossom yellow and stinking around him, knowing it would blanket his thoughts. He had no intention of giving Cernunnos the sword. Dee had spent centuries searching for Excalibur's twin blade and was not prepared to see it disappear into some distant Shadowrealm with the Horned God. His outrageous plan suddenly came together. "I would be honored to present the sword to you myself."

"I would allow that," the Archon said, a touch of arrogance in its voice.

Dee bowed his head so that the creature would not see the triumph in his eyes. He would stand before the Archon, Excalibur in his right hand, Clarent in his left. He would bow

271

to the Horned God and step forward . . . and then plunge both swords into Cernunnos. The Magician's brimstone aura flared brighter and brighter with excitement. What would it feel like, what would he learn, what would he know after he had killed the Archon?

# CHAPTER THIRTY-FOUR

Coughing, eyes streaming, Sophie, Josh and the three immortals scrambled away from the searing heat, slipping and falling on the muddy ground. They were safe behind the wall of fire, but they were also trapped.

Josh helped his sister to her feet. Her bangs had been seared to crispy curls and her cheekbones were bright red, her eyebrows little more than smudges.

Sophie reached out to trace a line over Josh's eyes. "Your eyebrows are gone."

"Yours too." He grinned. He touched his cheekbones. His face felt tight, his lips dry and cracked, and he suddenly realized how lucky they'd been. If he'd been standing a couple of inches closer to the moat, he would have been badly burned. Sophie reached out and pressed her little finger against his cheek and he smelled vanilla as a soothing coolness touched his scorched skin. He caught his sister's hand and lifted it away from his face; the pad of her little finger was coated with silver. "You shouldn't be using your powers," he said, concerned.

"It's a simple healing—laying on of hands, Joan called it. It uses little or no aura. We'll never have cuts or bruises again." She smiled.

"I've got a feeling we'll need to be worried about more serious things than cuts," Josh said. He turned to look through the burning curtain of fire. The Horned God stood patiently on the far side of the flames. Its arms were folded across its massive chest, and the smoldering ruin of its club lay at its feet. Although hundreds of the Wild Hunt had turned to dust, at least twice that number still remained. Most had gathered in a semicircle behind Cernunnos, either sitting or lying down, their shockingly human faces staring fixedly at their master. Josh turned in a complete circle. The rest of the Wild Hunt had taken up positions around the camp. They were completely surrounded. "What are they doing?" he wondered aloud.

"Waiting," Palamedes rumbled from behind him.

Josh turned. "Waiting?"

"They know the fire will not burn for long."

"How long?"

"An hour. Maybe two." He turned his face to the skies, gauging the time. "Maybe till midnight, but that's not long enough." He shrugged. The knight's black armor was streaked with mud and dirt and smelled of oil. It squeaked and creaked with every movement. "We built this fortress more for privacy than protection, though it has kept us safe

274

from some of the less savory creatures that haunt this land. It was never designed to keep something like Cernunnos away." He suddenly looked sidelong at Sophie as a thought struck him, his eyes liquid in the reflected firelight. "You have mastered Fire. You could keep the flames alive."

"No," Josh said immediately, instinctively moving in front of his sister. "Even attempting something like that could kill her, burn her up."

The Alchemyst nodded. "Sophie would need to keep the fires burning till dawn; she's not strong enough for that. Not yet. We need to find an alternative."

"I know some spells . . . ," Shakespeare began. "You too, Palamedes. And what of you, Nicholas? Working together, surely we three could—" And then the Bard's head snapped around, nostrils flaring, eyes narrowing.

"What is it?" Palamedes asked, turning to squint through the wall of fire.

"Dee," Shakespeare and Flamel said together. Even as they were speaking, the figure of a small man standing alongside the Archon was outlined in sulfurous yellow. He was holding a smoldering blue sword.

"With Excalibur," Flamel added.

As the group watched, the Magician plunged Excalibur into the fiery wall and twisted the blade. Hissing and sizzling, the stone sword pierced the fire, and then a sudden downdraft of icy wind opened a perfectly circular hole, like a window, in the raging flames. Dee peered through the opening and smiled, the fire reflecting off his teeth, bloodred. "Well, well, well, what have we here? Master Shakespeare—

apprentice to both the Alchemyst and the Magician. Why, it is practically a family reunion. And Palamedes, the Black Knight, reunited—almost—with the swords that ruled and ruined your master's life. And the twins, of course. So nice of you to bring them home to me, Nicholas, though it would have been so much more convenient if we had concluded this business on the West Coast. Now I'll have to return them to the States. However, surrender them now and we can avoid a lot of unpleasantness."

The Alchemyst laughed, though there was nothing humorous in the sound. "Aren't you forgetting something, John?"

The Magician tilted his head to one side. "You seem to be trapped, Nicholas, behind flames, and surrounded by the Wild Hunt." He jerked his thumb at the huge figure standing by his side. "And, of course, Cernunnos. This time, there is no escape. Not even for you."

"We three immortals are not without power," Flamel said quietly. "Can you stand against all of us?"

"Oh, I don't have to," Dee said. "All I have to do is douse the fire. Even you cannot prevail against an Archon and the Wild Hunt."

Josh stepped forward, Clarent a blaze of black light in his left hand, the dancing shadows making his face look older than its fifteen years. "And what about us? It would be a mistake to forget about us," he snapped. "You were in Paris. You saw what we did to the gargoyles."

"And Nidhogg," Sophie added, at his side.

Clarent moaned and then Josh snapped it forward toward

Excalibur. The swords met in the circular opening in the midst of the fire, the two blades crossing in an explosion of black and blue sparks.

And Dee's thoughts washed over Josh.

*Fear. A terrible all-consuming fear of beastlike creatures and shadowy humans.*

*Loss. Countless faces, men, women and children, family, friends and neighbors. All dead.*

*Anger. The overriding emotion was one of anger—a simmering all-consuming rage.*

*Hunger. An insatiable hunger for knowledge, for power.*

*Cernunnos. The Horned God. The Archon. Lying dead in the mud with Dee standing over him, holding Clarent and Excalibur in either hand, the swords blazing red-black and blue-white flames.*

The thoughts and emotions came at Josh like blows. He felt his head jerk with each startling image. But the most shocking of all was the sight of the Archon lying in the mud. Dee intended to kill Cernunnos. But to do that he needed Clarent. And Josh was not giving up the Sword of Fire. He tightened his grip on the hilt and pushed hard against Excalibur, but it was like pushing against a rock wall. Holding the sword in both hands, he pressed back against Dee's sword again, stone grating and sparking, but it didn't move. The reflected light turned Dee's face into a grinning skull.

Josh had seen Sophie focus her aura, had watched her shape it around her body; he'd felt its healing properties on his own skin, but he had no idea *how* she did it. Joan had trained her. But he'd had no one to train him. "Sis . . . ?"

"I'm here." Sophie was instantly by his side.

"How did you . . ." He groped for the right word. "How do you get your aura to focus?"

"I don't know. I just . . . I guess I just concentrate really hard."

Josh took a deep breath and frowned, forehead creasing, eyebrows knitting together, concentrating as hard as he could.

Nothing happened.

"Close your eyes," Sophie said. "Visualize really clearly what you want to see happen. Start with something small, tiny . . ."

Josh nodded. He took another deep breath and squeezed his eyes tightly shut. Sophie could focus her aura into her little finger, so why couldn't he just—

There was an instant when he felt something churn in his stomach; then it surged up through his chest, down along both arms, into his hands, which were wrapped around the hilt of the sword. His aura exploded into blazing, blinding light that flowed down the weapon.

Clarent moaned, the sound one of pure agony as the stone blade turned to solid gold. The instant it touched Dee's sword, it doused Excalibur's cold blue-white fire, turning it back to plain gray stone.

Josh blinked in surprise.

And his aura winked out of existence.

Instantly, the gold fire faded from Clarent and was replaced with crimson-black fire. Excalibur reignited in a huge explosion of sparks. Staggered and shaking, Josh managed to retain his grip on Clarent, but the shocking force had sent Dee flying backward, sending up a geyser of mud. He then slid on his back across the filthy oily ground, and Excalibur tumbled through the air to fall point-first into the mud close to his head.

It took a tremendous effort for Josh to pull Clarent back out of the fire. Immediately, the circular window in the flames snapped shut. The boy's face was ghastly, deep blue-black shadows under his eyes, but he still managed a shaky smile for his twin. "See: that was no problem."

Sophie reached out for her brother and put her hand on his shoulder. He felt a trickle of energy from her aura flow into his body, steadying his wobbly legs.

"I wonder what Dee will do next?" she said.

A heartbeat later, thunder boomed and rumbled and lightning flashed almost directly overhead. The rain that followed was torrential.

# CHAPTER THIRTY-FIVE

*P*erenelle sloshed through the muddy tunnel, heading back toward the ladder. In one hand she carried the spear; the other was clamped over her nose, but she could feel the nauseating fishy smell coating her tongue and taste it in her throat every time she swallowed.

Juan Manuel de Ayala floated beside her, facing back down the tunnel. There was no sign of the Crow Goddess.

"What are you frightened of?" Perenelle demanded. "You're a ghost; nothing can harm you." Then she smiled, and her voice softened. "I'm sorry. I didn't mean to snap. I know what an extraordinary effort it took for you to reach the cave mouth and warn me."

*"It was easier once you broke the Spell of Binding,"* the ghost said. Much of his essence had dissipated, leaving only the merest hint of his face and the outline of his head hanging in the air. His dark shining eyes were brilliant in the

gloom. *"Nereus is every sailor's nightmare,"* he admitted. *"And I am not frightened for myself; I fear for you, Sorceress."*

"What's the worst that can happen?" Perenelle asked lightly. "He can only kill me. Or try to."

The ghost's eyes turned liquid. *"Oh, he'll not kill you. Not immediately. He'll drag you down to some undersea kingdom and keep you alive for centuries. And when he is finished with you, he'll turn you into some sea creature—like a sea cow or a dugong."*

"That's just a story . . . ," Perenelle began, and then stopped, realizing just how ridiculous her statement was: she was running down an underground tunnel accompanied by a ghost, pursuing an ancient Celtic goddess and being followed by the Old Man of the Sea. Reaching the end of the tunnel, she craned her neck and looked up. Far above her, she could see a circle of blue sky.

She tore a narrow strip off the ragged hem of her dress and tied it around her waist. Shoving the spear into the back of the makeshift belt, she reached up to grab the slimy metal rungs of the rusting ladder.

*"Perenelle!"* de Ayala howled as he flowed upward.

"Leaving so soon, Sorceress?" The voice echoed down the corridor, liquid and bubbling, a gurgling, gargling sound.

Perenelle turned and tossed a tiny spark of light down the tunnel. Like a rubber ball, it bounced off the ceiling, hit a wall, then the ground, and bounced up again.

Nereus filled the darkness.

The instant before he reached out and crushed the light in his web-fingered hand, Perenelle caught a glimpse of a stocky, surprisingly normal-looking man, a head of thick curly hair flowing to his shoulders, mingling with a short beard that was twisted into two tight curls. He was wearing a sleeveless jerkin of overlapping kelp leaves and strands of green seaweed, and in his left hand he held a wickedly spiked stone trident. As the light faded and the tunnel plunged back into darkness, Perenelle realized that the Old Man of the Sea had no lower limbs. Below the waist, eight octopus legs writhed and coiled across the corridor.

The stink of rotting fish intensified, there was a flicker of movement and then one suckered leg wrapped itself around Perenelle's ankle and held fast. A second, sticky and slimy, attached itself to her shin.

"Stay awhile," Nereus gurgled. Another leg snapped around Perenelle's knee, suckers biting deep into her skin. His laughter was like a wet sponge being squeezed dry. "I insist."

# CHAPTER THIRTY-SIX

*J*osh sat, dazed, as the wall of fire started to die down in a billowing cloud of thick white steam. Rain churned the ground to thick sticky mud as thunder rumbled continuously overhead. Lightning flashed, painting everything ash white and ebony black.

"Time to go," Palamedes said decisively, rainwater running off his helmet. He turned to look at Sophie and Josh, Nicholas and Shakespeare. They were all soaked through, the twins' hair plastered to their skulls. "There is a time to fight and a time to run. A good soldier always knows when it is time to do either. We can stand here and fight Dee and Cernunnos and none of us will survive. Except you, perhaps," he said to the twins. Firelight ran amber off his dark skin and matching armor. "Though I am not sure what your quality of life would be in service to the Dark Elders.

Nor how long you would survive when they were finished with you."

Bitter smoke curled around them, thick, cloying and noxious, driving them back toward the metal hut.

"Will, take the Gabriel Hounds—"

"I'm not running," the Bard said immediately.

"I'm not asking you to run," Palamedes snapped. "I want you to regroup and not needlessly sacrifice our forces."

"*Our* forces?" Nicholas asked. "Don't tell me the Saracen Knight has finally chosen a side?"

"Temporarily, I assure you," Palamedes said. He turned back to the Bard. "Will, take the Gabriel Hounds through the tunnel under the hut. Gabriel," he called. The largest of the dogmen hurried over. The blue tattoos on his cheeks were covered in mud and speckled blood, and his dun-colored hair stuck up in all directions. "Protect your master. Get him out of London and bring him to the Great Henge. Wait for me there."

Shakespeare opened his mouth to protest but closed it when the Saracen Knight glared at him.

Gabriel nodded. "It will be done. How long should we wait at the Henge?"

"If I am not back by sundown tomorrow, then take Will to one of the nearby Shadowrealms; Avalon or Lyonesse, perhaps. You should be safe there."

Ignoring the Alchemyst, Gabriel turned bloodshot eyes to look at the twins. "And what of the two that are one?"

Josh and Sophie waited silently as Palamedes took a deep

breath. "I'm going to bring them back into London." He looked at the Alchemyst. "We'll take them to the king."

The dogman's savage teeth flashed in a smile. "Leaving them with Cernunnos might be safer."

Sophie and Josh sat in the back of the black London taxi and watched the Alchemyst, Shakespeare and Palamedes huddle together around a flaming barrel that was burning chunks of wood and strips of smoldering black tires. Rain steamed and hissed over the flames, and thick white smoke from the dying moat fires mingled with the greasy black fumes coming out of the barrel.

"I can see their auras," Josh muttered wearily. The unexpected appearance of his own aura had exhausted him. A sick headache pounded just over his eyes, the muscles in his arms and legs were burning and his stomach felt queasy, almost as if he was going to throw up. His hands were numb where they'd gripped Clarent's hilt.

Sophie turned to look out the steamed-up window. Josh was correct: the three immortals were outlined with the faintest of auras—Flamel's emerald green and Palamedes' deeper olive green bracketing Shakespeare's pale lemon yellow.

"What are they doing?" Josh asked.

Sophie hit the window button, but the car was turned off and the electric windows didn't work. She rubbed the palm of her hand across the glass to clear it, then caught her breath. The immortal's auras brightened, and she could feel the crawling trickle of power as it started to dribble from their hands like sticky liquid into the barrel. "Nicholas and Palamedes seem to be lending their power to Shakespeare. The Bard's lips are moving, he's saying something. . . ." She cracked open the door to listen, blinking as a sprinkling of rain spattered into the darkened interior of the car.

". . . imagination is the key, brother immortals," Shakespeare said. "All I need you to do is to concentrate and I can create a charm of powerful trouble."

"It's a conjugation," Sophie said in awe. She was abruptly conscious that this was a word she would never have used days earlier, one she wouldn't have even understood.

Josh slid over beside his sister to peer out into the wet night. "What's a conjur . . . conjurgate . . . ?"

"He's creating something out of nothing, shaping and making something simply by imagining it." She pushed open the door a little farther, ignoring the rain on her face. She knew—because the Witch knew—that this was the most arduous and exhausting of all the magics, requiring extraordinary skill and focus.

"Do it quickly," the Alchemyst said through gritted teeth. "The fire is nearly out and I'm not sure how much strength I have left."

Shakespeare nodded. He pushed both hands deep into the burning barrel. "Boil and bubble, boil and bubble," he whispered, his accent thickening, returning to the familiar Elizabethan he had grown up with. "First, let us have the serpent of the Nile. . . ."

Smoke twisted and curled around the barrel, which

suddenly boiled with hundreds of heaving snakes. They tumbled onto the ground.

"Snakes! Why are there always snakes?" Josh groaned and looked away.

". . . spotted snakes with double tongue . . . ," Shakespeare continued.

More snakes spilled from the barrel, writhing and slithering around the immortals' feet. The Gabriel Hounds silently backed away, red eyes fixed on the serpents.

"And now for some thorny hedgehogs, newts and blind worms . . . ," Shakespeare continued, his voice rising and falling in a singsong pattern, as if he were repeating a verse. His head was thrown back and his eyes were closed. ". . . and toads, ugly and venomous," he added, his voice becoming hoarse.

Creatures cascaded from the barrel, hundreds of fat hedgehogs, grotesque toads, slithering newts and curling worms.

". . . and finally, screech owls . . ."

A dozen owls erupted from the flames in a shower of sparks.

Shakespeare suddenly slumped and would have fallen if the Saracen Knight had not caught him. "Enough," Palamedes said.

"Enough?" The Bard opened his eyes and looked around. They were standing ankle-deep in the creatures that had burst from the burning barrel. The ground around them was thick with twisting snakes, hopping toads, curling newts and wriggling worms. "Aye, 'tis done." Lightning flashed overhead as he reached out to squeeze the Alchemyst's arm and quickly embraced the Saracen Knight. "Thank you, my brothers, my friends. When shall we three meet again?" he asked.

"Tomorrow night," Palamedes said. "Now go, go now." He carefully lifted his left leg. A black adder dripped from his ankle. "How long will these last?" he asked.

"Long enough." Shakespeare smiled. Brushing strands of lank hair out of his eyes, he raised his hand to the twins in the car. "We only part to meet again."

"You didn't write that," Palamedes said quickly.

"I know, but I wish I had." Then, surrounded by the hounds, William Shakespeare slipped under the metal hut and disappeared. Gabriel waited until the other hounds had followed him.

"Keep him safe," Palamedes called.

"I will protect him with my life," Gabriel said in his soft Welsh accent. "Tell me, though." He nodded to the mass of creatures in the mud. "These . . . things . . . ?" He left the question unfinished.

Palamedes' smile was ferocious. "A little present for the Wild Hunt."

The Gabriel Hound nodded, then stooped and transformed into his huge dog form before squirming under the hut and vanishing.

And then, with a final sizzling hiss, the moat fires went out. "Time to go," Flamel said, carefully picking his way through the creatures Shakespeare had conjured. "I didn't know he could do that."

"Created them entirely out of his imagination," Palamedes said. He held open the cab door and ushered the Alchemyst into the back of the car. "Buckle up," he advised, his black armor winked out of existence. "It's going to be a bumpy ride."

The torrential rain died as quickly as it had started, and then the wolves of the Wild Hunt leapt through the gray smoke.

A moment later, Cernunnos stepped across the moat, smoke twisting through its antlers. Throwing back its head, it bellowed a triumphant laugh. "And where do you think you are going?" it demanded, striding toward the car. "There is no escape from the Horned God."

# CHAPTER THIRTY-SEVEN

*H*olding tightly to the metal rung with one hand, Perenelle tugged the spear free and stabbed it hard into one of the octopus legs holding her. The metal barely touched the slimy skin, but the leg was abruptly snatched back, leaving the woman with a series of puckered sucker marks on her flesh. Before she could stab the creature again, the other two legs disappeared back into the dark tunnel.

"Sorceress, that was positively rude. You could have injured me. A little deeper and you would have cut my leg off."

"That was the idea," Perenelle muttered, shoving the spear back into the makeshift belt and pulling herself up.

"I have not lost a leg in centuries. And it takes such a long time to grow a new one," the creature added petulantly in Greek, its accent appalling.

Ignoring him, Perenelle climbed up another rung, moving closer to the light. She wondered if Nereus would even be able to fit into the narrow shaft. The creature's sickening stench rolled over her, making her eyes water. She swallowed hard as she felt her stomach protest. Shifting sideways in the narrow passageway, she looked down. Nereus was standing at the bottom of the shaft. She could just about make out his head and shoulders in the dim light from above; thankfully, everything below that was hidden in shadow. He raised his trident and waved. "It seems you are trapped, Sorceress. You cannot climb *and* stab me with your toothpick. But you are not beyond my reach. . . ."

Perenelle caught a glimpse of wriggling octopus legs at the bottom of the shaft. First one, then two, then four, began to snake their way toward her, curling and coiling, feeling along the dripping stones like creeping fingers. "Have you any idea just who I am?" she demanded in English. She repeated the question in ancient Greek.

Nereus shrugged, a movement that sent all his legs rippling. "I confess I do not."

"Then why are you here?" Perenelle asked, pulling herself up another rung of the rusting ladder. She thought he sounded like a bored academic.

"I am paying off an age-old debt," Nereus bubbled. "One of the Great Elders told me that my debt to them would be wiped clean if I returned to this world and came to this island with my daughters. I was told I could have you for myself and that while you would make only an average servant, you might, perhaps after a century or two, make a good wife. All I know is that you are called a sorceress."

"But do you know *which* sorceress?" Perenelle demanded.

The creature laughed. "Oh, humani, I do not know, nor do I care. In my time, the word had meaning. A sorceress was someone with power, someone to fear, someone to respect. But here, in this time and in this world, the old words, the old titles, mean nothing. Why, a magician, I have discovered, is nothing more than a children's entertainer, someone who pulls rabbits out of hats."

Perenelle's laugh shocked the Dark Elder to silence. "Then you should know this, Old Man: I am no entertainer. I'm surprised your Elder didn't tell you who you were facing on this island. Or perhaps not so surprised. Maybe if you had known, you would not have embarked on this foolish venture." Perenelle's voice echoed down the shaft. "I am the seventh daughter of a seventh daughter. I have lived upon this earth for nearly seven hundred years, and I carry within me the wisdom of the ages. I have trained with some of the finest sorcerers and magicians, wizards and enchanters who ever lived. Some even you will have heard of. I was apprenticed to the Witch of Endor and I am a pupil of two of the greatest sorceresses in history: Circe and Medea."

"Circe?" Nereus rustled uncomfortably, legs quivering. "Medea?" he added, sounding miserable.

"You, above all others, should know my teachers' reputations."

"And were you a good pupil?" Nereus inquired cautiously.

"The best. Know this, Old Man of the Sea: I will never be your wife. I am wed to the Alchemyst, Nicholas Flamel."

*"Oh,"* the Elder said very softly.

"I am the immortal human Perenelle Flamel."

"Ah—that sorceress," Nereus mumbled.

"Yes, that sorceress." Perenelle wrenched a metal spike from the wall, concentrated her aura in the palm of her hand and watched the rusty metal twist and curl, then melt into dirty brown liquid. "Let me show you a trick Circe herself taught me." Opening her hand, she allowed the metal droplets to dribble from her cupped palm. Scores of tiny golden-brown globes fell into the shadows. The molten rain hissed and sizzled as it scattered across Nereus's flesh, and the air suddenly filled with the reek of frying fish. Octopus legs thrashed and pounded against the stones as the Old Man of the Sea howled and squealed in a score of human and inhuman languages. Perenelle flicked the last droplet off her fingertips. She followed the golden teardrop as it plunged straight down . . . and landed right in the center of Nereus's forehead, just above his nose. This time he screamed so loudly Perenelle could actually hear the sudden explosion of wings as the thousands of seabirds gathered on the island above rose high into the air, crying and calling.

Nereus disappeared into the shadows, trailing the smell of burnt fish in his wake. "You have not heard the last of me, Sorceress Perenelle," he sobbed. "You will never escape alive!"

Fighting the wave of exhaustion that washed over her, Perenelle turned back to the ladder and pulled herself upward. "That's what everyone says," she murmured. "But I'm still alive."

✧   ✧   ✧

"You could have helped." Perenelle was sitting on one of the steps in the exercise yard. She turned her face to the afternoon sun and allowed the warmth to soak into her body and recharge her aura.

"Why?" Perched on a step below and to Perenelle's right, the Crow Goddess had spread her black cloak out about her and had also turned her face to the sunlight, eyes lost behind mirrored black sunglasses. Her skin had returned to its former alabaster and only the faintest hint of green remained, with the puckered suggestion of pimples around her lips.

Perenelle took a moment to consider and then she nodded. She had no answer to that. Nereus was not their enemy.

"We could have flown away, too," the Crow Goddess suggested without moving her head.

Perenelle was beginning to identify the voices; the Badb's was slightly softer than the harsher and more masculine Machas's.

"Why didn't you?" Perenelle asked. When she'd finally climbed out of the shaft, filthy and almost sick with exhaustion, she'd known that she was in no condition to fight the Crow Goddess. She hadn't expected to find the creature still on the island at all, but it had been crouched by the entrance to the shaft beneath the rusting water tower, carefully sewing long black feathers back onto its cloak. "Why did you stay?"

The Crow Goddess stirred. "We have been trapped within the Morrigan for a long time. She's had lifetimes of

294

fun; now it's our turn. And we decided that there would be no place more exciting than Alcatraz in the hours to come."

Perenelle eased herself up on her elbows to look down at the creature. "Exciting? I think we might have two different definitions of that word."

The Crow Goddess moved her head and eased her dark glasses down her nose with a long black-nailed finger. One red and one yellow eye blinked at the woman. "Remember, humani, we are the Badb and Macha. We are Fury and Slaughter. Our sister is Death. For millennia, we have been drawn to battlefields the world over, where we feasted on the pain and memories of the dead and dying." Black lips pulled back from long white teeth in a terrifying grin. "And right now, this island is exactly where we need to be." She licked her lips. "I think there is going to be a banquet for us soon!"

# CHAPTER THIRTY-EIGHT

$\mathcal{T}$ires spinning in the mud, the heavy taxicab lurched forward. Sophie gasped as her seat belt locked tight, pulling her back into the seat. Josh groaned as his jerked across his aching stomach.

"Sorry!" Palamedes shouted. "Hang on. Here they come. . . ."

Nicholas grabbed the rubber strap over the door and leaned forward. "We're heading straight toward them!" he said, voice rising in alarm.

"I know." Palamedes' bright teeth flashed in the gloom. "Best form of defense is . . ."

". . . attack," Josh finished.

A solid line of the human-faced wolves launched themselves at the cab. Barreling through the still-steaming fire, they did not see the carpet of snakes until it was too late. The serpents rose like question marks, mouths gaping, heads jerking . . . and the front line of the Wild Hunt dissolved into filthy dust that exploded onto the window, completely coating it. Palamedes calmly squirted water on the glass and hit the windshield wiper switch, but all he succeeded in doing was turning the gray dust into a thick paste.

A trio of huge wolves, bigger and broader than any of the others, leapt across the moat . . . and straight onto the hedgehogs. Bristling spines rose to pierce the wolves' legs and paws. The beasts crumbled to powder with looks of absolute surprise on their faces.

Cernunnos howled and bellowed as he blundered onto the carpet of serpents and hedgehogs. The snakes struck at him, hedgehog spines stabbed, but without any obvious effect. Josh shuddered and felt sick to his stomach as he watched snakes curl and twist up the Horned God's trunklike legs.

Palamedes revved the cab's engine, then threw it into gear and roared across the narrow metal bridge that spanned the moat, meeting another trio of the Wild Hunt head-on. Two disappeared beneath the tires in geysers of grit, while the third leapt onto the hood and hammered on the glass with jagged claws. The windshield cracked and the Saracen Knight stood on the brakes. The car screeched to a halt, sending the wolf sliding off the hood, straight into a nest of vipers.

Josh turned in his seat to watch more of the Wild Hunt fall as they brushed past the oily skin of the poisonous toads; he saw others turn to dust as they stumbled across the newts or trod on worms. The air grew thick and gritty with explosions of opaque dirt. Owls swooped out of the night air, claws

297

extended, scything through the beasts, leaving clouds of dust in their wake.

"Shakespeare created all these?" Sophie asked in wonder. She was staring out the back windshield and could see that the ground was carpeted with the heaving mass.

"Every single one," Palamedes said proudly. "Each one generated within his imagination and animated by his aura. And you have to remember, he is mostly self-taught." The knight glanced in the rearview mirror and caught the Alchemyst's eye. "Think what he could have achieved if he'd been properly trained."

Nicholas shrugged uncomfortably. "I could not have taught him this."

"You should have recognized his talent, though."

"Dee!" Josh snapped.

"Aye, Dee did," Palamedes agreed.

"No. Dee. Directly in front of you!" Josh shouted.

Dr. John Dee had crawled out of the smoke and was spinning Excalibur loosely in his left hand, turning it into a whirling circle of blue fire. His right hand dripped yellow energy. And he had taken up a position directly in front of the entrance to the compound, blocking their path.

"What—does he think I'll not run him down?" Palamedes said.

Dee pointed the sword at the cab and then lobbed a ball of energy. It hit the sodden ground, bounced once and then rolled beneath the car. The engine cut out and all the electricity in the vehicle died, sending the car coasting to a halt, power steering locked and useless.

Sophie caught a hint of movement behind them and turned . . . just as the snake-wrapped Archon stepped through the thick gray clouds. "This is no good," she muttered, tugging Josh's sleeve.

"This is bad," her twin agreed when he saw the Archon. "Very bad."

"What do we do now?"

"It's always best to fight just one battle at a time. You win more that way."

"Who said that?" Sophie asked. "Mars?"

"Dad."

# CHAPTER THIRTY-NINE

"Josh!" Nicholas shouted.

Josh Newman pushed open the left-hand door, checked to make sure there were no snakes underfoot and hopped out. Clarent whined and keened as he brought it around to bear on Dee. "I'll keep him busy," he shouted. "Can you get the car started?" he asked the knight.

"I'll try," Palamedes said grimly. He twisted around to look at the Alchemyst. "Battery's dead. Can you recharge it?"

"Josh Newman," Dee said pleasantly as the boy approached. "You cannot honestly be thinking about fighting me?"

Josh ignored him. Holding Clarent tightly, both hands wrapped around the hilt, he felt the sword settle comfortably into his grip.

Dee grinned and continued patiently. "I want you to take a moment and think about what you are contemplating doing. I've spent a lifetime with this weapon; you've had Clarent for little more than a day at most. There is no way you can defeat me."

Without warning Josh launched a blistering attack on the Magician. Clarent actually screamed when it hit Excalibur, a screeching cry of triumph. Josh didn't even try to remember the moves Joan and Scatty had taught him; he allowed the sword to take control, to jab and thrust, to cut and parry. And somewhere at the back of his mind, he knew he was analyzing Dee's every move, noting his footwork, how he held the weapon, how his eyes squinted just before he lunged.

Clarent tugged Josh forward as it slashed through the air. It was all the boy could do to keep both hands around the hilt. It was like trying to hold on to a lunging dog: a ravenous, rabid dog.

And for an instant, Josh had the ridiculous thought that Clarent was alive and hungry.

"Sophie!" Nicholas roared.

But she didn't hear him. Her only focus was her brother. Sophie pushed open the right-hand door and climbed out, her aura sparking the moment her feet touched the ground, sheathing her in a mirror image of the armor she'd seen Joan wear. Unlike Josh, she had no weapon, but she'd been trained in Air and Fire magic. The girl deliberately lowered the barriers Joan of Arc had put in place to protect her from the Witch of Endor's memories. Right now, she needed to know everything the Witch had known about the Archon Cernunnos.

*Rumors, fragments, whispered tales.*

*Once it had been beautiful. A giant; tall, proud and arro-gant. A respected scientist. It had experimented first on others, then, when that was forbidden, upon itself. Finally, it had be-come repulsive, bony outcroppings appearing from its skull, its toes fusing to thick hooves. Only its face remained, a hideous re-minder of its former beauty. The incomprehensible passage of time had destroyed its great intellect, and now it was little more than a beast. Ancient, powerful, still with the ability to warp humans into wolfkind, it inhabited a distant Shadowrealm of dank rotting forests. . . .*

No animal likes fire, Sophie reasoned, and if the Archon lived in a wet forest world, it was probably afraid of fire. She felt the briefest flicker of fear—what if her fire failed her again?—but she savagely quashed the idea. Her magic would not fail her this time. In the heartbeat before she pressed her finger against her tattoo, calling upon the Magic of Fire, she used a tiny portion of her aura to bring the Magic of Air to life.

A whipping tornado appeared around the Archon. The remnants of the Wild Hunt, every particle of dust and grit swirled up to surround Cernunnos in a thick buzzing blan-ket. Blinded, its mouth and nostrils filled with dirt, the crea-ture covered its face. Then Sophie pressed her thumb against the circular tattoo and ignited the dust cloud. In the last sec-ond before she slumped to the earth, unconscious, she was aware of the Horned God's scream. It was the most terrifying sound she had ever heard.

✦   ✦   ✦

"Josh," Dee gasped, desperately parrying the tremendous blows that actually numbed his arms. "There is so much you do not know. So much I can tell you. Questions I can answer."

"There's a lot I already know about you, Magician." Blue-white and red-black sparks exploded every time the twin blades met, showering the fighters with burning specks. Josh's face was flecked with black spots, and Dee's ruined suit was pitted with a score of holes. "You. Were. Thinking. Of. Killing. The. Archon." Josh drove home each word with a blow.

"You've held Clarent," Dee heaved. "You've had a taste of its powers. You know what it can do. Think of it: kill the Archon and you will experience millennia, hundreds of millennia, of knowledge. You will know the history of the world from the very beginning. And not just this world either. A myriad of worlds."

Suddenly, a huge explosion of vanilla-scented heat washed over them and drove them both to their knees. Dee was facing the Archon and crashed backward, hands over his face, blinded by the light. Josh rolled over, saw the Horned God engulfed in green-gold flames and then saw his sister slump unconscious to the ground. Sick with fear, he rolled over onto his hands and knees—and discovered Excalibur lying in the mud by his right hand. His fingers instantly wrapped around the hilt and a bolt of agony shot up through his left hand where he held Clarent. He attempted to drop the Coward's Blade, but he couldn't—it was stuck to his palm, sealed in his clenched fist. Bright red blood seeped between his fingers. He jerked away from Excalibur, and the searing pain in his left hand faded. Scrambling to his feet, he caught the edge of Excalibur's hilt with Clarent's blade, flicked the sword away, then ran around the car to his sister.

Dee scrambled to his knees, blinking glowing afterimages from his eyes. He saw Josh send Excalibur spinning through the air, watched it plop onto the gooey remnants of the steaming moat. It floated on the surface of the thick black oil for a single heartbeat; then the oil bubbled furiously and the blade sank.

Josh dropped to his knees, terrified. He pulled Sophie into his arms and then lifted her onto the backseat just as the engine coughed to life. A sick-looking Nicholas Flamel fell into the car, his hands streaming threads of the green energy he had used to recharge the car.

John Dee had to fling himself out of the way as the car, all its doors still flapping open, howled down the narrow alley, crushing arrows and spears under its wheels. The Magician desperately tried to focus his thoughts and gather enough energy to stop the cab, but he was physically and mentally drained. Pushing himself to his feet, he watched as the Archon crashed to the ground and rolled over and over in the sticky mud, extinguishing the flames that danced and flickered in the furs wrapping its body. Less than a handful of the Wild Hunt had survived the attack, and two of those disappeared into dust as Cernunnos accidentally crushed them.

Metal screaming, sparks fountaining from its fenders and open doors, the black cab scraped through the torn gate and fishtailed onto the damp street as it roared off into the night. Brake lights flared red; then the car turned a corner and vanished.

Standing concealed in the shadows, Bastet pulled a slender cell phone from her pocket and hit a speed dial. Her call was answered on the first ring. "Dee failed," she said shortly, and ended the call.

# CHAPTER FORTY

$\mathcal{S}$ophie woke up as the taxi rumbled over a speed bump. She was completely disoriented, and it took a long moment for what she first thought were fragments of dreams, and then realized were memories, to fade. She could still hear Cernunnos screaming in her head and, for a moment, actually felt sorry for the creature. Rising slowly and stiffly to a sitting position, she looked around. Josh lay slumped in the seat beside her, breathing heavily, face blackened and swollen where he'd been struck with sparks. The Alchemyst sat in shadow up against the window, staring out into the night. Hearing her move, he turned his head, his weary eyes catching reflections from the city lights.

"I was hoping you would sleep a little longer," he said quietly.

"Where are we?" she asked thickly. Her mouth and lips

were dry, and she imagined she could feel the gritty dust of the Wild Hunt on her tongue.

Flamel handed her a bottle of water. "We're on Mill-bank." He gently tapped the window with his finger and she looked out. "We've just driven past the Houses of Parliament."

Through the rear window, Sophie caught a glimpse of the spectacularly lit English parliament building. The lighting gave it a warm, almost otherworldly appearance.

"How are you feeling?" Nicholas asked.

"Exhausted," she admitted.

"I'm not surprised after what you've just done. You do know that what you did today is unique in human history: you defeated an Archon."

She swallowed more water. "Did I kill it?"

"No," Flamel said, and Sophie found she was secretly relieved. "Though I daresay you could if you were fully trained. . . ." The Alchemyst paused for a moment, then added, "Once you're trained, I don't think there is anything you—or your brother—could not do."

"Nicholas," Sophie said, suddenly sad, "I don't want to be trained. I just want to go home. I'm sick of all this, the running and fighting. I'm sick of feeling ill, of the constant headaches, the pains in my eyes and ears, the knot in my stomach." She realized she was on the verge of tears, and rubbed her face with her hands. She wasn't going to cry now. "When can we go home?"

There was a long silence, and when Flamel finally answered,

his accent had thickened, his French ancestry clearly audible. "I am hoping I can take you back to America soon—perhaps even tomorrow. But you cannot go back home. Not just yet."

"Then when? We can't run and hide forever. Our parents are already asking questions. What do we tell them?" She held out her hand and watched a smooth mirrorlike silver skin form over her soft flesh. "How do we tell them about this?"

"You don't," Nicholas said simply. "But maybe you won't have to. Things are moving quickly, Sophie." His accent made her name sound exotic. "Faster than I imagined or anticipated. Everything is coming to a head. The Dark Elders seem to have abandoned all caution in their desperation to capture you and the pages from the Codex. Look at what they have done: they have loosed Nidhogg, the Wild Hunt and even the Archon Cernunnos on the world. These are creatures and beings that have not walked this earth for centuries. For ages they wanted Perenelle and me captured alive for our knowledge of the Codex and the twins; now they want us dead. They do not need us anymore, because they have most of the Book and they know you and your brother are the twins of the prophecy." Nicholas sighed, an exhausted sound. "I once thought we had a month at the most—a month before the immortality spell failed and Perenelle and I dissolved into withered old age. I no longer think that. In little over two weeks it will be Litha: midsummer. It is an incredibly significant day; a day when the Shadowrealms draw close to this world. I believe it will all be over then, one way or the other."

"What do you mean, all over?" Sophie asked, chilled.

"Everything will have changed."

"Everything has already changed," she snapped, fear making her angry. Josh stirred in his sleep but didn't waken. "This is all normal for you. You live in a world of monsters and creatures and fairy tales. But Josh and I don't. Or didn't," she amended. "Not until you and your wife chose us. . . ."

"Oh, Sophie," Nicholas said very softly. "This has nothing to do with Perenelle and me." He laughed quietly to himself. "You and your brother were chosen a long time ago." He leaned forward, eyes bright in the darkness. "You are silver and gold, the moon and the sun. You carry within you the genes of the original twins who fought on Danu Talis ten millennia ago. Sophie, you and your brother are the descendants of gods."

# CHAPTER FORTY-ONE

"*Is there someone you could call upon for help?*" Juan Manuel de Ayala asked.

"I'm not sure there is." Perenelle was leaning on a wooden rail almost directly over the official sign that welcomed visitors to the island.

UNITED STATES PENITENTIARY

ALCATRAZ ISLAND AREA 12 ACRES

1½ MILES TO TRANSPORT DOCK

ONLY GOVERNMENT BOATS PERMITTED

OTHERS MUST KEEP OFF 200 YARDS

NO ONE ALLOWED ASHORE

WITHOUT A PASS

Over the sign the words *Indians Welcome* had been daubed in red paint and beneath it, in larger fading red letters, were the words *Indian Land*. She knew they had been

310

painted there in 1969 when the American Indian Movement had occupied the island.

The Sorceress had spent the remainder of the afternoon systematically going over the island, looking for some way to escape. There were no boats, though there was plenty of wood and lumber, and she briefly considered making a raft, using towels and blankets from the cell exhibits to lash the wood together. In 1962, three prisoners had supposedly escaped by building their own raft. But Perenelle knew that nothing was going to get past Nereus and his savage daughters. From her second-floor position on the dock over the bookshop, Perenelle could see the heads of the Nereids bobbing in the water directly in front of her, long hair floating behind them like seaweed. From a distance they might have looked like seals, but these creatures were unmoving, and fixed her with cold unblinking eyes. Occasionally, she caught a glimpse of jagged teeth as they chewed still-wriggling fish. No doubt they had heard what she'd done to their father.

She had found clothes on her tour of the island and was now dressed in a set of coarse prison trousers and shirt, both of which were at least two sizes too large for her and which scratched everywhere. The clothes had been part of the display that had once greeted the many visitors to the island. But since Dee's company had taken over, there had been no visitors to Alcatraz for months. Perenelle discovered that many of the cells were decorated with artifacts and items that would once have belonged to the prisoners. Going through the cells, she had found a heavy black coat hanging on a peg and taken that. Although it smelled musty and felt slightly damp, it was still a lot warmer than the light silk dress she'd been wearing, and meant that she would not have to expend her energy keeping warm. She had found no food but had discovered a dusty metal cup in the kitchen, and once she'd cleaned it out, there were plenty of rainwater pools scattered around the island. The water tasted slightly of salt, but not enough to make her feel ill.

As the afternoon had worn on, she'd finally ended up on the dock, where all the visitors—prisoners and tourists—to Alcatraz would have started and finished their journeys. She'd discovered a flight of stairs to the left of the bookshop that led up to the second floor, and had climbed up. Now, leaning on the rail, she looked out over the waves. The city was tantalizingly close, just over a mile and a half away. Perenelle had grown up on the cold northwestern coast of France, in Brittany. She was a strong swimmer and loved the water, but swimming the treacherous and chilly waters of the bay was out of the question—even if Nereus and his daughters had not been waiting. She realized she really should have learned how to fly when they were in India in the days of the Mughal Empire.

Water pounded against the dock, sending silver-white spray high into the air . . . and the ghost of de Ayala materialized out of the glistening water droplets.

*"There must be someone in San Francisco you can call upon for assistance,"* the ghost said. *"Another immortal, perhaps?"*

Perenelle shook her head. "Nicholas and I have always

kept very much to ourselves. Remember, most of the immortals are servants or even slaves of the Dark Elders."

*"Surely not all immortals are beholden to an Elder,"* de Ayala said.

"Not all," she agreed. "We are not; neither is Saint-Germain nor Joan. I have heard rumors of others like us."

*"And could some of these others be living in San Francisco?"* he insisted.

"It's a big city. Immortals prefer large cities with constantly shifting populations, where it is easier to remain anonymous and invisible. So, yes, there must be."

The ghost moved around to float on her left-hand side. "Would you recognize another immortal if you passed one in the street?"

"I would." Perenelle smiled. "Nicholas might not."

The ghost floated out directly in front of the Sorceress. *"So if you had no contact with others of your kind in the city, then how did Dee find you?"*

Perenelle shrugged. "That is a good question, is it not? We're always exceptionally careful, but Dee has spies everywhere, and sooner or later, he always finds us. In truth, I'm surprised we've managed to stay hidden here in San Francisco for so long."

*"But you have friends in the city?"* the ghost pressed.

"We know some people," Perenelle said, "but not many, and not well." Brushing stray wisps of silvered hair away from her face, she squinted up at the dead sailor. In the afternoon sunlight de Ayala was almost completely invisible, just a

313

wavering impression in the air, the hint of liquid eyes betraying his position. "How long have you been a ghost?" she asked.

*"Two hundred and more years . . ."*

"And in all that time have you ever wished for immortality?" she asked.

*"I have never thought of it,"* the ghost said slowly. *"There were times I wished I were still alive. On days when the fog rolls in across the bay, or the wind whips spray into the air, I have wished for a physical body to experience the sensations. But I am not sure I would like to be immortal."*

"Immortality is a curse," Perenelle said firmly. "It is heartbreaking. You cannot afford to get close to people. Our very presence is a danger to them. Dee has leveled entire cities in his attempts to capture us, has caused fire and famine, even earthquakes as he sought to stop us. And so Nicholas and I have spent our lives running, hiding, skulking in the shadows."

*"You did not want to run?"* the ghost asked.

"We should have stopped and fought," Perenelle said, nodding. Leaning her forearms on the wooden rail, she looked down over the landing dock. The air shimmered, and for an instant, she caught a fleeting glimpse of countless figures in the costumes and uniforms of the past, crowding the docks. The Sorceress focused and the ghosts of Alcatraz disappeared. "We should have fought. We could have stopped Dee. We had an opportunity in New Mexico in 1945, and twenty years earlier, in 1923, in Tokyo, he was at our mercy, weakened almost to the point of death following the earthquake he'd caused."

*"Why didn't you?"* de Ayala wondered aloud.

Perenelle examined the backs of her hands, looking at the new wrinkles and the tracery of lines that ran across once-smooth flesh. The blue-green veins of age were now clearly visible beneath her skin; they had not been there yesterday. "Because Nicholas said that we would then be no better than Dee and his kind."

*"And you did not agree?"*

"Did you ever hear of an Italian called Niccolò Machiavelli?" Perenelle asked.

*"I have not."*

"A brilliant mind, cunning, ruthless, and now, sadly—and surprisingly—working for the Dark Elders," the Sorceress said. "But many years ago, he said something like, if you have to injure someone, then make it so severe that his vengeance need not be feared."

*"He does not sound like a nice person,"* de Ayala said.

"He's not. But he's right. Three centuries ago, the immortal human Temujin offered to imprison Dee in some distant Shadowrealm for eternity. We should have accepted that offer."

*"And you wanted to?"* de Ayala asked.

"Yes, I was in favor of imprisoning him in Temujin's Mongol Empire Shadowrealm."

*"But your husband said no?"*

"Nicholas said we were tasked with protecting the Codex and finding the prophesied twins, not with warring with the Dark Elders. But I'll not deny, it would have been easier without Dee always after us. We had an opportunity in Tokyo to

315

strip Dee of his powers, his memory, possibly even his immortality. He would have been no threat to us. We should have done that."

"*But would it have stopped the Dark Elders?*" the ghost asked.

Perenelle took a moment to consider. "It would have inconvenienced them, slowed them down a little, but no, it would not have stopped them."

"*Would you both have been able to disappear completely?*"

Perenelle's smile was bitter. "Probably not. No matter where we had ended up, there would have come a time when we would have had to move on. Sooner or later, we always move." She sighed. "We had already been too long in San Francisco. Even the woman who owns the coffee shop across from our bookshop had started to comment on my unlined skin." Perenelle laughed. "No doubt she thinks I'm getting Botox injections." She held both hands up in front of her and examined them critically. "I wonder what she would say if she could see me now?"

"*Is this woman a friend?*" de Ayala asked quickly. "*Would she be able to help?*"

"She is an acquaintance, not a friend. And she is human. Trying to explain even the tiniest part of this to her would be impossible," Perenelle said, "so no, I'll not ask her. It would only put her in danger."

"*Think, madame, think: there must be someone you can call upon for help,*" de Ayala insisted desperately. "*What about an Elder friendly to your cause, an immortal who is not allied to the Dark Elders? Give me a name. Let me go find them. You are*

316

*strong and powerful, but even you cannot stand against the sphinx, the Old Man of the Sea and the monsters in the cells on your own. And whoever sent the flies this morning will be sure to try something else, something even more deadly."*

"I know that," Perenelle said glumly. The Sorceress stared at the Nereids bobbing in the sea and allowed her thoughts to wander. There must be immortals in San Francisco—in fact, she *knew* there were; earlier that day she had actually caught a fleeting impression of a young-looking dead-eyed boy staring at her. He'd been using a scrying bowl to watch her. The Sorceress's lips curled in a smile; he'd not be using that bowl again. There was something about him, though, something feral and deadly about the way he moved and watched her that reminded her of . . .

"There is someone," she said suddenly. "She has lived here for decades; I'll wager she knows every Next Generation and Elder in the city. She will know whom we can trust."

*"Let me go to this person,"* de Ayala said. *"I can tell her where you are."*

"Oh, she's not in San Francisco right now." Perenelle smiled. "But it matters not."

The ghost looked puzzled. *"Then how are you going to contact her?"*

"I will scry."

*"Whom will you call?"* the ghost asked, curious.

"The Warrior Maid: Scathach the Shadow."

317

# CHAPTER FORTY-TWO

$\mathcal{T}$he scarred and battered taxicab drove down Millbank past the Houses of Parliament and stopped at a traffic light and immediately, a wild-haired shaggy-bearded tramp wrapped in layers of clothing pushed away from the black metal railing and hurried over to the car. Dipping a squeegee in a blue plastic bucket, he slapped it across the cab's cracked windshield and dragged it back and forth in three quick movements, expertly scraping away mud and the clotted dust of the Wild Hunt. Palamedes rolled down the window and passed the old man a two-pound coin. "Seems we're both working late tonight, old man. You're keeping well?"

"Warm and dry and food in my belly, Pally. What more could I ask for? Nothing, really. Except maybe a dog. I'd like a dog." His voice rose and fell in a curious singsong rhythm. The tramp sniffed loudly, nose wrinkling in disgust. "Whoa!

Something smells. I think you might have driven over something. Bet it's stuck to the underside of the car. Best get it scraped off, otherwise you'll not get too many fares." He laughed, liquid gurgling in his chest. He blinked nearsightedly, suddenly realizing that there were passengers in the back of the cab. "Whoops, didn't see them there." He leaned closer to Palamedes and said in a hoarse but clearly audible whisper, "Guess they've no sense of smell."

"Oh, they know what it is, all right," Palamedes said lightly. The signal changed to green and he checked the rearview mirror, but there was nothing behind them and he remained at the intersection, car idling. "It's the remnants of the Wild Hunt. Or at least, those that didn't get out of my way quickly enough."

"The Wild Hunt, eh?" The tramp rubbed his thumb over the side mirror, scraping away grit and bringing it to his mouth. A pink tongue poked out from the knotted beard, tasting it. "You've got a little Hittite there, mixed with a Roman and a touch of Magyar." He spat it away. "Does that horned monstrosity still think he's master of the hunt?"

"He is."

"Never liked him," the tramp said shortly. "How is he?"

"On fire, the last time I saw him."

The tramp ran his hand across the scarred front driver's-side door. "That's not going to buff out." He grinned and winked. "I know a good scrap yard, might get a couple of spare doors there."

"The yard is no more," Palamedes said quietly. "Cernunnos

and the Wild Hunt paid it a visit a couple of hours ago. Cernunnos was burning in the middle of it when we left. I'm afraid he might guess we've come in search of you," Palamedes continued gently, the changing traffic light painting his face red, turning the whites of his eyes crimson.

"He's all bluster; he'll do nothing," the man chuckled, then turned suddenly serious. "He's frightened of me, you know."

"The English Magician, Dee, is with him," Palamedes added.

The tramp's surprisingly perfect teeth appeared in a spectacular smile. "And *he's* terrified of me." Then the smile faded. "But he's also stupid enough not to know that." Shoving the squeegee into the bucket, he padded back over to the railing and stuck his supplies behind a bush. "Hard to get a good squeegee nowadays," he said, returning to the car. "Takes ages to get them broke in." He pulled open the back door and peered inside. "Now, what have we here?"

The interior light had clicked on when the tramp opened the door, bringing Josh blinking awake, squinting, shielding his eyes. He sat up, startled to find a ragged and filthy-looking homeless person climbing into the car. "What's going on? Who . . . who are you?" he mumbled.

The tramp turned astonishingly blue eyes on the boy, then frowned. "I'm . . . I'm . . ." He looked at Sophie. "Do *you* know who I am?" When she shook her head, he turned to the shadowy figure of the Alchemyst. "You look like a man of learning. Who is it I am again?" he demanded.

"You are Gilgamesh the King," Nicholas Flamel said gently. "You are the oldest immortal in the world."

The tramp squeezed in between Sophie and Josh, smiling delightedly. "That's who I am." He sighed. "I am the King."

The light turned green and the cab pulled away. Behind them, Big Ben chimed midnight.

TUESDAY, _5th June_

# CHAPTER FORTY-THREE

*F*rightened, aching and exhausted, Sophie tried her best to edge away from the tramp. He had squeezed in between the twins and she could feel a chill damp seeping from his bundled overcoats into her jeans and across her left arm. On his opposite side she noticed her brother also inch away, and from the corner of her eye, she could see that Nicholas had pressed himself back into the shadows. She watched as he raised his right hand and let it casually rest across his mouth, covering the lower half of his face, and she got the feeling that he was trying to hide from the old man.

"Oh, but this will not do." Gilgamesh pushed himself up and flopped down into the small pull-down seat directly facing them. "Now I can see you properly." He clapped his hands lightly. "So what have we here?"

Sodium streetlights and the passing headlights of other cars briefly illuminated the interior of the cab. Tilting her head to one side, Sophie focused on the homeless man, her enhanced senses taking in every detail. Surely this couldn't be the person they had come to London to see, the immortal called Gilgamesh, the oldest human on the planet. Nicholas had called him a king, Palamedes had said he was insane; he looked neither, just a harmless old vagrant wearing too many clothes and in need of a haircut and beard trim. But if the last few days had taught her anything, it was that no one was what they seemed.

"Well, this is pleasant," Gilgamesh said, folding his hands in his lap. He smiled happily. He spoke English with a trace of an indefinable accent, vaguely Middle Eastern. "I always say you never know when you wake in the morning how the day will end. I like that: keeps you young."

"And how old are you?" Josh immediately asked.

"Old," Gilgamesh said simply, and grinned. "Older than I look, but not as old as I feel."

Random images flickered into Sophie's head. These were the Witch's memories. Joan of Arc had taught her how to ignore them and dismiss the constant buzzing voices and noises she heard in her head, but this time Sophie deliberately let her guard down. . . .

*Gilgamesh, ageless and unchanging.*

*Gilgamesh, standing tall and proud, a ruler, in the costumes of a dozen ages and as many civilizations: Sumerian and Akkadian, Babylonian, Egyptian, Greek and Roman, and then the fur and leather of Gaul and Britain.*

*Gilgamesh the warrior, leading Celts and Vikings, Rus and Huns into battle against men and monsters.*

326

*Gilgamesh the teacher, in the plain white robes of a priest, oak and mistletoe in his hands.*

Sophie's eyes blinked silver and she spoke in a hoarse whisper. "You are the Ancient of Days."

Gilgamesh drew in a quick breath. "It has been a long time since anyone called me that," he said very slowly. "Who told you that?" There was a note almost of fear in his voice.

The girl shook her head. "I just knew."

Josh smiled. "Are you as old as the pyramids?"

"Older, much, much older," Gilgamesh said happily.

"The king's age is measured in millennia and not centuries," Palamedes offered from the front of the car.

Sophie guessed that Gilgamesh wasn't much taller than Josh, but his thickly bundled clothing—coats worn on top of coats, multiple fleeces, T-shirts and hooded sweatshirts—bulked him out, and his mass of wild hair and ragged beard made him look like an old man. Eyeing him closely, trying to see beyond the hair, Sophie discovered that he reminded her of her father, with his high forehead, long straight nose and bright blue eyes peering out of a deeply tanned face. She thought he looked like he was around the same age, too: midforties.

They passed a brightly lit store. It illuminated the interior of the cab in bright yellow-white light, and Sophie also realized that what she'd first taken for dirty and stained patches on the king's bundled clothes were odd symbols and lines of script written onto the cloth in what appeared to be black felt-tip marker. Squinting, she recognized what looked like cuneiform and Egyptian hieroglyphics, and what she had first

327

assumed were tears or pulls in the fabric were long thick jagged stitches that looked almost like early writing. She was sure she had seen ancient clay tablets in her parents' study with similar scratches on them.

Sophie was conscious that the old man was looking at her and her brother, bright blue eyes flickering from her face to Josh's and back again, frown lines on his forehead and on either side of his nose deepening as he concentrated. And even before he spoke, she knew what he was going to say.

"I know you."

Sophie glanced at her brother. The Horned God had said exactly the same words. Josh caught the look, squeezed his lips tightly shut and shook his head slightly; it was a signal they'd used many times when they were growing up. He was telling her to say nothing. "Where did we meet?" he asked.

Gilgamesh put his elbows on his knees and leaned forward. He brought his palms together, fingers straight, and then pressed the two index fingers against the cleft beneath his nose and stared at them. "We met a long time ago," he said finally, "when I was young, young, young." Then his blue eyes clouded. "No, that's not right. I saw you fight and fall. . . ." His voice caught and suddenly his eyes shone with tears. His voice turned raw with pain. "I saw you both die."

Sophie and Josh looked at one another, startled, but Flamel moved in the shadows, forestalling their questions. "The king's memory is often faulty," he said quickly. "Do not believe everything he says." He made it sound like a warning.

"You saw us die?" Sophie asked, ignoring Flamel. Gilgamesh's words had awakened gossamer threads of memories, but even as she tried to focus on them, they slipped away and faded.

"The skies bled tears of fire. Oceans boiled and the earth was rent asunder . . . ," Gilgamesh said in a lost whisper.

"When was this?" Josh asked quickly, eager for more information.

"In that time before time, the time before history."

"Nothing the king says can be taken as accurate," Flamel said coldly, voice loud in the suddenly silent cab. His French accent had thickened, as it did when he was under pressure. "I'm not sure the human brain is designed to hold and store something like ten millennia's worth of knowledge. His Majesty often gets confused."

Sophie reached across the seat and squeezed her brother's hand. When he looked at her, this time *she* squeezed her lips tightly and shook her head, warning him not to say anything. She wanted time to explore the Witch's memories and thoughts. There was something at the very edge of her consciousness, something dark and ugly, something to do with Gilgamesh and twins. She saw her brother nod, a tiny movement of his head, and then he looked back at the tramp. "So . . . you're ten thousand years old?" he said carefully.

"Most people laugh when they say that," Gilgamesh said. "But not you. Why is that?"

Josh grinned. "In the last couple of days, I've been Awakened by a buried legend, ridden on the back of a dragon and fought the Horned God. I've been to a Shadowrealm and seen a tree as big as the world. I've watched men change into wolves and dogs, seen a woman with the head of a cat . . . or maybe it was a cat with the body of a woman. So, to be honest, a ten-thousand-year-old man isn't really that strange. And actually, you're probably the most normal-looking of all the people we've met. No offense," he added quickly.

"None taken." Gilgamesh nodded. "I may be ten thousand and more years old." Then his voice altered, suddenly sounding tired. "Or I may be just a confused old fool. Lots of people have called me that. Though they're all dead." He grinned, then twisted in the seat and tapped on the glass partition. "Where are we going, Pally?"

The Saracen Knight was a vague shape in the gloom. "Well, first we wanted to see you . . ."

Gilgamesh smiled happily.

". . . and then I want to get these people off the island. I'm taking them to the Henge."

"The Henge?" the tramp asked, frowning. "Do I know it?"

"Stonehenge," Flamel said from the shadows. "You should; you helped build it."

Gilgamesh's bright blue eyes turned cloudy. He squinted toward the Alchemyst, peering into the gloom. "Did I? I don't remember."

"It was a long time ago," Flamel murmured. "I think you started raising the stones more than four thousand years ago."

"Oh no, it's older," Gilgamesh said suddenly, brightening. "I started working on that at least a thousand years earlier. And the site was ancient even then. . . ." His voice trailed away and he looked at Sophie and then Josh. Then he turned back to Palamedes. "And why are we going there?"

"We're going to try and activate one of the ancient ley lines and get these people out of the country."

Gilgamesh nodded. "Ley lines. Yes, lots of ley lines in Salisbury. One of the reasons I raised the gates there. And why do we want to get them out of the country?"

"Because these children are the sun and the moon," Flamel said, "with auras of pure gold and silver. And they are being hunted by the Dark Elders, who this very night brought an Archon back onto the earth. Two days ago Nidhogg rampaged through Paris. You know what that means."

Something altered in the king's voice. It became cold and businesslike. "They've stopped being cautious. It means the end is coming. And soon."

"Coming *again*," Nicholas Flamel said. He leaned forward, and amber light washed across his face, turning it the color of old parchment; the shadows highlighted the wrinkles across his forehead and emphasized the bags under his eyes. "You could help stop it."

"Alchemyst!" Gilgamesh's eyes widened and he hissed in alarm. "Palamedes! What have you done?" he shouted, voice high and wild. "You have betrayed me!"

And suddenly, a long black-bladed knife appeared in the tramp's hand. It flashed in the light as Gilgamesh stabbed it toward Flamel's chest.

# CHAPTER FORTY-FOUR

*F*ilthy and disheveled, his clothing ripped and stained, hair wild about his head, Dr. John Dee skulked down the empty streets, keeping to the shadows as police, fire trucks and ambulances raced past, sirens howling. A series of rattling explosions lit up the night sky behind him as gas canisters ignited. The cool June night air stank of burning rubber and hot oil, seared metal and melted glass.

When Flamel and the others had escaped in the car, Dee had raced over to the moat, dropped to his belly in the mud and pushed his left arm down into the oily sludge where Excalibur had sunk. It was deeper than he'd expected and it swallowed his arm almost up to his shoulder. The liquid was thick and still warm where it had burned, and noxious bubbles burst under his nose, making him nauseous and lightheaded. His eyes stung furiously. He felt around, searching frantically, but touched nothing. He could hear sirens in the distance; the flaming moat must have been seen all across North London, and no doubt there had been scores of calls to the emergency services. Digging the fingers of his right hand into the soft muddy earth, he held on tightly as he leaned farther out over the edge, the side of his face actually touching the liquid. Where was it? He wasn't leaving without the sword. Finally, his fingers closed over a smooth length of cold stone. It took a tremendous effort to lift Excaliber out of the thick liquid. It came free with a pop. Rolling onto his back, he cradled it against his chest. Even though he was exhausted, Dee charged his palm with his aura and rubbed yellow power across the stone, wiping away the filthy muck.

Clambering to his feet, he looked around. But there was no trace of the Horned God or the Wild Hunt. The last of the menagerie Shakespeare had created—the snakes, hedgehogs and newts—were slowly winking out of existence, like bursting bubbles, leaving sooty outlines in the air. The car yard was a ruin, with scores of tiny fires burning everywhere, and black smoke billowed out from beneath the metal hut. Fire burned within. Somewhere off to the right a wall of cars creaked ominously, then swayed and crashed to the ground in a                                                  huge detonation of metal. Metal and glass shards whined through the air.

Dee turned and raced onto the street. He was unsurprised to find that Bastet and the car they'd arrived in had disappeared.

He'd been abandoned. More than that, he was truly on his own.

Dee was bitterly aware that he had failed his Dark Elder masters. And they had been very clear about what would happen to him. He had no doubt that Bastet had reported his failure. His lips twisted in an ugly smile. One of these days he was going to have to do something about that cat-headed creature. But not now, not yet. He had failed, but all was not lost, not unless his master withdrew the gift of immortality, and before his master could make him human again, he would have to touch him, lay both hands on him. That meant either his master would come out of the Shadowrealms or someone—or something—would be sent to capture Dee and drag him back to stand trial.

But that wasn't going to happen immediately. The Elders understood time differently than the humani; it would take a day, maybe two, to organize for his capture. And a lot could happen in that time.

Even in his darkest hour, Dr. John Dee had never admitted defeat, and he had always ultimately triumphed. If he could capture the twins and find the missing pages, then he was confident he would be able to redeem himself.

London was still his city. His company, Enoch Enterprises, had offices on Canary Wharf. He had a home here—more than one, in fact—and he had resources he could call upon: servants, slaves, allies and mercenaries.

Stupidity always angered Dee; especially his own stupidity. He had been overawed by the presence of Bastet and the appearance of the Archon and the Wild Hunt; he had not taken the proper precautions. On previous occasions the

Flamels had escaped by a combination of luck, circumstances or their own skills and powers. But Dee had never considered himself to blame. This time it was different. This was entirely his own fault. He had underestimated the twins.

Blue and white lights washed over boarded-up houses, and the Magician ducked down behind a wall as a trio of police cars screamed past.

He knew the girl had been trained in at least two of the magics—Air and Fire—and she'd demonstrated extraordinary skill and courage when she'd faced down the Archon. But if the girl was dangerous, then the boy . . . well, the boy was doubly so. He was an enigma. Newly Awakened, untrained in any of the elemental magics, he handled Clarent as if he'd been born to it, and fought with a skill that was far beyond him. And that should have been impossible.

The Magician shook his head. He knew the ultimate secret of the four Swords of Power; he knew what they did to normal humani. The swords were insidious and deadly, almost vampiric in nature. They whispered of victories to come, hinted at secrets beyond imagining and made promises of ultimate power. All the humani had to do was to keep using the weapon . . . and all the while, the sword was drinking the humani's memories, consuming their every emotion before it finally gorged upon their aura. At that stage the humani forgot to eat and drink. The strongest survived for a month; most didn't last ten days. Magicians like him spent decades of preparation before they even touched the cold stone weapons; it took months of fasting and practice before they learned the art of forging their auras into protective gloves. Even then, the swords were so powerful that many a magician and sorcerer had succumbed to them.

So how was the boy able to handle Clarent?

And how had he known that Dee intended to kill the Archon?

The Magician cut through a narrow trash-filled alley and slunk down a deserted street. He pressed his hand to his side, where he could feel Excalibur's warmth beneath his filthy coat. All four swords were very similar, though each was unique in ways he could not even begin to understand. Excalibur was the best known of all the swords, and while it was not the most powerful, it had attributes the other swords lacked. Ducking into another deserted alley, John Dee pulled the sword from beneath his coat and set it on the ground at his feet. His little fingernail glowed yellow, and the smell of brimstone was lost amid the stinking refuse as he touched the blade with his finger and whispered, "Clarent."

The stone sword trembled and vibrated and then slowly turned, the blade pointing south. Excalibur always pointed toward its twin. Dee snatched up the weapon and hurried on.

The Magician had spent centuries collecting the Swords of Power. He had three of the four, and he'd just come frustratingly close to adding Clarent to his collection. Neither Elders nor Next Generation were immune to the lure of the Swords. It was said that Mars Ultor had worn both Excalibur and Clarent in matched scabbards across his back. He had been the champion of the humani before he'd carried the twin blades; afterward he became a monster. And if the two swords had corrupted the Elder, then what chance had an untrained humani boy? Every time the boy held it, every time he touched the hilt, it drew him deeper under its control. And so long as he carried it, Dee would always be able to find him.

# CHAPTER FORTY-FIVE

*N*iccolò Machiavelli sat back in his chair and focused on the largest of the high-definition LCD screens on the wall before him. He was watching the English satellite news service Sky News. The two a.m. headlines showed an aerial shot of a fire raging through an industrial area. The line of text crawling across the bottom of the screen announced that the fire was in a car yard in North London. Machiavelli had seen enough castle fortifications in his time to recognize the design, even though this one was made of cars rather than slabs of stone. The black outline of a moat was still clearly visible, gray smoke curling from it.

Machiavelli grinned as he reached for the remote control and brought up the volume. That particular location sounded familiar. On a separate screen he activated his encrypted database of Elders, Next Generation and immortals and typed in the location in North London. Two names immediately popped up: Palamedes, the Saracen Knight, and the Bard, William Shakespeare.

Machiavelli scanned both files: Shakespeare had been Dee's apprentice for years, until he'd suddenly turned against the Magician. He was immortal, though how he'd become so was a mystery, since he was associated with no known Elder. Palamedes was an enigma. A warrior-prince of Babylon, he'd fought with Arthur and had been there at the end, when the king had been killed. Again, there was no record of who had made him immortal, and traditionally the Saracen Knight had remained neutral in the wars between the Elders and the Dark Elders.

Machiavelli had never met either immortal, though he had known about them for generations and had longed to meet the Bard. Machiavelli had always wondered how and when and where Shakespeare and Palamedes had originally met. According to his files, their first recorded meeting was in London in the nineteenth century, but Machiavelli suspected they'd known one another a long time before that; there was some evidence to suggest that the Bard had originally written the part of *Othello* for Palamedes early in the seventeenth century. Shakespeare had turned up in London sometime in the middle of the nineteenth century as a ragpicker, a dealer in secondhand clothing. At least sixty barefoot urchins worked for him, sleeping in the attic of his warehouse on the docks, then going out during the day to scour the city for cast-off clothing and rags. There was a police report on file that the warehouse was suspected of storing stolen goods, and it had been raided at least twice. The Saracen Knight had been in

London at the same time, earning his living as an actor in theaters in the West End. He specialized in monologues from Shakespeare's plays.

Machiavelli examined a grainy photograph of the man identified as William Shakespeare. Taken with a telephoto lens, it showed a rather ordinary-looking man dressed in stained blue overalls, bending over the engine of a car, a scattering of tools and car parts by his feet. Two dogs were visible in the background, and the photography had given both dogs red eyes. The second photograph was higher resolution. It showed a huge dark-skinned man leaning against the side of a gleaming London taxi, drinking tea from a white paper cup. The wheel of the London Eye was just visible in the background.

A male reporter's voice filled the room. *". . . raging for the past two hours in this car yard. At this time, no bodies have been removed from the scene, and officers do not expect to find any. Officials have expressed concern because of the huge amount of combustible material in the area, and firemen are using breathing apparatuses to enter the yard. There is a fear that if the stacked tires start to burn, they will release noxious gases. There is some consolation, however, that in this run-down part of London, most of the houses are abandoned and derelict. . . ."*

Machiavelli hit the Mute button. Leaning back in his leather chair, he ran his hands over his close-cropped white hair, hearing it rasp in the silence. So, had Dee killed the Alchemyst and captured the twins?

The reporter appeared on-screen holding a handful of

what looked like flint arrowheads, and Machiavelli almost fell off the chair in his haste to turn on the sound.

"*. . . and bizarrely found hundreds of what look like flint arrowheads.*" The camera panned around and showed broken arrows and spears scattered all over the ground. Machiavelli recognized the stubby lengths of crossbow bolts.

Well, if Dee *had* captured the twins, it hadn't been without a fight.

Machiavelli's cell phone buzzed, startling him. Pulling it out of his inner pocket, he stared at the screen, immediately recognizing the overlong number and impossible area code. He took a deep breath before answering. "Yes?"

"*Dee has failed.*" Machiavelli's Elder's voice was little more than a thready whisper. He spoke in Late Egyptian, the language used in the New Kingdom over three thousand years ago.

Machiavelli responded in the formal Italian of his youth. "I'm watching the news. I see there's a fire in London; I know that location is associated with two neutral immortals. I assume there is some connection to the two events."

"*Flamel and the twins were there. They escaped.*"

"It looks like the location was defended; the television report is showing evidence of a fight—arrows, spears and crossbow bolts. Perhaps we should have given the English Magician more resources," Machiavelli suggested carefully.

"*Bastet was there.*"

Machiavelli kept his face impassive; he despised the cat-headed goddess but knew she was close to his Elder master.

"And Cernunnos was tasked with helping the Magician."

Machiavelli came slowly to his feet. "The Archon?" he asked, struggling to keep the shock out of his voice.

"And the Archon brought the Wild Hunt. I did not authorize this; none of us did. We do not want the Archons back in this world."

"Who did?"

"The others," the voice said shortly. "Dee's masters and their supporters. This could work to our advantage; now that the Magician has failed, they must order his destruction."

Machiavelli placed the phone on the table and hit the Speaker button. Straightening his suit jacket, he folded his arms across his chest and looked at the wall of television and computer screens. Most of the news channels had started to show video of the fire in North London. "Dee is no fool, he must know that he is in danger."

"He does."

Machiavelli placed himself in Dee's position, wondering what he would do if the roles were reversed. "He knows he has to capture the twins and those pages," he said decisively. "It is the only way to get back into his Elders' good graces. He will be desperate. And desperate men do stupid things."

The reporter was talking to an excitable bearded man, who was holding up one of the spearheads and waving it around.

"What do you want me to do?" Machiavelli asked.

"Is there any way you can help us locate Flamel and the twins in England before Dee does?"

"I do not see how . . . ," Machiavelli began.

"*Why is Flamel in London? Why risk bringing the twins into the heart of Dee's empire? We know he is trying to train the twins. So, who—amongst the Elders, Next Generation or immortals—could he be planning on meeting?*"

"It could be anyone." Machiavelli blinked in surprise. Not taking his eyes off the TV screens, he continued, "I am head of the French secret service. How would I know who is even in London?" He was pleased that his voice remained neutral and calm.

"*Surely the information is in your database?*" the voice on the phone asked, and the Italian was sure he could *hear* the smile in the comment.

"My database?" he asked carefully.

"*Yes, your secret database.*"

Machiavelli sighed. "Obviously not that secret. How many know about it?" he wondered aloud.

"*The Magician knows,*" the voice said, "*and he told his masters . . . and I . . . well, let us say I discovered it from them.*"

Machiavelli kept his face carefully neutral, just in case his master could actually see him. He had always known about the different factions within the Dark Elders. He wasn't surprised. The Dark Elders had once been rulers, and where there were rulers, there were always others waiting, plotting, planning to take over. This was the type of politics Machiavelli understood and excelled in.

The Italian sat down and rested his fingers on the keyboard. "What do you want to know?" he asked with a sigh.

"*London belongs to the Magician. But Flamel has the two that are one, and both have been Awakened. The girl knows Air*

343

*and Fire, the boy knows nothing. Who, in London, has mastery of any of the elemental magics and, more importantly, would be sympathetic enough to Flamel and his cause to train the twins?"*

"Surely you have other means of discovering this?" Machiavelli asked, fingers moving over the wafer-thin keyboard.

*"Of course."*

Machiavelli understood. His Elder did not want the others to know he was looking for the information. A screen of names, some with attached photographs, appeared: Elders in London with control over one or more of the elemental magics. "There are twelve Elders in London," he said, "and they are all loyal to us."

*"What about Next Generation?"*

Sixteen names appeared on the screen. Machiavelli checked their allegiances and again shook his head. "All loyal to us," he repeated. "Few who side against us choose to live in England, though there are some in Scotland and one in Ireland."

*"Try immortal humans."*

Machiavelli's fingers danced across the keys and half a screen of names appeared. "There are immortal humans scattered all across England, Wales and Scotland . . . ," he said, fingers moving on the keyboard as he narrowed the search, "but only five in London."

*"Who are they?"*

"Shakespeare and Palamedes . . ."

*"Shakespeare has disappeared, possibly dead in the fire in London,"* Machiavelli's master said immediately, *"and Pala-*

344

*medes was seen with the Alchemyst. Neither has mastery of an elemental magic. Who else?"*

"Baybars the Mamluk . . ."

*"Friend of Palamedes and no friend to us. He has no knowledge of the elemental magics."*

"Virginia Dare . . ."

*"Dangerous, deadly and loyal to none but herself. Her master is dead; I believe she may have killed him. She is a Mistress of Air, but she has no love for Flamel and has fought alongside Dee in the past. Flamel will not go to her."*

Machiavelli looked at the final name blinking on the screen. "And then there is Gilgamesh."

*"The king,"* the voice sighed, *"who knows all the magics, but has no power to use them. Of course."*

"Where do his loyalties lie?" Machiavelli wondered aloud. "His name is not associated with any Elder."

*"Abraham the Mage, the creator of the Codex, is responsible for Gilgamesh's immortality. I believe the process was flawed. It fractured his mind, and the centuries have made him both mad and forgetful. He might teach the twins, though he could just as easily refuse. Do you have an address?"*

"No fixed abode," Machiavelli said. "Looks like he's living on the streets. I have a note here that he is usually to be found sleeping in the park close to the Buxton Monument, which is in the shadow of the Houses of Parliament. If Flamel and the twins were at that car yard in North London, it will take them some time to get across the city."

*"My spy reported that a black vehicle left that location at high speed."*

345

Machiavelli looked up at the photo of Palamedes standing alongside a black London cab. He scrolled down until he found the license plate. "The English capital has more traffic and security cameras than any other city in Europe," he said absently. "Even more than Paris. However, they use the same traffic monitoring system that we use here." Two of the screens turned black, and then short lines of code started to appear as Machiavelli hacked into London's traffic cameras. "And the same software."

The Italian brought up a high-resolution map of London, found the Buxton Monument in Victoria Tower Gardens alongside the Houses of Parliament and then pinpointed the nearest traffic lights. Sixty seconds later he was looking at the live feed from the traffic camera. Watching the time code, he started running it in reverse: 2:05 . . . 2:04 . . . 2:03 . . . Traffic was sparse, and he sped up the digital video, jumping backward in five-minute intervals. The time code had reversed to 00:01 before he finally found what he was looking for. A black taxicab had stopped at the lights almost directly opposite the monument and a homeless man had shuffled out of the park to wipe the windows. The cab had sat at the light even though it had changed from red to green. Then the same homeless man climbed into the back of the cab and it pulled away.

"I've got him," he said. "They're heading west toward the A302."

*"Where are they going?"* Machiavelli's master demanded. *"I want to know where they're going."*

"Give me a minute. . . ." Using illegal access codes,

Machiavelli hopped from traffic camera to traffic camera, tracking the cab by its number plate across Parliament Square, Trafalgar Square, into Piccadilly and onto the A4. "He's heading out of London," he said finally.

*"Which direction?"*

"West onto the M4."

*"Where are they going?"* the Elder snarled. *"Why are they leaving London? Surely if they are trying to convince Gilgamesh to teach the twins one of the elemental magics, they could do it at a safe house in the city?"*

Machiavelli increased the resolution on the map, looking for items of significance on their route. "Stonehenge," he said suddenly. "I'll wager they are going to Stonehenge. He's heading for the ley lines on Salisbury Plain," he announced confidently.

*"Those gates have been dead for centuries,"* the Elder said. *"Assuming he chose the correct gate, it would still need a powerful aura to activate them."*

"And Gilgamesh has no aura," Machiavelli said very softly. "The Alchemyst would have to do it himself. But that would be madness; in his weakened state, the effort would burn through his aura and consume him in seconds."

*"That might be just enough time to open the gate and push the twins through,"* the Dark Elder said.

Machiavelli looked up at the screen, tracking the black cab as it drove down the A4, washed yellow in the glare of sodium light. "Would Nicholas Flamel sacrifice himself for the twins?" he wondered aloud.

*"Does he believe—truly believe—these to be the real twins?"*

"Yes. Dee also believes that, and so do I."

*"Then I have no doubt that he would sacrifice himself to save them."*

"There is one other option," Machiavelli said. "Could he not have the twins open the gates? We know their auras are powerful."

There was a long silence on the other end of the line. The Italian heard ghostly snatches of song, like the sounds of a distant radio. But the song was a Spartan marching ballad. *"The gate on Salisbury comes out on the West Coast of America, north of San Francisco."*

"I could have told you that," Machiavelli said.

*"We will lay our plans accordingly,"* the Elder said.

"Well, what exactly does that mean . . . ," Machiavelli began, but the phone was dead.

# CHAPTER FORTY-SIX

Josh's right hand shot out, fingers wrapping around Gilgamesh's wrist. He squeezed and twisted all in one movement and the knife fell from the king's hand, embedding itself point-first in the rubber matting on the floor. Sophie bent down and quickly scooped it up.

"Hey," Palamedes shouted at the sudden commotion. "What's going on back there?"

"Nothing," Flamel answered quickly, before Josh or Sophie could say anything. "Everything is under control."

Gilgamesh sat back in the seat, nursing his bruised wrist, glaring at the Alchemyst. He looked at the knife in Sophie's hands. "I want that back."

Ignoring him, she passed it to her brother, who handed it to Nicholas. She was shaking with the shock of what had just happened . . . and something else, too: fear. She had never seen Josh move like that before. Even with her enhanced senses, she had barely registered that Gilgamesh had a knife in his hand and then Josh had struck, neatly disarming him without saying a word or even rising from his seat. Drawing her legs up to her chest, she wrapped her arms around her shins and rested her chin on her knees. "Do you want to tell us what that was all about?" she asked quietly.

"It took me a while," Gilgamesh said grimly, staring at Flamel. "But I knew there was something about you, something familiar." He wrinkled his nose. "I should have recognized your foul stench." He sniffed. "Is it still mint or have you changed it to something more appropriate?"

Both twins automatically sniffed the air but could smell nothing.

"It is still mint," the Alchemyst said softly.

"I see you know one another," Josh said.

"We've met over the years," Nicholas agreed. He looked at the king. "Perenelle told me to say hello."

Streetlights ran liquid down Gilgamesh's face as he turned to look at the twins. "And I knew I'd met you before," he snapped.

"We've never seen you before in our lives," Josh said sincerely.

"Honestly, we haven't," Sophie agreed.

A look of confusion passed across the immortal's face; then he shook his head. "No, you're lying. You're Americans. We've met before. All of you." He pointed at each of them in turn. "You two were with the Flamels. That's when you tried to kill me."

"It wasn't these twins," Nicholas said quietly. "And we weren't trying to kill you. We were trying to save you."

"Maybe I didn't want to be saved," Gilgamesh said petulantly. He dipped his head so that his hair fell over his forehead, covering his eyes. Then he peered out at the twins. "Gold and silver, eh?"

They both nodded.

"The twins of legend?"

"So we're told." Josh smiled. He glanced sidelong at his sister and saw her nod; she knew the question he was about to ask. She focused on the Alchemyst as Josh spoke, watching his reaction, but his face was a mask, and the passing streetlights turned it dark and ugly. Her brother leaned toward Gilgamesh. "Do you remember when you met the other American twins?"

"Of course." The king frowned. "Why, it was only last month . . ." His voice trailed away into silence. When he spoke again, there was a note of terrible loss in his voice. "No. It was not last month, or last year, or even in the last decade. It was . . ." His gaze drifted and he turned to look at the Alchemyst. "When was it?"

The twins both turned to Flamel.

"In 1945," he said shortly.

"And it was in America?" Gilgamesh asked. "Tell me it was America."

"It was in New Mexico."

The king clapped his hands. "At least I was right about that. What happened to the last pair?" he suddenly asked Flamel.

The Alchemyst remained silent.

"I think we'd like to hear the answer too," Sophie said coldly, eyes blinking silver. "We know there've been other twins."

"Lots of other twins," Josh added.

"What happened to them?" Sophie demanded. Somewhere at the back of her mind she thought she already knew the answer, but she wanted to hear Flamel say it out loud.

"There have been other twins in the past," Nicholas admitted finally. "But they were not the right twins."

"And they all died!" Josh said, a crack of anger in his voice. The scent of oranges filled the cab, but the odor was sour and bitter.

"No, not all," Flamel snapped. "Some did, and some went on to live to old age. Including the last pair."

"And what happened to the ones who didn't survive?" Sophie asked quickly.

"A few were damaged by the Awakening process."

"Damaged?" She picked up on the word, determined not to let him get away with anything.

The Alchemyst sighed. "Anyone can be Awakened. But no two people react to the process in the same way. Some were not strong enough to handle the wash of emotions. Some fell into comas, others ended up lost in dreams or unable to cope with the real world, or their personalities split and they spent their days in institutions."

Sophie began to tremble. She felt physically sickened by what Flamel was saying. Even the way he reported it—coldly, without emotion—frightened her. She knew now that Josh's suspicions were justified: the Alchemyst was not to be trusted. When Nicholas Flamel had brought them to the Witch of Endor to be Awakened, he had been fully aware of the terrible consequences of a failed Awakening. But he'd still been willing to go through with it.

Josh slid across the seat, moving closer to his sister, wrapping his arms around her, holding her. He couldn't speak. He knew that he was close, dangerously close, to hitting the Alchemyst.

"How many other sets of twins have there been, Flamel?" Gilgamesh asked. "You have lived on this earth for more than six hundred and seventy years. Was there one set a century? Two? Three? How many lives have you destroyed trying to find the twins of legend?"

"Too many," the Alchemyst whispered. He sat back into the shadows, and the passing streetlights painted his wet eyes sulfurous yellow. "I have forgotten my father's face and the sound of my mother's voice, but I remember the name and face of every twin, and not a day goes by that I do not think of them and regret their loss." And then the hand holding the black bladed knife jabbed out of the gloom at Sophie and Josh. "But every mistake I made, each failed Awakening, gradually and inexorably led me to these, the real twins of legend. And this time, I have no doubts." His voice rose, becoming harsh and raw. "And if they are trained in the elemental magics, then they will be able to stand against the Dark Elders. They will give this world a chance of survival in the battle to come. And then all the deaths and lost lives will not have been in vain." He leaned forward out of the shadows and glared at Gilgamesh. "Will you train them? Will you help them fight the Dark Elders? Will you teach them the Magic of Water?"

"Why should I?" Gilgamesh asked simply.

"You could help save the world."

"I saved it before. No one was grateful. And it is in worse shape today than it has ever been."

The Alchemyst's smile turned feral. "Train them. Empower them. We will take back the Codex from Dee and his Dark Elders and reunite it with the last two pages. I will surrender the Book to the twins: you know there are spells within the Book of Abraham that could return this world to a paradise."

The king leaned closer to the twins. "And there are spells within the Codex that could turn this world to a cinder," he said absently. His finger began moving, pointing to each of them in turn as he repeated the ancient verse. " 'And the immortal must train the mortal and the two that are one, must become the one that is all.' " He sat back. "One to save the world, one to destroy it. But which one?"

The Witch's memories battered at Sophie's thoughts, random images leaking into her consciousness.

*A tidal wave racing across a lush landscape, crashing into a forest, sweeping away everything before it . . .*

*A line of volcanoes erupting in sequence, tearing out huge chunks of landscape, the sea foaming white-hot against the red-black lava . . .*

*The skies boiling with storm clouds, raindrops dark with grit, snowflakes black with soot . . .*

"I have no gift of foresight," Flamel snapped. "But this I know to be certain truth: if the twins are not trained and cannot protect themselves, then the Dark Elders will take them, enslave them and use their incredible auras to open the gates to the Shadowrealms. The Dark Elders are missing the Final Summoning from the Codex, but once they have these pages, then they will be able to reclaim this earth again."

"Even without the Codex, the Dark Elders could begin the process if they had the twins," Gilgamesh said, voice calm and even. "The Final Summoning is designed to open all the doors to the Shadowrealms simultaneously."

"What would happen to us afterward?" Josh asked, breaking the long silence that followed. He pressed his hands against his chest, feeling beneath his T-shirt, where he carried the two pages he'd torn from the Book of Abraham.

"There is no afterward, not for you or for any other human."

Palamedes drove for nearly ten minutes in silence, and then Gilgamesh cleared his throat and said, "I will train you in the Magic of Water on one condition."

"What condi—" Josh began.

"Agreed," Sophie interrupted. She turned to look at her brother. "There are no conditions."

"When all of this is over, and if we have survived, then I want you to promise that you will return here to me with the Book of Abraham," the king told them.

Josh was about to ask another question, but Sophie squeezed his fingers as hard as she could. "We'll come back, if we can."

"There is a spell in the Codex right on page one." The king closed his eyes and tilted his head back. His words were precise, his voice little more than a whisper. "I stood by Abraham's shoulder and watched him transcribe it. It is the formula of words that confers immortality. Bring that to me."

"Why?" Josh asked, puzzled. "You're already immortal."

Gilgamesh opened his eyes and looked at Sophie and she suddenly realized why he wanted the Book. "The king wants us to create the formula in reverse," she said softly. "He wants to become mortal again."

Gilgamesh bowed. "I want to live out my life and die. I want to be human again. I want to be normal."

Sitting facing him, Sophie Newman nodded in silent agreement.

# CHAPTER FORTY-SEVEN

*E*ven though the late-afternoon sun was warm on her face, Perenelle suddenly felt chilled. "What do you mean, you're not with Nicholas and the children?" she asked in alarm, staring intently into the flat metal plate filled with faintly discolored water. Wisps of her white aura crawled across the surface of the liquid.

Grass green eyes, huge, magnified and unblinking, stared out of the water. "We got separated." Even though it was barely audible, Scathach's voice sounded miserable. "I had a spot of bother," she admitted, embarrassment thickening her Celtic accent.

The Sorceress was sitting with her back to the warm stones of the Alcatraz lighthouse, staring into the liquid in front of her. Taking a deep breath, she raised her head to look at the city across the bay. The realization that Nicholas and the children were unprotected had set her heart thumping.

When she'd been talking to him earlier, she'd just assumed Scathach was there, somewhere in the background, but she'd been distracted talking to William Shakespeare and then the vetala had attacked. She looked down again. Scathach had stepped back from whatever reflective surface was carrying the image and Perenelle was able to see more of her face. There was a quartet of long scratches like claw marks on Scatty's forehead, and one cheekbone looked bruised. "A spot of bother. Are you all right?" she asked. She had trouble trying to decide what the Shadow might call *bother*.

The Shadow's vampire teeth appeared in a savage inhuman smile. "Nothing I could not handle."

Perenelle knew she needed to remain calm and focus her aura. She was concentrating so hard on scrying and keeping the connection with Scathach that her other defenses were failing, and already she could see the flickering movement of the ghosts of Alcatraz in the air around her. As more and more of the protective layers of colors fell away from her aura, the ghosts would start to flock around her, disturbing her, and she'd lose the link with the Warrior Maid. "Scathach, tell me," she said calmly, staring hard at the water, "where are Nicholas and the twins?"

The Shadow's bright red hair swam into view. "London."

"I know that. I spoke to him earlier." Perenelle had picked up on the slightest hesitation in the Warrior's voice. "But . . . ?"

"Well, we *think* they are still in London."

"Think!" The Sorceress drew in a deep breath and bit

back a wave of anger. A tremor of white light curled across the surface of the water and the image rippled and fragmented. She was forced to wait until the image re-formed. "What's happened? Tell me everything you know."

"There have been some reports on the news channels of odd disturbances in the city last night. . . ."

"Last night?" Perenelle asked, confused. "What time is it? What day?"

"It's Tuesday here in Paris. A little after two in the morning."

Perenelle did the calculation, working out the time difference: it was still Monday on the West Coast, and now around five p.m. "What sort of odd disturbances?" she continued.

"Sky News reported a thunderstorm and torrential downpour over one tiny section of North London. Then euronews and France24 carried a story about a huge fire in a derelict car yard, also in North London."

"That could be nothing," Perenelle said, though she instinctively knew it was somehow connected to Nicholas and the twins.

On the other side of the Atlantic, Scatty shook her head. "Flint arrowheads, bronze spears and crossbow bolts were found all around the burning yard. One of the news reporters showed a handful of the arrowheads to the camera. They looked brand-new. Some local historian dated them back to the Neolithic Period, but said the bronze spears were Roman and the crossbow bolts were Medieval. He claimed they were all genuine."

"There was a fight," Perenelle said curtly. "Who was involved?"

"Impossible to say, but you know what lives in and around that city."

Perenelle knew only too well. Scores of creatures had settled on the British Isles, drawn there by the abundance of ley lines and the Shadowrealms. And most were loyal to the Dark Elders.

"Were there any bodies found at this car yard?" she asked grimly. If anything had happened to Nicholas or the twins, she would tear the city apart looking for Dee. The hunter would discover what it was like to be hunted. And she had more than six hundred years of sorcerous knowledge to draw upon.

"The car yard was deserted. What looked like a moat of oil had been set alight, and everything was covered in a thick layer of gray ash."

"Ash?" Perenelle frowned. "Have you any idea what left it?"

"There are several creatures who turn to ash when they are killed," Scatty said slowly.

"Including immortal humans," Perenelle added.

"I do not believe Nicholas was killed," Scatty said quickly.

"Nor do I," the Sorceress whispered. She would know if anything had happened to him, she would *feel* it.

"Could you try to contact him?" Scatty asked.

"I could try, but if he's on the run . . ."

"You found me." The Warrior smiled. "Though you did give me quite a start." The Warrior had been standing before a bathroom mirror, rubbing antiseptic cream on her cuts, when the glass had fogged over, then cleared to reveal Perenelle Flamel. Scatty had almost stuck her finger in her eye.

Perenelle had got the idea to try scrying from the immortal human with the Anasazi bowl she'd caught spying on her earlier. She'd chosen the warmest spot on the island, where the white stones of the lighthouse were baked by the sun. Filling a shallow plate with water, she'd sat down and allowed the afternoon sun to charge her aura. Then she'd asked de Ayala to keep the rest of the ghosts of Alcatraz away from her as she lowered her defenses. She'd also asked him to warn her if the Crow Goddess approached. Perenelle didn't entirely trust the creature.

Creating the link with the Shadow had proven to be surprisingly easy. Perenelle had known Scathach for generations. She could clearly visualize everything about her: her bright red hair and brilliant green eyes, her round face and the dusting of freckles across her straight nose. Her fingernails were always ragged and chewed. She looked to be a girl around seventeen years old; in truth she was more than two thousand five hundred years old and was the finest martial artist in the world. She had trained most of the great warriors and heroes of legend and had saved the Flamels' lives on more than one occasion. They had returned the favor. Even though the Shadow was more than eighteen hundred years her senior, Perenelle had come to think of her if not as a daughter, then certainly as a niece. "Tell me what happened, Scatty," Perenelle demanded.

"Nicholas and the children escaped to London. He was taking the twins to see Gilgamesh."

Perenelle nodded. "I know that. Nicholas told me. He also said that both twins have been Awakened," she added.

"Both," Scatty agreed. "The girl has been trained in two of the elemental magics, but the boy has no training. However, he has Clarent."

"Clarent," Perenelle murmured. She'd watched her husband sink the ancient blade into the lintel over the window of their home on the Rue du Montmorency. She'd wanted to destroy it; he'd refused. He'd argued that it was older than a score of civilizations and they had no right to break it; he'd also argued that it was probably impossible to harm the blade anyway.

"So where are you?" Perenelle asked.

"Paris." Scathach's face swam in and out of focus. "It's a very long story. Parts of it are quite boring. Especially the bit where I was dragged into the Seine by Dagon . . ."

"You were dragged into the Seine!" Nicholas hadn't told her that.

Scatty nodded. "That happened just after I'd been rescued from the Nidhogg, which had rampaged through the streets of Paris."

Perenelle stared at her openmouthed. Finally, she said, "And where were Nicholas and the twins while all this was happening?"

"They were the ones who chased the Nidhogg through the streets and rescued me."

The Sorceress blinked in surprise. "That does not sound like my Nicholas."

"I think it was more the twins' doing," Scathach said. "Especially the boy, Josh. He saved my life. I think he slew the dragon."

"And then you fell into the river," Perenelle said.

"I was pulled," Scathach corrected her immediately. "Dagon came up like a crocodile and grabbed me."

"Did you not once fight him and a school of Potamoi fishmen on the Isle of Capri?"

Scatty's savage vampire teeth flashed again. "Now, that was a good day." Then her smile vanished. "Anyway, he turned up working with Machiavelli in Paris."

"I'd heard the Italian was in Paris." Perenelle nodded.

"Head of the secret service or something. I was only semiconscious when Dagon pulled me into the water. But the Seine was so cold that the shock brought me wide awake. We fought for hours while the currents dragged us downriver. It wasn't the toughest battle I've ever fought, but Dagon was in his element and the water took a lot of the force out of my blows."

"I see he managed to scratch you."

"Lucky hits," Scatty snorted, dismissing them. "I lost him somewhere around Les Damps, and it took me two days to get back to the city."

"Are you safe now?"

"I'm with Joan." The Shadow smiled. "And Saint-Germain, too." Her smile broadened. "They got married!"

She pulled her head back and a second face swam into view in the water, huge gray eyes dominating a small boyish face. "Madame Flamel."

"Joan!" Perenelle smiled. If she considered Scatty to be a niece, then Joan was the daughter she never had. "You finally married Francis?"

"Well, we have been seeing one another for centuries. It was time."

"It was. Joan, it is good to see you," Perenelle continued. "I just wish it were in better circumstances."

"I agree," Joan of Arc said. "These are indeed desperate times. Especially for Nicholas and the children."

"Are they the twins of legend?" Perenelle asked, curious to hear what her friend thought.

"I am convinced of it," Joan of Arc said immediately. "The girl's aura is stronger and purer than mine."

"Can you get to London?" the Sorceress asked.

The tiny face in the water blurred as the woman on the other side of the world shook her head. "Impossible. Machiavelli controls Paris, and he has locked this city down tightly, claiming a matter of national security. The borders are closed. All flights, ferry sailings and trains are being carefully monitored, and I'm sure they have our descriptions—Scatty's certainly. There are police everywhere; they're stopping people on the streets, demanding to see identification, and there is a nine o'clock curfew in effect. The police have released grainy security-camera video of Nicholas, the twins, Scatty and me taken from in front of Notre Dame."

Perenelle shook her head. "Do I want to know what you were doing in front of the cathedral?"

"Battling the gargoyles," Joan said lightly.

"I knew I shouldn't have asked. I'm concerned about Nicholas and the children. Knowing Nicholas's sense of direction, they're probably lost. And Dee's spies are everywhere," Perenelle added miserably. "No doubt he knew the moment they arrived."

"Oh, don't worry, Francis arranged for Palamedes to pick them up. He's protecting them. He's good," Joan assured her.

Perenelle nodded in agreement. "Not as good as the Shadow."

"Well, no one is," Joan declared. "Where are you now, madame?"

"Trapped on Alcatraz. And I'm in trouble," she admitted.

Scatty's face pushed in alongside her friend's. "What sort of trouble?"

"The cells are full of monsters, the seas are full of Nereids. Nereus guards the water and a sphinx roams the corridors. That sort of trouble."

Joan of Arc's smile turned brilliant. "Why, if you are in trouble, then we must help you!"

"That, I fear, is impossible," Perenelle said.

"Ah, but madame, you were the one who taught me a long time ago that the word *impossible* is meaningless."

Perenelle smiled. "I did say that. Scatty, is there anyone you know in San Francisco who could help me? I need to get off this island. I need to get to Nicholas."

"No one I trust. Maybe some of my students—"

"No," Perenelle interrupted. "I'll not endanger any humans. I mean any Elders loyal to us, any of the Next Generation?"

Scatty considered for a minute, then slowly shook her head. "No one I trust," she repeated. She turned her head to listen to a conversation behind her, and when she looked back, her savage smile was brilliant. "We've a plan. Or rather, Francis has a plan. Can you hang on for a little while longer? We're on our way."

"We? Who's we?" Perenelle asked.

"Joan and I. We're coming to Alcatraz."

"How can you get here if you cannot even get to London?" Perenelle began, but then the water shivered and trembled and suddenly the myriad ghosts of Alcatraz rose around her, clamoring and crying out for attention. The connection was lost.

# CHAPTER FORTY-EIGHT

*D*r. John Dee stood before the huge plate-glass window on one of the topmost floors of the Canary Wharf Tower, the London headquarters of Enoch Enterprises. Sipping a steaming mug of herbal tea, he watched the first glimmers of dawn appear on the eastern horizon.

Freshly showered, hair pulled back off his face, dressed in a tailored gray three-piece suit, he looked nothing like the filthy vagabond who had arrived at the parking-lot security booth less than an hour earlier. The Magician had taken great care to avoid the cameras, and a simple mesmerizing spell had focused the guard's attention on the black-and-white squares of his newspaper's crossword puzzle. Even if he'd wanted to, the man wouldn't have been able to look away from it. Sticking to the shadows in the empty parking lot, Dee had made his way into the private elevator and used his personal security code—13071527—to go straight up to the penthouse suites.

Dee's Enoch Enterprises occupied an entire floor of the Canary Wharf Tower, the tallest building in Britain, right in the heart of London's financial district. He had similar offices scattered around the world, and although he only rarely visited them, the Magician kept a luxurious private suite in every one. Built into each office was a tall safe that opened only to Dee's handprint and retina scan. It contained clothes, cash in assorted currencies, credit cards and a variety of passports in a dozen different names. He'd been trapped without money and clothes in the past and had sworn it would never happen again.

It was only when he was standing under the scalding shower, water running filthy and black from his body, that he'd had a moment to consider his options. He had to admit that they were extremely limited.

He could find the Alchemyst, kill him, retrieve the missing pages and secure the twins.

Or he could run.

He could flee Britain on a false passport and hide in a quiet out-of-the-way place, and spend the rest of his life in fear, unable to use his aura in case it revealed his location, constantly looking over his shoulder, always waiting for one of his masters to appear to lay their hands on him. The moment they touched his bare flesh, the immortality spell would be broken and he would age and die. Or maybe they would keep their promise: render him mortal and allow his nearly five hundred years to consume his physical body . . . and then make him immortal again in the last moments of extreme old age. Dee shuddered. It would be a living death.

Stepping out of the shower, he ran his hand across the steamed-up mirror and stared at his reflection in the glass. Was it his imagination or were there new wrinkles on his forehead and alongside his eyes? He had spent centuries running—running from danger or chasing the Alchemyst and the others like him. He had skulked and hidden, cowered in fear of his Elder masters, done their bidding unquestioningly. Condensation ran down the mirror, making it look as if he were crying. But the Magician did not cry anymore; the last time he had shed tears was when his baby son, Nicholas, had died in 1597.

He would run no more.

The study of magic and sorcery had taught the Magician that the world was full of limitless possibilities, and the years spent researching alchemy with Flamel had shown him that nothing—not even matter—was fixed and unalterable. Everything could be manipulated. He'd lived his long life dedicating himself to changing the world, bettering it by returning it to the Dark Elders. On the surface it was an impossible task, the odds stacked against him, but over the centuries he had nearly succeeded, until now the Elders were poised to return to the earth.

His situation was desperate and dangerous, but he could fix it. The key to his own survival was simple: he had to find Flamel.

He dressed quickly, relishing the feel of clean clothes, and made himself some tea, then went to look out over the city he controlled. Standing before the window, staring across the sprawling streets, he realized the enormity of the task before him; he had no idea where the Alchemyst had taken the children.

He did have agents—both human and inhuman—in London. Next Generation and immortal mercenaries were on the streets. They all had the latest descriptions of the Alchemyst and the children, and he would add Palamedes and the Bard to that list. He would double—no, triple—the reward. It was only a matter of time before someone spotted the little group.

But he had no time.

Dee's cell phone buzzed in his breast pocket, then played the opening bars of the theme to *The X-Files*. He made a face; suddenly that didn't seem so funny anymore. He put the cup of tea down, fished the phone out of his inside pocket and held it clenched in his fist before looking at the screen. It was the impossibly long and ever-changing number he'd been expecting. He was surprised it had taken them until now to get to him; maybe they'd been waiting for him to make a report. His finger hovered over the green Answer button, but he knew that the moment he hit it, the Elders would know his location. He doubted he'd live long enough to finish his tea.

Dr. John Dee returned the phone to his pocket unanswered and picked up his cup.

Then, a moment later, he plucked the phone back out and dialed a number from memory. His call was answered on the first ring. "I need a favor."

✧   ✧   ✧

Niccolò Machiavelli shot out of his chair. *"Favore?"* he said, unconsciously slipping into Italian.

"A favor," Dee said in the same language. "No doubt you have heard about my little difficulty."

"I'm looking at news of a fire in London," Machiavelli told Dee cautiously, aware that everything he said could be recorded. "I guessed you were involved."

"Flamel and the others fled in a car," Dee continued. "I need to contain them."

"So you are still pursuing them?" Machiavelli said.

"To my death," the Magician said. "Which could be sooner than I wish," he added. "But I am sworn to do my duty to my masters. You understand duty, Machiavelli, do you not?"

The Italian nodded. "I do." He sat back in the chair. "What do you want me to do?" He glanced at the clock. It was 5:45 a.m. in Paris. "Be aware that I'm flying to San Francisco in a few hours."

"I need you to make a phone call, that's all."

Machiavelli remained silent, unwilling to commit. He knew that this conversation could be very dangerous. His master and Dee's were somehow opposed, but they both wanted the same thing: the return of the Dark Elders to the earth. And Machiavelli knew he must be seen to support that in every way possible. Once the Dark Elders returned, then the real power struggle for control of the planet would take place. Naturally, he was hoping that his master and his master's followers would be triumphant, but if Dee's masters took control, then it might be useful to have Dee as an ally. Machiavelli grinned and rubbed his hands together; his scheming reminded him of the good old days of the Borgias.

"As head of the French secret service," Dee continued, "you must have contacts with your British counterparts."

"Of course." He started nodding. He suddenly knew what the Magician was about to ask. "Let me contact them," he said quickly. "I'll inform them that the terrorists who attacked Paris are now in London. I am sure the British authorities will move swiftly to close the airports and train stations."

"We need roadblocks and checkpoints, too."

"That should be possible." Machiavelli chuckled. "I will make that call now."

Dee coughed slightly. "I am in your debt."

"I know that." Machiavelli grinned.

"Let me ask a final favor, then," Dee said. "Could you delay informing our Elders of my location? Give me this one last day to find the Alchemyst."

Machiavelli hesitated; then he said, "I'll not tell your Elder," he said, "and you know me to be a man of my word."

"I do."

"You have one final day," the Italian began, but Dee had already hung up. Machiavelli sat back and tapped the phone against his lips. Then he started to dial a number. He had promised the Magician that he would not inform *his* Elder; but Machiavelli's own Elder master would certainly want to know.

✧　✧　✧

In London, bands of orange and pink shot through with purples and blacks appeared on the horizon. The Magician stared hard at the sky, his gray eyes picking up the colors, watching them intently while his tea grew cold in his hands. He knew that if he did not find the Alchemyst and the twins, then this could be the last sunrise he would ever see.

# CHAPTER FORTY-NINE

*O*nce the sun had set, temperatures had fallen quickly, and the breeze whipping in off San Francisco Bay was cold and salty. From her position in the watchtower over the wharf, Perenelle peered down on the island. Although she was wearing bundles of clothing and had gathered all the blankets from the cells to wrap around her, she was still freezing. Her fingers and toes were so numb she had lost all feeling in them, and she'd actually bitten down hard on a moldy blanket to keep her teeth from chattering.

She dared not use her aura to warm up—the sphinx had freed itself from its icy tomb and was prowling the island.

Perenelle had been standing before Areop-Enap's cocoon looking for any sign of movement when she had smelled the distinctive scent of the creature on the salt air, a rancid mixture of snake and lion and musty feathers. A heartbeat later, de Ayala had blinked into existence before her.

374

"I know," she said before he could speak. "Is all in readiness?"

"*Yes,*" the ghost said shortly. "*But we tried this before . . .*"

Perenelle's smile was brilliant. "The sphinx are powerful and terrifying . . . but not terribly bright." She wrapped a blanket more tightly around her shoulders and shivered with the chill. "Where is it now?"

"*Moving through the shell of the Warden's House. A hint of your odor must remain there. No offense intended, madame,*" he added quickly.

"None taken. That's one of the reasons I've chosen to stay outdoors tonight. I'm hoping that the gusting wind will blow away any scent."

"*It is a good plan,*" de Ayala agreed.

"And how does the creature look?" the Sorceress wondered out loud. She patted Areop-Enap's thick cocoon, then turned and hurried away.

The ghost smiled delightedly. "*Unhappy.*"


The sphinx lifted a huge paw and put it down carefully, wincing as the most extraordinary sensation—pain—shot up her leg. She had not been injured in three centuries. Any wound would heal, cuts and bruises would quickly fade, but the memory of her injured pride would never go away.

She had been bested. By a *humani.*

Throwing back her slender neck, she breathed deeply and a long black forked tongue protruded from humanlike lips. The tongue flickered, tasting the air. And there it was: a hint, the merest suggestion of a humani. But this building was roofless and open to the elements, constantly scoured by the sea breezes, and the trace was very faint. The female humani had been here. The creature padded over to a window. Right here, but not recently. A forked tongue tasted the bricks. She had rested her hand here. The head turned toward the huge opening in the wall. And then the humani had gone out into the night.

The sphinx's beautiful human face creased in a frown. Folding tattered eagle's wings tightly against her body, she pushed through the ruined house and out into the cool night.

She could not sense the humani's aura. Nor could she smell her flesh.

And yet the Sorceress had to be on the island; she could not have escaped. The sphinx had seen the Nereids in the water and had smelled the fishy odor of the Old Man of the Sea lingering on the air. She had spotted the Crow Goddess perched like a hideous weathervane on top of the lighthouse, and though the sphinx had called out to her in a variety of languages, including the lost language of Danu Talis, the creature had not responded. The sphinx was unconcerned; some of the Next Generation, like herself, preferred the night; others walked in the sunlight. The Crow Goddess had probably been sleeping.

Despite her bulk, the sphinx moved swiftly down to the wharf, claws clicking on the stones. And here she caught the faintest wisp of the odor of a humani, the smell of salt and meat.

And then she saw her.

A movement, a shadow, a hint of long hair and a flowing dress.

With a terrifying screech of triumph, the sphinx set off after the woman. This time she would not escape.

From her high vantage point in the watchtower, Perenelle watched the sphinx race off after the ghost of a long-dead warden's wife.

The merest suggestion of de Ayala's face appeared out of the night, little more than a shimmering disturbance in the air. *"The ghosts of Alcatraz are in place. They will lead the sphinx away to the far end of the island and keep it busy down there for the rest of the night. Rest now, madame; sleep if you can. Who knows what the morrow will bring?"*

# CHAPTER FIFTY

"Where are you taking us?" Nicholas asked softly. "Why have we left the main road?"

"Trouble," Palamedes said quietly. He tilted the rearview mirror to peer into the back of the cab.

Only the Alchemyst was awake. The twins were slumped forward, held in place by seat belts, while Gilgamesh was curled up on the floor, twitching and mumbling in Sumerian. Nicholas looked at the Saracen Knight's deep brown eyes in the mirror.

"I knew something was wrong when traffic was so heavy," the knight continued. "Then I thought there might have been an accident." They were taking seemingly random turns, heading down narrow country lanes, lush green hedgerows battering against the side of the car. "All the main roads are blocked; police are searching every car."

"Dee," Flamel whispered. Unclipping his seat belt, he

slipped into the jump seat just behind the driver, twisting around to look through the glass partition at the knight. "We have to get to Stonehenge," he said. "That is our only way out of this country."

"There are other leygates. I could take you to Holyhead in Wales, and you could get the ferry to Ireland. Newgrange is still active," Palamedes suggested.

"No one knows where Newgrange comes out," Nicholas said firmly. "And the ley line on Salisbury will take me just north of San Francisco."

The knight turned down a road marked PRIVATE and stopped before a five-barred wooden gate. Leaving the engine running, he climbed out of the car and unlatched it. Flamel joined him, and together the two men pushed it open. A rutted track led down to a ramshackle wooden barn. "I know the owner," Palamedes said shortly. "We'll hide up here until everything calms down."

Flamel reached out and caught Palamedes' arm. There was a sudden odor of cloves and the Alchemyst jerked his fingers away as the knight's flesh turned hard and metallic. "We need to get to Stonehenge." The Alchemyst gestured toward the road they'd left. "We can't be more than a couple of miles away."

"We're close enough," Palamedes agreed. "Why the rush, Alchemyst?"

"I've got to get back to Perenelle." He stepped in front of the knight, forcing him to stop. "Look at me, Saracen. What do you see?" He held up his hands; blue veins were now clearly visible, and there were brown age spots scattered across his flesh. Tilting his head back, he exposed his wrinkled neck. "I'm dying, Palamedes," the Alchemyst said simply. "I don't have very long left, and when I die, I want to go with my own dear Perenelle. You were in love once, Palamedes. You understand that."

The knight sighed and then nodded. "Let's get into the barn and wake the twins and Gilgamesh. He agreed to train them in the Magic of Water. If he remembers and if he does it, then we'll press on to Stonehenge. I'm sure I can work out a route with the GPS." He reached out and caught Flamel's arm. "Remember, Nicholas. Once he starts the process, the twins' auras will blaze up, and then everyone—and everything—will know where they are."

# CHAPTER FIFTY-ONE

At 10:20 a.m., five minutes later than its scheduled departure time, the Air France Boeing 747 lifted off from Charles de Gaulle airport, bound for San Francisco.

Niccolò Machiavelli settled into his seat and adjusted his watch nine hours back to 1:20 a.m., Pacific Standard Time. Then he reclined his seat, laced his fingers together on his stomach, closed his eyes and enjoyed the rare luxury of being uncontactable. For the next eleven hours and fifteen minutes, no one would be able to phone, e-mail or fax him. Whatever crisis arose, someone else would have to handle it. A smile formed on his mouth: this was like a mini-vacation, and it had been a long time—more than two centuries, in fact—since he'd had a proper rest. His last holiday, in Egypt in 1798, had been ruined when Napoléon had invaded. Machiavelli's smile faded as he shook his head slightly. He had masterminded Napoléon's plan for a "federation of free peoples" and the

Code Napoléon, and if the Corsican had only continued to listen to him, France would have ruled all Europe, North Africa and the Middle East. Machiavelli had even drawn up plans for an invasion of America via sea and down through Canada.

"Something to drink, monsieur?"

Machiavelli opened his eyes to find a bored-looking flight attendant smiling down at him. He shook his head. "Thank you. No. And please do not disturb me again for the duration of the flight."

The woman nodded. "Would you like to be awakened for lunch or dinner?"

"No, thank you. I am on a special diet," he said.

"If you had let us know in advance, we could have organized an appropriate meal. . . ."

Machiavelli held up a long-fingered hand. "I am perfectly fine. Thank you," he said firmly, eyes moving off the woman's face, dismissing her.

"I will let the others know." The attendant moved away to check on the three other passengers in the l'Espace Affaires cabin. The rich smell of freshly brewed coffee and newly baked bread filled the air, and the Italian closed his eyes and tried to remember what real food—fresh food—tasted like. One of the side effects of the gift of immortality was the diminishing of appetite. Immortal humans still needed to eat, but only for fuel and energy. Most food, unless it was highly spiced or sickly sweet, was tasteless. He wondered if Flamel, who had become immortal by his own hand rather than by an Elder's, suffered the same side effect.

And thinking of Nicholas made him focus on Perenelle.

Dee's Elder had been quite clear: *"Do not attempt to capture or imprison Perenelle. Do not talk to her, bargain with her or reason with her. Kill her on sight. The Sorceress is infinitely more dangerous than the Alchemyst."*

Machiavelli had trained himself to become a master of both verbal and body language. He knew when people were lying; he could read it in their eyes, the tiny movements of their clenching hands, twitching fingers and tapping feet. Even if he could not see them, several lifetimes of listening to emperors, kings, princes, politicians and thieves had taught him that it was often not what people said, but what they did *not* say that revealed the truth.

Dee's Elders had warned that the Sorceress was infinitely more dangerous than the Alchemyst. They had not indicated exactly how . . . but they *had* revealed that they were frightened of her. And why was that? he wondered. She was an immortal human: powerful, yes; dangerous, certainly; but why should she frighten the Elders?

Tilting his head, Machiavelli looked through the oval window. The 747 had risen above the clouds into a spectacularly blue sky, and he allowed his thoughts to wander, remembering the leaders he had served and manipulated down through the ages. Unlike Dee, who had come to fame as Queen Elizabeth's personal and very public advisor, he had always operated behind the scenes, dropping hints, making suggestions, allowing others to take the credit for his ideas. It was always better—safer—to be overlooked. There was an old Celtic saying he was particularly fond of: *It is better to exist unknown to the law.* He'd always imagined that Perenelle was a little like him, happy to stay in the background and allow her husband to take all the credit. Everyone in Europe knew the name Nicholas Flamel. Few were even aware of Perenelle's existence. The Italian nodded unconsciously; she was the power behind the man.

Machiavelli had kept a file on the Flamels for centuries. The earliest notes were on parchment with beautifully illuminated drawings; then had come thick handmade paper with pen-and-ink sketches and later still, paper with tinted photographs. The most recent files were digital, with high-resolution photographs and video. He had retained all his earlier notes on the Alchemyst and his wife, but they had also been scanned and imported into his encrypted database. There was frustratingly little information on Nicholas, and very, very little devoted to the Sorceress. So much about her was unknown. There was even a suggestion in a fourteenth-century French report that she had been a widow when she had married Nicholas. And when the Alchemyst had died, he had left everything in his will to Perenelle's nephew, a man called Perrier. Machiavelli suspected—though he had no evidence to back up his supposition—that Perrier might be a child from her first marriage. Perrier took possession of all the Alchemyst's papers and belongings . . . and simply vanished from history. Centuries later, a couple claiming to be the descendents of Perrier's family appeared in Paris, where they were promptly arrested by Cardinal Richelieu. The Cardinal had been forced to release them when he realized that they knew nothing about their famous ancestor and possessed none of his books and writings.

Perenelle was a mystery.

Machiavelli had spent a fortune paying spies, librarians, historians and researchers to look into the mysterious woman, but even they had found astonishingly little on her. And when he had fought her face to face in Sicily in 1669, he had discovered then that she had access to extraordinary—almost elemental—power. Drawing upon more than a century of learning, he had battled her using a combination of magical and alchemical spells from around the globe. She had countered them all with a bewildering display of sorcery. By evening, he had been exhausted, his aura dangerously depleted, but Perenelle had still looked fresh and composed. If Mount Etna had not erupted and ended the battle, he was convinced she would have destroyed him, or caused his aura to spontaneously combust and consume his body. It was only later that he'd realized that the energies they had both released had probably caused the volcano to erupt.

Niccolò Machiavelli settled a soft wool blanket up around his shoulders and hit the switch that gently converted his comfortable seat into a six-foot-long bed. Lying back, he closed his eyes and breathed deeply. He would think about the problem of the Sorceress for the next few hours, but one thing was already crystal clear: Perenelle frightened the Dark Elders. And people were usually afraid only of those who could destroy them. One final thought hovered at the edge of his consciousness: who—or what—was Perenelle Flamel?

# CHAPTER FIFTY-TWO

$\mathcal{T}$he cab hit a pothole and the jolt woke the twins. "Sorry," Palamedes called back cheerfully.

Moving stiffly, arms and necks aching, Josh and Sophie both stretched out. Josh automatically ran his hand through the bird's nest of his hair, yawning widely as he squinted out the window, blinking in the sunlight. "This is Stonehenge?" he asked, peering out at the field of tall grass speckled with wildflowers. Then reality hit him and he answered his own question, his voice rising in alarm. "This isn't Stonehenge." Twisting in the seat, he looked at the Alchemyst and demanded, "Where are you taking us?"

"Everything is under control," Palamedes said from the front. "There are police checkpoints on the main road. We've just taken a little detour."

Sophie hit a button and the power window whined down, flooding the car with the scent of grass. She sneezed, and as her sinuses cleared, she realized that she could pick out the scents of individual wildflowers. Leaning her head out the window, she turned her face to the sun and the cloudless blue sky. When she opened her eyes, a red admiral butterfly danced past her face. "Where are we?" she asked Nicholas.

"I've no idea," he admitted quietly. "Palamedes knows this place. Somewhere close to Stonehenge."

The car rocked again and Gilgamesh came slowly, noisily awake. Lying on the floor, he yawned hugely and stretched, then sat bolt upright and looked out the window, squinting in the bright light. "I haven't been out to the country for a while," he said happily. He looked at the twins and frowned. "Hello."

"Hi," Josh and Sophie said simultaneously.

"Has anyone ever told you that you look alike enough to be twins?" he continued, sitting cross-legged on the floor. He blinked and frowned. "You are twins," he said slowly. "You are the twins of legend. Why aren't you called the legendary twins?" he asked suddenly.

They looked at one another and shook their heads, confused.

Gilgamesh tilted his head to look up at the Alchemyst and his expression soured. "You I know. You I will never forget." He turned back to the twins. "He tried to kill me, you know that?" He frowned. "But you do know that, you were there."

They shook their heads. "We weren't there," Sophie said gently.

"Not there?" The ragged king sat back on the floor and pressed both hands against his head, squeezing hard. "Ah, but you must forgive an old man. I have lived for . . . for a long time, too long, too, too long, and there is so much that I remember, and even more that I forget. I have memories and dreams and they get confused and wrapped up together. There are so many thoughts whirling around inside my head." He winced, almost as if he were in pain, and when he spoke, there was nothing but the sadness of loss in his voice. "Sometimes it is hard to tell them apart, to know what really was and what I have only imagined." He reached into his voluminous coats and pulled out a thick sheaf of paper held together with string. "I write things down," he said quickly. "That's how I remember." He thumbed through the pages. There were scraps from notebooks, covers torn from paperbacks, bits of newspapers, restaurant menus and napkins, thick parchment, even scraps of hide and wafer-thin sheets of copper and bark. They had all been cut or torn to roughly the same size and they were covered in miniscule scratchy writing. He looked closely at each of the twins in turn. "Someday I'll write about you, so that I'll remember you." He glared at Flamel. "And I'll write about you, too, Alchemyst, so that I never forget you."

Sophie suddenly blinked and the image before her fragmented as tears came to her eyes. Two perfect silver drops slid down her cheeks.

The king came slowly to his knees before her and then, gently, carefully, reached out to touch the silver liquid with his index finger. The tears twisted and curled like mercury across his fingernail. Concentrating fiercely, he rubbed the tears between forefinger and thumb. When he looked up, there were no signs of confusion in his eyes, no doubts on his face. "Do you know how long it has been since anyone has shed a tear for Gilgamesh the King?" His voice was strong and commanding, and there was the tiniest accent when he said his name and title. "Oh, but it was a lifetime ago, in that time before time, the time before history." The silver droplet pooled in his palm and he closed his hand into a fist, holding the tear. "There was a girl then who shed silver tears, who wept for a prince of the land, who wept for me, and for the world she was about to destroy." He looked up at Sophie, blue eyes huge and unblinking. "Girl, why do you weep for me?"

Unable to speak, Sophie shook her head. Josh put his arm around his sister.

"Tell me," Gilgamesh insisted.

She swallowed hard and shook her head again.

"Please? I would like to know."

Sophie drew in a deep shuddering breath, and when she spoke her voice was barely above a whisper. "I have the Witch of Endor's memories inside me. I spend all my time trying to keep thoughts away and ignore them . . . but here you are, trying to remember your own life, writing your thoughts down so that you don't forget. I suddenly realized what it would be like not to know, not to *remember*."

"Just so," Gilgamesh agreed. "We humans are nothing more than the sum of our memories." The king sat back against the door, legs stretched straight out in front of him. He looked at the bundled pages in his lap, then pulled out a tiny stub of a pencil and started writing.

The Alchemyst leaned forward, and for a moment, it looked as if he was about to put his hand on the king's shoulder. Then he drew it back and asked gently, "What are you remembering now, Gilgamesh?"

The king pressed his index finger into the page, rubbing silver tears into the paper. "The day someone cared enough to shed a tear for me."

# CHAPTER FIFTY-THREE

"End of the road." Palamedes hit the brakes and the cab skidded to a stop in front of the barn. A cloud of dust from the baked-hard earth plumed upward, billowing out around the windows. Gilgamesh immediately pushed open the door and stepped out into the still morning, turning his face to the sun and stretching his arms wide. The twins followed him, pulling the cheap sunglasses the Alchemyst had bought them from their pockets.

Flamel was the last to exit, and he turned to look at the knight, who'd made no move to turn off the engine or get out of the cab. "You're not staying?"

"I'm going into the nearest village," Palamedes said. "I'll pick up some food and water and see if I can find out what's going on." The Saracen Knight allowed his eyes to drift toward the king and lowered his voice. "Be careful. You know how quickly he can turn."

The Alchemyst moved the side mirror slightly, angling it to be able to see Gilgamesh and the twins exploring the barn. The building sat in the middle of the grassy field. Ancient and overgrown, the walls were constructed of thick black timbers and mud. The doors were of a more recent vintage, and he guessed that they'd probably been put up sometime in the nineteenth century. Now they both hung askew, the right door attached by only a single leather hinge. The bottoms of both doors were rotted to ragged splinters by weather and the gnawings of animals.

"The boy will be first inside," Palamedes said, looking over the Alchemyst's shoulder.

Flamel nodded silently in agreement.

"You need to be careful of him also," Palamedes advised. "You need to separate him from the sword."

Nicholas adjusted the mirror slightly. He saw Josh tug Clarent from its map tube and slip into the barn, followed a moment later by his twin and then the king. "He needed a weapon," the Alchemyst said, "he needed something to protect himself with."

"A shame it was *that* weapon. There are other swords. They are not quite so dangerous, not quite so . . . *hungry* as that one."

"I'll take it back when he learns one of the elemental magics," Flamel said.

Palamedes grunted. "You'll try. I doubt you'll succeed." He put the car in gear. "I'd best go. I'll be back as soon as I can."

"Are we safe here?" Flamel asked the knight, looking around. The field was surrounded by ancient twisted oaks; he could see no signs of nearby buildings or power lines. "Any chance of the owner turning up?"

"None at all," Palamedes said with a grin. "Shakespeare owns it, and everything for miles around. He has properties all across England." The knight tapped the satellite navigator stuck to his cracked windshield. "We have them all entered in here; that's how I was able to get you to safety."

Nicholas shook his head. "I never imagined Will as a property investor, but then I never imagined him as a car mechanic either."

The knight nodded. "He was—and still is—an actor. He plays many roles. I know he started buying properties back in the sixteenth century, when he was writing. He always said he made more money from property than he did from his plays. But you don't want to believe half of what he says; he can be a terrible liar." Palamedes eased on the gas and turned the wheel, rolling the big black taxi around in a half circle, Flamel walking alongside the open window. "The barn is invisible from the road, and I'll lock the gate after me." The knight glanced sidelong at Flamel, then jerked his chin in the direction of the dilapidated structure. "Did you really try to kill the king the last time you met?"

Nicholas shook his head. "In spite of what you think of me, Sir Knight, I am not a killer. In 1945, Perenelle and I were working in Alamogordo, in New Mexico. It was, without doubt, the perfect job for an alchemyst. Even though our work was classified as above top-secret, Gilgamesh somehow discovered what we were planning."

"And what were you planning?" Palamedes asked, confused.

"To detonate the first atomic bomb. Gilgamesh wanted to be standing underneath when it went off. He decided it was the only way he could truly die."

The Saracen Knight's broad face creased in sympathy. "What happened to him?" he asked softly.

"Perenelle had him locked up in an institution for his own protection. He spent ten years there before we thought it was safe enough to allow him to escape."

Palamedes grunted. "No wonder he hates you," he said. And before the Alchemyst could answer, the knight revved the engine and drove off in a plume of dust.

"No wonder indeed," Nicholas murmured. He waited until the dust had settled and then he turned and headed for the barn. He was hoping Gilgamesh wouldn't remember everything—especially the part about being locked up—until after he had taught the twins the third of the elemental magics. A thought hit him as he slid through the doorway of the barn: given the fractured state of his mind, would the king even *remember* the ancient Magic of Water?

# CHAPTER FIFTY-FOUR

*J*osh walked cautiously through the barn, Clarent still and quiet in his hands, the tiny quartz crystals in the stone blade dull and lifeless. He inched along on the balls of his feet, suddenly struck by how acutely conscious he was of his surroundings. Though he knew he'd never been here before, and had thus far only had a quick glimpse of the interior, he also knew with absolute certainty that he could navigate the space with his eyes closed.

The barn was warm and close, heavy with the scent of old hay and dry grass. Unseen creatures rustled in corners, doves cooed in the rafters and Josh could clearly hear a drone from a large wasps' nest built high in a corner. A stream of insects moved in and out of the nest. Farm machinery had been stored here and abandoned; Josh thought he recognized an old-fashioned plow, and the squat remains of a tractor, its knobbly tires rotted to black strips. Every scrap of metal was

395

covered in thick brown-red rust. Wooden crates and empty barrels lay scattered around, and a crude workbench—nothing more than two strips of wood resting on concrete blocks—had been constructed up against one wall. The planks had warped and curled up at both ends. The frame of a black bicycle was tucked under the bench, almost invisible behind a heavy covering of grass and nettles.

"This place hasn't been used in years," Josh said. He was standing in the center of the barn, turning in a complete circle as he spoke. He drove Clarent into the dirt floor between his feet and folded his arms across his chest. "It's safe."

Gilgamesh wandered around the space, slowly peeling off layers of clothing, letting them fall on the ground behind him. Beneath all the coats and fleeces he was wearing the remains of what had once been a smart suit. The pinstripe jacket was greasy with wear, and the matching trousers had thin knees and a shiny seat. The king wore a grubby collarless shirt underneath the coat. The ragged remains of a knitted scarf wound around his neck. "I like places like this," he announced.

"I like old places too," Josh said, "but what's to like about a place like this?"

The king spread his arms wide. "What do you see?"

Josh made a face. "Junk. Rusted tractor, broken plow, old bike."

"Ah . . . but I see a tractor that was once used to till these fields. I see the plow it once pulled. I see a bicycle carefully placed out of harm's way under a table."

Josh slowly turned again, looking at the items once more.

"And I see these things and I wonder at the life of the person who so carefully stored the precious tractor and plow in the barn out of the weather, and placed their bike under a homemade table."

"Why do you wonder?" Josh asked. "Why is it even important?"

"Because someone has to remember," Gilgamesh snapped, suddenly irritated. "Someone has to remember the human who rode the bike and drove the tractor, the person who tilled the fields, who was born and lived and died, who loved and laughed and cried, the person who shivered in the cold and sweated in the sun." He walked around the barn again, touching each item, until his palms were red with rust. "It is only when no one remembers that you are truly lost. That is the true death."

"Then you will always be remembered, Gilgamesh," Sophie said quietly. She was sitting on an overturned barrel, watching the king carefully. "*The Epic of Gilgamesh* is still in print today."

The king stopped, his head tilted to one side, considering. "I suppose that is true." He grinned and wiped his hands on his trousers, leaving red streaks on the stained cloth. "I read it once. Didn't like it. Only some of it is true, and they missed the good parts."

Flamel pushed the barn door closed, shutting out the sunlight. "You could write your own version," he offered. "Tell your story, the true story."

The king laughed, the booming sound setting the doves flapping from the rafters. "And who would believe me, eh,

397

Alchemyst? If I were to put down half of what I know, I would be locked up. . . ." His voice trailed away and his eyes clouded.

Nicholas quickly stepped forward and bowed deeply, an old-fashioned courtly movement. He knew he had to take control of the situation before Gilgamesh began to remember too much. "Majesty, will you keep your promise and teach the twins the Magic of Water?"

Still staring at Flamel, the king slowly nodded. "I will do that."

Flamel straightened, but not before the twins had seen the look of triumph on his narrow face. "Sophie has been trained in Air and Fire. Josh has no training, so he has no idea what to expect," he warned.

Josh stepped forward. "Just tell me what to do," he said eagerly, eyes bright with excitement. He grinned at his twin. "We'll start becoming real twins again," he announced.

Sophie smiled. "This isn't a competition."

"Maybe not for you!"

Gilgamesh picked up a barrel and set it on the ground next to Sophie. "Come sit by your sister."

"What do you want me to do?" Flamel asked, leaning back against the door, his hands shoved into the back pockets of his jeans.

"Say nothing and do nothing except stay out of my way," Gilgamesh snapped. He looked over at the Alchemyst, his blue eyes blazing. "And when this is over, you and I will have a little talk . . . about the decade I was incarcerated. We're due a reckoning."

Nicholas Flamel nodded, his face expressionless. "This process," he said. "Will it activate the twins' auras?"

The king tilted his head to one side, thinking. "Possibly. Why?"

"Their auras would act as a beacon. Who knows what they will attract."

Gilgamesh nodded. "Let me see what I can do. There are different ways to teach." The king sank cross-legged onto the floor in front of the twins and briskly rubbed his hands together. "Now, where do we begin?" he said.

Josh suddenly realized that they were surrendering themselves to a mad vagrant who sometimes forgot his own name. How was this man going to remember age-old magic? What would happen if he forgot the process halfway through? "Have you done this before?" he asked, growing increasingly worried.

The king reached out and took Sophie's right hand and Josh's left hand and looked at them seriously. "Just once. And that didn't end well."

"What happened?" Josh attempted to pull his hand away from the immortal's, but Gilgamesh gripped it tightly, his flesh as rough as tree bark.

"He flooded the world. Now, close your eyes," the king commanded.

Sophie immediately shut her eyes, but Josh kept his open. He stared at the king. The man turned to look at him, and suddenly his bright unblinking blue eyes seemed huge in his head and Josh felt a nauseating twist of vertigo. He felt as if he were falling forward . . . and down . . . and rising up all at once. He squeezed his eyes closed in an attempt to shut out the sickening sensations, but he could still see the king's huge blue eyes burning into his retina, growing larger and larger, white threads starting to twist and curl across them. They reminded him of . . . of . . . of . . . clouds.

Gilgamesh's voice boomed. "Now, think of . . ."

# CHAPTER FIFTY-FIVE

"*. . . Water.*"

Josh opened his eyes.

A huge blue planet floated in space. White clouds swirled across its surface; ice glittered at its poles.

And then he was falling, plunging toward the planet, hurtling toward the bright blue seas. Strong and commanding, Gilgamesh's voice boomed and roared around him, rising and falling like the waves of the ocean.

"*It is said that the Magic of Air or Fire or even Earth is the most powerful magic of all. But that is wrong. The Magic of Water surpasses all others, for water is both the lifegiver and the deathbringer.*"

Mute, unable to move, to even turn his head, Josh fell through the clouds and watched as the world grew larger, vast landmasses appearing, though there was none that he recognized. He raced toward a red speck on the horizon, the clouds dark and thick above it, flying high over churning grass green seas.

Volcanoes. A dozen stretched along a ragged coastline, huge monsters belching fire and molten rock into the atmosphere. The seas roared and foamed around the red-hot rock.

*"Water can extinguish fire. Even lava from the molten heart of the planet cannot stand against it."*

When the lava hit the pounding seas, it cooled in a detonation of smoke. A steaming black landscape of congealed magma appeared out of the waves.

Josh was soaring again, the only sound the heartbeat-like throb of the king's voice, powerful yet soothing, like the crash of waves on a distant shore. The boy rose high over the ring of fire, heading east, toward a dawn. Clouds gathered beneath him; wisps giving way to fluffy balls that thickened into clumps and then blossomed into an expanse of roiling storm clouds.

*"Without water, there is no life. . . ."*

Josh fell through the clouds. Lightning flashed silently around him, and torrential rain washed down onto lush green primordial forests, where impossibly tall trees and enormous ferns covered the earth.

The landscape changed again, images flickering faster and faster. He soared across a desert wasteland where vast dunes undulated in every direction. A single spot of color drew him down, down, down toward an oasis, vibrant green trees clustered around a sparkling pool.

*"Mankind can survive with little food but cannot survive without water."*

Josh rose and dropped down onto a mighty river cutting

through high ragged hills. Dotted along its curved banks were tiny habitations, lit by fires sparking in the gloom. Racing low along the length of the river, he was aware that time was speeding up. Decades, then centuries, passed with each heartbeat. Storms lashed across the mountains, weathering them, softening them, wearing them down. Straw huts changed to mud, to wood, to stone; then clusters of stone houses appeared, a wall wrapped around them; a castle appeared and crumbled, to be replaced by a larger village, then a low town of wood and stone; then a city grew, polished marble and glass windows winking in the light before it transformed into a modern-day metropolis of glass and metal.

*"Mankind has always built his cities on riverbanks and sea-coasts."*

The river opened out to a vast ocean. The sun streaked across the sky, moving almost too fast to see as time raced by.

*"Water has been his highway . . ."*

Boats moved on the water, canoes first, then rowboats, then ships with banks of sails, and finally vast oceanliners and supertankers.

*". . . his larder . . ."*

A flotilla of fishing boats pulled huge nets from the ocean.

*". . . and his doom."*

The ocean, huge and churning, the color of a bruise, battered an isolated coastal village. It swamped boats, swept away bridges, leaving devastation in its wake.

*"Nothing stands against the power of water. . . ."*

A vast wall of water rolled down a modern city street, flooding homes, washing away cars.

Suddenly, Josh was soaring upward, the earth falling away beneath him, and the king's voice faded to a whisper, like the hiss of surf on sand.

*"It was water which brought life to the earth. Water which very nearly destroyed it."*

Josh looked down at the blue planet. This was the world he recognized. He saw the shapes of continents and countries, the sweep of North and South America, the curl of Africa. But then he suddenly realized that there was something wrong with the outlines of the land. They weren't the way he remembered them from his geography class. They seemed larger, less clearly defined. The Gulf of Mexico looked smaller, the Gulf of California was missing entirely and the Caribbean was definitely smaller. He couldn't see the distinctive shape of Italy in the Mediterranean, and the islands of Ireland and Britain were one misshapen lump.

And as he watched, the blue of the sea began to seep over the land, drowning it, flooding it. . . .

He fell toward the water, into the blue.

And Gilgamesh blinked and looked away.

And then both twins woke.

# CHAPTER FIFTY-SIX

*F*rancis, the Comte de Saint-Germain, turned in the driver's seat to look over his shoulder at Scathach. "And you cannot see it?"

Scathach leaned forward between Saint-Germain and Joan, who was sitting in the passenger seat, and stared through the windshield. Directly in front of her was the ruined façade of the great cathedral of Notre Dame. The world-famous gargoyles and grotesques that had decorated the front of the ancient building now lay in heaped rubble on the parvis. Groups of academics from across France, surrounded by volunteers and students, milled around in front of the cathedral, attempting to put the shattered pieces of stone back together again. All of the larger lumps of stone had little numbered stickers on them.

"What am I looking for?" she asked.

Saint-Germain rested both hands on the steering wheel of

the black Renault and raised his sharp chin, pointing it toward the center of the rock-strewn square. "Can you not see a faint golden pillar of light?"

Scathach squinted her grass green eyes, turned her head from side to side, searching, then finally said, "No."

The count looked at his wife.

"No," Joan of Arc said.

"It's there," Saint-Germain insisted.

"I've no doubts about that," Scathach said quickly. "I just cannot see it."

"But I can," Saint-Germain mused aloud. "Now, that's a mystery," he said delightedly. "I just assumed everyone could see it."

Joan reached out, clamped iron-hard fingers over her husband's arm and squeezed tightly enough to silence him. "You can puzzle it out later, dear. Right now we need to go."

"Oh, absolutely." The count brushed his long black hair off his forehead and then pointed to the center of the square. "Two ley lines connect the West Coast of America to Paris. Both are incredibly ancient, and one—this one, in fact—circumnavigates the globe, linking together all the primeval places of power." He tilted the rearview mirror to look at Scathach. "When you, Nicholas and the twins arrived, you came in on the line that ends at the Sacré-Coeur basilica in Montmartre. Theoretically, it should not have worked, but obviously the Witch of Endor was powerful enough to activate it."

"Francis," Joan warned, "we don't have time for a history lesson."

"Yes, yes, yes. Well, the other line, the much more powerful ley line, is here at Point Zero outside Notre Dame in the center of the city."

"Point Zero?" Scathach asked.

"Point Zero," the count repeated, pointing toward the cathedral. "The very heart of Paris; this place has been special for millennia. This is the place from which all distances to Paris are measured."

"I've often wondered why this particular spot was chosen," Joan said. "It wasn't some accident or random choice, then?"

"Hardly. Humans have worshipped here since before the Romans arrived. They have always been drawn to this place and the others like it. Perhaps, deep down in their DNA, people remembered that there was a leygate here. There are Point Zeros or Kilometer Zeros in just about every capital city in the world. And there are nearly always leygates nearby. There was a time when I used them to travel the globe."

Joan looked at her husband. Although they had known one another for centuries, they had only recently married, and she realized that there was still much she didn't know about him. She pointed toward the cathedral. "What do you see?"

"I see a golden column of light shining up into the heavens."

Joan squinted out into the early-afternoon sunlight, but she saw nothing. Her eye was caught by a flash of bright red over her shoulder as Scathach also shook her head. "These columns: are they always gold?" she asked.

"Not always: they are either gold or silver. On my travels into the Far East, I saw silver spires. Once, before he lost the ability to see clearly, I believe that ancient man would have been able to identify leygates by simply looking to the skies to find the nearest gold or silver shaft of light." He turned to look at Scathach. "Can the Elders see leygates?"

Scathach shrugged. "I have no idea," she said dismissively. "I cannot, and before you ask, I've never heard of any Next Generation who was able to see them either." The young-looking woman settled a black backpack onto her shoulders, then pulled a wide black bandana down over her forehead, completely concealing all traces of her red hair. Her matching short swords were wrapped up in a rolled blanket tied across the top of the backpack. "So what do we do?"

The count looked at his watch. "This gate will activate at precisely one-forty-nine p.m., which is solar noon over Paris—that's the time the sun is at its zenith."

"I know what solar noon means," Scatty muttered.

"Walk straight up to Point Zero and stand there. Set into the cobblestones you will find a circle surrounding a miniature sunburst. The circle is divided into two parts. Make sure both of you have one foot in each section. I'll do the rest," Saint-Germain said. "Once the gate is active, I can send you on your way."

"And the gendarmes?" Joan asked, pulling on a matching backpack. She carried her sword in a thick tube that had once held a camera tripod.

"I'll take care of them, too." Francis grinned, revealing his crooked teeth. "Stay in the car until you see the police talking to me, then move. And no matter what happens, don't stop until you reach Point Zero. Then wait."

"What then?" Scatty demanded. She hated using leygates. They always made her feel seasick.

The count shrugged. "Well, if everything goes according to plan, you will instantaneously arrive on the West Coast of America."

"And if it doesn't?" Scatty asked in alarm as Saint-Germain climbed out of the car. "What happens if it doesn't go as planned: where do we end up then?"

"Who knows?" Francis threw up his hands. "The gates are solar- or lunar-powered, depending on the direction they run. I suppose there is always the possibility that if something went wrong, you could emerge in the heart of the sun or on the dark side of the moon. This line runs east to west, so it is a sun line," he added, then smiled. "You'll be fine. He drew Joan into his arms, held her tight, then kissed her lightly on both cheeks and whispered in her ear. Then he twisted around in the seat to look at the Warrior Maid. "Stay safe. Get Perenelle off the island and contact me. I'll come and get you." The count climbed out of the car, shoved both hands in the pockets of his long black leather coat and sauntered over to the nearest gendarme.

Joan turned to look at her friend. "You've got that look about you," she said.

"What look?" Scatty asked innocently, green eyes glittering.

"I call it your battle face. I first saw it the day you rescued me from the fire. Something happens to your face, it be-comes . . . sharper." She reached back and ran a finger along

Scathach's cheek. It was as if the flesh had tightened on her bones, clearly defining the skull beneath. Her freckles stood out on her pale skin like drops of blood.

"It's my vampire heritage." The Shadow grinned, long teeth savage in her mouth. "It happens to my clan when we are excited. Some of the blood drinkers cannot control the change and it alters them utterly, making them monsters."

"You're excited to be going into battle?" Joan asked quietly.

Scatty nodded, happy. "I'm excited to be rescuing our dearest friend."

"It will not be easy. She is trapped on an island full of monsters."

"What about them? You are the legendary Jeanne d'Arc, and I am the Shadow. What can stand against us?"

"A sphinx?" Joan suggested.

"They're not so tough," Scatty said lightly. "I fought the sphinx and her appalling mother before."

"Who won?" Joan asked, biting back a smile.

"Who do you think?" Scatty began, then corrected herself. "Well, actually, I ran away. . . ."

# CHAPTER FIFTY-SEVEN

Sitting with their backs against the wall of the barn, legs stretched out in front of them, the twins watched Nicholas and Gilgamesh arguing outside. The Alchemyst was standing still and silent; the king was gesticulating wildly.

"What language are they speaking?" Josh asked. "Sounds almost familiar."

"Hebrew," Sophie said without thinking.

Josh nodded. He settled himself more comfortably against the wall. "You know, I thought . . . ," he began slowly, struggling to find the words through a blanket of exhaustion. "I thought it would be more . . ." He shrugged. "I don't know. More spectacular."

"You saw what I saw," Sophie said with a tired smile. "You don't call that spectacular?"

He shrugged again. "It was interesting. But I don't feel any different. I thought . . . I don't know, I thought that after learning one of the magics, I'd feel . . . stronger, maybe. And how do we even use this Water magic?" he asked, holding both hands straight out in front of him. "Do we do something with our auras and think about water? Should we practice?"

"Instinct. You'll know what to do when the time is right." Sophie reached out and pushed her brother's hands down. "You can't use your aura," she reminded him, "it will reveal our location. This is the third of the elemental magics I've learned," she said, "and you're right, it's not spectacular, but neither were the others. I didn't feel any stronger or faster or anything like that when I learned Air or Fire. But I do feel . . ." She paused, looking for the right word. *"Different."*

"Different?" He looked at his twin. "You don't look different, except when your eyes turn silver. Then you're scary."

Sophie nodded. She knew what he meant; she had seen her brother's eyes turn to flat gold discs and it had been terrifying. Leaning her head back against the smooth wood, she closed her eyes. "Do you remember when you had the cast taken off your arm last year?"

Josh grunted. "Never forget it." He'd broken his arm in a bad tackle the previous summer and had spent three months in a cast.

"What did you say when the cast was cut off?"

Josh unconsciously raised his left hand, turning it in a half circle, closing his fingers into a fist. The cast had been incredibly irritating; there were so many things he just couldn't do with it, including tying his shoelaces. "I said I felt like me again."

"That's how I feel." Sophie opened her eyes and looked at her brother. "With every magic I learn, I feel more and more complete. It's as if parts of me have been missing all my life and now I'm becoming whole again, piece by piece."

Josh tried a laugh, but it came out sounding shaky. "I guess by the time you learn the last magic you won't need me anymore."

Sophie reached out and squeezed her brother's arm. "Don't be silly. You're my twin. We are the two that are one."

"The one that is all," he finished.

"I wonder what it means," Sophie whispered.

"I have a feeling we'll find out—whether we want to or not," Josh said.

# CHAPTER FIFTY-EIGHT

Saint-Germain was a rock star, famous throughout Europe, and the young police officer recognized him immediately. He came forward, snapped a quick salute and then pulled off his leather glove as the count stretched out his hand. Behind the smoked glass in the car the two women—Next Generation and human immortal—watched as Francis shook the man's hand and then deftly turned him so that he was facing away from the road.

"Let's go." Joan eased open the car door and slipped out into the warm afternoon air. A heartbeat later, Scathach joined her, gently pressing her door closed behind her. Side by side the two young-looking women walked toward the cathedral. They passed close enough to Francis and the gendarme to hear part of the conversation.

". . . a disgrace, a national tragedy. I was thinking I should have a concert to raise money for the repair of the cathedral. . . ."

"I'd go," the gendarme said immediately.

"I would insist on free entrance for our brave police, ambulance and fire officers, of course."

Joan and Scathach slipped under the flapping police tape and started to step through the piles of stone. Much of the rubble was dust, but some of the larger fragments still retained ghostly images of the figures they'd been before the twins had unleashed their elemental magic. Scatty saw traces of claws and beaks, sweeping horns and curling tails. A stone ball lay alongside a weathered hand. She glanced at Joan and both women turned to look at the front of the cathedral. The devastation was incredible: huge chunks of the building were missing, scraped or torn off, and portions looked as if it had been attacked by a wrecking ball.

"In all my years, I've never seen anything like it," Scathach murmured, "and that was only with two powers."

"And only one twin had those powers," Joan reminded her.

"Can you imagine what would happen if they possessed all the elemental magics?"

"They would have the power to destroy the world or remake it," Joan said.

"And that's the prophecy," Scathach said simply.

"Hey, you! You two. Stop there!"

The voice came from directly ahead of them.

"Stop. Stop right there." The second voice came from behind them.

"Keep going," Scatty muttered.

Joan glanced over her shoulder to see the young police officer attempting to extricate himself from Francis's viselike grip. Suddenly, the count released him and the man tumbled to the ground. In attempting to help him to his feet, Francis stepped on the hem of his long black coat, stumbled and fell on top of the man, pinning him down.

"You two. You don't belong here." A shaven-headed, shaggy-bearded middle-aged academic jumped to his feet before them. He'd been lying on the ground, piecing together tiny fragments of an eagle's wing. He came forward, waving a clipboard in their faces. "You are trampling over priceless historical artifacts."

"I'm not sure we could damage them any further if we tried." Without breaking stride, Scatty snatched the plastic clipboard from the man's grasp and tore it in two as easily as if it were a sheet of paper. She tossed the pieces at his feet. The man looked at what had been his clipboard lying on the ground, then turned and ran off, shouting.

"Very subtle, very discreet," Joan said.

"Very effective," Scatty said, and strode onto Point Zero.

Point Zero was in the middle of the square. Set into the cobbles was a circle of flat gray stone, divided into four parts. In the center was a circle of brighter stone with a sunburst design cut into it. The sunburst had eight arms radiating from its middle, though two were worn smooth by the passage of

416

countless feet and rubbing fingers. The words *Point Zero Des Routes De France* were cut into the outer stones. There was plenty of space for Scathach and Joan to stand within the circle back to back, a foot on each section.

"What happens . . . ," Scathach began.

# CHAPTER FIFTY-NINE

"... *Now*?" Scathach finished.

Then she squeezed her eyes shut, pressed one hand to her stomach and the other to her mouth and collapsed to her knees. Scathach felt the world tilt and fought the urge to throw up, until she suddenly realized she was kneeling on soft earth. With her eyes still tightly shut, she patted the ground and felt long grass beneath her fingers. Then strong arms pulled her to her feet and cool hands cupped her face. Scathach opened her eyes to find Joan's face inches from her own. There was a smile on the Frenchwoman's elegant mouth.

"How do you feel?" Joan asked in French.

"Seasick."

"You'll live," Joan laughed. "I used to tell my troops that if they could still feel pain, they were alive."

"I bet they loved you," Scatty grumbled.

"Actually, they all did," Joan said.

"So we didn't fall into the sun." Scathach straightened and looked around. "We made it," she sighed. "Oh, it's good to be back home."

"Home?" Joan asked.

"I've lived on the West Coast for a long time; San Francisco is as much of a home to me as any other place. I was once told I would die in a desert, so I've always chosen to live on the coasts."

The two women were standing on the side of a gently sloping mountain. After the humid pollution-tainted air of Paris, the cool breeze was sweet, rich with the smell of vegetation, and although it had been early afternoon when they'd left Paris a heartbeat ago, the sun had not yet risen on the West Coast of America. "What time is it?" Scatty wondered aloud.

Joan checked her watch and then reset it. "It's ten minutes to five in the morning." She nodded toward the east, where the heavens were beginning to lighten to purple, though the sky over their heads was black, speckled with misty distant stars. Thick gray-white fog had settled farther down the mountain. "The sun will rise in about an hour." The Frenchwoman turned to look up the slopes of the mountain, which was barely visible in the gloom. "So this is Mount Tamalpais. I thought it would be . . . bigger."

"Welcome to Mount Tam," Scatty said with a flash of white teeth, "one of my favorite spots in America." She pointed into the blanket of thick mist. "We're about fifteen miles north of San Francisco and Alcatraz." The Shadow settled her knapsack more comfortably on her back. "We can jog. . . ."

"Jog!" Joan laughed. "The last thing Francis said to me was that you would probably want to jog into the city. We're hiring a car," she said firmly.

"It's really not that far . . . ," Scatty protested, and then stopped.

Directly below them, a huge shape moved through the fog, sending it swirling and curling. "Joan . . . ," she began.

More figures moved, and abruptly the mist parted like a torn curtain to reveal an enormous herd of woolly mastodons grazing at the foot of the mountain. Then the Warrior spotted two saber-toothed cats lying flat in the tall grass, watching the herd intently, black-tipped tails twitching.

Joan was still looking up the mountains. She pulled her cell from her pocket and hit a speed dial. "I'll just let Francis know we've arrived. . . ." She held the phone to her ear and then checked the screen. "Oh, no signal. Scatty, how long will it take us to get to . . . ?" The shocked expression on her friend's face made her turn to see what she was looking at.

It took a heartbeat for Joan's eyes to adjust to the sheer scale of the mastodon herd that was now moving slowly through the shreds of predawn mist. A suggestion of movement caught her attention and she looked up: floating silent and high on invisible thermals, a trio of giant condors soared directly overhead.

"Scathach?" Joan breathed in a horrified whisper. "Where are we?"

"Not where, but *when*." The Shadow's face turned sharp

and ugly, eyes glittering green and pitiless. "Leygates. I hate them!" One of the huge cats raised its head to look in the direction of the voice and yawned, savage seven-inch-long teeth glinting. The Warrior stared it down. "We may be on Mount Tamalpais, but this is not the twenty-first century." She indicated the mastodons, tigers and condors with a sweep of her hand. "I know what these are: they're megafauna. And they belong to the Pleistocene Epoch."

"How . . . how do we get back . . . to our own time?" Joan whispered, clearly upset.

"We don't," Scathach said grimly. "We're trapped."

Joan's first thoughts were for the Sorceress. "And what about Perenelle?" She started to cry. "She's expecting us. She's waiting on us."

Scatty drew Joan into her arms and held her close. "She might have a long wait," she said grimly. "Jeanne, we've gone back in time maybe a million years. The Sorceress is on her own."

"And so are we," Joan sobbed.

"Not really." Scatty grinned. "We've got one another."

"What are we going to do?" the immortal Frenchwoman wondered, angrily brushing her tears away.

"We will do what we have always done: we will survive."

"And what about Perenelle?" Joan asked.

But Scathach had no answer to that.

# CHAPTER SIXTY

illy the Kid glanced at the black-and-white photograph cupped in the palm of his hand, fixing Machiavelli's severe appearance in his head. The short white hair should be
easy to spot, he decided. Tucking the image into the back
pocket of his jeans, he folded his arms across his thin chest
and watched the first passengers appear in the arrivals hall of
San Francisco International Airport.

The tourists were easy to pick out; they were casually
dressed in jeans or shorts and T-shirts, most with baggage
carts piled high with far too many suitcases full of clothes they
would never wear. Then there were the businessmen in light-
colored suits, or slacks and sports jackets, carrying briefcases
or pulling small overnight bags, striding out purposefully,
already checking their cell phones, Bluetooth earpieces blinking in their ears. Billy paid particular attention to the fami-
lies: elderly parents or grandparents greeting grandchildren,

young men and women—maybe students—returning home to their parents, couples reuniting. There were lots of tears, shouts of joy, smiles and handshakes. Billy wondered what it would be like to be met like that, to step out into an airport arrivals hall and scan the faces, *knowing* that you would find someone genuinely pleased to see you—a parent, a sibling, even a friend, someone with whom you shared a history and a past.

He had no one. There hadn't been anyone for a very long time. Even during his natural life, he'd had few friends, and most of those had tried to kill him. None had ever succeeded.

Finally, tall and elegant in a smart black suit, a black leather computer bag over his shoulder, the white-haired man in the photograph came into the hall. Billy bit down on the inside of his cheek to prevent himself from smiling: maybe in some European airport Machiavelli would pass unnoticed, but here, amid all the color and casual clothes, he stood out. Even if Billy hadn't seen the photograph, he would have known that this was the European immortal. He watched Machiavelli put on a pair of plain black sunglasses and scan the crowd, and even though he showed no sign of recognition, the Italian turned and made his way toward Billy. The American wondered if he would shake hands. Many immortals were reluctant to touch other humans, and especially other immortals. Though he'd met the English Magician a few times, Billy had never seen Dee take off his gray gloves.

Machiavelli stretched out his hand.

Billy smiled, quickly rubbed his palm on the leg of his jeans and stretched out his hand in turn. "How did you know

423

it was me?" he asked in passable French. The Italian's grip was firm, his flesh cool and dry.

"I usually just follow my nose," Machiavelli replied in the same language, and then slipped into accentless English. He breathed deeply. "The hint of cayenne pepper, I believe."

"Just so," Billy agreed. He tried breathing in to catch the Italian's scent, but all he could smell were the myriad odors of the airport, plus—bizarrely—the faint odor that every cowboy associated with rattlesnakes.

"And of course I looked you up online," Machiavelli added with a wry smile. "You still resemble the famous photograph. Curious, though; you knew me the moment I stepped through the door. I could feel your eyes on me."

"I knew who I was looking for."

Machiavelli's eyebrows raised in a silent question. He pushed his sunglasses up onto his high forehead, gray eyes flashing as he looked down. He was at least a head taller than the American. "I take great care to ensure that no photographs of me appear online or in print."

"Our employers sent this to me." Billy fished the photo out of his back pocket and handed it over. Machiavelli looked at it, then the tiniest of smiles creased his mouth. They both knew what it meant. The Dark Elders were spying on Machiavelli . . . which probably meant that they were also watching Billy. Machiavelli went to return the photo, but Billy shook his head. Looking into the Italian's eyes, he said, "It served it's purpose. You might find another use for it."

Machiavelli's head moved in a slight bow that dropped his sunglasses back onto his long nose. "I am sure I will." They both knew that when the Italian returned to Paris, he would do everything in his power to find out who had taken the photograph.

The American looked at the single bag in Machiavelli's hand. "Is that all your luggage?"

"Yes. I had packed a larger case, but then I realized I would not be here long enough to use even a tenth of the clothing I intended to bring. So I left it all behind and just brought a change of socks and underwear. And my laptop, of course."

The two men made an odd couple as they headed for the exit, Machiavelli in his tailor-made black suit, Billy in a faded denim shirt, battered jeans and down-at-heel boots. Although the airport was packed, no one came close enough to brush against them, and the crowd unconsciously parted before them.

"So this is just a quick in-and-out trip?" Billy asked.

"I hope to be on the first available flight home." Machiavelli smiled.

"I admire your confidence," the American said, keeping his voice neutral, "I'm just of the opinion that Mrs. Flamel may not be so easily defeated." He pulled an ancient pair of Ray Bans from his shirt pocket as they stepped out into the brilliant early-afternoon sunshine.

"Is everything in readiness?" Machiavelli asked as they walked into the dimness of the parking garage.

Billy tugged his car keys out of his pocket. "I've hired a boat. It will be waiting for us at Pier Thirty-nine." He stopped, suddenly realizing that the Italian was no longer standing beside him. He turned, the key to the bright red Thunderbird in his hand, and looked back to find the Italian staring admiringly at the convertible, which was a dramatic splash of color and style in the middle of all the other ordinary cars.

"Nineteen fifty-nine Thunderbird convertible—no, nineteen sixty," Machiavelli amended. He ran a hand across the gleaming hood and over the lights. "Magnificent."

Billy grinned. He'd been prepared to dislike Niccolò Machiavelli, but the Italian had just gone up a notch in his estimation. "It's my pride and joy."

The immortal walked around the car, stooping to examine the wheels and the exhaust. "And so it should be: everything looks original."

"Everything is," Billy said proudly. "I've replaced the exhaust twice, but I made sure the replacements were from an identical model." He climbed into the car and waited while Machiavelli strapped himself in. "I'd have pegged you for a Lamborghini driver, or an Alfa Romeo, maybe."

"Ferarri, maybe, but never an Alfa!"

"Do you own many cars?" Billy asked.

"None. I have a company car and a driver. I don't drive," the Italian admitted.

"Don't or can't?"

"I do not like to drive. I'm a really bad driver," he admitted with a wry smile. "But then, I did learn to drive in a three-wheeled car."

"When was that?" Billy asked.

"In 1885."

"I died in 1881." Billy shook his head. "I can't imagine not being able to drive," he murmured as they pulled out of the parking lot. "Like not being able to ride." He hit the accelerator and the car surged forward and slotted into the heavy airport traffic. "Do you want to get something to eat?" he asked. "There's some good French and Italian restaurants. . . ."

Machiavelli shook his head. "I'm not hungry. Unless you want to eat."

"I don't eat much these days," Billy admitted.

Machiavelli's cell phone pinged. "Excuse me." He pulled out the wafer-thin phone and stared at the screen. "Ah," he said in delight.

"Good news?" Billy asked.

Machiavelli sat back in the seat and grinned. "I set a trap yesterday; it was sprung a couple of hours ago."

Billy glanced sidelong but remained silent.

"The moment I discovered the Alchemyst's wife was being detained in San Francisco, I knew that either he or some of his allies would attempt to make their way back here. They had two alternatives: the flight on which I've just come in, or the Notre Dame leygate."

"I'm going to guess you did something to this leygate." Billy grinned. "That sounds like the sort of thing I'd do."

"The gate is activated at Point Zero in Paris. I simply coated the stones with an alchemical concoction made from ground-up mammoth bones—bones from the Pleistocene Epoch—and added a simple Attraction spell to the mix."

The light changed to red and Billy brought the car to a

427

stop. Tugging on the hand brake, he swiveled in his seat to look at the Italian with something like awe. "So whoever used the leygate . . ."

". . . was pulled back in time to the Pleistocene Epoch."

"Which was when?" Billy asked. "I never did get much schooling."

"Anywhere between one point eight million and maybe eleven thousand five hundred years ago." Machiavelli smiled.

"Oh, you're good." Billy shook his head. "So, do you have any idea who activated the gate?"

"A security camera has been trained on the spot for the past twenty-four hours." Machiavelli held up his phone. It showed an image of two women standing back to back in the middle of a rock-strewn square. "I've no idea who the smaller woman is," Machiavelli said, "but the one to the left is Scathach."

"The Shadow?" Billy whispered, leaning forward to look at the screen. "That's the Warrior Maid?" He looked unimpressed. "I thought she'd be taller."

"Everyone does," Machiavelli said. "That's usually their first mistake."

Car horns blared behind the Thunderbird as the lights changed, and someone shouted.

Machiavelli glanced at the American immortal curiously, wondering how he'd react. But Billy the Kid had tamed his famous temper decades ago. He raised his hand and waved an apology in the air, then took off.

"So with the Shadow out of the picture, I take it that our job is much easier."

"Infinitely," Machiavelli agreed. "I had a vague suspicion that she'd somehow turn up on Alcatraz and spoil the party."

"Well, that ain't going to happen now." Billy grinned, then got serious. "Under your seat you'll find an envelope. It contains a printout of an e-mail I received from Enoch Enterprises sometime yesterday afternoon, giving us permission to land on Alcatraz. Dee's company currently owns the island. You'll also find a photograph that came attached to an anonymous e-mail that arrived this morning. I'm guessing it's for you. Means nothing to me."

Machiavelli shook out the two pages. On Enoch Enterprises letterhead was a long legal-looking document giving the bearer permission to land on the island and carry out "historical research." It was signed *John Dee, PhD*. The second sheet was a high-resolution color photo of the images on the wall of an Egyptian pyramid.

"Do you know what it means?" Billy asked.

Machiavelli turned the page sideways. "This is taken from the pyramid of Unas, who reigned in Egypt over four thousand years ago," he said slowly. A perfectly manicured nail traced a line of hieroglyphs. "These used to be called Pyramid Texts; nowadays we call them the Book of the Dead." He tapped the photograph and laughed softly. "I do believe this is the formula of words for awakening all the creatures sleeping on the island." He slipped the pages back into the envelope and looked over at the younger man. "Let's get out to Alcatraz. It is time to kill Perenelle Flamel."

429

# CHAPTER SIXTY-ONE

*D*r. John Dee examined the business card in his hand. It was exceptionally beautiful, silver ink embossed on thick handmade rag paper. He turned it over; there was no name on the card, only the stylized representation of a stag with flaring antlers enclosed in a double circle. Leaning forward, he pressed the intercom button. "Send the gentleman in; I will see him now."

His office door opened almost immediately, and a nervous-looking male secretary appeared and ushered a tall sharp-faced man into the room. "Mr. Hunter, sir."

"Hold my calls," Dee snapped. "I do not wish to be disturbed under any circumstances."

"Yes, sir. Will that be all, sir?"

"That will be all. Tell the staff they can go home now." Dee had insisted that everyone remain long after normal office hours.

"Yes, sir. Thank you, sir. Will you be here tomorrow?"

Dee's look sent the secretary scurrying. The Magician knew the entire office were on tenterhooks because he had turned up unexpectedly. Rumors were flying around the building that he was going to close the London branch of Enoch Enterprises. Even though it was now ten o'clock in the evening, no one had complained about staying late.

"Take a seat, Mr. Hunter." Dee indicated the low leather and metal chair before him. He remained seated behind his desk of polished black marble, watching the newcomer carefully. There was something *wrong* about him, the Magician decided. The planes and angles of his face were awry; his eyes were slightly too high, each one was a different color and his mouth a little too low and wide. It was almost as if he had been created by someone who had not seen a human for a long time. He was dressed in a pale blue pinstripe suit, but the trousers were just a little too short and showed a flash of white flesh just above his black socks, while the sleeves of his jacket ended below his knuckles. His shoes were filthy, thickly caked with mud.

Hunter folded himself into the seat, the movement awkward and stiff, as if he wasn't quite sure what to with his arms and legs.

Dee allowed his fingers to brush against Excalibur, which was propped under his desk. He also knew half a dozen auric spells, any one of which was designed to overload an aura and bring it to blazing life. Then the only problem would be cleaning the dust out of the carpet. The chair would probably melt.

"How did you know I was here?" Dee asked suddenly. "I rarely visit this office. And it is a little late in the evening for a meeting."

The tall pale-faced man tried to smile, but instead twisted his lips oddly. "My employer knew you were in the city. He presumed you would make your way to this office inasmuch as it gives you access to your communications network." The man spoke English with clipped precision, but in a slightly high-pitched voice that made everything sound faintly ridiculous.

"Can you not speak plainly?" Dee snapped. He was tired and running out of time. Despite the hours of roadblocks and countless police checkpoints, there was still no sign of Flamel and the children. The British government was coming under pressure to remove the checkpoints. All roads leading in and out of the city were still gridlocked, and London itself was at a standstill.

"You had a meeting with my employer late last night," the pale man said. "It was terminated before it had reached a satisfactory conclusion, due to circumstances entirely beyond your control."

The Magician rose and walked around the desk. He was holding Excalibur in his right hand, tapping the stone blade gently against his left. The seated man showed no reaction. "What are you?" Dee asked, curious. He had come to the conclusion that the creature was not entirely natural and probably not even human. Going down on one knee, he stared into the man's face, looking at the mismatched eyes.

Green and gray. "Are you a tulpa, a Golem, simulacrum or homunculus?"

"I am a Thoughtform," the figure said, and smiled. Its mouth was filled with stag's teeth. "Created by Cernunnos."

Dee was scrambling back even as the figure changed. The body remained that of a tall ill-dressed man, but the head altered, became beautiful and alien, even as great antlers sprouted. The Horned God's mouth moved in the tiniest of smiles and its slit-pupiled eyes expanded and contracted. "Lock your door, Doctor; you would not want anyone to walk in now."

Giving the creature a wide berth, keeping Excalibur between them, Dee moved around to snap the lock on the door. What Cernunnos had just done was remarkable. Using its imagination and the power of its will, the Archon had created a being entirely out of its aura. The creation wasn't perfect, but it was good enough. Dee knew that humani never really looked at one another anymore, and even if someone had noticed that something was wrong with the man's appearance, they would have looked away, embarrassed.

"I'm impressed," Dee said. "I take it that you are controlling the Thoughtform from a distance?"

"Farther than you can imagine," Cernunnos said.

"I had come to the conclusion that you did not have any mastery of magic," Dee admitted, returning to his desk. The fancy silver business card was slowly steaming, curls of off-white smoke drifting away to be absorbed by the stag-headed man sitting on the opposite side of the desk.

"Not magic, just Archon technology," Cernunnos said simply. "You would find the two indistinguishable."

"I assume you are here for a reason," Dee said, "and not just to demonstrate this . . . this technology."

The stag nodded, smiling brilliantly. "I know where Flamel, Gilgamesh, Palamedes and the twins are."

"Right now?"

"Right now," the creature agreed. "They are an hour from here."

"Tell me," Dee demanded, then added, "please."

The Archon held up its right hand. Dee noticed that it had one too many fingers. "My terms remain the same, Magician. I want Flamel, Gilgamesh and Palamedes alive. And I want Clarent."

"Agreed," Dee said without hesitation. "All yours. Just tell me where they are."

"And I want Excalibur."

At that moment the Magician would have promised the creature anything. "Done. I will put it in your hands myself, the moment Flamel is dead. How many others are with him?" he asked eagerly.

"None."

"None? What about the Gabriel Hounds?"

"The Ratchets and their master, the Bard, have vanished. The Alchemyst, the knight and the king are with the twins."

"How did you find them?" Dee asked. He had to admit he was impressed. "I've looked everywhere."

The creature was changing again as it stood, horns retracting back into its skull. A head and face that was subtly, disturbingly different from its previous head appeared. "I went back to their metal fortress, and then I simply followed their scent."

"You tracked them across this city by smell?" Dee found that an even more astonishing feat than controlling the Thoughtform. He bit back a smile at the sudden image of the Horned God on all fours running through traffic, sniffing after a car.

"Archon technology. It was simplicity itself," the Thoughtform said. "Now, if you will just accompany me, I will endeavor to arrange for you to be transported. . . ."

"The Thoughtform is impressive," the Magician said sincerely, "but if you intend to pass among the humani, you really need to work on the voice. And the clothes."

"It is of little consequence," the creature said. "Soon the humani will be no more."

# CHAPTER SIXTY-TWO

*P*erenelle Flamel was disappointed.

Huddled in the watchtower where she had spent the night, the Sorceress had been hoping against hope that any one of the small sailing boats scattered across the bay would suddenly veer toward the island, and Scatty and Joan would come ashore.

But as the day wore on, she'd realized that they were not coming.

She had no doubts that they had tried, and she knew that only something terrible could have kept them away. But she was also a little annoyed with herself for getting her hopes up.

*"Boat coming!"* de Ayala's voice whispered behind her left ear, startling her.

"Juan!" she snapped. "You're going to be the death of me!" She pushed to the edge of the watchtower, feeling a wave of relief wash over her, along with the tiniest twinge of guilt that she had ever doubted her friends. The Sorceress's face broke into a cruel smile; with Joan of Arc and Scathach the Shadow by her side, nothing—not even the sphinx and the Old Man of the Sea—would be able to stand against her.

Huge black wings flapped and snapped, and she watched the Crow Goddess come spiraling down off the top of the lighthouse and float gently to the wharf almost directly below her. Perenelle frowned; what was the creature thinking? Scathach would probably feed her to the Nereids, who were none too fussy about what they ate.

She was just about to stand up and climb out of the tower when de Ayala's face partially materialized in front of her. The ghost's eyes were wide with alarm. *"Down. Stay down."*

Perenelle flattened herself against the floor. She heard the bubbling of an outboard motor and the scrape of wood against wood as the boat bumped up against the dock. And then a voice spoke. A male voice.

"Madam, it is an honor to find you are here."

There was something about the voice, something dreadfully familiar. . . . Perenelle crept over to the edge of the watchtower and peered down. Almost directly below her, the Italian immortal Niccolò Machiavelli was bowing deeply to the Crow Goddess. The Sorceress recognized the young man who climbed out of the boat as the immortal she'd caught spying on her the previous day.

Machiavelli straightened and held up an envelope. "I have instructions from our Elder master. We are to awaken the sleeping army and kill the Sorceress. Where is she?" he demanded.

The Crow Goddess's smile was savage. "Let me show you."

# CHAPTER SIXTY-THREE

The twins slept, and their dreams were identical.

They dreamt of rain and pounding water, towering water-falls, vast curling waves and a flood that had once almost destroyed the earth.

The dreams left them twitching and mumbling in their sleep, muttering in a variety of languages, and once, Sophie and Josh simultaneously called out for their mother in a tongue Gilgamesh recognized as Old Egyptian, a language first spoken more than five thousand years ago.

A dozen times during the course of the long day, Nicholas Flamel had been tempted to wake the twins, but Gilgamesh and Palamedes stood guard over them. The king had pulled a barrel alongside Josh; the knight had squatted down on a broken box beside Sophie. The two men scratched out a square board in the dirt and played endless games of checkers with stones and seeds, rarely speaking except to keep score with scraps of broken twig.

The first time Flamel had approached the twins, the two men had looked up, matching expressions of distrust on their faces. "Leave them be. They must sleep," Gilgamesh said firmly. "The Magic of Water is unique. Unlike the other magics, which are external—spells that can be memorized, an aura that can be charged and shaped—the power of Water magic comes from within. We are all creatures of water. This is the magic we are born with. I have awakened that knowledge deep within their cells, their DNA. Now their bodies need to adapt, adjust and absorb what they have just learned. To awaken them now would be just too dangerous."

Flamel folded his arms and looked down at the sleeping twins. "And how long are we expected to sit here, waiting?"

"All day and all night, if we have to," Gilgamesh snapped.

"Dee is tearing this country apart looking for us, my Perenelle is trapped on an island full of monsters. We can't just—" Flamel began angrily.

"Oh yes we can. And we will." Palamedes slowly rose to his full height, towering over the Alchemyst. There was an expression of disgust on his face, and the scars under his eyes were bright against his dark skin. "You told me earlier that you did not kill people."

"I don't!"

"Well, I do."

"Are you threatening me?"

"Yes," the knight said simply. "Impatience and stupidity claim more victims than any weapon. You will heed the king.

Wake the twins now and you will kill them." He paused and then added bitterly, "Just as you killed the others before them." He turned his head to look down on Sophie and Josh. "Have you ever wondered if some of those who died might have been the twins of legend, and it was your eagerness that caused their deaths or was responsible for their madness?"

"Not a day passes that I do not think about them," Flamel said sincerely.

The Saracen Knight sat down and stared at the game board carved into the earth. He moved a piece, then looked up again and spoke very softly. "And if you take a step closer, I will kill you."

The Alchemyst had no doubt that he meant it.

Flamel spent most of the day in the taxicab, listening to the news on the radio, hopping from station to station, looking for any clue to what was happening. Speculation was running wild, and the talk shows and phone-ins were full of the most outrageous theories. But there was little real news. Alerted by their colleagues in France of a major terrorist threat, the British authorities had closed down all of Britain's air- and seaports. There were checkpoints on all major roads, and the police were advising people not to travel unless it was absolutely necessary. Nicholas had always known that the Dark Elders were powerful and had agents at every level of human society, but this was the clearest demonstration he had seen of that power.

As the afternoon wore on into evening, the Alchemyst wandered through the field of tall grass that surrounded the barn, drinking the bottled water Palamedes had bought in the nearby town. Usually, Nicholas was the most patient of men—alchemy by its very nature was a long slow process—but the delay was infuriating. Stonehenge was less than a mile away, and within the broken circle of standing stones was a leygate that connected with Mount Tamalpais. Flamel was aware that he no longer possessed the strength to open the gate, but the twins did. He was sure they would be as eager as he was to return home. Then he could set about rescuing Perenelle. He would either free her or die trying. And even if he succeeded and managed to get Perry off the island, he was beginning to believe that there was little left for them to do but die.

The Alchemyst stopped by one of the ancient oaks that bordered the field and leaned back against it, staring up at the skies through the thick covering of leaves, before sinking down to the hard dry earth. He held both hands up to the light: they were the veined hands of an old man. He brushed his fingers across his scalp and saw tiny strands of short hair drift away in the sunlight. His knuckles were swollen and stiff, and there was a stabbing pain in his hip when he stood or sat. Old age was catching up with him. Since last Thursday, when Dee had walked into his bookshop, he must have aged a decade, though it was beginning to feel like two. He'd used so much of his aura without allowing it to recharge that the aging process had accelerated. His energy levels were dangerously depleted, and he was conscious that if he used much more of his aura anytime soon, there was a very real danger that he would spontaneously combust.

Without the Codex, both he and Perenelle would die. The Alchemyst's lips curled in a wry smile. The Book of Abraham was with Dee and his masters, who were not likely to return it. Nicholas stretched out his legs, closed his eyes and turned his face to the sun, letting it's warmth embrace him. He was going to die. Not someday, not at some vague point in the future—he was going to die very soon. And what would happen to the twins then? Sophie had two magics left to learn, Josh still had four to master; who would continue their training? If they survived their present predicament, he knew he would need to make some decisions before death claimed him. Would Saint-Germain be willing to mentor the twins? he wondered—though he was unsure whether he entirely trusted the count. Maybe there was someone in America he could ask, maybe one of the Native American shamans could . . .

A bone-deep exhaustion coupled with the heat and stillness of the day made the Alchemyst drowsy. His eyelids blinked, then closed, and he fell asleep sitting up against the tree.

The Alchemyst dreamt of Perenelle.

It was their wedding day—August 18, 1350—and the priest had just pronounced them man and wife. The Alchemyst trembled in his sleep; this was an old dream, a nightmare that had once haunted him every night for centuries, and he knew what was coming.

Nicholas and Perenelle turned away from the altar to face the church and found that the small stone building was packed with people. As they came down the aisle, they discovered that the church was filled with twins—boys and girls, teenagers, young men and women—all with blond hair and blue eyes. They all looked like Sophie and Josh Newman. And they all had the same expression of horror and disgust on their faces.

Nicholas jerked awake. He always awoke at the same point.

The Alchemyst remained unmoving, allowing his thundering heart to slow. He was startled to discover that night had fallen. The air was cool and dry against his sweat-damp skin. Overhead leaves rustled and whispered, the scent of the forest heavy and cloying. . . .

That was *wrong*. The night should have smelled of trees and grass, but where was the scent of the primal forest coming from?

A branch snapped to his left, dried leaves crunched somewhere off to the right and the Alchemyst realized that something was moving through the field toward the barn.

# CHAPTER SIXTY-FOUR

"The Sorceress is in a cell in D Block," the Crow Goddess said. "This way." She stood back and allowed Machiavelli and Billy the Kid to precede her. Then she turned her head and looked over her shoulder, up at the watchtower, red and yellow eyes bright against her pale skin. She raised her pencil-thin eyebrows, her black lips curled in a slight smile and then she dropped her sunglasses on her face. The Crow Goddess tugged her black feathered cloak high on her shoulders and strode after the two immortals, boot heels clicking on the damp stones.

*"What just happened?"* de Ayala asked, confused.

"A debt was paid," Perenelle said softly, her eyes following the creature as she disappeared directly below the watchtower. "Unasked and unexpected," she added with a smile. The Sorceress grabbed her spear, wrapped a blanket around her shoulders and climbed down the metal ladder onto the wharf. She breathed deeply; there were traces of Machiavelli's serpent odor and his companion's scent—red pepper—lingering on the air. She would not forget them.

*"You should wait until they are in the cells below before attacking,"* de Ayala said, materializing beside her. He was now wearing the more formal costume of a lieutenant in the Spanish navy. *"Take them unawares. Is your aura strong?"*

"As strong as it is going to get, I believe. Why?"

*"Strong enough to bring the ceiling down on top of them?"*

Perenelle leaned on the spear and stared at the sea-rotted buildings. "Yes, yes, I could do that," she said carefully. The onshore breeze whipped strands of hair across her face. She brushed them away, realizing there was more silver than black in them. "I need to conserve my aura, but I'm sure I could find a little spell to eat away at the concrete and metal supports. . . ."

The ghost rubbed his hands gleefully. *"All the spirits of Alcatraz will assist you, of course, madame. Just tell us what we need to do."*

"Thank you, Juan. They have already helped enough." Perenelle took off after the trio, moving silently in her battered shoes. She stopped at the corner of a building and peered around. The Crow Goddess and the immortals had vanished.

De Ayala floated up. *"And what of the ice you used against the sphinx? That was successful; how about sealing the entire corridor in solid ice?"*

"That might be a little trickier," the Sorceress admitted, turning and heading purposefully back toward the wharf, past

446

the bookshop. A wicked smile tugged at the corners of her mouth. "However, there is something I can do that will most certainly upset them."

*"Which is?"* de Ayala asked eagerly.

Perenelle pointed with the wooden spear. "I'm going to steal their boat." The ghost looked so disappointed that the Sorceress laughed for the first time in days.

# CHAPTER SIXTY-FIVE

*M*int green light blazed through the barn's warped walls, incandescent shafts and bars lighting up the interior in solid beams.

Outlined by the light, its antlers huge and terrifying, was the Archon, Cernunnos. Shadows of wolves' heads danced on the walls.

Sophie woke up with a scream, shining silver armor winking into existence around her body as her aura sparkled over her flesh. Josh's eyes snapped open and he scrambled to his feet, his left hand automatically reaching for Clarent. The stone sword hummed and hissed as his fingers closed around the hilt, the blade crackling, a sheen of colors running along its length.

Palamedes' smooth black armor grew over his body and he dragged his enormous claymore sword off his shoulder and positioned himself in front of the twins. Gilgamesh silently reached over and pulled the curved shamshir sword from the knight's belt. "Where's the Alchemyst?" Palamedes demanded.

"I can smell mint," Sophie said quickly, breathing deeply. The distinctive odor permeated the night air. She was aware of the solid thumping of her heart, but even though she knew what was outside, she was not frightened. They had defeated the Archon once already, and that was before they had the Magic of Water.

"That light is the same color as Nicholas's aura," Josh added. "He must be outside."

"We need to get out," Palamedes said urgently, "we can't be trapped in here." He turned and launched himself at a wall. Rotten wood gave way in a burst of splinters, sending him crashing out into the field.

"Go!" Gilgamesh shouted, catching Sophie's arm and pushing her through the ragged opening ahead of him. "Josh, come on!"

Josh was turning to follow when the barn doors were ripped off their hinges. Cernunnos ducked its head to peer into the barn, only its huge rack of antlers preventing it from coming through the doorway. The beautiful face smiled and the voice buzzed and trembled in Josh's head. "So, we meet again, boy. I've come for my sword."

"I don't think so," Josh said through gritted teeth.

"I do. And I came prepared this time." Cernunnos drew back its right arm, and Josh saw that the Horned God had a bow and arrow in its hand. Josh heard the twang of a bow-string and he caught the flicker of an arrow arcing through the air directly toward him.

Clarent moved, coming up and across Josh's body, blade flat over his heart.

The bone-tipped arrow shattered harmlessly against the stone blade, but with enough force behind it to send the boy staggering back. Cernunnos bellowed in frustration. He notched another arrow and fired.

Clarent shifted in Josh's hand, blade singing as it cleaved the arrow in two.

Two of the huge human-faced wolves pushed past the Horned God and slunk into the barn. They spread out to come at Josh from either side, and he backed up until his legs hit the ancient tractor. He could go no farther. Planting his feet firmly, holding the sword in both hands in front of him, he stood and watched the wolves of the Wild Hunt creep toward him, and saw the Archon ready another arrow.

"How fast are you, boy?" Cernunnos bellowed. It shouted an unintelligible word as it loosed the arrow and the two wolves launched themselves, jaws wide.

Gilgamesh came out of the shadows, the heavy curved Persian sword whistling as it cut through the air. The first wolf didn't even see the immortal, but the moment the cold steel touched its flesh, it dissolved to dust.

The second wolf darted at Josh. Clarent moved, stabbing outward, and the creature exploded into grit. "Gilgamesh!" Josh shouted. "Look out!"

But the Archon's arrow took the immortal high in the

chest, spinning him around, dropping him to the ground. Cernunnos grabbed another arrow, leveled it at the king and fired.

Sophie's scream was terrifying: fear and loss and rage wrapped up in one sound. Jerking away from the Saracen Knight, she pushed back through the broken wall, silver aura hard and shining around her flesh as she raced to the fallen king and threw herself on top of him. Cernunnos's arrow hit her in the center of the back, its flint head shattering to powder against her armor, but the force of the blow broke her concentration and her aura faded and fizzled out, leaving her defenseless.

The Archon flung the bow aside; it had no more arrows. Then it started to rip the front of the barn apart with its huge hands, bellowing, stamping and roaring in delighted rage.

Sophie knelt beside Gilgamesh, lifting his head off the floor, cradling it. Josh placed himself between the Archon and his sister, eyes darting, looking for an attack. He planted his feet and his body automatically moved into a battle stance: weight shifted slightly to one side, sword in both hands, tilted up and across his chest. He felt a sudden sense of peace settle over him, and he knew that this was nothing to do with the sword buzzing and sizzling in his hands. It was the recognition that there were no choices, no decisions to make. There was only one thing he could do: he would stand and fight the Archon, and he was prepared to die defending his sister.

Gilgamesh's lips moved, and Sophie bent her head to hear his words. "Water," he whispered, his breath warm on her face.

"I don't have any," she said tearfully. She knew she should

451

be doing something, but she couldn't think, couldn't focus. All she could see was the old man in her arms, the terrible black arrow protruding from his chest. She wanted to help him; she just didn't know how.

The king's lips moved in a painful smile. "Not to drink," he rasped. "Water: the ultimate weapon."

Before she could respond, the Archon tore away the entire front of the barn. She spun around, and through the gaping hole she could see what was happening outside. Nicholas Flamel, his aura green and glowing, was battling with Dr. John Dee, who was wrapped in smoking sulfurous yellow. Dee fought with a long whip of sallow energy while the Alchemyst tried to keep him at bay with a solid spear of green light. Palamedes was surrounded by the remainder of the Wild Hunt, the huge wolves darting in to snap and claw at him, threatening to overwhelm him as he slashed and cut with the longsword.

"Josh." Sophie was calm. "The king said we should use water."

"Water?" Her twin glanced down. "But I don't know how. . . ."

"Remember what I said about instinct?" She stretched up her right hand and her twin reached down with his left to take it.

Cernunnos finished demolishing the front of the building and pulled a savage-looking stone-headed club out of its belt. "You cannot defend yourself *and* the girl," it grunted.

"I only have to defend the girl," Josh whispered.

Cernunnos took a step forward . . . and then the ground opened up beneath it. What had been hard-baked earth turned to a sticky quagmire, swallowing its ankles. Water, thick and muddy, bubbled up from beneath the ground. A tiny geyser squirted from a fissure, and then a whole section of the earth cracked and suddenly dissolved into muck. The Archon lurched forward, the club falling from his hand. Another patch of earth turned to soupy marsh and the creature sank up to its knees, then its hips. Grimly silent now, its oval amber eyes fixed on the twins, blazing with hate, Cernunnos dug its huge hands into the ground and attempted to heave itself up.

"Mistake," Josh whispered.

The ground liquefied around the Archon's hands.

"We just need a little more water," Sophie whispered.

Josh actually *felt* the water surging through the hard-baked earth, experienced its power as it pushed its way upward, driven by incredible pressure from below, slicing through mud, pulverizing the soil, pushing rocks and tree roots ahead of it.

The Archon howled and bellowed as it sank to its chest in mud, its huge bulk driving it deeper into the ground. The creature's hands battered the sticky earth, sending it spraying everywhere. It grabbed for purchase, but found nothing but mud. A bubble popped behind it, a stone emerging to the surface of the mire, and another and then a third. And suddenly, sticky brown-black mud spewed upward, raining down to coat the creature in filth, battering it with scraps of tree roots and chunks of stone. A circular depression opened up around Cernunnos and the Archon was swallowed, mud flowing over its head, until only the very tips of its antlers showed.

Sophie jerked her hand away from her brother's and splayed her silver metal fingers. An intense blast of white-hot fire blazed over the swampy circle, the searing heat baking the ground iron-hard in an instant.

"We did it," Josh laughed. "We did it! I could feel the power flowing through me. The Magic of Water," he said in wonder.

"Josh, get out there. Help them," Sophie commanded, all the color draining from her face as her aura depleted.

"What about you?"

"Do it," she snapped, eyes winking silver.

"You're not the boss of me." He grinned.

"Oh yes I am." She smiled and reached up to squeeze his fingers. "Remember, I'm older."

Smiling, Josh turned and raced out into the field, Clarent whistling before him, cleaving a path toward Palamedes. Part of him wanted to help the Alchemyst, but an instinct deep down told him it made more sense to rescue the knight first; two warriors were better than one.

Gilgamesh's grip tightened on Sophie's fingers. "You must go now," he said in a hoarse whisper. "Get away from here."

"I'm not leaving you. You're injured."

"You will never leave me," the king said, "you will live

forever in my memory." He suddenly grabbed the arrow protruding from his chest, pulled it out and flung it away. "And this, hah, it will slow me down for a bit, but it will take more than this to kill me. You go, go now. Your aura, the Alchemyst's and the Magician's will have called every evil thing in this county. And probably the authorities, too." His eyes flickered toward the green and yellow light blazing from the immortals' weapons. "I'm sure that light can be seen from miles away." The king squeezed Sophie's hand. "Know this: if we meet again, I may not remember you." He pulled the thick sheaf of mismatched pages from under his shirt, extracted the topmost sheet and pressed it into her hand. "And if I do not, then give me this. It will remind me of the girl who shed a tear for the lost king. Go now. Get to the leygate."

"But I don't know where it is," Sophie said.

"The Alchemyst does. . . ." He turned to look at Flamel, and Sophie followed his gaze. At that moment Flamel's aura winked out as he crumpled to the ground. Dee shouted in triumph and drew the crackling yellow whip back over his head.

# CHAPTER SIXTY-SIX

*F*rom the corner of his eye, Josh saw the Alchemyst's aura die and turned to watch him fall.

And he knew he was too far away to get to him in time.

He spun around and Clarent sliced a mangy one-eyed wolf to dust, and then, pivoting on his heel as if he were throwing a discus, he flung the sword at Dee. The blade sounded like a cat as it screamed through the air, the stone glowing red-black. The Magician saw it at the last moment. The whip in his hand became a glowing circular shield and Clarent hit its center in an explosion of black and yellow sparks that hammered the Magician to the ground. His aura crackled, then died. And he didn't get up.

A child-faced wolf leapt at Josh, its jaws gaping, and he hissed in pain as its claws raked his arm. Abruptly, the wolf exploded to dust. Sophie shook black soot off the metal shamshir blade Gilgamesh had given her. "Get the car, we've got to get out of here."

Josh hesitated, torn between retrieving Clarent and getting to the car. Wings flapped overhead and a six-foot-tall rat-like creature dropped out of the night sky, claws extended toward Sophie. Its hiss of triumph became a gurgle as the iron blade drove upward, turning it to gritty sand. "Now, Josh!" Sophie demanded, spitting dirt from her mouth.

Her twin turned and ran for the car. The night had come alive with a cacophony of sounds: howling, yipping and barking. Hooves clattered on the hard earth. The noises were getting louder, closer.

Palamedes had left the key in the car's ignition. Josh slid into the driver's seat, took a deep breath and turned it. The car started on his first try. Gripping the wheel tightly, he floored the accelerator. Two wolves disappeared under the wheels in puffs of dust. Another leapt onto the hood, but he jerked the steering wheel and it slid off, leaving long claw marks across the metal. He ran down a coal black wolf that was creeping up on Sophie and hit the brakes. "You called for a cab?"

But Sophie didn't climb in. "Get Palamedes," she snapped. Running alongside the car, she slashed and cut her way through the wolves of the Wild Hunt with the metal blade until they reached the Saracen Knight, who was standing ankle-deep in black dust.

"Get in, get in!" Josh shouted.

Palamedes wrenched open the door, pushed Sophie in

first, then threw himself into the back of the cab. Josh took off with a wheel-spinning lurch. He pulled up to Nicholas, who was lying unmoving on the ground. Sophie leaned out of the back of the cab, caught him by his shoulders and tried to haul him into the car, but he was too heavy. Palamedes reached out and even in his exhausted and weakened state dragged the Alchemyst in with one hand.

Sophie slapped the glass partition with the palm of her hand. "Go, Josh, go!"

"I've got to get Clarent."

"Look *behind* you!" she screamed.

In the rearview mirror, Josh could see that the field was full of monsters. They looked like they were part of the Wild Hunt, but these wolves were black, with brutish, almost ape-like faces, and were twice the size of the gray wolves. Running alongside them were huge coal-colored cats with blazing red eyes.

"What are they?" Josh shouted.

"Aspects of the Wild Hunt from all across the country," Palamedes said tiredly.

Josh glanced at the long grass where he knew Clarent was lying and made a decision. It would take only a moment to get to it . . . but doing so would endanger everyone. Even as he floored the accelerator, he recognized that the old Josh Newman would have put his own needs above others and gone for the sword. He had changed. Maybe it had to do with the magic he'd learned, but he doubted it. The experiences of the past few days had taught him what was important.

Sophie leaned out the window, gathering strength she didn't know she possessed, and pressed her thumb against the circle on her wrist. An arrow-straight line of raging vanilla-scented fire blazed into six-foot flames, bringing the charging creatures to a halt.

"What do I do?" Josh shouted. "Where do I go?" A wooden gate appeared in the headlights. Josh held on, hunched his shoulders and drove straight through it, shattering it into splinters. A length of timber snapped back and punched a hole through the windshield.

Palamedes grabbed the Alchemyst and none too gently shook his head. Flamel's eyes cracked open and his lips moved, but no sound came out. "Where are we going?" the knight demanded.

"Stonehenge," Flamel mumbled.

"Yes, yes, I know that. Where, specifically?"

"The heart of the Henge," the Alchemyst whispered, head lolling. Sophie saw that there were long tears in his clothing where Dee's whip had sliced at him. The skin beneath was blistered and raw. Focusing the remnants of her aura into the tip of her index finger, Sophie drew it along one of the nastier cuts, sealing and healing it.

"Where's Gilgamesh?" Palamedes asked.

"He was wounded. He told me to go; he made me go." Sophie's voice caught. "I didn't want to."

The Saracen Knight smiled kindly. "He's impossible to kill," he said.

"Where do I go?" Josh called again from the front seat.

"Just follow my directions," Palamedes said, leaning forward. "Go left. Stick to the back roads, there should be no traffic. . . ."

The road behind them suddenly lit up with blue and white light. Headlights flashed and sirens blared. "Police," Josh said, unnecessarily.

"Keep going," Palamedes commanded. "Stop for nothing." He looked out the rear window at the police cars and turned to Sophie. "Is there anything you can do?"

Sophie shook her head. "I have nothing left." She lifted her hand. It was trembling violently, and tiny wisps of smoke curled off her fingertips.

"We have three police cars closing in on us," Josh yelled back from the front seat. "Do something!"

"*You* do something," Palamedes said. "Sophie has no power left. It's up to you, Josh."

"I'm driving," he protested.

"Think of something," the knight snapped.

"What should I do?" he asked desperately.

"Think of rain," Sophie murmured.

Josh kept his foot pressed to the floor, the cab roaring down the road, speedometer touching ninety. Rain. OK, they'd lived in Chicago, New York, Seattle and San Francisco. He knew all about rain. The boy imagined water falling from the skies: thick fat drops of rain, torrential rain, misty summer rain, frozen winter rain.

"Nothing's happening," he called.

Abruptly, a torrential downpour washed across the road behind them, sluicing from a cloud that hadn't been there a heartbeat earlier. The nearest police car hit a patch of water and skidded sideways, and the second car crashed into its back passenger door. A tire exploded. The third car rear-ended the second and the three cars slid across the road, completely blocking it in a tangle of metal. The sirens died to squawks.

"Nicely done," Palamedes commented.

"Where to now?"

The knight pointed. "Over there."

Josh ducked his head to look to the left. Stonehenge was smaller than he'd imagined, and the road came surprisingly close to the standing stones.

"Stop here. We'll get out and run," Palamedes said.

"Stop where?" Josh asked, looking around.

"Right here!"

Josh hit the brakes and the car skidded to a halt. Palamedes leapt from the car, the Alchemyst unceremoniously draped over his shoulder. "Follow me," the knight shouted. His huge sword slashed a metal fence to ribbons.

Josh grabbed the Persian sword and wrapped his arm around his sister, who was struggling to stay conscious, holding her as they raced across the grass toward the circle of standing stones.

"And whatever you do," the Saracen Knight shouted, "don't look back."

Sophie and Josh both looked back.

# CHAPTER SIXTY-SEVEN

"*Y*ou know her?" Billy the Kid asked, dipping his head and speaking out of the corner of his mouth. He was looking at the back of the woman they were following through the maze of stone and metal corridors.

Machiavelli nodded. "We've met on occasion," he said quietly. "She is the Crow Goddess, one of the Next Generation."

The woman's head swiveled around like an owl's to regard the two men. Her eyes were hidden behind mirrored wraparound sunglasses. "And my hearing is excellent."

Billy grinned. He took two quick steps forward and fell in alongside the woman in black leather. He stuck out his hand. "William Bonney, ma'am. Most people just call me Billy."

The Crow Goddess looked at the hand and then she smiled, overlong incisors pressing against her black lips. "Don't touch me. I bite."

Billy was unfazed. "I haven't been immortal for long, a mite over a hundred twenty-six years, in fact, and I've not met that many Elders or Next Generation. Certainly no one like you . . ."

"William," Machiavelli said quietly, "I think you should stop bothering the Crow Goddess."

"I'm not bothering her, I'm just asking . . ."

"You're immortal, William, not invulnerable." Machiavelli smiled. "The Morrigan is worshipped in the Celtic lands as a goddess of death. That should be a clue to her nature." He suddenly stopped walking. "What was that?"

Billy the Kid's hand dipped under his coat and came out with a fifteen-inch-long bowie knife. His face changed, instantly becoming hard. "What?"

Machiavelli held up his hand, silencing the American. Head tilted to one side, he concentrated. "It sounds like—"

"—an outboard engine!" Billy took off at a run. Machiavelli cast a quick suspicious glance at the Crow Goddess and turned to race back down the corridor.

Moments later the sphinx padded around the corner. She spotted the Crow Goddess and stopped, and the two women bowed politely. They were distantly related through a complex web of Elder relationships. "I thought I heard something," the sphinx said.

"So did they." The Crow Goddess's smile was savage.

Nicholas had never learned to drive, but Perenelle had finally taken lessons ten years ago and, after six weeks of driving school, passed her test on the first attempt. They had never bought a car, but Perenelle had forgotten none of her lessons. It took her a few moments to work out how to control the small bright yellow motorboat. She turned the key in the ignition and pushed the throttle, and the outboard motor foamed white water. Spinning the wheel, she pushed the throttle farther and the boat roared away from Alcatraz Island, leaving a V of white water in its wake.

De Ayala's face coalesced out of the spray spitting in over the bow. *"I thought you were going to fight."*

"Fighting is a last resort," she shouted above the wind and the roar of the engine. "If Scathach and Joan had joined me, perhaps then I would have gone up against the sphinx and the two immortals. But not on my own."

*"What about the Spider God?"*

"Areop-Enap can take care of itself," Perenelle said. "They'd best hope they're not on the island when it awakes. It'll be hungry, and the Old Spider has a voracious appetite."

A tiny distant shout made her turn. Machiavelli and his companion were on the docks. The Italian was standing still, and the smaller man was waving his arms, sunlight glinting off a knife in his hand.

*"Will they not use their magic?"* de Ayala asked.

"Magic is not really effective over running water." Perenelle grinned.

*"I fear I must leave you, madame. I need to return to the island."* The ghost's face started to dissolve into spray.

"Thank you, Juan, for all that you have done," Perenelle said sincerely in formal Spanish. "I am in your debt."

*"Will you be back to Alcatraz?"*

464

Perenelle looked over her shoulder at the prison. Knowing now that the cells held a collection of nightmares, she thought the island itself looked almost like a sleeping beast. "I will." Someone would have to do something about the army before it was awakened. "I will be back. And soon," she promised.

"*I will be waiting,*" de Ayala said, and vanished.

Perenelle angled the boat in toward the pier and eased back on the throttle. A delighted smile crept across her face. She was free.

Niccolò Machiavelli took a deep breath and calmed himself. Anger clouded judgment, and right now he needed to be thinking clearly. He had underestimated the Sorceress, and she'd made him pay for that mistake. It was unforgivable. He'd been sent to Alcatraz to kill Perenelle and he'd failed. Neither his master nor Dee's master was going to be happy, though he had a feeling that Dee himself would not be too upset. The English Magician would probably gloat.

Although he feared the Sorceress, Machiavelli had really wanted to fight the woman. He had never forgiven her for defeating him on Mount Etna and over the centuries had spent a fortune collecting spells, incantations and cantrips that would destroy her. He was determined to have his revenge. And she had cheated him. Not with magic, or with the power of her aura. But with cunning . . . and that was supposed to be his specialty.

"Stop her," Billy shouted. "Do something!"

"Will you be quiet for a moment?" he snapped at the

465

American. He pulled out his phone. "I need to make a report, and I'm really not looking forward to it. One should never be the bearer of bad news."

And then, across the bay, the Old Man of the Sea exploded out of the water, directly in front of the boat. Octopus tentacles wrapped tightly around the small craft, bringing it to a shuddering halt. Perenelle disappeared, flung back by the sudden stop.

Machiavelli put his phone back in his pocket; maybe he would have some good news to report after all.

Nereus's voice trembled across the water, his words vibrating on the waves. "I knew we would meet again, Sorceress." Machiavelli and Billy watched as the hideous Elder flowed up out of the sea and squatted across the prow of the boat, legs writhing. Wood creaked and cracked, the small windshield shattered and the weight of the creature in the front of the vessel brought the stern right up out of the waves, its outboard engine still whining.

Shading his eyes, Machiavelli watched the Sorceress climb to her feet. She was holding a long wooden spear in both hands. Sunlight winked golden off the weapon, which trailed white smoke into the air. He saw her stab once, twice, three times at the creature's legs before bringing the spear around to jab at Nereus's chest. Water fountained, spraying high, as the Old Man of the Sea desperately scrambled away from the blade. The Elder fell off the prow of the boat and disappeared back under the waves in an explosion of frothing bubbles. The boat settled back in the water, engine foaming and churning, and then shot forward again. Three long still-wriggling legs peeled off the motorboat and drifted away on the tide. The entire encounter had taken less than a minute.

Machiavelli sighed and pulled out his phone again. He had no good news to report after all; could this day get any worse? A shadow appeared overhead and he looked up to see the huge shape of the Crow Goddess flying by. She soared high, black cloak spread like wings, then swooped down to land neatly on the back of the yellow motorboat.

The Italian started to smile. Of course, the Crow Goddess would simply pull the Sorceress out of the boat and then the Nereids could feast. The smile faded as he watched the two women—Next Generation and immortal human—embrace. By the time they turned to wave back at the island, his face was a grim mask.

"I thought the Crow Goddess was on our side," Billy the Kid said plaintively.

"It seems you just cannot trust anyone these days," Niccolò Machiavelli remarked, walking away.

# CHAPTER SIXTY-EIGHT

*T*he Wild Hunt raced across Salisbury Plain.

The creatures Sophie and Josh had only briefly glimpsed earlier were closer now. Some were recognizable: black dogs and gray wolves, enormous red-eyed cats, massive bears, curled-tusked boars, goats, stags and horses. Others had joined the Hunt: human-shaped figures carved from stone; creatures with bark for skin, leaves for hair and branches for limbs raced after them. Sophie and Josh recognized more of the Genii Cucullati, the Hooded Ones; they saw shaven skin-head cucubuths wielding chains, and knights in stained and rust-eaten armor. Tattooed warriors in furs and Roman centurions in broken armor limped after red-haired Dearg Due. And running among the monsters were perfectly normal-looking humans, carrying swords, knives and spears; Josh found these the most frightening of all.

The twins looked to where Stonehenge loomed dark and

468

indistinct in the night, and knew that they were not going to reach it in time. "We'll stand and fight," Josh panted, analyzing their situation and their limited options. "I've got a little strength left. . . . Maybe I can call up some more rain. . . ."

A savage high-pitched howling echoed across Salisbury Plain. Josh's heart sank as he saw movement to their right— another group was moving in to cut them off. "Trouble," he stated.

"On the contrary." Palamedes grinned. "Look again."

And then Josh recognized the figure leading the group. "Shakespeare!"

The Bard led the Gabriel Hounds in at an angle. The well-disciplined Ratchets crashed into the mismatched army, bringing it to a shuddering halt. Iron spears and metal swords flashed in the night and a pall of dust quickly rose up over the plain.

William Shakespeare, in full modern police body armor and visored helmet, fell into step with Palamedes. "Well met," he said.

"I thought I told you not to wait past sundown," the Saracen Knight said.

"Oh, everything comes to he who waits," Shakespeare said. "And you know I never listen to you anyway," the Bard added with a shy smile. "Besides, with nothing moving on the roads, I guessed you would find a place to hide until dark."

Palamedes dumped the unconscious Alchemyst on the ground and started slapping Flamel's cheeks. "Wake up, Flamel. Wake up. We need to know which stone."

Nicholas's pale eyes blinked open. "Get to the Altar Stone," he whispered hoarsely.

Gabriel appeared out of the night. His bare flesh was streaked with black soot. It caked his long hair. "There are just too many of them, and more coming every minute," he panted. "We can't hold them."

Josh pointed toward the circle of stones. "Pull everyone back to Stonehenge." The same feeling of peace he'd felt earlier had washed over him again. There were no more decisions left to make. Once again all he had to do was to stand and fight. He would protect his sister to the end. Pressing his hand against his chest, he felt the two pages of the Codex crinkle under his shirt. Maybe it was time to destroy them, though he wasn't entirely sure how. Maybe he could eat them. "Everyone back," he shouted. "We'll make our last stand there."

# CHAPTER SIXTY-NINE

"That may not be necessary," Shakespeare snapped. "The Wild Hunt and these other creatures are here for you and your sister, drawn by the smell of your auras and the huge reward Dee has put on your heads. They've no interest in us. So all we have to do is to get rid of you. Palamedes, Gabriel," the Bard commanded. "Buy us some time."

The Saracen Knight nodded. His dented armor formed and re-formed around his body, turning smooth, black and reflective. Gripping his huge longsword in both his hands, he launched himself toward the wolves and black cats. Gabriel led the surviving Ratchets after him.

Shakespeare supported the Alchemyst and Josh held Sophie upright, and the four made their way between two tall sandstone columns into the heart of Stonehenge.

The moment Josh stepped into the circle, he felt the

ancient buzz of power. It reminded him of the sensations he'd experienced when he'd held Clarent in his hands, the feeling that there were voices just at the edge of his hearing. He looked around, but it was hard to make out the shapes of the stones in the night.

"How old *is* this place?" he asked.

"The earliest site is perhaps five thousand years old, but it may be older," Shakespeare answered. He suddenly bumped into a stone lying flat on the ground. "Here's the Altar Stone," he said to the Alchemyst.

Nicholas Flamel sank onto the stone, breathing heavily, one hand pressed against his chest. "Orient me," he wheezed. "Which way is north?"

Both Shakespeare and Josh instinctively looked to the heavens, searching for the polestar.

A huge black cat suddenly leapt through the gates, mouth gaping, paws extended toward the Alchemyst. Flamel threw up his hands and razor-sharp claws scored his palm; then Shakespeare's police baton snapped out, knocking the creature out of the air. The cat crashed onto the huge stone and dissolved to dust. "Like metal, the stones are poisonous to them," the Bard said quickly. "They cannot touch them; that's why they're not rushing us. Alchemyst, if you are going to do anything, then you need to do it now." He pointed. "This way is north."

"Look for the third perfect trilithon to the left," Flamel whispered.

"The third what?" Josh asked, confused.

"Trilithon. Two uprights and a lintel," Shakespeare explained. "Greek for 'three stones.' "

"I knew that . . . I think," Josh whispered. He counted. "This one," he said decisively, pointing. "Now what?"

"Help me," Nicholas said.

Shakespeare caught the Alchemyst and half carried him to the two huge uprights. Pushing into the narrow gap between the stones, Nicholas put a hand on each, reaching as high as he could, then stretched his legs wide until he had assumed an X shape in the middle of the stone.

The faintest hint of mint touched the cold night air.

A huge bear reared up, claws slashing toward the Alchemyst's head. And then the creature was jerked back by the Saracen Knight and tossed to the Gabriel Hounds. They fell on it with savage howls. Dust billowed.

A trio of wolves raced toward Flamel. Josh caught one with the shamshir sword and Gabriel brought down another. Josh sliced out at the third wolf and it ducked the blow, but in avoiding the blade it brushed against the tall stone—and crumbled to powder.

Josh suddenly realized that there were less than a handful of Gabriel Hounds still alive and they were being driven back into the circle of standing stones. A skeletal horse ridden by a headless horseman reared up, flailing hooves catching one of the hounds, sending it crashing back onto a stone. The hound vanished, leaving only a dusty outline in the air.

"Alchemyst," Shakespeare warned, "do something."

Nicholas slumped to the ground. "I cannot."

"Are you sure it's the right gate?" Josh asked.

"I'm sure. I've nothing left." He looked up at the twins, and for an instant Josh thought he saw something in the immortal's eyes. "Sophie, Josh, you will have to do it."

"The girl is drained," the Bard said quickly. "Use her and she will burst aflame."

Nicholas reached out and took Josh's hand, pulling him forward. "Then it will have to be you."

"Me? But I'm . . ."

"You're the only one with the aura to do this."

"What's the alternative?" Josh asked. He had the distinct impression that this was what the Alchemyst had planned all along. Flamel had never had the power to activate the gate.

"There is none." The Alchemyst indicated the creatures crowding just outside the stones. Then he pointed to the heavens. A spotlight was picking its way across the landscape toward them. There were two others close behind. "Police helicopters," he said. "They'll be here in minutes."

Josh handed Flamel the battered and slightly bent shamshir sword. "What do I do?"

"Stand between the uprights with your arms and legs outstretched. Visualize your aura flowing out of your body into the stones. That should be enough to activate them."

"And be quick about it," Shakespeare said. Less than half a dozen Gabriel Hounds remained, and Palamedes was now cut off, surrounded by bogmen who flailed at him with flint daggers that screamed and struck sparks from his armor. Wolves and cats prowled just outside the stone circle.

"Let me help my brother," Sophie whispered.

"No," Shakespeare said. "It's too dangerous."

Josh's aura started to steam the moment he squeezed between the stones, lifting off his flesh like golden smoke. Reaching out, he placed his palms flat against the smooth sandstone and the fragrance of oranges grew stronger.

The smell sent the creatures outside the circle into a frenzy. They redoubled their efforts to get to the twins. Shakespeare and Gabriel took up positions on either side of the stone, desperately trying to keep them away from Josh.

Josh stretched his left foot to touch one upright, and as soon as his right foot touched the other upright stone, the voices he'd been hearing in his head from the moment he had stepped into the ancient circle clarified. He suddenly realized why they had sounded so familiar. They were all one voice—the voice of Clarent. He realized then that Clarent and Excalibur had been shaped from the same igneous rock as the great blue stones that had once composed the ancient circle. He saw the faces, both human and inhuman, and some that were a terrible mixture of both, of the original creators of the Henge. Stonehenge was not five thousand years old; it was older than that, much, much older. He glimpsed Cernunnos, shining and beautiful, without its horns, dressed entirely in white, standing in the center of the circle, a simple undistinguished sword held high in both hands.

But while the pillar to Josh's left crackled and blazed with golden light, the right pillar remained dark.

Flamel cut down a boar that had broken through the circle. He turned to Sophie. "You need to help your brother."

The girl was so exhausted she could barely stand. She

475

looked at the Alchemyst, trying to shape words in her head. "But Will said if I use any more of my aura, I could burst into flames."

"And if the gate doesn't open, then we're all dead," Flamel snarled. Catching Sophie by the shoulder, he propelled her toward the stone. She stumbled on the uneven ground, tripped and fell forward, arms outstretched . . . and her fingertips brushed the stone. There was a burst of vanilla, and then the stone started to glow. Muted silver mist curled off the stone and then it lit up from within, until the pillars of the trilithon throbbed gold and silver, the lintel over them glowing orange.

It was night on Salisbury Plain, but between the stones, a lush sunlit hillside appeared.

Josh stared in wonder at the scene. He could actually smell grass and greenery, feel summer heat on his face and taste the faintest hint of salt in the air. He turned his head; behind him it was night, stars high in the heavens; before him it was day. "Where?" he whispered.

"Mount Tamalpais," Flamel said triumphantly. Pulling Sophie to her feet, he dragged her toward the opening and the light. The moment her fingertips left the pillar, it started to fade.

"Go," Shakespeare said. "Go now. . . ."

"Tell Palamedes—"

"I know. Get out of here. Now."

"What a play you would have got out of this!" the Alchemyst said, wrapping his arm around Josh's waist, pulling the twins between the blazing stones and into the grassy landscape on the other side of the world.

"I never liked writing tragedies," William Shakespeare whispered.

The golden light faded the moment Josh's hand was pulled away, and the smells of orange and vanilla vanished and were replaced by the musky scent of Gabriel and the single surviving Ratchet.

The Wild Hunt and the Next Generation, the immortals and human attackers immediately faded back into the night, leaving behind them nothing but dust, and green fields tramped to muddy ruin. Palamedes staggered up out of the night. His armor was scratched and dented, his huge claymore snapped in two. Exhaustion thickened his accent. "We need to get out of here before the police arrive."

"I know a place," Shakespeare said. "It's close by, a perfectly preserved Edwardian barn."

Palamedes squeezed the Bard's shoulder. "Not quite so perfectly preserved, I'm afraid."

# CHAPTER SEVENTY

"*M*ount Tam," Nicholas Flamel said, falling to his knees, breathing in great lungfuls of warm air. "San Francisco."

Dizzy and disoriented, Josh too stumbled to his hands and knees and looked around. While there was still brilliant sunshine on the mountainside, swirling tendrils of mist were creeping in farther down the slopes.

Sophie crouched beside her brother. Her flesh was chalky white, her eyes sunk deep in her head, her blond hair flat and greasy on her skull. "How do you feel?"

"About as bad as you look, I'm guessing," he answered.

Sophie climbed slowly to her feet and then helped her twin up. "Where are we?" she asked, looking around. But there were no landmarks she recognized.

"North of San Francisco, I believe," he said.

A shape moved below them, sending the mist billowing in

great sweeping curves. The trio turned to face the figure, knowing that if it was an enemy, they had nothing left to fight it with. They were too tired even to run.

Perenelle Flamel appeared, looking poised and elegant even though she was dressed in a dirty black coat over a coarse shirt and trousers. "I've been waiting here for ages," she called, a huge smile on her face as she strode up the hillside.

The Sorceress wrapped her arms around the twins, squeezing them tightly. "Oh, but it is good to see you safe and well. I've been so worried." She touched the bruises on Sophie's cheek, a scrape on Josh's forehead, the cuts on his arm. They both felt a tingling crawling heat, and Josh actually watched the bruises fade from his sister's flesh.

"It's good to be back," Josh said.

Sophie nodded in agreement. "It's good to see you again, Perry."

Nicholas gathered his wife into his arms, holding her tight for what seemed like a long time. Then he stepped back, his hands on her shoulders, and looked at her critically. "You're looking good, my love," he said.

"Admit it, I'm looking old," she said. Then her green eyes moved across his face, noting the new lines and deep creases in his skin. Her index finger trailed white aura across his numerous cuts and bruises, healing them. "Though not as old as you. You are a decade younger," she reminded him, "though today"—she smiled—"for the first time in all our years together, you do look older than me."

"It has been an interesting few days," Flamel admitted. "But how did you get here? The last time we spoke you were a prisoner on Alcatraz."

"I can now claim to be one of the very few prisoners to have escaped the Rock." Slipping her arm into his, she walked him down the mountain through the early-afternoon mist, the twins following a few steps behind. "You should be very proud of me, Nicholas," she said. "I drove here all by myself."

"I'm always proud of you." He paused. "But we don't have a car."

"I borrowed a rather nice Thunderbird convertible I found at the pier. I knew the owner wouldn't be using it anytime soon."

# EPILOGUE

$\mathcal{D}$r. John Dee lay in the soft grass and looked up at the night sky, watching the gold and silver glow fade from the heavens and smelling, even from this distance, the hint of vanilla and orange. Police helicopters vibrated in the air, and sirens sounded everywhere.

So the twins and Flamel had escaped.

And they'd taken with them his life and his future. He had been living on borrowed time since the failed attack the previous night; now he was a dead man walking.

The Magician sat up slowly, cradling his right arm. It felt numb from fingertip to shoulder, where it had taken the full force of the blow from Clarent. He thought it might be broken.

*Clarent.*

He'd seen the boy throw the sword . . . but he hadn't seen him pick it up. Dee rolled over in the mud and discovered

481

the blade lying on the ground next to him. Gently, almost reverently, he lifted it out of the dirt and then lay back on the earth, the blade flat on his chest, both hands resting across the hilt.

Five hundred years he had been searching for this weapon. It was a quest that had taken him all over the world and into the Shadowrealms. He laughed, the sound high-pitched, almost hysterical. And he had finally found it back almost where it started. One of the first places he'd looked for the blade was under the Altar Stone at Stonehenge; he'd been fifteen years old at the time, and Henry VIII had been on the throne.

Still lying on the ground, Dee reached under his coat and pulled out Excalibur, holding it in his right hand. Then he raised both weapons aloft. The swords moved in his grasp, twitching toward one another, the round hilts rotating, blades gently smoking. An icy chill started up one side of his body; a searing warmth flowed up the other side. His aura popped alight, steaming off his flesh in long yellow tendrils, and he felt his aches fade, his cuts and bruises heal. The Magician brought the two swords close, blade crossing blade.

And then they suddenly snapped together, as if magnetized. He tried to pull them apart, but they slotted together, fitting one into the other, then clicked and fused, blade to blade, hilt to hilt, to create a single rather ordinary-looking sword, that leaked gray smoke.

A figure shuffled out of the darkness, an old man bundled up in dozens of coats. Yellow light danced off his wild hair and unkempt beard, and his bright blue eyes were lost and

482

distant. He looked at the sword, focusing, concentrating, re-membering. He reached out with one trembling finger to stroke the cold stone, and then his eyes filled with tears. "The two that are one," he mumbled, "the one that is all." Then the Ancient of Days turned and shuffled off into the night.

# End of Book Three

# AUTHOR'S NOTE
## STONEHENGE AND POINT ZERO

It is nighttime when Sophie and Josh arrive at the prehistoric circle of standing stones on Salisbury Plain, England, and they only catch glimpses of these remnants of a once-great monument, one of the most recognizable archaeological sites in the world.

Stonehenge was built in three reasonably distinct phases. What remains today are the tumbled ruins of all the stages. Although there is evidence to suggest that humans were active around the area of Salisbury Plain (which would have been wooded at the time) about eight thousand years ago, the first building phase dates back over five thousand years. Using deer antlers, stones and wooden tools, the earliest builders scraped out a huge ring 6 feet wide and 320 feet in diameter. Its center was nearly 7 feet deep in places. One arc was left open and two stones were erected as gateposts. One of these stones survives: the Slaughter Stone.

The next phase began around five thousand years ago. Nothing from this phase remains visible, but there is archaeological evidence that a wood structure was erected within the circle. Shards of pottery and burnt bone have been found here, and there is a suggestion that Stonehenge may have been a place of burial or possibly sacrifice.

Over the next thousand years, Stonehenge was enlarged, altered and changed. The great stones that survive today date from this period of building.

It is estimated that up to eighty bluestone pillars were set up in the center of the circle. The pillars formed two half circles, one inside the other. Each of these huge stones weighed at least four tons and had been quarried from a site in the Preseli Mountains in Wales, more than 240 miles away. Just transporting the huge slabs of stone through densely wooded countryside, across mountains and rivers, was an extraordinary feat and shows how important Stonehenge was to the ancient peoples who built it. The enormous Altar Stone, which Nicholas Flamel lies down on, may well have stood as a huge upright. It weighs six tons.

Around this time, the entranceway was widened, and sunrise—especially on the morning of the summer solstice— would have sent long shadows spiking deep into the heart of the circle. At sunset in midwinter, the sun would have sunk between the stones.

Later still, perhaps a little over four thousand years ago, a circle of thirty capped stones was erected. This was another extraordinary feat. Each of the standing stones weighs around twenty-five tons. The stones came from a quarry more than twenty miles north of Stonehenge and were carefully cut, polished and shaped. Within this circle there were five trilithons arranged in a half circle, with the smallest at the outermost edges and the largest in the middle. The "smallest" trilithon was twenty feet tall.

Over the centuries, the site was abandoned and fell into disarray. Nature, the elements and the great weight of the stones pulled some of them to the ground, and gradually the order and arrangement of the circle became confused and was lost.

Stonehenge is striking, spectacular and mysterious, and despite centuries of research, we still do not know what it was used for. Was it a burial site or, as many suggest, a place of worship? It is now associated with druidism, the religion of the ancient Celts, and while the Celts certainly used it, and many of the other stone circles and monuments that littered the countryside, they did not construct it. There are countless myths and legends associated with the site; it is even linked with Merlin and the Arthurian cycle.

One of the most shocking surprises people discover when visiting Stonehenge is just how close the roads are to this ancient monument. The A344—the road where Josh finally abandons the car—runs remarkably close to the original five-thousand-year-old circle.

Stonehenge is now a World Heritage Site.

Point Zero also exists.

The official center of Paris, France, is located on the square in front of Notre Dame Cathedral and is exactly as described in *The Sorceress*. Set into the cobblestones is a circle composed of four segments. Inscribed on the four segments are the words POINT ZERO DES ROUTES DE FRANCE. In the middle of the circle is a sunburst design with eight spiked arms radiating from its center.

There are Point Zero or Kilometer Zero markers in many cities around the world, and these are the locations from which all distances in these cities are measured. Some are stones set into the ground, while others are plaques or monuments.

Standing on the Paris stone at the solar noon is not recommended—you know what happened to Scathach and Joan!

A special preview of

# THE
# NECROMANCER

Book Four of

{ *The Secrets of*
THE IMMORTAL
NICHOLAS FLAMEL }

I am frightened.

Not for myself, but for those I will leave behind: Perenelle and the twins. I am resigned that we will not recover the Codex in time to save my wife. I have perhaps a week left, certainly no more than two, before old age claims me; Perenelle has no more than two weeks.

I do not want to die. I have lived upon this earth for six hundred and seventy-six years, and there is still so much that I have never done, so much that I wish I still had time to do.

I am grateful, though, that I have lived long enough to discover the twins of legend, and proud that I began their training in the elemental magics. Sophie has mastered three, Josh just one, but he has demonstrated other skills, and his courage is extraordinary.

We have returned to San Francisco, having left Dee for dead in London. I am hoping we have seen the last of him. I am disturbed, however, that Machiavelli is here in the city. Perenelle trapped him and his companion on Alcatraz along with the other monsters, but I am unsure how long the Rock can hold someone like the Italian immortal.

And both Perenelle and I are agreed that Alcatraz is a threat we will have to deal with while we still can. Just knowing that the cells are full of monsters is chilling.

More disturbing, however, is the news that Scathach and Joan of Arc have gone missing. The Notre Dame leygate should have brought them to Mount Tamalpais, but they never turned up. Saint-Germain is frantic with worry, but I reminded him that Scathach is over two and a half thousand years old, and she is the ultimate warrior.

My real concern lies with the twins. I am no longer sure how they view me. I always knew Josh harbored reservations about me, but now I am sensing that they are both fearful and mistrustful. It is true that they discovered portions of my history I would have preferred left uncovered. I am not proud of some of the things I did, but I regret nothing. I did what I had to do to ensure the survival of the entire human race, and I would do it all again.

The twins have gone back to their aunt's house in Pacific Heights. I will give them a day or two to rest and recuperate. Then we will begin again. Their training needs to be completed; they need to be ready when the Dark Elders return.

Because that day is almost upon us.

*From the Day Booke of Nicholas Flamel, Alchemyst*
*Writ this day, Tuesday, 5th June, in*
*San Francisco, my adopted city*

TUESDAY, *5th June*

# CHAPTER ONE

"Never thought I'd see this place again," Sophie Newman said.

"Never thought I'd be so happy to see it," Josh added. "It looks . . . I don't know. Different."

"It looks the same," his twin said. "We're the ones who have changed."

Sophie and Josh Newman walked down Scott Street in Pacific Heights, heading for their aunt Agnes's house on the corner of Sacramento Street. Five days ago—Thursday, May 31— they had left for work, Sophie at the coffee shop, Josh at the bookstore. It had been just an ordinary day . . . and yet it had been the last ordinary day they would ever experience.

That day their world had changed forever; they too had changed, both physically and mentally.

"What do we tell her?" Josh asked nervously. Aunt Agnes was eighty-four, and although they called her aunt, she was not actually related to them by blood. Sophie thought she might have been their grandmother's sister . . . or cousin, or maybe just a friend, but she wasn't sure. She was a sweet but irascible old lady who fussed and worried if the twins were even five minutes late. She drove them both crazy, and reported back to their parents about every single thing they did.

"We keep it simple," Sophie said. "We stick to the story we told Mom and Dad—first the bookshop closed because Perenelle wasn't feeling well, and then, when she got out of the hospital, the Flamels—"

"The *Flemings*," Josh corrected her.

"The *Flemings* invited us to stay with them in their house in the desert."

"And why did the bookshop close?"

"Gas leak."

Josh nodded. "Gas leak. And where's the house in the desert?"

"Joshua Tree."

"OK, I got it." He grinned. "You know we're going to get a grilling."

"I know. And that's even before we talk to Mom and Dad."

Josh nodded. "I've been thinking," he said slowly. "Maybe we should just tell them the truth."

The twins walked across Jackson Street. They could see their aunt's white wooden Victorian house three blocks away.

Sophie nodded. "Let me get this straight. You want to tell Mom and Dad that their entire life's work has been for nothing. That everything they have ever studied—history, archaeology and paleontology—is wrong." She grinned. "Great idea. You go ahead and do that. I'll watch."

Josh shrugged uncomfortably. "OK, OK, so we don't tell them."

"Not just yet, in any case."

"Agreed, but it'll come out sooner or later. You know how impossible it is to keep secrets from them."

A sleek black stretch limousine with tinted windows drove slowly past them, the driver leaning forward, checking house numbers on the tree-lined street. The car signaled and pulled in farther down.

Josh indicated the limo with a jerk of his chin. "It looks like it's stopping outside Aunt Agnes's."

Sophie looked up disinterestedly. "I just wish there were someone we could talk to," she said. "Someone like Gilgamesh." Her eyes filled with tears. "I hope he's OK." The last time she had seen the immortal, he had been wounded by an arrow fired by the Horned God. She looked at her brother, irritated. "You're not even listening to me."

"That car *did* stop outside Agnes's house," Josh said slowly. He watched a slender black-suited driver get out of the car and climb the steps, black-gloved hand trailing lightly on the metal rail.

The twins' Awakened hearing clearly picked up the knock on the door. Unconsciously, they both increased their pace.

Aunt Agnes opened the door. She was a slight, bony woman, all angles and planes, with knobby knees and swollen arthritic fingers. Josh knew that in her youth she had been considered a great beauty. He was guessing that her youth had been a long time ago. She had never married, and there was a family story that she had been left at the altar when she was eighteen.

"Something's not right," Josh muttered. He broke into a jog, Sophie easily keeping up.

The twins saw the driver's hand move and Aunt Agnes take something from him. She leaned forward, squinting at what looked like a photograph. When the woman had looked down, the driver had slipped around behind her and darted into the house.

"Don't let the car leave!" Josh shouted at Sophie, racing across the street and darting up the steps and into the house. "Hi, Aunt Agnes, we're home," he called as he ran past her.

The old woman turned in a complete circle, the photograph fluttering from her fingertips.

Sophie raced across the road, stooped down and pressed her fingertips against the rear passenger tire. Her thumb brushed the circle on the back of her wrist and her fingers glowed white-hot. She pushed, and with five distinct popping sounds, they punctured the rubber tire. Air hissed out and the car sank onto the metal rim.

"Sophie!" the old woman shrieked as the girl darted up the steps and grabbed her confused aunt. "What's going on? Where have you been? Who was that nice young man? Was that Josh I just saw?"

Without a word Sophie drew her aunt away from the door just in case Josh or the driver came rushing out and she was pushed down the steps.

Josh stepped into the darkened hallway and then pressed flat against the wall, waiting until his eyes had adjusted to the light. Last week he wouldn't have known to do that, but then last week he wouldn't have run into a house after an intruder. He would have done the sensible thing and dialed 911. He reached into the umbrella stand behind the door and lifted out one of his aunt's thick walking sticks. It wasn't Clarent, but it would have to do.

Josh remained still, head tilted to one side, listening. Where was the intruder?

There was a creak on the landing, and then a slender young man in a simple black suit, white shirt and narrow black tie came hurrying down the stairs from the second floor. He slowed when he spotted Josh, but kept coming. He smiled, but it was a reflex and didn't move past his lips. Now that the man was closer, Josh saw that he was Asian; Japanese, maybe.

Josh stepped forward, the walking stick held out in front of him like a sword. "Where do you think you're going?"

"Past you or through you, makes no difference to me," the young man said in perfect English, but with a strong Japanese accent.

"What are you doing here?" Josh demanded.

"Looking for someone."

The intruder stepped off the bottom stair into the hall and went to walk out the front door. Josh barred the man's route with the stick. "You owe me an answer."

The black-suited young man grabbed the stick, yanking it from Josh's grip, and snapped it across his knee. Josh grimaced; that had to hurt. The man tossed the two pieces on the floor. "I owe you nothing."

He swept from the house and moved swiftly down the steps, but stopped when he spotted the punctured back tire. Sophie smiled and waggled her fingers at him.

The rear passenger window eased down a fraction and the Japanese man spoke urgently into it, gesturing toward the tire.

Abruptly, the door opened and a young woman climbed out. She was dressed in a beautifully tailored black suit over a white silk shirt. She was wearing black gloves, and there were tiny round black sunglasses perched on her nose. But it was her spiky red hair and pale freckled skin that gave her away.

"Scathach!" both Sophie and Josh cried in delight.

The woman smiled, revealing a mouthful of vampire teeth. She pushed down the glasses to reveal brilliant green eyes. "Hardly," she snapped. "I am Aoife of the Shadows. And I want to know what you have done with my twin sister."

# ACKNOWLEDGMENTS

To acknowledge everyone would be to create a list of names longer than the book. *The Sorceress* would not have happened without the help, support, guidance, cajoling and understanding of so many people.

Especially and particularly:

Beverly Horowitz, Krista Marino and Colleen Fellingham at Delacorte Press

And

Barry Krost at BKM and Frank Weimann at The Literary Group

Then are the others who make it possible:

Claudette Sutherland and Michael Carroll

Those who make it easier:

Patrick Kavanagh, Libby Lavella and Sarah Baczewski

Those who make it interesting:

Simon and Wendy Wells, Hans and Suzanne Zimmer, Kelli Bixler, Kristofer Updike and Richard Thompson

And of course:

Julie Blewett-Grant, Tammy Weisensel, Marci Kennedy, Jeffrey Smith, Sean Gardell, Jamie Krakover, Roxanne Renaud-Coderre and Kristen Winsko-Nolan

# ABOUT THE AUTHOR

An authority on mythology and folklore, Michael Scott is one of Ireland's most successful authors. A master of fantasy, science fiction, horror, and folklore, he has been hailed by the *Irish Times* as "the King of Fantasy in these isles." *The Sorceress* is the third book in the series The Secrets of the Immortal Nicholas Flamel. The first two books, *The Alchemyst* and *The Magician,* are also available. You can visit Michael Scott at www.dillonscott.com.